A NOVEL OF LOVE AND DEATH

DRAGONS IN SHALLOW WATERS

CLARE KANE

Dragons in Shallow Waters

By Clare Kane

ISBN-13: 978-988-8552-27-6

FICTION / Historical

EB117

Published by Earnshaw Books Ltd. (Hong Kong)

London, July 1902

My dear Alistair,

Let us dance once more with flames licking our heels, let us mock the black night of death, let us drown in shallow waters until we are reborn dragons! I have read it all, and I say tell the world our story, let them live our suffering, our hope, our love and our despair.

Publish it and let us be damned!

Nevertheless, I agree that you are quite right to change the names. We must think of Charlotte, if nothing else.

Yours always,
Nina

I

It was a hot summer of fear in Peking, a season of distrust and despair, a fairground of vicious rumors, illicit liaisons and empty stomachs. That summer the China of tennis matches and tea parties was revealed as a mirage of hazy imperialism, and as the gilded scales faded from our collective vision I found myself confronting not only the darker aspects of our enclosed community, but also those more obscure elements of my own character. For that was the summer I learned the true meaning of loyalty, and discovered an astonishing capacity for betrayal.

Yet one was not to know, not in the first, uneventful months of the year, how the summer of 1900 would unfold. The spring had brought a hot, hostile dust and stubborn, scorched skies from the Gobi, but murmured complaints of dry heat do not a rebellion make. Setting down the story of that torrid time impels me, then, to select a point of departure, a moment that might be identified as the exact juncture at which normal life was suspended and our Boxer story began. This story is an exception to the habitual style of my journalistic narratives, for my usual position requires a cultivated observation of people, a close, unobtrusive and unceasing watch of my surroundings, while in this particular case events compelled me rather rapidly to adopt the uncomfortable role of the actor. Each of those little actions taken on my behalf, starting with the innocuous introduction of Nina Ward to Oscar Fairchild, I see now as part of a chain of unintended and unstoppable consequences, and I wonder which of those unconscious yet ultimately grave decisions might have been left unheeded, providing me with no story to write beyond that factual recording of the rebellion printed according to my editor's preferences upon the sober pages of the *London Herald*.

After much reflection I have decided to begin my tale with the celebration of Queen Victoria's birthday held, as one might expect, in May. I am a man of sometimes sentimental notions, and recalling that event now, I imagine that some frisson, a charge, a premonition of sorts, permeated the party, an event that appeared at its surface almost indistinguishable from that which had taken place the previous year. The party, held at the ostentatiously grand residence of the British Minister, brought together the sixty or so British subjects who called Peking home. These were almost all men of government: tax officials, interpreters and other such uninteresting types. I found them indistinguishable, particularly after the consumption of wine, when their pallid faces turned puce and their opinions colored the same shade of disagreeable. It was with surprise and delight, then, that while we were eating I spied amidst these anonymous civil servants the figure of academic Nicholas Ward, accompanied by his nineteen-year-old daughter Nina. Following pudding and port the crowd trickled outside to the Legation grounds, where a band had started up by the tennis courts.

"I did not expect to see you here this evening," I greeted Nicholas.

"Neither did I, Alistair," Nicholas said drily. "I must admit that I was rather flattered into attending by a young banker visiting from Hong Kong. Barnaby George, he said. Came to visit me yesterday, and even claimed to have read one of my books. How then might one refuse such an invitation?"

"A banker who indulges Chinese philosophy," I mused. "Truly all the world exists under Peking's eaves. And you decided to come too, Nina?"

"Yes, Mr Scott," Nina said. "Mr George suggested I might enjoy it, even though Father and I rarely attend these kind of events."

Nicholas had raised his daughter alone since his wife's sudden departure from China shortly following Nina's birth. The girl's education, overseen by her father only, had been something of a patchwork delivered by a succession of local governesses and her father's best students from the university. As a result, Nina boasted an unrivaled knowledge of Chinese literature, philosophy and myth, but lacked the most basic of European manners and niceties. Needlework and dance, French and piano-playing were as alien to her as they were useless, and it was this lack of interest in maintaining the old ways, the absolute refusal to cocoon themselves in the comforts of a world five thousand miles away, that led much of the foreign community to complain that the Wards held themselves aloof. In fact, it was this distance at which the Wards kept themselves from the others that had first attracted me to them. They were the eccentrics I had hoped to meet in China, and who were largely absent from the administrative and political center of Peking. The old China hands, the unconventional, the interesting and the dissolute, were spread across the booming coastal towns to which I only ventured occasionally from the interior seat of government. Perhaps it was the journalist's natural sympathy for the outsider that drew me to the Wards; whatever the case, I preferred them to the others, and my intimacy with this unusual family meant that Nina was the sun around which spun the planets of my particular experience of the Boxer Rebellion.

Mr Barnaby George approached us then. A man of plain and pleasant features, he reached out his hand to shake mine.

"You succeeded where almost all have failed," I said to him.

"You tempted Nicholas Ward from his bureau."

"I am most glad he indulged my suggestion," Barnaby said. "I have been in the city only a week and no one speaks of anything but the Boxers. The foreign community ought to engage Mr Ward more on this matter. After all, he is the greatest living expert on the Chinese people."

"Oh, come," Nicholas said. "I imagine any Chinese might be better qualified than I in that particular domain."

The young man's words were effusive, but not insincere. Nicholas was an eminent Sinologist and an exceptionally gifted linguist who had settled in China three decades earlier. His particular expertise lay in Chinese religion and philosophy and a pair of popular texts about Taoist thought had brought Nicholas as close to commercial success as an academic liked to stray. His daughter Nina had been born in Peking, and had not once visited her father's native England. As Barnaby and Nicholas continued their exchange of pleasantries, I summoned Oscar Fairchild, the recently-arrived First Secretary and second-in-command of the British diplomatic delegation, to join us by the tennis courts. I had no motive to speak with Fairchild beyond the professional; as a man dedicated to the gathering of news no event was ever strictly social for me.

And so was my first unthinking tinkering with the Fates. Neither Nina nor Oscar might have realized the gravity of their first meeting that evening when Fairchild and his wife, a tall, fair woman in a dress of Indian silk, entered our conversation with polite smiles and firm handshakes. I noted that Fairchild's eyes lingered a little longer upon Nina when I pronounced her name; this was not a surprise. Nina was a beauty by any standards, and a true belle by those of Peking, where foreign women tended to fall into one of two unappealing categories: dour-faced missionary or plain wife of official. My historic friendship with

4

the family meant my bond with Miss Ward was warmly platonic, and yet even I could not deny her blossoming loveliness, the unassuming allure of her flecked eyes, the subtle comeliness of her figure. Perhaps the most appealing of Nina's many qualities was that she remained delightfully, innocently unaware of the delicate power she yielded by her physical attractiveness.

I asked Fairchild what news he had of the Boxers. Word had reached Peking of the murder of a French missionary in the hinterlands, and while party guests valiantly constructed a veneer of civil cheeriness, none could resist the topic of this latest anti-foreign outrage for long. The Boxers, a violent conglomerate of young men in the arid countryside to the north of the capital who practiced sinister calisthenics inspired by China's long history of martial arts, were determined to uproot all imperialist and Christian elements from their native soil. They were angered by the appearance of menacingly unfamiliar technologies such as telegraph poles and dismayed by the sight of their starving countrymen kneeling before a foreign god in exchange for bread. They expressed their disenchantment with fire, swordplay and, in the most gruesome instances, beheadings. Thrillingly barbarous from a safe distance, the Society of the Righteous and Harmonious Fist was a generous source of relished indignation and priggish pondering upon the future of China for Peking's foreigners.

"I do not deny that the missionary's death was most unfortunate, but I do wonder if it really ought to be of such concern to us here in Peking," Oscar Fairchild said, cradling a pipe between long, elegant fingers. The French demanded action, he said, but the British questioned the wisdom of retaliation for crimes that had not yet touched the heart of imperial China.

"I believe it ought be of grave concern to us all," Nicholas said solemnly. "That the Boxers have only killed in the countryside so far is a matter more of convenience than conviction."

Barnaby George, bestowed with a false sense of security provided by his residence in the safe harbor of Hong Kong, expressed disbelief that the Boxers would dare to attack Peking.

"They believe bullets cannot pierce their skin," Nicholas said with gentle, fatherly patience. "I imagine they think themselves quite capable of penetrating the city walls."

"If we learned anything in India," said Fairchild's wife sharply, "it was that native unrest must be quelled immediately. Otherwise they can quite quickly lose all respect for the law of the land."

Oscar nodded lightly, approvingly. Nina, uncharacteristically quiet in these novel surroundings, listened to the back and forth with her head cocked to one side, the hint of a smile on her lips.

"What do you think, Miss Ward?" Oscar Fairchild asked her directly. Perhaps he too had perceived the quizzical knit of her eyebrows, possibly he also sensed the formation of some thought on Nina's behalf, and intuited that it would be more incisive than the rehashing of platitudes and the repetition of shallow truths offered by Mrs Fairchild and Mr George.

"Well," Nina began. "The stance of the Chinese people, particularly in the countryside, is entirely understandable. How should we like it if England were overrun by Chinese showing scant regard for our traditions, forcing us to practice their religions, laying railway tracks in places we held dear?"

"I think we shouldn't like it at all," Oscar conceded. "But there is a reason why we are here and they are not there. We have a duty to these countries, you understand. We are helping them to embrace the twentieth century."

"By what means?" Nina asked curtly. "With guns and opium? The Chinese invented gunpowder centuries before the Europeans did, yet they felt no duty to tell anyone else about it."

Violet Fairchild frowned slightly, but Oscar only laughed softly and drew leisurely on his pipe. "Surely you don't believe the Boxers justified?" he countered. "They are simple ruffians, intent upon sowing fear amongst the population and murdering any European unfortunate enough to cross their path. And their beliefs are quite absurd. Tricks and spells and ghost soldiers descending from the heavens."

"I do not say that they are justified in their actions or right in their beliefs, only that I understand their motives," Nina said.

Poor Barnaby did not know how to respond to this show of disagreement, however cordial in nature, and shifted nervously.

"Oh, come," Violet Fairchild said, urging her husband by the crook of his arm. "Let us speak no more of such horrors. We have yet to greet the Moores and I see Beatrice there by the band."

Oscar smiled broadly at us all as the couple departed, glancing over his shoulder at Nina and shaking his head with benign incredulity. Likely he considered their interaction a good piece of intellectual sparring; certainly the dichotomy of Nina, who presented a familiar exterior that belied her interior sympathies, had charmed the First Secretary.

"Nina," Nicholas said in soft reprimand.

"Father, you agree with me," she said, not looking at Nicholas but directing her gaze towards an abashed Barnaby George. "And perhaps if he pays my words any heed, Mr Fairchild shall come to agree with me too."

In recalling that first interaction for myself, I wonder how often Oscar and Nina might have returned in their minds to that moment. Likely Fairchild summoned the image of Nina's face in the days that followed, resurfacing, as men do, the face of a woman he considered lovely. Nina, soon distracted by an unexpected petition, most likely did not dwell upon their exchange. And yet in those brief moments their lives had already begun to unfold towards unstoppable, irrevocable change, and my part in it, by way of innocuous introduction, had already been decided.

Around noon the following day I raised my heavy head and left home. I lived just beyond the border of the Legation Quarter in a quaint Chinese street that today arranged itself in the usual moving tapestry of exoticism before me: snaking rows of children played a raucous game of catch the dragon's tail, traveling merchants led mangy and unwilling camels over gray cobbles, silver-haired women chopped bloody meat on rickety tables erected outside their homes. On the best days, Peking's distinctive unfamiliarity flooded you with vitality, on the worst it left you drained, cold, a stranger in an unfathomable city, longing for your native Edinburgh. That day, my mind fogged from the previous evening's intemperance, my morning's writing lost to sleep, the neighborhood pulled me gratefully awake. Still, it took a moment to recognize the figure of Barnaby George as he crossed the narrow *hutung* alley before me.

"Mr George," I called. "You have decided to brave life outside of the Legation Quarter?"

Barnaby explained that he was on his way to visit the Wards. In keeping with Nicholas' general attitude towards the other foreigners in China, he had elected not to live in the officially sanctioned foreigners' quarter, but to reside instead amongst the Chinese, in a traditional neighborhood of sloping roofs said to date back to the Ming dynasty. I noticed a nervous tension in Barnaby's voice, a strain at its edges, and imagined that perhaps he too was suffering from the effects of overindulgence. I wished him well, suggested a shortcut through Clear Sky *hutung* and proceeded to the Grand, an establishment on the edge of the Legation Quarter managed by my friend Edward Samuels and his German wife Hilde.

A hotel is of eternal interest to a man like me; a high incidence of one particular nationality or profession provides the first clues to a news story still in its infancy. But lately Edward Samuels had informed me only of the most ominous of all indications to any hotelier: a distinct lack of reservations. To a journalist this suggested one of two things: either Peking had become a backwater town of no interest to the outside world and I ought to pack my belongings and head south, or something great and unpleasant was expected within the city's walls, in which case I couldn't have found myself in a better position. Edward was not present when I stepped into the welcoming cool of the Grand. His wife, Hilde, stout and serious, polished the snout of a gun behind the reception desk.

"Mr Scott," she said lightly. "To what do I owe the pleasure?"

"Is your husband here?" I asked.

Hilde shook her head.

"We have had a visit that I imagine you might find most interesting," she said, her lips curling towards a smile. "From a Belgian engineer."

"I can't quite decide whether I care less for the nation of Belgium or the welfare of its engineers," I said. "Why do you smile so, Mrs Samuels?"

Hilde laughed warmly and told me that an hour before my arrival a distraught Belgian of around thirty wearing a tattered, blood-splattered shirt, had stumbled into the Grand, spluttering and coughing. Between choked breaths the man explained that he had been engaged in the construction of a new railway line by Fengtai when Boxer rebels set upon him and his colleagues.

"It is a shame you were not here to interview him," she said. "What descriptions he had of the Boxers, teeth gnashing, wild dancing. He said they ripped the railway tracks from the ground with their bare hands, pulled down telegraph polls."

"Where is the man now?" I asked.

"He led Edward to Fengtai. They have gone to see if the others might be rescued. Some of the engineers had families living in the village there."

"I must go," I said. "At once."

"Please, Mr Scott," Hilde said. "Something to steady your nerves."

She handed me a glass of whisky, I drank it in steady gulps and felt my head clear. The story forming before me had yet to arrange itself into the linear simplicity with which I would later have to write it, but the motives of the Boxers in this outrage were evident enough that I might pre-empt the outline of a narrative. The foreign powers invested heavily in infrastructure projects in China; developments such as railway lines they believed to be positive symbols of progress, enterprises conceived in the service of those most noble of secular aims: trade and civilization. The Boxers, meanwhile, perceived only the perils of unnatural technology and the egotism of profit-hungry invaders, and had decided to make clear their discontent by painting a horrific landscape at Fengtai station from their familiar palette of violence and terror.

I do not consider myself brave, only unafraid. It has been both a privilege and a curse to witness much war over the course of my career. In chronicling the misadventures of the British in Burma, in Africa, in every hot, uninhabitable and exploitable God-forsaken corner of the Earth, I have become quite accustomed to violence and the bloody traces left in its wake. I remain composed in the face of almost any danger, knowing that every body ends the same: rigid and lifeless, crawling with flies. And so it was without hesitation that I took one of Edward's horses and crossed the Legation Quarter at a quick trot. On the way I passed Barnaby and Nina. They were walking together in the shaded area beside the chapel, chatting animatedly as Nina twirled an ivory parasol between her fingers. I waved to the pair, but did not break to speak with them. I galloped across the racecourse in the direction of Fengtai station, where an hour later I encountered a small hell. The station was ablaze, the ground dredged up, splinters of torn railway line cleft under our horses' hooves. Distraught villagers streamed around me in the thick smoke, their curses deafening. *Huozai!* Fire! Calamity! I found Edward watching the scene and came to a stop beside him.

"They've really done it now," he said.

"And so close to Peking," I replied. "Might we still believe ourselves safe in the capital?"

One Boxer charged out of the mist towards us, wielding a long, curved sword. He thrust the blade towards us, close enough that I might observe the rusted blood that stained its crested edges, near enough my flesh that I could imagine its cool, deadly impact. The Boxer was young, his eyes glinted with conviction. Slowly he waved the sword in hypnotic circles before us, slicing silently through the air before eventually retreating, watching us still with narrowed eyes. Our horses neighed wildly, shifting beneath us. I have said that I was unafraid, and that is true, but I was no Boxer: I did not believe myself immortal. The infernal tableau spread before us was beyond the resolve of two well-intentioned British men, and so Edward and I set back towards Peking, hoping to raise the powers of the few military men stationed around the city.

I had been writing about the Boxers for some months by then, sending telegraphs to London that detailed their practices of spirit possession, sorcery and martial arts in as much depth as the medium of the foreign correspondent permits, and reporting on the sporadic killings of missionaries across the northern expanse of China, but this was my first direct experience of the warriors. The Boxers had long fascinated me with their visceral, unapologetic response to foreign expansion. While the Manchu government crumbled quietly in the face of foreign aggression, sinking gradually beneath the pressure of lopsided treaties and economic muscle, these peasant boys had organized themselves into ragtag militias scattered across the parched countryside. If they hadn't been quite so set upon murdering us all, I might have quite admired their pluck.

As Edward and I entered the Legation Quarter, I recognized the floral splash of Nina's parasol by the tennis courts and called out to her. She walked with determination, taking quick, sharp steps, and did not turn to greet me.

"Nina!" I tried again. "Stop. It's not safe for you to walk alone."

Edward nodded to me and I quickened my pace, leaving him behind and quickly catching up to Nina.

"I have just come from Fengtai," I said, and finally she turned to face me. "There has been a Boxer attack. It is not safe for you to walk alone. Come, let me see you home."

Nina frowned, considered this offer.

"Oh, fine," she said, resigned in tone. "I suppose it is rather hot to walk."

"Where is Mr George?" I asked as I stepped down from the horse, and lifted Nina into the saddle.

"How should I know?" she replied.

"Well, you were with him earlier. He ought not to have left you alone on a day like today."

I pulled on the reins and walked alongside Nina. We returned to the Ward household in comfortable silence; I knew that Nina, like her father, preferred to dwell in the realm of thoughts, and imagined that whatever had passed between her and Barnaby George would now be subject to intense scrutiny in her mind.

Always encouraged by her father to speak her thoughts, Nina often appeared capricious in her opinions, and an observer of her character could fall under the erroneous impression that she was wont to speak without consideration. In fact, Nina liked to weigh new information until her opinions were so well-defined, so unassailable in their logic, that she might never be persuaded away from her stance on a matter. She was irritated, irked by Mr George, that much she was willing to unburden upon me, but her disinclination to speak more suggested something unusual had occurred during their time together that afternoon, some turn of events for which she had no readily-prepared response. She smiled kindly while guarding her wordlessness, and I knew that she would share whatever troubled her when she was ready, and not a moment before.

I accompanied Nina through the red-painted door that marked the entrance to the Wards' courtyard home. Together we crossed the wide, breezy patio and Nina breathed a consoling sigh. We walked towards the drawing room, where Nicholas reclined in an armchair, a thick book in his lap.

"Mr George asked me to marry him," Nina said, taking a seat opposite her father. "I refused."

Surprised, I stood between father and daughter, watching as Nicholas slowly removed his reading spectacles to regard his daughter. Nina, after her moments of quiet reflection upon the horse, was spirited now. Her cheeks were flushed a rosy pink and she met her father's eye with absolute confidence.

"You refused him?" Nicholas said with a wry smile. "I had a suspicion you might."

"Why did you suggest he speak with me if you already knew what was in my heart?" Nina protested. "You could have spared us all much embarrassment." She looked to me. "Does that not strike you as most unthinking of my father, Mr Scott?"

"Never have I met someone who thinks more than your father, Nina," I said, settling myself into a chair by Nicholas' side.

"I suggested he talk to you because as much as I enjoy postulating as to what may exist in that mind of yours, Nina, you remain a mystery even to me," Nicholas said. "I only wished you to have the chance to explore his proposal yourself."

Nina stood, circled the room on restless feet. She enjoyed an unusually frank relationship with her father as for most of her life they had been bound together without anyone to intrude upon their exclusive intimacy. In recent years Nicholas Ward had acquired a woman, a former concubine called Pei, who rounded out the small family as a replacement wife and mother, but who had not disturbed the unusually equal balance of that unconventional father-daughter connection.

"But the very idea of getting married now is quite ridiculous," Nina said. "And what's more, he is to move to England shortly. He suggested I might go with him!" She walked untiringly, fingers winding around themselves. "He wants to stop by later this summer before he returns to England for good. To see if I have changed my mind."

"And do you think you might?" I asked.

"I doubt that very much. He was quite cruel when I refused him." Nina stopped before a scroll decorated with sloping calligraphy. "I have told him that he may come to Peking in the summer if he wishes to see the city in its hottest months, but to expect nothing of me. China is my home and I have no desire to leave it."

"Oh, Nina," her father said with a gentle laugh. "Sometimes I think perhaps it is you who is cruel."

Pei entered the drawing room then, taking small, hushed steps on bound feet. Nina told her of the proposal, and as they spoke in the convivial tones of the informal Mandarin that I had learned in my first months in the country, crossing the mountains of Shantung with a parade of coolies in tow, I took the opportunity to describe my experience at Fengtai to Nicholas.

"I am not in the least surprised," Nicholas said, his voice inked with disappointment. "It astounds me that the foreign powers have continued unabashed with these plans in the countryside, believing against all evidence that the development of such technologies will provoke no reaction amongst the Chinese."

"Nicholas, you know as well as I do that our leaders consider that they help the Chinese. The majority will laud the medicinal benefits of opium given half the chance."

Nicholas shook his head with reconciled sorrow and we returned once more to the women's conversation.

"You are a strong girl," Pei was saying admiringly. "But you must be careful. Love touches everyone in the end. Look, it even happened to me." She walked behind Nicholas, and stroked his white hair with tenderness.

"My dear Pei," Nina replied. "I will do my best to avoid being touched by love for quite some time yet."

II

THE DANGER in Peking grew undeniably, tangibly real in the days following Barnaby George's ill-fated proposal. The Boxers, emboldened by their successful destruction at Fengtai and their increased tally of felled foreign devils, intensified their activities. They had reached the outer edges of Peking, and by night we heard them circling the city, calling in low and liturgical tone: *Sha! Sha!* Kill! Kill! That single, chilling syllable was to become the drumbeat to our cracked, dry summer, each cry accompanied by discordant clashing of drums and piping of flutes. The very real threat of the Boxer presence was further intensified by gruesome rumors that grew more outlandish with each retelling, stories of priests beheaded on street corners and milky-skinned babies snatched out of cots by night. It became impossible to keep a level head amid such feverish irrationality and a general hysteria set in amongst the foreign population of the city.

Claude MacDonald, the British Minister, decided the best course of action was to invite all British nationals to the relative safety of the Legation Quarter. The British Legation, that tiny area of Peking under the auspices of a fluttering Union Jack and nestled alongside the missions of a handful of other nations, habitually housed only a few dozen people, mostly in government accommodation, but MacDonald promised that residents would accommodate their compatriots at this time of great need. It did not surprise me to hear that Nicholas Ward had politely declined the offer, saying he saw no reason to leave his home.

It was on one of those cacophonous, sleepless nights that I saw Oscar Fairchild again. I had taken to stopping by the Grand Hotel before returning home each evening, knowing that Hilde would always provide a generous serving of whisky while Edward would pass on intelligence gleaned from diplomatic and commercial conversations overheard in the dining room. The three of us were discussing the early departure of an American couple visiting from Shanghai and Edward's concerns that his accounts for the month of June would fall short of previsions, when Oscar crossed the lobby with a close group of secretaries and trade officials. He separated from his colleagues and hastened to join me at the bar.

"Please do take a seat," I said, surprised by his attention. "Though I shan't be staying long."

It was in my professional interest to cultivate good relations with anyone close to the nexus of power in Peking, but the toll of the recent days' turmoil made the idea of engaging in that breed of speech favored by officials - light, inoffensive and incurably dull - vastly unappealing in comparison to the silent company of whisky.

"There is something I wish to discuss with you," he started. "I know you to be a close friend of Mr Ward. We have invited him to take up residence in the Legation Quarter. I have personally offered rooms in my own residence for him and his daughter, but he refuses to leave his home. I may not know them well, but we are all concerned for the safety of both Mr Ward and Miss Nina. I wondered if you might be able to persuade them to join us in the Legation Quarter."

I laughed, telling Oscar that unlikely as anyone was to persuade Nicholas Ward of anything, I would pay him a visit on my way home and suggest he give some further thought to the offer. Oscar urged me to tell the Wards that the Chinese had permitted the presence of three hundred soldiers to protect the various nationalities within the Legation Quarter, and they were due to arrive the next day.

"We believe everyone inside the Legation Quarter shall be safe," he said. "You, of course, are also encouraged to join us here."

Politely I told Oscar that I preferred to remain in my own accommodation as long as circumstances allowed, but I agreed that we must think of Nina's welfare. Fairchild rose and bade me good night, waving to Edward Samuels as he left.

"He seems pleasant enough," Edward said.

"For an official he appears quite human," I agreed, swirling the last of the amber liquid around my glass.

Finding a rickshaw was more challenging than usual that night, and my courageous driver's tread fell on silent streets. Doors were bolted, children quietened, stoves unlit, as residents prepared themselves for another night of baleful piping and menacing cries as the Boxers marched closer to the perimeter of the Legation Quarter. The Ward household, however, remained warm and inviting; from the dim *hutung* I detected the pleasant murmur of conversation, and noted the orange light that seeped around the corners of the vermilion-painted doorway, pooling across the stone steps that led to the neatly-maintained courtyard. Head servant Yang led me to the drawing room, where I found that Nicholas and Nina had received two student interpreters, James Millington and Hugo Lovell. Each year a handful of young men was dispatched to Peking to learn the basics of Chinese before being posted to a more lucrative position in one of the country's commercial centers. I was surprised by their presence; Nicholas had never displayed any prior interest in these novices of the Chinese language, and I doubted Nina had previously made their acquaintance.

"Good evening," I said from the doorway. "I hope I do not interrupt."

"Never," Nicholas said. "Please, take a seat. These two young men came to me with questions about the Boxers. You ought to speak to Mr Scott, boys. He has seen this many times before."

"The Boxers also bring me here," I said. "You shall be a popular man if they carry on this way."

"And you wonder why I have always been suspicious of popular individuals," Nicholas said lightly. "Go on, Alistair."

I repeated Oscar Fairchild's invitation and suggested Nicholas reconsider the idea of moving to the Legation Quarter.

"The Boxers are growing more confident," I said. "You cannot be sure that you will be safe here."

"I absolutely agree," Hugo Lovell said quickly. "We have already suggested such a course of action to Mr Ward."

"Three decades I have lived in this house," Nicholas said. "No harm has come to me yet, unless you consider that inflicted by my wife."

The two young men smiled uncomfortably, unsure whether to laugh.

"Please, Nicholas, think of Nina," I said.

"Mr Scott, you know Father and I are not enemies of the Chinese. What would anyone want with us? We are not missionaries, we are not officials, we are just ordinary people," Nina said. "Ordinary people who like China, who speak the language, who have never built a railway line or erected a church in our lives."

"You are not ordinary people to the Boxers, Nina. You are the enemy. In fact," I turned to Hugo and James, "I imagine you two young men ought to leave soon. It's rather late."

"How can they become future leaders of empire if they're scared of a Boxer or two?" Nina said, gently mocking.

James Millington nodded fiercely.

"I am not afraid," he said. "And we wish to hear more from Mr Ward. Mr George did not lie when he said that Mr Ward was perhaps the world's leading expert on the Chinese and the Manchu ruling class. Already he has explained the ambivalence of the Empress Dowager to us. Should she protect the foreigners and risk the wrath of the Boxers? A most serious conundrum."

"Well, in that case I shall take my leave," I said, rising. "I have spent most of the day thinking of nothing but the Boxers." I took a last look at Nicholas. "Please consider the offer. You would be far safer in the Legation Quarter."

"And you, Mr Scott? Shall you move to the Legation Quarter?" Nina asked.

"I have thought about it," I lied. I would not admit my foolhardiness to young Nina, but I was resistless to story, and a secret, heedless part of myself willed the Boxers to my door, wished their destruction to my street, so that I might see it, and survive long enough to record that historic sight never to be witnessed by men of prudence and providence. "And I shall not rest until I know you are safe there."

The morning carried with it the unmistakable smell of war. The station at Machiapu was crowded; curious locals jostled with imperial officials who had crossed south of the Tartar Wall to await the arrival of the troops sent to safeguard the Legation Quarter. Oscar Fairchild had secured a first-line vantage point, and I stood beside him as we waited for the incoming train, noticing the crease in his forehead and the muted tone of his conversation.

"I suppose China has proved rather a difficult post," I suggested.

He shook his head.

"Every post has its challenges. India certainly was not without its difficulties. I'm sorry that you have detected my lack of animation, it is rather a personal matter. My wife's father has fallen ill and she has left for the coast. I suppose it is best for her to be in England at a time like this," he said.

"I'm terribly sorry to hear that," I replied. "If there's anything I might do…"

"You might mention the troops in your next dispatch," Fairchild said. "Reassure those at home that we shall be quite safe."

The train pulled in to a smattering of applause from gathered foreigner onlookers, but when the soldiers stepped down from the train cars, stiff and stony-faced in the regalia of their respective countries, they attracted loud jeers from many of the Chinese spectators. *Yang guizi!* Foreign ghosts! they called as the soldiers marched down the platform. The troops, wrong-footed by this negative reception, tried to progress steadily forward as the crowds swarmed around them. Fairchild and his colleagues shook hands with the most senior officers, chaotically leading them out of the station in what ought to have been a glorious arrival and now appeared to be something of an uncontrolled scrum. Dozens of foreign residents had come out to line the streets, but they strained now to see the faces of their promised saviors. I spied Nina in the crowd; she stood with the student interpreters, Hugo and James. The boys whistled and cheered, but Nina's smile was tight and small.

Violence simmered as more Chinese pushed behind the soldiers. These locals weren't necessarily Boxers, but the sentiments of the gathered mob were vociferously anti-foreign. They whistled and chanted; their insults and cries eclipsed the good-spirited welcome planned by officials. *Hongmao guizi!* Red fur devils! Such phrases were not new to me. Upon my arrival in China I had undertaken my journey across Shantung, where peasants watched wide-eyed as I circled their villages, beginning my travels simply with the idea of seeing Mount Tai and later continuing directionless but happy. Their gazes had followed me, their words had trailed my steps, and yet I had never heard those vivid descriptions spoken with such venom as that day by the station, vowels guttural and thick, catching foul and ugly in throats. The troops picked up speed on approach to the Legation Quarter, and Oscar walked more rapidly, following the pace of the new arrivals as they attempted to outpace their detractors. I fell behind, keeping an eye on Nina, who moved joylessly with the foreign crowd. I was shocked to see one of the disgruntled spectators turn to her, unleashing a torrent of threatening words. I saw Nina's mouth move in pleading shape, but could not hear her words. The young man bared his teeth in response, and grabbed at Nina's necklace, ripping the string of pearls from around her neck before sprinting away.

"Hey!" Nina shouted after him in indignant Chinese. "Don't you dare run away! Give that back!"

She lunged after him, only to be immediately restrained by Hugo and James. The man dangled the necklace in the air; its constituent pearls dropped and scattered, rolling over the ground.

"Look, *gaobi*, I have your pearls!" he called. His unpolished country accent was impenetrable even to the student interpreters, but I witnessed the reference cut close to Nina's core. The man had referred to Nina's high-set nose, a common insult thrown at usually uncomprehending Westerners. She responded with a torrent of indignant Mandarin and he leapt towards her again, this time producing a small knife. I started, and wished I might do something to protect her, but the surge of people between us pushed me ever closer to the Legation Quarter, and I could only watch helplessly. The blade glinted in the uncompromising sunlight, its clean tip aimed squarely at the pale skin exposed above the circular sweep of Nina's summer dress. She stumbled as she stepped back, falling into the embrace of Hugo and James. The man ran on, dropping pearls as he sprinted, his head whipping round for one last look at his victim. The crowd closed densely around Nina, emitting sounds soothing and sympathetic. I struggled against the direction of those around me in an attempt to reach her, and quickly realized my efforts were futile. I saw Nina swallowed by the crowd and turned away, watching as the last of the grim-faced soldiers marched into the Legation Quarter.

Nicholas and Nina seemed to expect me that evening. Their home offered none of the bright and hospitable warmth it had provided just the night before. Instead, a single dim light glowed in the drawing room; doors and windows were tightly closed against the night. Nina greeted me in embarrassed tones.

"I suppose you know what happened," she said quietly.

"And I suppose you know why I am here," I said. "First Secretary Fairchild has told me once again that both of you are very much welcome to stay with him."

"I hate to leave my home," Nicholas said. "But we must do all we can to keep Nina safe. It is as the Chinese say: squid make fools of dragons in shallow waters. These are our shallow waters." He gestured at the room around him, the scrolls of calligraphy hung carefully against white walls, the delicately painted vase atop a panelled cabinet, the jade lion roaring silently by the fireplace.

"I never thought such a thing might happen," Nina said, her voice small. "I understand that he might have seen me and thought that I...that I was one of them, a missionary or the wife of some senseless official. But I spoke to him, I tried to make him see that I was...I was different. It was as though he couldn't hear me."

Nina looked at the floor as she spoke, her lips pulled tight and thin. Her posture, quiet and rounded, saddened me.

"I am afraid we are all the enemy now," I said. "That is what happens in wars. A terrible business."

"Let us not get carried away, Mr Scott," Nicholas said. "This is far from a war. Nina and I shall go temporarily to the Legation Quarter until such a time as we might live here in absolute safety. I expect we shall be home within the week, isn't that right, Nina?"

"Yes, Father," Nina said. She stepped suddenly towards me and I embraced her, let her head rest gently on my shoulder, noting how fragile her form felt against mine. Nicholas met my eye with grave expression.

The Wards conducted no great ceremony upon leaving their home. Although I had increasingly come to believe that we faced a serious and possibly protracted conflict, I likewise found it hard to imagine the Wards would be absent from their *hutung* for long. The arrival of the troops should render it impossible for the Boxers to reach their ultimate target of the foreign population, I reasoned, and ought to repel them from Peking, perhaps allowing a half-peace to settle upon the city even as the hinterlands blazed. The household staff was instructed to stay and carry out a lighter roster of duties, an order to which they readily agreed. They had no desire to enter the Legation Quarter, where servants could expect to be packed into hellish accommodation with the native Christians, who sought sanctuary in the quarter after abandoning the tumultuous countryside. As Yang led us silently through the courtyard to the familiar front door with its golden lion knockers, Nicholas passed me a piece of thin, poor quality paper: a poster, torn at its corners and with a scrawl of chaotic characters coiling across it from top to bottom.

"I saw this today. The translation is on the other side," he said. "A little color for one of your stories, perhaps."

I glanced at the words written in Nicholas' looping cursive:

Their men are immoral, their women truly vile,
For the Devils mother-son sex is the breeding style.

I folded the paper and placed it in my pocket, reaching to take Nina's small and hastily-prepared leather bag from Yang's grip. The servant secured the door decisively behind us and the *hutung* lay gloomy and deserted, stretching desolate ahead of our party. We passed through the shadows of the city, the echoing trundle of our rickshaws bound by the walls of opaque courtyards, each corner causing us hold our breath, wondering if a Boxer lay in wait, Peking's unnatural obscurity providing ideal shelter for the magical warriors.

Dinner was drawing to a close when we arrived at Oscar Fairchild's home. The First Secretary greeted us with earnest cordiality, and ordered his staff to arrange three additional chairs around the long table, where the dining party was looked over by a large and imperious portrait of Queen Victoria. The other guests watched with curiosity as we took our places at the mahogany table. They were three women: one I knew as Lillian Price, cousin of Fairchild's wife Violet and heiress to an American railroad fortune on a coming-of-age tour of the Far East, while another was Beatrice Moore, wife of a British trade official and widely known as a something of a gossip. The other woman was unknown to me. Her clothes were homespun and plain, her hair graying and parted down the middle. She was, I suspected, a woman of God.

"I am so very glad Mr Scott was able to change your mind," Fairchild said to Nicholas.

"Mr Scott made valiant efforts to do so," Nicholas said. "But I am afraid it was rather the unfortunate events of the day that changed my position on the matter. Nina had quite a fright, as you might imagine."

"Oh, really?" Lillian Price said, smiling broadly. "I heard it was quite to the contrary, that the poor Boxer was more afraid after receiving such a scolding from Miss Ward!"

The American girl rose then from her seat and assuredly shook Nicholas' hand .

"Lillian Price," she declared with conviction.

"How do you do," Nicholas said.

"Phoebe Franklin," the other woman said. "I have come from Chihli."

A missionary, then, escaping the flames and fury of the rainless interior.

Oscar Fairchild explained that while Nicholas had been designated his own room, Nina was expected to share Violet Fairchild's bedroom with Lillian. The First Secretary had a fine house; not as large, of course, as the British Minister's, but with a number of spare rooms to accommodate the needy. He had hosted Lillian Price for three weeks already, and she now remained indefinitely in the company of strangers, the arrival of the Boxers having stymied plans to join her brother in Tokyo. Miss Price had been joined under Fairchild's roof by the American missionary two days previously. Oscar called for a servant to show Nina to the room, suggesting that she must be tired after a long day, without making explicit reference to the event that had led her to his door. I appreciated his tact, and I am sure that Nina, the stiffness of whose carriage hinted at some remaining shame, also liked that he avoided mention of the altercation.

"I shall accompany her," Lillian said, rising from her seat. "I have everything arranged just so, and a lovely screen to separate our two beds."

The pair followed a servant upstairs, and I heard Lillian ask Nina if she knew James Millington and Hugo Lovell.

"Miss Ward should be safe here," Oscar said to Nicholas. "I am so glad that you and your daughter have decided to join us. I very much hope that you shall both be comfortable here."

Nicholas thanked Oscar for his hospitality.

"This is something of a luxury for Nina," he said warmly. "Prior to this, the only time she has spent away from home has been in the most humble of villages, helping me with my work."

"Miss Ward seems a most spirited young woman," Beatrice Moore said, fixing her round, brown eyes upon Nicholas. "How surprised we were to see a young woman shouting at a dangerous Boxer!"

"Miss Ward was very brave," Oscar said evenly. "Might I offer anyone a drink?"

Nicholas scratched his beard and shook his head.

"Time to retire, I think," he said.

Beatrice Moore, who had attended the dinner in her role as friend and confidante to the young Miss Price, also excused herself, saying she must return to her children whom she had left in the care of the servants at the Bloomfield household, where she and her husband had recently taken up residence. Beatrice had made evasive references to the inferiority of the Bloomfields' domestic arrangements throughout the evening, taking care to make use of that special brand of English delicacy that avoided any outright criticism, any material utterance about which one might be accused of ill-feeling, while making clear one's displeasure.

"Well, Mr Fairchild, it is not in my nature to refuse the offer of a drink," I said. "If it is no trouble to you, of course."

"Never."

I followed Oscar to the drawing room. To my surprise, the missionary Phoebe Franklin also decided to join us. Rapidly it transpired that Mrs Franklin desired neither port nor brandy, but rather wished to persuade Fairchild of the urgent need for the British government to quash Boxer activity in the countryside. Somewhat reserved at the dining table, Phoebe spoke now with assured righteousness, demonstrating the flame-blooded passion of the proselytizer as she detailed the horrors to which she and her heavenly colleagues had been subject.

"The deaths I saw!" she cried. "They burnt down our church, but that was not enough, no, they mutilated the bodies of worshippers, they emptied their pockets for worthless coins and crumbs of mouldy bread."

"I know the French wish to take some kind of retaliatory action, but they must realize these deaths are insignificant if one is to consider the wider situation in China," Oscar said, tapping ash from his pipe into a jade-trimmed dish. "We risk provoking a more violent reaction from the Boxers. God knows, we have unsettled the Chinese enough by parading our troops through the city today."

"The Boxers are murdering people who believe in the Christian God, Mr Fairchild. Is that something your government will really allow to continue?" Phoebe leaned forward in her chair, heavy jaw and high forehead glaring in the orange flicker of candlelight.

My prejudices against the offices of both Phoebe and Oscar allowed me to listen detachedly to their arguments, half-agreeing with each interlocutor while experiencing no compulsion to demonstrate my support for either.

"But most of the deaths are *Chinese*, Mrs Franklin," Oscar responded. "Natives killing natives, and that always happens, regardless of whichever God they might profess to believe in." He stopped, his neck craned towards the doorway. "Is that you, Miss Ward?"

None of us had heard Nina approach, but now through

the half-open door I perceived her standing uncertainly in the darkened corridor, her figure ghostly pale, a jug of water clutched between her fingers. Sheepishly, she stepped into the room.

"I'm sorry, Mr Fairchild, I came downstairs for water and heard your conversation. I couldn't help but to overhear…"

"Quite right," Oscar said, standing up and lifting the jug from her hands, setting it down upon a mahogany table. "Please, Miss Ward, sit with us a while. And in future you may call a servant for water. You are a guest in this house."

"Oh, really, I ought to sleep," Nina began, but Oscar gestured once more for her to sit. She obeyed, taking a seat next to mine, offering me a small, familiar smile.

"We have been talking, Miss Ward, about the deaths in the countryside. We are all in agreement that there is little we might do to prevent such terrible events," Oscar said.

Phoebe frowned.

"While it is most distressing to see the deaths of so many innocent Chinese," he continued, "these native killings are not an issue for our governments. The Chinese shall always kill each other, shall they not?"

"Just as Englishmen shall always kill Englishmen, yes," Nina said. "I suppose every man has his sunless side."

"And in any case the death of a Christian is a tragedy, regardless of the color of his skin or the language upon his tongue," Phoebe said.

Oscar, looking inquisitively towards Nina, did not respond to the missionary.

"Yet the rates of murder witnessed here, Miss Ward, are not comparable with those of England," he continued. "One cannot deny that life is rather less valued in China. That is not something the foreign powers might change, however strong our good will towards the Chinese."

"And yet the Boxers would not exist if the Europeans had not tried to impose their way of life on the Chinese," Nina protested. "Is theirs not a natural reaction? Extreme, yes, but absolutely natural. Step on a dog's tail and he shall bite you."

"Quite," I said in support of Nina, but I was prevented from speaking more by Phoebe Franklin.

"Whatever do you mean, child?" the missionary said to Nina, her voice steady and stern. "There is absolutely nothing natural about the Boxers. We have worked to liberate the natives from devil worship. We have saved them from the superstitious culture that has allowed such nonsense as the Boxers to flourish. Invulnerability rituals, nefarious magic, innumerable gods. The religion of poverty and backwardness."

"I do not wish to speak out of turn," Nina said, setting her spine tall against the high-backed chair, eyes traveling calmly between Oscar and Phoebe without a break in her young voice. "But I do not believe the converts have been saved from anything. They are dying precisely because they believe in a God they would not even know to worship if they had not been told to do so by foreigners."

"Miss Ward," Phoebe said primly. "We enlightened the Chinese. We brought them faith and education and health where before there was only poverty, ignorance and sickness. I have heard such attitudes as yours among the heathens themselves, of course, but never from one of our own people. Such audacity!"

"Mrs Franklin is right, is she not?" Oscar said, turning to face Nina, eyebrows arched questioningly above the glacial blue of his eyes. "The Boxers, with their magic and their martial arts, show just how primitive China would be without us. We build a railway track, they tear it up, we give them telegraph poles, they tear them down. It is as though they don't want China to prosper."

"I do not believe they wish any ill on China, Mr Fairchild," Nina said quietly. "Excuse me, I must go to bed."

"Nina, stay a while," I suggested.

"No, really, I must return to Miss Price. She waits for the water."

"Very well, Miss Ward," Oscar said with sincere warmth. "But allow me, please, to tell you frankly that I find something refreshing in your ideas. Perhaps we might talk more tomorrow. I am new to China, as you know, and someone as knowledgeable as you might help me understand better this unusual situation that we face."

"Blasphemy," Phoebe said sharply. "Refreshing, indeed."

"Good night." Nina dipped her head in the missionary's direction and fled upstairs. Only when we heard the closing of the bedroom door did Phoebe note that Nina had forgotten the jug of water. I offered to take the jug upstairs to her, and left Oscar and Phoebe to continue their discussion.

I stood outside Violet Fairchild's bedroom, my hand raised to knock on the door, when I heard the unmistakably poised tones of Lillian Price.

"Imagine Mr Fairchild taking advice from you. Do you suppose he shall formulate military strategy according your opinions?" she asked Nina.

"Oh, no, Mr Fairchild is very polite. A necessary quality for diplomats, I suppose," Nina said quietly, and I felt impelled to save her from this shame with which she had unwittingly tarred herself. How might a young woman like Lillian Price, blonde, vivacious and rich, a product of the most elite institutions of the New World, an heiress not only of financial security but also of such elevated social status, ever understand such a strange creature as Nina? I knocked loudly upon the door and called Nina's name.

"You forgot the water," I said, and Nina slipped out of the room to meet me in the dark corridor.

"Hello, Mr Scott," she said, with uncharacteristic formality. We were both aware of the figure of Lillian Price behind the dark wood door. "How very careless of me."

"We all have rather a lot on our minds," I said carefully.

Nina took the jug from me, but made no move to return to the bedroom. Rather she looked at me in a manner almost beseeching. Nina's pride would not allow any petition to be written plainly upon her face, instead the suggestion that she was burdened by words unspoken was evinced in the slightly awkward manner in which she stood, the swaying of her weight from hip to hip, the tilt of her head.

"Miss Ward," I said, feeling myself an actor for the benefit of Miss Price, "won't you accompany me to the front door?"

Nina followed me downstairs, together we paused outside the drawing room.

"Are you all right?" I asked in low tones. "You have been most courageous, you and your father, leaving your home to reside with strangers. I know it has not been easy, dear Nina, but it is for the best."

"How like me these people look," Nina said in whispered wonderment, "yet how differently to me they think."

I pitied Nina: Europeans had featured so little in her young life that of course the temperaments and characteristics of the individuals around her were shrouded in codes and signs that she struggled to decipher. The lives lived by these people of her own lily-colored race were unknowable, impenetrable.

"I am very proud of you," I said. "You defended your views and there is nothing wrong with that. If you ask me, these people will benefit very much from your experience. They live in a China without Chinese, caring only for the natives when they are of use to them, to be taxed or converted or sold something. You remind them of the existence of another country and it is not your fault if it results in their discomfort."

"Really? I would so hate to embarrass Father, and I feel that perhaps I said too much. The way that woman, the missionary, the way she regarded me as though I were the Devil Himself!"

I shook my head, clasped her shoulder.

"Come, I must bid goodnight to our host. Sleep well, Nina, and do not concern yourself further with such thoughts."

Nina turned to ascend the stairs once more, but stopped, one foot hovered over the bottom step.

"I did not say goodbye to Chang," she said slowly. "She might wonder where I am. Father said I ought not to leave the Legation Quarter alone, but perhaps you might accompany me to her home tomorrow?"

I replied in the affirmative: Chang was Nina's best friend, the daughter of a Chinese academic and sometime political reformer who lived in the same neighborhood as the Wards. Nina had known her so long she did not remember meeting her; like her father, Chang was simply a fact of Nina's existence. I imagined Nina, a square peg forced suddenly into a round hole, felt the steady rhythm of her existence suddenly jangled and discordant, and I wished to offer her some comfort. Steadily, calmly she climbed the stairs, and I called to Oscar that I was to leave.

The First Secretary led me to the front door, one hand placed familiarly upon my back.

"What an extraordinary young woman Miss Ward is," he said.

"Quite." I puzzled at his expression, but Oscar Fairchild possessed the diplomatic ability to conceal any motive behind a pleasantly neutral arrangement of features. I wondered if there might be some hint of condescension in his words, some disapproval couched in layers of most polite deception, but he betrayed no such ironic feeling.

"Two Italian guests arrive tomorrow evening," he said. "Would you care to join us again for dinner?"

"I would be most obliged," I said, and it was not much of a lie, not for a man like myself. I did not care for Lillian Price or Phoebe Franklin and certainly not for Beatrice Moore, but officials such as Oscar lived close enough to the kindling of events to prove useful to my work, and the Wards were my most intimate acquaintances in an increasingly hostile city. "Good night, Mr Fairchild."

III

I WAITED as Nina knocked on her best friend's door. The entrance was painted a deep red like the Wards' and framed by scrolls decorated with New Year couplets, their corners curled in the months that had passed since the Spring Festival. I watched a servant open the door with a show of lavish caution, head appearing warily around the edge of the hatch.

"*Zao,*" Nina wished him good morning in her enviable Mandarin, smooth and standard where mine, cultivated by coolies and inelegant as the villages in which I had learned it, was rough and rudimentary. "*Chang zai ma?*"

I could not make out the servant's mumbled reply from my position a few feet behind Nina.

"When will she return? Shall I wait for her?" Nina asked.

The servant spoke no words, dipped his head and gently levered the door closed. The house was sealed now, its thick walls impenetrable to Nina. With reluctant tread she stepped back into the lane and faced me. The day's heat rose already from the dust and beaded sweat atop her lip.

"I thought I saw her," Nina said glumly. "Running across the courtyard."

The commitment of Chang's family to modernity and emancipation was writ in flesh and bone in their daughter's freedom to wriggle her toes and roll her ankles; Chang had escaped the common fate of bound feet, and was, I suppose, quite unlike her Chinese peers. That was what made the friendship of

Chang and Nina, two cranes amongst their respective hordes of chickens, so successful.

"I'm sorry, Nina. You must be terribly disappointed," I said. She nodded heavily. "Well, as we are so close to your home perhaps you might like to collect some more of your belongings. Then the morning is not lost." Chang lived only two lanes west of the Wards.

"I suppose so," Nina sighed.

Languidly we walked together, following east the twists of the *hutung,* noting the unusual silence of the streets, the paucity of life around us. No old women gossiped in doorways, no rag-and-bone men rang their bells, no familiar click of mahjong tiles sounded beneath the curved eaves. And then, the sound of quick strides. We turned to see Chang, hair loose about her shoulders, long dress pooling around her feet as she ran.

"Chang. They told me you were not at home," Nina said.

"They won't let me see you." Chang came to a halt, her chest rattled by short, shallow breaths. "Father says it is too dangerous."

"Too dangerous?" Nina repeated.

"To consort with foreigners." Chang's eyes swept the length of the lane and she chewed her bottom lip. A rabbit, I thought, innocent and true, but capable just the same of fear. "Nina, this shall pass, I know it shall, and after the bitter shall come the sweet. But I fear I may not be able to see you for some time. "

"Chang..." Nina faltered. "Father and I are staying in the British Legation," she said finally.

"Good," Chang said. "You ought to be very careful. When the Boxers have been defeated all shall be as it was before. Hopefully soon enough that we might still take the boats out on Houhai."

Nina reached for her friend's hand, gripped it tightly. The previous summer she had spent many breezy afternoons on the lakes with her friend, wide-brimmed parasols shading them from the sun as they sailed in dallying circles on the placid waters. Chang pressed a kiss against Nina's cheek, and waved shyly to me.

"Take care." And then she was gone, running quickly in the direction from which she had come.

Nina looked wordlessly at me and it was in that moment that I witnessed the fear seize her. Its shadow may have crossed her before, when the troops arrived in their neatly-pressed uniforms, buttons tightly fastened and shining for war, when the blade of the man's knife had glinted in the sunlight yesterday, its tip sharp and unforgiving, when Nina woke in Fairchild's house and felt the bed beneath her strange and uncomfortable. Yet it was only now, as she stood before me in this neighboring lane, its every brick and gutter as familiar as the lines of her own palm, the figure of her friend vanished, the houses all around shuttered and mute, that true fear descended, choking and fetid upon her. This girl, who had known no home beyond Peking, this girl, whose tongue danced effortlessly to the tones of Chinese, this girl was to be avoided by the people she had known all of her life. With wild eyes she reached for my arm and together we sped towards her home, our fear carrying us from a beast we could not name.

Nina, Nicholas and I walked together to the Fairchild house for dinner. Nicholas had returned home for the day to continue working on his current book despite my insistence that he would be safer within the Legation Quarter. As long as the Boxers did not sound their drums or twirl their knives during daylight hours, Nicholas said, he would return to his study as normal. Given my fervent determination to remain in my own house I could not protest his decision too strongly.

We joined the other guests around the dining table, where

our pre-dinner conversation concerned, as one might expect, the Boxers. Mention was made of an Italian couple due to join us, a countess and her diplomat husband, but talk focused on anything but our enemy withered quickly in the febrile, expectant atmosphere of those first days in the Legation Quarter. Lillian told us of a visit she had paid to the student interpreters; she had learned that they were to be given leave of their lessons for some time, with the understanding that they might well be expected to take up arms. She was lamenting James Millington's poor backhand at tennis, suggesting he might lack the coordination for battle, when La Contessa came into view. Standing respectfully behind Oscar Fairchild, her hands clasped neatly by her waist, she wore a silk dress of deep forest green. Her figure was full and exuberant and her very presence overwhelmed that of the man by her side, slight as he was, with a sharp-cut nose and an expression of earnest nervousness.

"I present to you Mr Pietro Mancini and his wife, La Contessa Chiara," Fairchild said.

"Good evening," La Contessa said, her accent rising and falling over each syllable like fingertips upon the keys of a flute.

"*Buona sera*," I said amidst the chorus of *good evenings*, and thrilled as Chiara rewarded me with a smile both indulgent and dazzling.

Oscar gestured for the couple to be seated. I watched, enchanted, as La Contessa lowered herself precisely into the seat next to Lillian, arranging her skirts around her with collected purposefulness. Once settled, she rose again suddenly with sharp, feline movement.

"I forgot," she said. "We have some gifts." She left the room, dress cascading around her, each crease glimmering as it caught the light. Pietro Mancini shook his head as she left.

"My wife...She is a little disturbed," he explained. "There

38

have been many problems in our Legation. The servants…" He pulled his finger in swift motion across his throat. "All of them. She is very happy to leave. Thank you for your kindness and hospitality."

"What are you saying, Pietro?" La Contessa returned with a bottle of champagne in each hand, dust obscuring the French names printed on their labels. She tapped the door closed with a gracefully extended leg. "We had so many in the cellar I thought I must bring some. Oh, Mr Fairchild, please be a darling and ask the servants for some glasses. We shall make a toast to peace!"

What pleasure it brings me now to recall the unrepentant display of life performed that first night by Chiara, her spirit vivid and undeniable, her essence frivolous and light, under the disapproving glare of Beatrice Moore and the austere portrait of Queen Victoria that looked imperiously down upon us all. La Contessa insisted upon filling each glass herself, seeming neither to notice nor to care when drops of champagne dribbled and pooled over the linen tablecloth, dismissing the servants when they offered assistance. Perhaps she did not perceive Beatrice Moore dabbing at the spilled droplets. More likely she preferred not to pay her any heed.

"*Alla salute,*" La Contessa crowed when all glasses were full. "*Cento di questi giorni!*"

When dinner was finished and each glass was dry, Nicholas announced that he would retire for the night. Oscar invited Pietro and I to join him in his study for port, and the women moved to the drawing room, where La Contessa promised them Swiss chocolates rescued from her abandoned pantry. Phoebe Franklin declined the offer, saying she had no interest in fiddling while Rome burned and left instead to check the conditions of some of the Chinese Christian refugees housed elsewhere in the Legation Quarter.

Oscar's library was low-lit and decorated in comfortably dark, masculine tones. I felt quite at home as I received a glass of port and allowed myself to skim the titles on his shelves. The spines of the most serious tomes were unbent, but one volume upon his desk appeared well-thumbed.

"*Far From The Madding Crowd*," I said, touching the corner of the novel.

"How pleasant I found it to lose myself in those bucolic English scenes when the heat of the Subcontinent raged," Oscar replied. "And each time I read it I fall in love once more with Bathsheba Everdene."

"And how does Mrs Fairchild feel about that?" I asked.

Oscar gave a low laugh and lit his pipe.

"She was something of a Bathsheba herself before we married," he said. "Violet was widowed at a very young age, you see, and I feared no suitor would ever win her affections again."

I was tempted to press further; one never knows when personal information regarding a man with official capacities may prove useful, but Pietro Mancini interrupted, demanding Oscar set out the British government's position on the protection of missionaries in the countryside. We sat in a loose circle, and talked of the latest Boxer developments. Each new day only brought more of the same: reports of atrocities in the hinterlands, sightings of Boxers ever closer to the Legation Quarter, the arrival of more Chinese Christians to Peking and official befuddlement across the representatives of all nations about what exactly ought to the done next. Pietro wore his customary expression of stalk-eyed surprise; a bird-like, small man, he seemed perpetually startled by events. Yet it was possible to read even in his face a profound sense of shock when Oscar suggested we call for Nina to join our discussion.

"Miss Ward? Whatever for?" I asked.

"The Wards are experts on the Chinese, are they not? They live amongst them, and Mr Ward has written profoundly about their belief systems and philosophy. What's more, Miss Ward is most frank in her opinions," Oscar said.

Pietro protested that we ought to call for Nicholas instead, an opinion I happened to share, but Oscar, undeterred, summoned a servant and demanded Miss Ward be brought to the library. This was a most unusual suggestion. While women were permitted, perhaps even encouraged, to speak of the Boxer threat in the most general terms of unease and anxiety, they were seldom included in conversations of strategy and defense. Only women of God, who through chastity and hardship had made themselves almost akin to men, were allowed within such circles, and even then only when the occasion called for their particular brand of expertise. War and politics were men's matters; publicly we declared that women were excluded to protect their dignity and prevent their becoming afraid, while reason unspoken ruled that no woman would have anything of import to contribute to such discussions. For a senior British official to call upon a young woman of no special position was so very unconventional that I found myself rather intrigued by Oscar Fairchild. His hitherto pleasant and upstanding character was shrouded suddenly in an elusive, unorthodox air and suggested to me he possessed rather more layers of personality to unravel than I had first estimated.

Nina followed the servant into the room with precise, careful step, her brow lightly creased.

"Thank you, Lin. You may leave," Oscar said to the servant, who bowed and retreated. The First Secretary turned his attention to Nina with an easy smile.

"Miss Ward," he began.

"Perhaps we ought to ask for the girl's father," Pietro said in sharp, but somewhat pleading, tone. "He is the scholar, after all."

"I shouldn't like to disturb him," Oscar replied mildly. "Besides, in my admittedly limited experience, Miss Ward has no trouble speaking her mind. She is a native of this place, Mr Mancini, but one who is not against us. That makes her, in my judgement at least, one of the most valuable individuals in Peking at present. Miss Ward, kindly take a seat."

Nina, hesitant, remained standing.

"Miss Ward, we wouldn't wish to trouble you," Pietro Mancini continued.

Oscar raised a hand to silence him.

"Miss Ward, I wish to ask your counsel," he said.

I gestured for Nina to take a seat by me, with a grateful smile she lowered herself by my side.

"You are likely aware that we are presently in negotiations with our Chinese counterparts with regards the Boxer question," Oscar continued. "We are to meet Prince Ching in the coming days to discuss the murder of two missionaries south of Peking."

"Missionaries?" Nina repeated.

"Two British missionaries. Slaughtered in a most terrible way," Oscar said, and Pietro Mancini shook his head gravely. "Circumstances grow more terrible by the minute, and yet the Chinese seem absolutely uninterested in preventing Boxer destruction of their own country. These ruffians shall burn the place to the ground if we do not impel the Chinese to act at once. You are familiar with the etiquette of the Chinese, are you not?" He fixed his eyes upon her.

"Mr Fairchild, I am not sure I am the right person to advise on matters of statecraft," she began.

"She admits it herself!" Pietro interjected.

"Statecraft is only a matter of people and, in this case, the people of China," Oscar said. "Miss Ward, it seems to me that you have an understanding of the Chinese. I ask only how you would conduct a meeting with Prince Ching as a person, not as a diplomat. No further expertise is required on your part." He leaned back in his chair, invited Nina to speak.

I nodded my encouragement, puzzled still by Oscar's decision to invite Nina to participate in the conversation. Yes, she lived almost as a Chinese, but was the Legation Quarter not already crowded with real Chinese by the names of Wang and Hong and Li, any of whom might have accurately described China through the eyes of a native? And what of my expertise, I asked myself in a pique of chagrined pride. Was my very position not that of observer and interlocutor of the Chinese, translator of events and customs, narrator of the country's unfolding story?

"Let me share, then, my most inexpert opinion," Nina said deliberately. "There are as many philosophies of life as there are men in China, and I cannot speak for all. Even if I were to consider myself an expert on the Chinese character, one has to recognize that the ruling classes are Manchu, and not Han Chinese, with the subtleties of culture and history such differences entail. Yet if I were to draw a general conclusion, I would hazard that the only way to quell the Boxers is through softness and comprehension, not hardness and combat. The Boxers see no advantage in the presence of foreigners, they only see them casting Chinese gods as devils or constructing railways in sacred places. A harsh or punitive approach to negotiations with the Qing government would only further justify the Boxers' cause."

She paused. Oscar listened intently with thoughtful expression, but I detected amusement in the countenance of Pietro Mancini. Nina looked in the direction of the Italian and swallowed nervously.

"I appreciate that you are short on time," she continued. "As such, I suggest only that you remember to give the prince face.

Do not pressure him or his officials with impossible deadlines or extreme demands. Imagine the negotiation as a stream. Drop a boulder into the stream and the water shall find a new course around it. The Manchus avoid confrontation where possible, so do not raise your voice. If you shout, they shall plan your downfall in whispers." Nina stopped, lightly cleared her throat. "I am sure there are many scholars who might tell you far more than I am able to share. My father is the real expert on these matters, perhaps you ought to talk to him tomorrow."

"Thank you, Miss Ward," Oscar said sincerely.

"Do not expect any decisions immediately. I have no doubt that all shall be reported to the Empress Dowager and that she will take any final decision," Nina added. "Allow the water to settle and the mud to clear, and do not force action."

"Oh yes, the famous Empress Dowager. What are your thoughts on the her, Miss Ward?" Oscar asked.

Pietro sighed deeply, raised his eyes to the gold cornice that lined the library ceiling.

"She is the first woman to rule China since the Tang dynasty," Nina began, trying to ignore the dubiety with which Pietro Mancini regarded her. "She has the will to survive this new century, but not the support of the court; at least this is what my father says. Her feelings towards the Boxers are rather ambivalent. When they are a useful political tool she does not hesitate to make use of them."

Nina stood, suddenly aware of Pietro staring at her, his expression unreadable now. "Perhaps I have said too much, I really have very little idea of these things. I ought to excuse myself," she said.

"Thank you, Miss Ward," Oscar said sincerely.

"You are your father's daughter," I said. "A most incisive analysis."

"Good night." Nina stood to leave, and I rose with her, saying to Fairchild that I ought to return home. The night had yet to unveil its dark heart, we were still an hour or two from the velvety moments when the Boxers took to the streets, and I had no desire to cross paths with the enemy. As we reached the door Nina paused and looked back at Oscar and Pietro, bowed silently over their drinks.

"Mr Fairchild, if I may," she said. "You said that statecraft was a matter of people. The Chinese are people. Think of them as humans, not two-headed dragons, and perhaps you shall have more success." She pursed her lips, thinking she had perhaps gone too far, but Oscar laughed genially.

"You are quite right. Thank you, Miss Ward, for your candid observations. Good night."

Nina closed the door quietly behind her, and together we crossed the dark corridor.

"Oh, Mr Scott," she whispered fiercely to me. "Did I say too much? Why do you think Mr Fairchild called for me?"

I told her that I did not know why he had summoned her, and urged her not to worry about what she had said, which, after all, had been eminently sensible, if rather unexpected from the mouth of a nineteen-year-old woman. We stopped outside the drawing room, and I bowed my head goodnight.

"Until tomorrow, then," I said, catching, as I leaned towards her, fragments of the women's conversation inside the room.

"It is quite improper," I heard Lillian say.

"It only encourages her," Beatrice Moore agreed. "She understands nothing. It is as though she is neither English or Chinese but rather something *feral*."

"Miss Price, did you not say she is to be married?" La Contessa asked.

I pulled back. Nina stood unnaturally still, her lips frozen in a half-smile. I observed the first hot springs of tears in her eyes.

"Nina," I started, but she only lifted a finger hurriedly to her lips, and turned to climb the stairs quickly, not turning back to look at me as she ascended them two at a time. I heard the bedroom door close, and thought for a moment of saying good night to the ladies in the drawing room, before dismissing the idea on the basis of my loyalty towards Nina. I hurried towards the night dark and foreboding, the first echoes of the Boxers already in the air. *Sha! Sha!* Kill! Kill!

IV

THE NEXT DAY brought rumors of a Boxer incident at the racecourse, and I was, in the contrary manner of a newspaper man, quite happy to hear it. Finally, a promising story within striking distance of Peking's foreign village, terrible and pertinent enough to stir the masses back home so far largely unmoved, according to my editor, by the second-hand stories of torture, beheadings or kidnapping passed to me from the hinterlands. The racecourse offered powerful symbolic value; in Peking, as in every corner of empire, the British had found a likely piece of land upon which to impress a circuit, construct a stand and cement a clocktower. The racing ground lay to the west of the city, a good five or six miles from the Legation Quarter, where dry, dusty paths at last gave way to the flat green of the countryside. The races functioned as the axis of a familiar life recreated under foreign skies, and in China the pastime was popular with both the British and European communities, as well as a small number of wealthy Chinese. The Qing authorities, however, bristled at the sight of their citizens queuing eagerly to hand over their money to foreigners and nurtured suspicions that the unfamiliar sport was rigged somehow against the locals. It was logical to me, then, that the burning of the grandstand could be no accident, and surely constituted a Boxer attack against the outsiders. The fire beckoned me closer with curls of black smoke that wavered across the horizon as scores of grim-faced men, impatient to confirm whether the Boxers had succeeded in razing that old place of sunny days and civilized society, surged through the streets alongside me. I spied some of the student interpreters riding a little further ahead, their indignation palpable as they forged an unyielding course southwards.

The body of the grandstand had fallen swiftly and its structure was crumbling still. Rogue pieces tumbled to the trampled lawn in charred, blackened lumps. Horses had bolted from the stables and they galloped wildly across the course, leaving spirals of upturned mud behind their nervous hooves. The Boxers, most of whom had taken rapid retreat, could be spied running further south, the red rags of their informal uniform billowing behind them. A handful of the most courageous warriors stood challenging and triumphant around the far edges of the course.

With the destruction of grandstand almost complete and most of the Boxers escaped, the only role any of us might serve would be that of a passive witness to the horror. I recognized James Millington and Hugo Lovell amongst the crestfallen faces of the gathered Englishmen. James, normally circumspect, was warrior-like now upon his horse, his face rubicund and scowling under dense, slate-colored hair. Impatiently he tugged on the reins wrapped between his fingers, determinedly he pressed against his horse's flank with tensed thighs. Hugo, fair and slight, appeared feeble and impotent by his side.

"This is a bad business." Edward Samuels stopped beside me. "We could hear the Boxers so clearly last night, it was as though they were inside the hotel with us. They appear absolutely fearless."

My eyes were fixed still on James and Hugo. Their horses were agitated, offering occasional flashes of teeth.

"I have said to Hilde that we will be safe within the Legation Quarter, but I wonder if I ought to have sent her away like the other wives," Edward continued. "Not that she would have gone, I suppose."

"Hilde does not strike me as a woman who would be afraid of a few Boxers," I said.

"She is not afraid, but..." He faltered. "I have been here almost twenty years, but this, this is a bloody mess. Where are the soldiers?" Edward shook his head. "For what purpose did they bring troops here? Only to antagonize the Chinese? It is utterly senseless."

The most foolhardy Boxers came closer then, a gaggle of fewer than a dozen men who had stayed to relish the despondency their violence had bred in the enemy. They surrounded the Englishmen, moving in a dire, dizzying dance, mocking and scoffing in coarse language I was sure the interpreters had yet to study in their Chinese classes. James Millington's complexion grew ever more rufescent and his expression more brutal as his lips twitched with whispered curses. And then a shot. Clearly, it rang out across the racetrack. A rapid, remorseless shot, with long, hollow echo.

"What was that?" Edward Samuels started.

We saw the body of the Boxer, suddenly, shockingly lifeless, splayed and expired amidst the muddle of horses and men. I moved towards the melee but Edward stopped me, held his arm across my chest. And quite right he was to do so: my instinctive reaction to an injured man is not, I am ashamed to say, to tend to his wounds or to offer honeyed visions of the realm that lies beyond death. No, it is my habit instead to try to wring one last word from his soon-to-be-silenced mouth, it is my aim to have him, in his last expiring breath, reveal to me the purpose, the core, the truth of his life and the reason why I might record its passing in text. This selfish interest in the last moments of another's life endears me neither to his friend or to his foe, each of whom regard my actions with great suspicion. And so I stopped myself, though I couldn't help but to lean forward in the saddle, to glance more closely upon the Boxer's dim face, to wonder if he had felt, as the bullet pierced his supposedly unassailable skin, that this generational struggle against the foreign justified the termination of his existence.

The muttering, indignant crowd of Englishmen reluctantly parted as a single Boxer leapt from his horse and hurried towards the corpse. The Boxer shouted to his companions to help him retrieve the body, but they, apparently cowed by the death of a peer, allowed this single most valiant of their number to trail the man's limp, motionless form over the grass. The man's skin was still slick with sweat. His face fell slack, but a flush lingered upon his cheeks. I lifted my eyes from the body and saw James, cavalier and imperious on his horse, his face a canvas of triumph and terror. I had seen that very mien before: the countenance of the man who has taken his first life. And then suddenly James was pulled from his saddle, wrenched from his gun, set upon by two Boxers in a confusion of strikes and kicks. Limp and defenseless he lay upon the ground, his being fading, receding like that of the man he had killed.

"Edward," I said. "We must act now. They shall kill the boy!"

A thundering of hooves announced the arrival of real troops. The Boxers ceased their hail of violence and raced away, leaving behind a victory still evident in the rusty smell of burning wood and charred metal, their glory only gently dimmed by the loss of one of their men. James Millington stirred, ragged breaths swelled his chest. The troops put out the fire with little heart and methodically Hugo and friends lifted James atop his horse once more, talking of doctors and bandages and Chinese firewater to clean the wounds. Resignation dampened the smoky air, the shame of defeat reduced those usually brash, confident English tones to nothing more than vexed mutterings. The stand was devastated, and whilst it was unlikely that any of us would have spent the summer at the races in the current circumstances, seeing its cragged remains, watching as its rows of splendid seats collapsed upon one another, constituted an undeniable wound to our pride.

James Millington survived. He was safely returned to the Legation Quarter, where a Russian doctor treated his wounds. Hastily I recorded my account of events, writing word after hurried word until they blurred before my eyes, trying to pull a string of sense through the disparate elements before me. A racecourse, a dead Boxer, a halo of magic. And what of James' role? It had unnerved me, that shot of his. James was a boy, really, had only recently finished his university studies. Over the course of my career I had seen many boys fail to mature to men, fossilizing instead as stumps of unrefined masculinity, stunted by violence. James' actions had not been heroic; the graceless tumble from his horse, the dislodging of his gun, were more farcical than noble. And so I omitted his name, saying only that a Chinese had been shot, leaving unspecified whose finger had pulled the trigger. I wondered then, as I wonder now, if James appreciated the protection I afforded him by withholding his name. But perhaps, in that secret and proud heart possessed by many young men, he experienced disappointment that his vanquishing of another had escaped official record. The decisions we must make as journalists are immediate but enduring; our light choices weigh heavily on the existence of others.

My work complete, I instructed one of my boys to carry the article to the city borders where it might be transported to the nearest town with a functioning telegraph system, which rumors had informed me might not be for two hundred miles. Then I called at the Grand Hotel, hoping to catch Edward. Instead his wife Hilde served at the bar, and greeted me with raised eyebrows.

"An interesting day for you, Mr Scott," she said, and I noticed the gun strapped around her waist.

"Where is Edward?" I asked.

"Asleep," she said lightly. "I fear today's activities rather exhausted him."

Oscar Fairchild was seated at the bar, half-way finished a generous serving of gin. His still youthful face was pinched and gray following two days of discussions with the Manchu authorities; unceasingly his fingers circled smarting temples.

"And just when I thought things could not become any more complicated," he said to me. "Now this damned racecourse. Mr Millington, a simple student...At least he is alive, and the Russian doctor says he shall stage a speedy recovery, but really, this incident does rather complicate matters."

"You experienced similar in India, did you not?" I suggested, taking a seat beside him. "I've heard it said that you crushed an insurgency or two in your time there."

There was truth in my words, and Fairchild did strike me as a considered and competent official. What I did not say, although both Fairchild and I were painfully, politely aware of the fact, was that in the shadow of South Africa's Boer War, official decisions about China had of late been taken in haste and without discernment. Fairchild's predecessor had retired to Yorkshire three months earlier and Fairchild's name had immediately been suggested by Foreign Office mandarins in London amongst whom he had garnered respect following the quashing of a small local uprising in India triggered by intrusive British tactics in controlling an outbreak of plague. He was now expected to work similar miracles of repression and subjugation further east, yet Fairchild's career in India had been a slow burn up to a pair of blazingly successful years, and now his reputation loomed too large, eclipsing, perhaps, his abilities.

"I had Violet in India. She had been there for so long," he said softly. "I felt I understood the Indians. And they didn't speak this fiendish Mandarin." Oscar released a long, low groan, a bodily exhalation of several days of frustration. "I suppose I am accustomed to people who recognize that we are in charge. In Peking it feels rather as though everyone is still deciding whom to obey."

"The Manchus are in charge," I said plainly. "As they have been since the seventeenth century."

"I spoke to the Ward girl and her father about it," Oscar continued. "Sometimes I feel that the Wards are the only ones here who understand the Chinese, who even respect them a little."

I agreed that Nicholas was more than a simple scholar.

"He lives his work," I said. "He loves China, he does not simply tolerate her."

"And young Nina, she's very eloquent. Humorous even, sometimes." He stopped. "Nicholas is the real expert, I suppose. I wonder what they might make of the incident at the racecourse."

"There is no mystery to it, Mr Fairchild," I said. "A token of empire reduced to ashes."

Oscar drained his glass and left.

The sun rose unfeeling and bright over Peking the next day. In the Legation Quarter, talk was muted, and in soliciting opinion I was greeted by a succession of downcast eyes and mumbled responses rehearsed from a script of understatement. How fortunate no one was seriously hurt, they said. The stand had always been unstable, they conceded, and would have required fortification soon in any case. The Boxers shall be crushed in a matter of days, they consoled themselves. They wished to believe what they told me, those earnest trade officials and steadfast diplomatic secretaries, they longed to sweep away the destruction as nothing more than a native jape gone awry. Perhaps the most committed believed the plain, unfeeling words they spoke, but their discomfort under questioning suggested quite the opposite. Trouble had taken residence in our town, and heavily he dwelt in our bosoms.

The news created a great and strange sense of animation in the Fairchild household. For days its residents had anticipated some Boxer occurrence and reports of the fire were greeted with a sentiment not unlike relief. Their fear, previously of the abstract variety, had been cast now in flesh and bone, their dread justified, its growth fomented. I paid a visit after lunch and found them all, with the exception of Nicholas who still insisted on returning to his own home to continue his work, gathered together on the verandah, talking in hushed, frantic tones. I had hoped I might see Nina alone and offer some succour following her exposure the previous evening to those forthright comments not intended for her ears. I was pleased to find that she sat quite comfortably amongst the other guests and hoped that her shame and dismay had lessened overnight. And yet I noted that while she was physically in the presence of Phoebe Franklin, La Contessa and Lillian Price, Nina's companionship was rather uncommitted. Listlessly her gaze wandered the horizon, thoughtlessly her head tilted to the side, betraying her disinterest in the conversation of her neighbors. She looked, I felt, a little peaked. Her pale skin usually possessed a smooth, almost glassy texture, but today it appeared coarse under the glare of the afternoon sun. She smiled towards me and I crossed the verandah to greet her.

"We decided to come out here," she said quietly to me. "Although we cannot go anywhere, we might at least feel as though we aren't trapped inside the house."

"Quite right," I said, but already her eyes roamed the dense, unyielding walls that encircled the Legation Quarter. I wondered if she thought of the home that lay beyond their reach.

"Did you know, Mr Scott, that Mr Millington shall today come here, where we might care for him properly?" Lillian Price said. "Mr Fairchild thought it a wonderful idea that we remove him from the student residence and see he is provided with adequate care."

"Really?" I asked. I silenced my next thoughts, but saw in the delicate arch of La Contessa's eyebrows that she shared my bewilderment. James Millington's actions had further complicated the ongoing negotiations with the Chinese authorities. The authorities claimed now that the dead Boxer had been a mere passerby, an innocent intrigued by the smoke billowing menacingly from the racecourse, a regular citizen shot by a zealous English student for demonstrating concern for the destruction of his own city. This was nonsense, of course, I had seen the man with my own eyes and known by his characteristic costume that he could be nothing but a Boxer, I had witnessed the red turban wound closely around his head, recorded in my mind the folds of his loose red robes, their edges stained by the blood that flowed from his fatal chest wound. And yet such was the frustrating, fantastical nature of negotiations that the Boxer had become for the Chinese an anonymous symbol of a nation downtrodden by the unforgiving foreigner, while the British had repainted him a fanged, brutal barbarian, his death a much deserved inevitability.

"Naturally, Mr Scott," Lillian said. "We cannot leave a young man far from home to rot under the disinterest of a Russian doctor. He shall arrive shortly and we shall nurse him ourselves if we must. I requested he have a nurse by his side at all times, but I am told," and here she leaned forward conspiratorially in her chair, "that they are too occupied with care of Chinese from the countryside. Now, I am most glad that they care for these people, but oughtn't the Chinese have their own doctors and nurses?"

"Those Chinese are Christians," Phoebe Franklin said severely. "Persecuted Christians deserving of our care and attention."

"I do not believe Mr Millington's injuries severe enough to require twenty-four hour nursing, Miss Price," I said, finding myself once more in the uncomfortable position of agreeing with an ocean-crossing proselytizer. "I hear he is recovering well."

Lillian sighed, her eyes shot heavenward.

"Come," she said, rising to her feet, "come and help me finalize the preparations for Mr Millington's arrival."

Phoebe and Nina followed the American girl, but La Contessa, with a sharp shake of the head, stayed behind. Boldly she arranged herself in a chair opposite me, her lips hinting at a smile as she curled and uncurled a loose tendril of hair with jeweled fingers.

"They do not know," La Contessa said softly. "That is why they are so sweet."

"Know what?" I watched as La Contessa languidly removed her shoes, exposing the pale topsides of her feet to the sun.

"That Mr Millington shot the Chinese," she said simply and bent to light a cigarette. "My husband tells me very little, but he was so enraged last night when Miss Ward requested Mr Millington come here, so angry, my Pietro, that he could not keep it even from me, what the boy had done."

"Nina requested that Mr Millington come here?" I asked. "Are you quite sure?"

"Quite sure." La Contessa took a first inhale from her cigarette and looked up at me with coquettish expression. "Please do not tell my husband that you have seen me smoking, he disapproves so."

"I shan't," I said. "It is a secret of mine that I believe women smoking to be quite becoming."

She sat suddenly upright, scattering ash across the verandah, and posed a smile so inviting I allowed myself to imagine for a moment that this sentiment I perceived growing between us, fragile and promising, was the product of desire on both our parts, and not merely my own wishful thinking.

"Mr Scott! La Contessa! Mr Millington has arrived," Lillian Price called and reluctantly I stood and turned towards the house. Slowly La Contessa rose, extinguishing the last embers of her cigarette as she slipped her feet once more inside her shoes.

We joined the small committee by the front door. James, supported in his unsteady steps by Hugo Lovell and an antique walking stick, limped past us, his head bowed. The servants watched at some distance, their bodies lined neatly down the hallway formed a silent welcoming party. Lillian stepped forward to embrace James.

"Oh, Mr Millington! Come, we have prepared a bed for you. You shall be comfortable here amongst friends," she said, guiding him and Hugo down the hallway. The rest of us followed a little further behind. The servants stood by, unmoving.

Lillian settled James in the makeshift bed by a window in Oscar's study. The sun shone brilliantly, allowing me to see the room with fresh perspective, its corners lit now where they had lain dark and unknown the night before. James squinted as his head rested upon the pillow and Lillian hastily drew the velvet curtains closed, casting crimson shadows over the room.

"Poor Mr Millington," she said. "Now, you just tell us what we might do for you. Nina, where are the servants? Someone ought to be here. What if Mr Millington is hungry?"

"Please, do not trouble them. I wish only to sleep," James said, his voice weak.

Phoebe Franklin settled on folded knees by the young man's bedside.

"Mr Millington, let us praise God for sparing your life," she said, each word weighty and sober.

"Thank you," he said, looking in befuddlement at the group gathered in the room. I observed James as he received the missionary's prayers, noting the raging laceration across his forehead, the bloated distention to his misshapen cheeks, the fluttering of his eyelids as he struggled to stay awake.

"Oh, these Puritan prayers!" La Contessa whispered furiously to me. "At least in Italy we pray with our souls. Excuse me." She left the room with a vivid sweep of skirt, pushing past Hugo, who shifted from foot to foot, hands fumbling in his pockets. Nina and I turned to follow.

"Miss Ward," James said, his voice stronger now. "Won't you stay?"

"Naturally, Mr Millington." Nina stopped, turned back to the patient.

"They tell me that you asked Mr Fairchild if I might come here," James said to Nina, who edged closer now to the bed. "That was most kind of you."

"Really it was Miss Price who brought you here. You ought to thank her," Nina said, taking a step backwards.

"I was most moved by the gesture, Miss Ward. Thank you."

"Sleep well, Mr Millington." Nina bowed her head.

"Miss Ward," he tried, but she ignored his call and crossed the room to the door.

"I did not know Mr Millington was such a close friend," I said to Nina as we walked together the length of the hallway.

She frowned.

"He is not," she said. "It is just as I said now; Miss Price brought him here. She is close to him, I believe, she played tennis with him and Hugo when circumstances were... normal."

"Yet you asked Fairchild if he might stay?"

We descended the stairs together, Nina slow and deliberate in her movements, her face angled away from me.

"Miss Price asked me to speak with him, yes," Nina said as we reached the bottom step. Her words were unnatural and stilted, her personality paled. Increasingly in the Fairchild house I felt we each performed roles: I held myself at more of a distance from Nina than my intimacy with the family required, and she redacted her thoughts, reduced her usual flowering sentences to the barest bones, and pronounced them in detached, polite tones. Only when we reached the drawing room did she drop her voice to a whisper and explain that Miss Price had insisted she speak with Mr Fairchild.

"I did not wish to bother him," she said, "and I thought Mr Millington would be fine at the residence, but Miss Price found the idea of him staying there most unpalatable."

Fortunately, Oscar had received the request with magnanimous courtesy, Nina said, although Pietro Mancini had staged voluble protest at the idea.

"I do not really understand," she said, "what is polite and what is impolite, what is expected and what is unusual."

"Nor do they," I said. "They are only more practiced at the pretense."

Nicholas was still working, a servant informed me when I paid a visit late in the afternoon, although I was welcome to wait for him to finish. Contentedly I sat in the shade of the Wards' courtyard, sipping green tea and admiring the comfortable silence maintained in the neat, enclosed space as the world raged beyond its perimeter. Around half past four Nicholas joined me, taking a seat sheltered by the curve of a pomegranate tree.

"I write against time," he mused. "I write of the Boxers, of China, of belief, and it is a game I am destined to lose. These things change form before me, my pen cannot so speedily record their transformation."

"And yet you must try," I said.

"Perhaps it is men like you who are best placed to record history," Nicholas said. "Paragraphs, not pages, allow for the twin virtues of quality and urgency."

"Paragraphs are for amateurs, Nicholas," I said warmly. "And you are an expert."

Nicholas shook his head, dismissive of my compliment, and in the intensity of his gaze I intuited that this would not be one of our habitual wandering, open-ended conversations of unhurried intellectual flavor. Instead, he hastily shared his experience of the Fairchild house so far: he was, he admitted, finding the company of so many unfamiliar women somewhat trying. He missed Pei, whom he had not seen since moving to the Legation Quarter, despite hoping each time he returned home that she might be there, and he found it increasingly difficult to carve out any time alone with Nina.

"I have never taught her of these things," Nicholas said. "The inanities of which women talk, dresses and servants and popular novels. I see how she exerts herself, how delightful she is, and how it pains me then to see them watch her askance, to recoil at her opinions, to reject all those things that I have taught her with such pride. I am not blind to it, Alistair, I know that amongst these people my daughter is an oddity."

"A delightful oddity," I said.

"An oddity all the same. I never imagined that we might live amongst such people, and yet now that I see how unprepared

Nina would be to live in England, or even to reside in a place such as Hong Kong, I fear that I have failed her. A mother might have helped her more."

I attempted to reassure Nicholas that his daughter was faring well in her unfamiliar environment, but my words were hollow; I too had witnessed her uncomfortable adjustment to such strange surroundings. I suggested then that we return to the house together, and perhaps find some time to talk with Nina.

"Another man at the dinner table would be most welcome in my eyes," Nicholas said. "Besides Mr Millington. Do you know, the servants told me that he murdered an innocent Chinese at the racecourse yesterday? Naturally I told them that it must be nonsense, but one still worries of course, and wonders what Fairchild was thinking in inviting him to stay."

I hesitated, recalled the expression on James' face the day before, the terror of success in death, and decided to say nothing. It was the first time that I had withheld information of any sort from Nicholas, with whom I shared great confidence, and I see now as I apply retrospective reason to my actions, that I did it for Nina, for her protection, that she might not learn of the gravity of her misstep from her father and feel further embarrassment. And so as Nicholas and I walked the desolate, deserted streets to the Legation Quarter together, dusk settling pink over the gray roofs of the city, James' misdeed remained a truth unspoken upon my tongue.

La Contessa languidly reclined in a chair, and I admired the manner in which her long, slender fingers gripped the stem of a glass of vermouth. Nina called for a servant as Nicholas and I stepped onto the verandah, but before one could attend to us La Contessa had already poured me a generous serving from her bottle of Cinzano. Gladly I accepted it from her, while Nicholas politely declined the offer. His eyes stayed upon

James Millington, who was propped uncomfortably in a chair, a light blanket spread over his knees, a cup of black tea held between grazed knuckles. Phoebe Franklin cradled a Bible in her lap, and glanced up every so often from her verses to observe us, the damned who drank before the dusk. I noticed that La Contessa consumed alcohol in the same manner as did I, and I liked her for it. It was unusual to find women who would really give themselves to drink, who would open their spirits and let alcohol lift them, carry them away from reality. Women drinkers so regularly face disapprobation, but La Contessa, as her very name suggested, was of a class where the approval or disapproval of others had very little bearing on her fate. As such, she was open-minded yet opinionated, questioning but certain, the kind of foreigner that proliferated on the seductive shores of treaty port China, the characters so keenly missed amidst the guarded and conservative society of Peking.

"From the rising of the sun to its setting, the name of the Lord is to be praised," Phoebe Franklin read from her Bible.

"Come, Mr Millington, have a little of La Contessa's chocolate," Lillian said. "The sugar shall make you feel stronger."

James, a lock of hair slick against his damp forehead, struggled to lean forward to accept the offering.

"It seems the Italians have the best of everything," Lillian said as she placed the chocolate in James' open palm. "When I go to Europe I must stop there. Do you suppose Rome is as beautiful as Paris, La Contessa?"

"Infinitely more so," La Contessa said.

"I suppose both cities are more beautiful than London at least," Nina said, closing the book she held in her hands. The faded blue of its cover and the dim gilt of its title were familiar; I looked closer and saw it was Fairchild's copy of *Far From The Madding Crowd,* the very volume I had discovered on the desk in his study.

"Miss Ward," James said, laughter in his voice. "You mustn't be so hard on London. England is a beautiful place. Green. Not like Peking."

"Like Shantung province?" Nina asked him.

"Sorry?"

"Is England green as Shantung is green?" Nina insisted. She spoke in earnest, but I saw the brief pain that crossed Nicholas' face as his daughter, that delightful oddity, sent gentle ripples of distaste through her new community of half-strangers.

"You mean to say the province from which the Boxers hail?" James asked.

"Well, yes. It is also the birthplace of Confucius, but I suppose that is irrelevant to our concerns. Shantung is beautiful and green. Father and I went there last summer. Perhaps I might imagine England that way. Is Shantung like England, Father?"

Nicholas coughed and shook his head briefly.

"I don't suppose England is anything like Shantung province, Miss Ward," Lillian said crossly. "What a ridiculous comparison to make. Don't you agree, Mr Millington?"

James did not speak, but looked ahead, a distance in his eyes. Lillian wiped his brow with a towel. There seemed no natural way to continue the conversation, though I felt obliged to fill the silence that followed Nina's questions, heavy and uncomfortable. I wished to introduce some uncontroversial subject, but La Contessa spoke first.

"It is strange, isn't it, to suppose they watch the same sun as we do?"

She met my eye with bold, almost brash, assurance. I endeavored then as I do now to resist vanity; I knew that as a man already past forty that it constituted folly to assume that all female interest displayed towards me might be romantic, and

"Unfortunately not," Oscar said. "We have received word, however, that soldiers dispatched from Tientsin shall arrive tomorrow. They shall secure the Legation Quarter and we have their word that they shall remove any of you who so wish to safety. Away from Peking."

"Wonderful!" La Contessa raised her glass. "Let us enjoy a celebratory dinner. Pietro, go and fetch that special wine."

Her husband turned quietly to follow her command. La Contessa met my eye extravagantly. I was first to look away.

"Oh, what excellent news," Lillian said delightedly, her hand reaching in manner unthinking and automatic to take James', before quickly dropping his fingers from her grip.

"Be sober, be vigilant; because your adversary the devil, as a roaring lion, walketh about, seeking whom he may devour," Phoebe said quietly, unnoticed or ignored by all, even when she closed the heavy shell of her Bible with a hollow clap.

V

OUR PROMISED hope had yet to arrive; no hooves sounded beyond the city walls, no swarms of weapon-bearing men appeared on the horizon. The inhabitants of the Legation Quarter grew restless, chattering, bickering amongst themselves as the afternoon deepened and the temperature remained stubbornly elevated. I had spent the bulk of the day at the Grand, drinking one bitter coffee after another, each served with warm efficiency by Hilde, and becoming increasingly agitated. There is nothing a newsman hates more than waiting; those wasted hours before an event during which speculation, that sly, alluring temptress, writes for us stories extravagant and fantastic that humble reality later forces us to discard. And so when trade official Benjamin Moore hurried in at the hottest hour of the afternoon, flustered, sweat pooling in the hollows of his jowls, I stood immediately to attention.

"They're here?" I said, my coffee cup clattering against the saucer.

"The Japanese!" he cried.

Heads turned in the bar.

"The Japanese?" I repeated. While no one could describe the Japanese as exactly innocent of aggression in China, they were, for the time being, considered allies in the fight against the Boxers.

"They killed him. Cut him to pieces." Moore's words were spiked, senseless. "They took him…"

"Sit." I lowered Moore into a chair and signaled to Hilde to pour the man a drink. "Take a breath and tell me what happened."

"They got him. A Japanese...He..." Benjamin shook his head, his mouth hung slack and dumb. "A bad business. They tore him to pieces."

"The Boxers?"

"The Boxers," he breathed. "We mustn't leave. Lock the doors!"

"Get a hold of yourself," I said to him. I adopted the quiet but firm tones I had learned in the course of my two decades of talking to witnesses to human tragedy, the patient insistence required to extract my narrative from their devastating reminisces. The other patrons had gathered around us, expressionless faces peering at Benjamin, a man we knew as serious and sensible, even a little pompous, gibbering now, stuttering and halting. "You shall cause nothing but hysteria carrying on like this. Now, are you absolutely sure that this happened? You saw it with your own eyes?"

"Yes, absolutely. I saw..." Benjamin heaved a breath. "I saw him, I saw his limbs, the blood...They showed no mercy."

"Mr Moore," I said finally, passing him a generous glass of gin prepared by Hilde. "I think you ought to go home. You wouldn't like Beatrice and the children to worry, would you?"

The other patrons murmured in cool-headed agreement, but I could see the light in their eyes, the glittering delight, that vile excitement. Barbarity and blood and Boxers, it had finally happened, and, even better, the first victim was Japanese. We Europeans could retell events, we could grow ever more fearful reliving the terrible, grim little details of it all, smugly aware that the victim had not been one of ours. Benjamin Moore stood, legs shaky under his portly carriage.

"Yes, quite right," he said, straightening and lengthening

himself, returning to his customary dignified posture. "I do apologise. A most terrible fright."

"Quite, quite." I ushered Benjamin out of the bar with the aid of one of his colleagues.

"I must tell Kitty," he muttered. "Warn her."

"Who?" I asked, but Benjamin's face was clouded, impassive. I departed, leaving him on the arm of the other trade official; I was by then far more concerned with the welfare of Nicholas Ward.

Stubborn Mr Ward would be at home as usual, I was sure, unwilling as he was to allow anything, be it rainstorm or Boxer uprising, to cleave him from his work. But the moment had arrived for Nicholas to abandon his noble charade of normality. I hurried towards his home, horribly aware that once humanity has shed its first skin in a conflict it tends to rapidly disappear altogether, powerless against the beasts of brutality. Nearing the edge of the Legation Quarter, I stopped suddenly. Before me stood a Boxer in distinctive red garb, the first I had glimpsed within the Legation Quarter itself. He was alone, a carving knife grasped tightly in his right hand. A rag was knotted loosely around his head, and scarlet ribbons fluttered from his wrists. His face was steely and hard-set, his long, black queue brushed his shoulder. We regarded one another warily as foxes meeting in the night. He lifted his knife, stroked the blade with the calloused fingers of his left hand.

A roar sounded behind me. Baron von Ketteler, the German Minister, barrelled towards the Boxer, pushing me to the side, a band of uniformed marines close behind him. I had never studied German, but von Ketteler's cries were intuitive to decipher. *Da ist her!* There he is! *Töten ihn!* Kill him!

The German lunged towards the Boxer, who, with a quick,

clean turn, sprinted rapidly towards the outer walls of the Legation Quarter. While I didn't believe in the supernatural power of the Boxers, I had to admit that this particular one ran as though flying. He skipped down an alleyway, the Germans giving chase. The Boxer's long plait swung behind him, his form seemingly weightless as he hopped and jumped out of reach of his assailants. The Germans in their heavy uniforms and thick boots struggled to match the Boxer's velocity under the relentless sun. Von Ketteler led the marines, brandishing a long stick, waving it wildly and calling so loudly for the man's head that his shouts followed me all the way to Nicholas' door.

"Nicholas!" I was surprised to see him open the familiar red door himself.

"The servants have gone," he said matter-of-factly. "I arrived this morning and there wasn't a trace of them. They haven't even had their wages for the month."

"Did they take anything?" I stepped into the cool relief of the courtyard. Two swallows chirped from the sloping, curved eaves.

"No," he said.

"The Boxers killed a Japanese," I said, mirroring his neutral tone.

"Is that so?"

"Yes. And there is a Boxer in the Legation Quarter. I left von Ketteler and a crowd of Germans chasing after him."

"A Boxer in the Legation Quarter," Nicholas said. "I suppose it is really happening then."

I urged Nicholas to return to Fairchild's house, offering to help carry any books or other items he wished to take with him. I noted his reluctance as his fingers worried his white beard, his gaze falling upon the peaceful courtyard around him.

"I suppose if the servants have gone," Nicholas said, his voice faraway. "Only for you, Alistair. And Nina."

I held Nicholas' rigid, proud arm as we stepped out to the street. A wild surge of people, their faces covered in soot, their voices rising in a shared, shrill cry, descended upon the Legation Quarter from each of the city's four corners. They were Chinese converts, fleeing their homes to seek sanctuary after the Boxers, rampaging across Peking, had razed their homes. The warriors had not abandoned the chase, and gripping knives between white-knuckled fingers, they followed the displaced Christians towards the Legation Quarter, their swift, agile forms identifiable by the red rags wound around their heads. The Chinese Christians moved together, an irrepressible tide, crashing over the streets of the city, ferocious in their distress. Even the women with bound feet tottered quickly over the cobbles, their fear overpowering the stabbing pain of crushed bones and rotten flesh. The Boxer cry of *Sha! Sha!* swirled and swelled thick as cloud around us, growing more menacing with each repetition. Flames licked hungrily at the edges of the Legation Quarter, climbed its walls.

"The road to hell is rather crowded," Nicholas said.

As we reached the gate of the Legation Quarter, I was surprised to see James Millington approaching the same horrific spectacle from inside. Sprinting towards us, he appeared to be evading a pursuer unseen; frantically his head turned back and forth, and valiantly he struggled against the crowds, a boat batted against the current. It was odd, I thought, that Mr Millington, not only injured but also jealously protected by the women of the Fairchild house, should have braved the streets on a day as bloody as this. Chinese converts pounded down the street towards James and wavering, he pressed himself against the wall to let them pass. A pair of Boxers stopped their chase of the Chinese Christians to regard this big-nosed white devil, alone and defenseless, standing before them. Then I lost sight of him in the melee, and my honesty compels me now to admit that my only interest lay in safely returning Nicholas to the house, where he might bolt the door and remain inside with the women.

I suggested we take shelter in the nearest home, thankfully, eerily abandoned, and there we waited for the crowds to pass. We sat on two squat armchairs, our heads lowered, Nicholas' labored breathing echoing in our warm, dark surroundings. If such chaos had not reigned outside, it may have proved an opportune moment for a nap, so pressing was the heat, so seductive was the darkness. When the noise outside subsided, I led Nicholas back to the street. He followed me with unsteady steps. He flinched as we passed inside the Legation Quarter. On the ground before us lay the body of a young Chinese girl, her coarse, plain clothes soaked in blood. Her face, grubby with soot, was tranquil.

"She looks as though she were sleeping," Nicholas said.

We pressed on the short distance to the Fairchild residence, and it was only a few steps beyond the body of the young girl that we found James.

"God Almighty," Nicholas said, his fingers digging into my arm. "That's…"

"Go inside," I instructed him. "I will move the body. We mustn't let the girls see him."

"No, no, I won't leave you."

"Nicholas," I said firmly. "Nina must be worried for you. Please, go inside. I shall come as soon as I can."

Nicholas left me, looking twice over his shoulder, thinking about returning. I waved him away.

James was not only dead, but also in pieces. The Boxers, in their exuberant savagery, had reduced him to a collection of crude parts, and seeing him so mutilated I was unsure as to how to proceed. How confident I had sounded when I sent Nicholas away, but I thought now of Nina, innocent of such brutishness, mere moments from this grotesque horror, and realized that I would need help to rapidly move evidence of this Boxer atrocity. I ran towards the Grand Hotel, where Edward Samuels paced before the entrance, shaking his head and muttering to himself.

"Alistair!" he called. "I am glad to see you. What are we going to do about the converts?"

"The converts?" I replied.

"The Chinese converts," he said. "They have nowhere to go. I am prepared to offer our rooms as lodgings, but I cannot house them all."

"James Millington is dead," I said. "I need your help."

"What?" Edward placed his arm around my shoulders and guided me inside the hotel. "Come, have some water."

I followed him to the lobby, where Hilde was inspecting a collection of guns laid upon the reception desk.

"Hello Mr Scott," she said, not lifting her eyes from the guns. "Quite a day we're having."

"Yes." I gulped down the water Edward served me, brushing the back of my hand over dry lips. I explained that James had been killed in the most brutal manner and that his body now lay in pieces just yards from Fairchild's home. "I must move it, but I have nothing."

Hilde, staring down the barrel of a gun towards me, carefully placed the weapon back upon the desk and ascended the stairs.

"Millington?" Edward said softly. "Isn't he the one that shot a Boxer?"

"Yes."

"A terrible shame," Edward said. We were silent a moment, listening to Hilde opening and closing cupboards upstairs. She appeared then at the foot of the stairs, a large trunk held in her thick, sturdy arms.

"It feels rather unceremonious," she said, handing it to me. "Packing up a young man's life, but it is the best we have for now."

"Thank you, Hilde."

"Be careful," she said with a curt nod. "Edward shall accompany you."

She bolted the door behind us with grave finality.

James' body remained in position. Edward and I labored together wordlessly, carefully lifting each severed part into the trunk. An involuntary urge to vomit rose within me when I was forced to place James' head, empty now of thoughts and dreams, inside it, and my fingers brushed his dark hair, matted with blood. Swallowing down the sour viscosity, I fastened the boy's remains inside the trunk. Edward asked what we might do with the body now and I was forced to admit that my plans were not yet so advanced.

"I suppose we ought to take him to a church," I suggested. I am not a religious man, and under the circumstances I felt very much prepared to sacrifice the following of traditional burial rites, but life is brutish, and I have always felt some dignity ought to be awarded to men in its passing. More pressingly, I could not think of anywhere in the heat and the chaos of the Legation Quarter where we might deposit the remains of the deceased young man.

"Well, we cannot take him to the church here," Edward said. "Word would spread immediately, and they are overwhelmed by the arrival of so many native Christians."

"Then where shall we take him?" I asked, and heard impatience in my voice. "We cannot hand him over to his friends in pieces."

"I know Bishop Laurent at the Peitang," Edward said slowly. "We would have to leave the Legation, but perhaps he would allow us to bury the body there, as long as we do not alert the women and children in the church. It's a terrible scene there too."

"Terrible scenes are my business," I said, as much to convince myself as Edward.

"Millington wasn't a Catholic, was he?" he asked.

"Not as far as I know."

Edward shrugged.

"Let us go. One would hope that God might overlook such divisions at a time like this," he said.

Taking a handle each, we shared the weight of the James' soul between us, winding slowly, cautiously through the blood-stained streets to the edge of the Legation Quarter. The crowds had thinned somewhat, but the air remained hazy with smoke, and no one else dared leave the Legation Quarter. The body swung heavy between us, and a dull ache spread from my wrist to my shoulder. Short of breath and damp with sweat, we exited the Legation Quarter against the best advice of a young soldier who stood guard before one of its imposing gates, and Edward hurried to find a rickshaw. I waited for the best part of ten minutes, warily watching the streets in their curious quiet, before Edward returned with a hesitant coolie prepared to take us to the Peitang for four times the going rate. Finally we reached the Northern Church, somehow sinister today, its two symmetrical towers spears piercing the ashen sky. A chaotic crowd milled around its elegant entrance. Many of the Chinese gathered under those divine arches wore the weather-beaten faces of rural poverty, and the bulging cloth bags they hugged under their bony arms confirmed their status as refugees from some Christianized hinterland. Amongst them too existed city-dwellers, identifiable by their garments of fine cloth, only lightly rumpled and gently stained, and their pale faces that indicated customary shelter from the elements. Together these displaced people, united by faith if not by wealth or dialect, numbered at least one hundred. They became to me then, I am ashamed to say, an impersonal mass. I have seen it many times, tragedy multiplied so greatly it becomes diluted, horror so inconceivable it is rendered mundane. They represented to me then an obstacle only, a wall to be broken through to secure the safe deposit of James' body.

"Hold the trunk behind you, don't let them see it," Edward said, letting go of it, and surprising me with the morbid weight I now sustained. "Poor Laurent. He has done so much already, and he will not want to turn them away."

The bishop opened the elaborately carved doors, stepped out to address the crowd, appealed for calm. A group of women seized this opportunity to push past him into the dark promise of the cathedral. The others remained outside, but gesticulated forcefully, clasping their hands in prayer, falling to their knees, reaching for the bishop's arm, his shoulder, pulling even on his hair as they entreated him to let them inside. Perhaps most disconcerting were those who spoke no words, who stood unstirred, their expressions entirely dispassionate, their instinct for survival nearing extinction.

"*Lai, lai,*" the bishop was saying to them as we approached. "Come, come. Each one shall find a home in the house of the Lord." He followed his invitation with qualifications, explaining that space was limited, food was scarce and that he could not promise absolute safety, but the refugees were deaf to this, joyous in their small salvation. They charged into the cathedral, leaving the bishop alone to face us.

"Mr Samuels," he said.

Bishop Laurent was a Frenchman of around forty, with ginger beard and a belly that strained the seams of his cassock.

"We are very sorry to bother you at this very difficult time,

Bishop Laurent," Edward said. He pointed at the trunk, which I eased from behind me, felt its unbearable weight as I placed it on the floor before the bishop. "We are in need of a place to put…a young man."

"No, no young men." The bishop shook his head vehemently. "I have accepted only women and children, a handful of elderly men. Some of the women here, they have seen things that mean they might never wish to set eyes upon another man in their lives. Who can blame them?"

"No," I interrupted, wishing to speak before Edward, knowing that he would fumble over his words; while he was unaccustomed to death, the quitting of life furnished my home and clothed my body. "The young man of whom we speak is dead. His body is in pieces inside this very trunk. We have no desire to burden you, but we are at a loss as to where to take his corpse."

The bishop raised his eyes heavenwards and made the sign of the cross across his barrel chest.

"Who?" he asked.

"James Millington. A student interpreter."

"Follow me." The bishop led us into the cathedral.

I had only visited the Peitang two or three times before and on each of those occasions the absolute silence of the place had impressed me, the intractable stillness that filled the cavernous space between its stone walls. Now that silence was replaced by the thick, pressing clamour of hundreds of people, their desperate bodies covering every inch of the flagstone floor. Still more lay on the pews, surrounded by blankets and pots and pans, items seized in haste when they had abandoned their homes.

"My God," I said.

"They have been coming for weeks," Laurent said, advancing through the space with careful tread, sure to avoid stepping on the bodies that dotted the floor. "Mostly from the countryside. Today, of course, we have welcomed many from Peking. Neighbours. The German is to blame, naturally."

"German?" Edward repeated.

"Yes, you know him. Mr von Ketteler. Very foolhardy, he chased after a Boxer who proved too fast for him, and so he took a young boy instead. Held him prisoner. Most foolish." We passed outside into the small churchyard where a smattering of headstones rose above the dry scrub of a lawn. "I fear many more shall have to flee their homes." He ran his foot along a patch of rainless grass. "Now, gentlemen, if one of my boys can dig something here would that be sufficient for your young friend?"

"Yes, absolutely. Thank you, Bishop," I said. The hubbub inside continued, carrying over the stale air to reach us outside. "Is there anything we might do to help? These circumstances appear rather untenable."

"Food," he said, exasperated and defeated in tone. "That is what we need." He looked skywards, watched the ripple of orange and red flames turning black as they spiralled higher. "A ceremony shall be expected at some point, I imagine."

A young girl dressed in what looked like a school uniform padded out into the yard.

"Bishop Laurent," she addressed him in lisping French. "There are more people from the countryside. Shall we let them in?"

The bishop looked down at his feet.

"They are knocking on the door," the girl continued. "They are shouting very loudly."

"Go inside, Ling," he said finally. "I will be right along."

The girl, who looked around eight or nine, with sweet little pigtails bobbing by her ears, nodded obediently and proceeded towards the cathedral.

"You see?" The bishop looked between me and Edward. "This shall not cease. And how could I turn them away?"

"Bishop Laurent," I said. "There must be something we can do."

"Unless you know of some place where these good people might go, I'm afraid there is little any of us can do to alleviate their suffering. Come, please, gentlemen. I will take care of young James. He, at least, shall rest in peace."

There were more than fifty refugees gathered on the steps to the Peitang, shouting, weeping and begging to be let in. Bishop Laurent opened the door just slightly, glancing between the anguished refugees on his doorstep and the wretched and demoralized who filled the cathedral behind him. Just as he stepped back to allow the newcomers inside, I stopped him. Now we had safely deposited James' body, the refugees appeared to me once more as individual vessels of tragedy and I could not disregard the desperation in their hoarse voices or the anguish in the coarse hands they clasped tightly in prayer. "I have an idea," I said.

In the Legation Quarter stood the residence of a suave and somewhat pliable courtier by the name of Prince Su. The prince's mansion, an expansive palace of low, sloping roofs and open courtyards, was situated just across the Imperial Canal from the British Legation. I had met Su in my reporting efforts, and knew him to have both a taste for the finer things in life and a very flexible backbone. The Manchus might have advocated bamboo-like adaptability in political maneuvers, but Su was unique in his utterly brazen lack of convictions, his selfish desire to move with the wind wherever he thought more favor might shine upon him. He had provided me with valuable information on a number of occasions, expecting little more than a lavish dinner or debauched evening in the company of enchanting women in return for stories that might have terminated his career had their source been discovered.

"Edward," I said, lowering my voice. "Let us take them to the Su mansion."

Bishop Laurent looked perplexed.

"Are you quite sure, Mr Scott?" he asked in quiet tones.

"Absolutely," I said. Whatever I lacked in conviction, I compensated for in bluster. With Edward by my side, I led the throng of rootless, unsettled travelers through the streets until we stopped outside the gates of Su's palace. A neatly-dressed servant approached the entrance, his face drawing pale when the dozens of people gathered behind me came into his line of sight.

"Yes?" He opened the door only slightly, addressed me charily through this slender gap.

"Please call for Prince Su," I said, sanguine and assured. My Mandarin remained awkwardly accented, but I succeeded in issuing this instruction with confidence. "Tell him his friend Mr *Si-Kao-Te* has come to see him."

"*Si-Kao-Te*," the servant repeated, chewing nervously over the transliterated syllables of my name.

The servant retreated. We waited. The women and children grew restless, some of the smallest infants keened and whimpered. Ten minutes passed before the servant returned, and invited me to an audience with the prince.

"Mr Scott," Prince Su said carefully, receiving me in a cool, shaded room. The courtier, dressed in a lightweight robe of jade silk, did not stand, but gestured for me to sit before him. His fingernails were long, curved crescents and his queue hung silken and gleaming down his spine. "You wished to speak with me?"

"Prince Su," I started. "Your people are being massacred. The Peitang is full of people forced to abandon their homes and leave the remains of their murdered families behind. We seek some place where they may finally find safety."

The prince smiled doubtfully.

"Here, Prince Su, you have ample space, a palace far beyond the needs of any one man. I believe it is only right that you, in accordance with your role as servant to the Qing government, offer these hopeless people a sanctuary in your home. In fact, Prince Su, I would go so far as to suggest it is your duty to protect them."

The prince considered, crossed his hands, unlined and smooth, in his lap.

"Mr Scott," he began, his lips stretched thin.

"Prince Su," I said. "I know you to be a reasonable man. Do you want your legacy to be that of a man who let his fellow citizens be slaughtered, beheaded, torn limb from limb by some Shantung bandits? I very much doubt that." I took a breath. Su let me continue. "I know you are a good man, Prince Su, a scholar, a gentleman in the finest Confucian tradition. That is why I have come alone, with only Mr Samuels for company, knowing how distasteful, how unthinkable it would be to pay visit to a man as cultivated as your highness accompanied by soldiers."

The prince considered the threat, sitting absolutely still before me, only the gentle furrow across his brow betraying his hesitance.

"It would be an honor," he said at length. "Nothing could please me more than to allow these defenseless women and children into my home."

Prince Su called the servant to his side and whispered a low command into his ear. The man nodded, and Su dismissed me. I followed the servant to the palace entrance, where with hesitant movement and an expression of distaste, he eased the doors open and I ushered the refugees through the gaping entranceway.

They followed me through the courtyard to the mansion proper, awe-struck at what awaited them inside. I lead them through the hallways and high-ceilinged rooms, past the Prince's collections of lustrous jade, burnished gold and serpentine calligraphy. A half hour later Prince Su returned momentarily to bid me farewell.

"Goodbye, Mr Scott," he said graciously. "I trust you shall care for the palace in my absence."

"Naturally, Prince Su."

I marveled at how easily the prince had been displaced. He departed, supported by four bearers in an elaborate palanquin fringed with red tassels, leaving Edward and I to walk through the palace trailed by our assorted followers. We discovered the lingering members of Su's harem, fair-skinned beauties draped in colorful, shimmering silks who flitted from corner to corner as nervous butterflies. Their delightfully decorated faces fell with sharp disquiet when they caught sight of the grimy-faced children, some with their clothes in rags, struggling behind us.

"I cannot believe the prince simply up and left," Edward said to me as we completed our circuit of the palace and its expansive grounds. "How on earth did you know he would agree to our demands?"

"Prince Su is a man too exceedingly easy to comprehend," I said. "He will have been desperate to flee, mark my words. Peking is too dangerous, too febrile, for a man who desires only to enjoy women and wine. It is much to his advantage to depart in the role of hero."

"I daresay not all the ladies here consider him a hero," Edward said, grinning broadly.

"Quite," I agreed. "Now, Mr Samuels, if you don't mind, I ought to pay a visit to the Wards."

"Go! You have done more than could have been expected. I

shall remain to see them settled." Edward accompanied me to the exit, waving warm-heartedly as I left him behind in that palace of lost souls.

Lillian Price, her eyes fierce and swollen, took a deep, ungracious gulp of gin, her hand trembling slightly where she gripped the fine-cut crystal glass. Encircled by Phoebe Franklin, La Contessa and a wide-eyed Beatrice Moore, the American girl sat silently against a straight-backed chair, her chest fluttering still in the half-calmed corollary of tears.

"Don't you think her parents would object?" Phoebe Franklin ventured. "Gin is not a drink for young ladies."

"We live in extraordinary times, Mrs Franklin," I said as I stepped into the drawing room.

Indeed, we were not aware of it then, but we would soon justify all kinds of ignoble actions in that experiment in co-existence we unwittingly conducted. Our community wouldn't become entirely lawless; my experiences have taught me that even the most desperate, bloody and primitive societies adhere to shared codes of human behavior. But our common laws would nonetheless be rewritten. The boorish ways of the Boxers would succeed in destabilizing our own civilization, in sweeping away the enlightened principles that we believed divided us from them. The beginnings of this process were evinced, too, in La Contessa's sudden sweep across the room, in the intimate placing of her arms around my neck, in the relief in her voice as she cried: "Oh, you are well!"

Immediately she corrected herself, stepped back from me and assumed formal posture. "It is only, Mr Scott, that we hadn't seen you yet today and with this terrible news..."

"Naturally," I said magnanimously. "Mrs Moore, have you seen your husband? He received something of a fright earlier today."

"Yes," she said coolly. "He was rather flustered. He is sleeping it off now. We are rather more concerned that Mr Millington did not return to the residence, and is feared dead."

Lillian watched me as might a hunted animal, with expression both accusing and besieged. I approached the ignoble throne upon which she sat, her grief visceral, naked, inglorious, and my tongue failed me. What words might I offer this eternal recipient of privilege and prestige, this holder of a young life so carefully protected, so far unassailed by the brutish horrors of existence? None would provide a salve, I knew, and so I tried for phrases plain and un-elaborate, attempted to avoid those pathetic, flat and well-meaning utterances so commonly expressed in the wake of tragedy.

"I am sorry, Miss Price," I said simply. "I know Mr Millington was a friend of yours. I can confirm that he has indeed passed away."

"You do not need to be sorry, Mr Scott," she said.

I made then to touch her shoulder, but she angled her frame out of my reach.

"Miss Ward is outside on the verandah," La Contessa said gently.

I nodded and turned to leave, starting when Lillian emitted a crude sob, a noise strangled and private, wrenched from her wretched gut.

"A time to be born and a time to die," Phoebe Franklin said to her. "Do not fight the Lord's plan. Do not try to understand. Only ask for strength."

"Take another sip," La Contessa said, smiling tenderly towards me as she stroked Lillian's blond head.

Nina stood absolutely still, her back to the house, straight and ungiving, her silhouette burning orange as the sun dipped towards the walls of the Legation Quarter. She looked to the horizon, where smoke drifted lazily above defeated streets and the silence of a spectral city was punctuated still by the occasional cry of *Sha! Sha!*

"Nina," I said.

Slowly, agonizingly, she turned to me. Her face, usually animated and expressive of spirit, surprised with vacant countenance.

"Alistair," she said quietly, her voice splintered. "Oh, Alistair, I killed him."

"Nina, whatever do you mean?"

"That is what she said to me," Nina said, steady and low. "She said I sent him away."

I reached for her hand, guided her to a seat, implored her to explain. Avoiding my eyes, her face fixed desperately upon the disappearing sun, its last rays throwing her mournful features into pallid relief, Nina explained that Lillian had suggested she go to see James the previous evening.

"I was ready to sleep when she came back from the library. She said James wished to see me, and in such a sharp tone that I felt I really must go," Nina said. "I protested, it was late, I said, and he ought to sleep. And she said, quite mocking, quite cruel in tone, *'The invalid requires a nurse, and only Miss Ward shall do.'* And so I went to see him."

James was reading in bed when Nina arrived at the library. She spoke pleasantly with him for a few moments, asked if she might request anything for him, some tea or another pillow or some balm for his wounds, but he only motioned for her to come closer and with reluctant step she approached, sensing that he required something of her that she was not able to give. He spoke rapidly, hurried to share heavy, expectant words with her. He had felt stirrings of emotion towards her, he explained, ever since he had seen her at the celebration of Queen Victoria's birthday in May, and had even persuaded Hugo to accompany him in paying a visit to Nicholas just for the opportunity to see her again.

"He did not ask me to marry him, or tell me that he was in love with me," Nina said, "but his words echoed those spoken to me by Barnaby George. I feared what he might say if I allowed him to continue, and so I excused myself."

"And what of it?" I said. "One cannot pretend to love every man who makes such a declaration."

"No, but… he left. He came out to the verandah this morning and thanked us all very much for our hospitality, told us that he wished to return to the student residence."

The women of the Fairchild residence at first protested this idea, relenting when James insisted no harm would come to him during a short walk across the British Legation. Naturally they had weighed the wisdom of his departure with no knowledge of the bloody events that had taken place on the streets of Peking that day, even within the ringed defense of the Legation Quarter. Had they known of the day's happenings, without doubt the hitherto most horrifying of the Boxer standoff, they would not have even remotely entertained the possibility of an injured party stepping out into that scorched battlefield.

"Oh, Nina," I said. "It is not your fault. Mr Millington was foolish to leave the house unaccompanied and foolish to speak to you as he did last night, but you mustn't blame yourself. No one was to know what would come to pass in the Legation Quarter today."

Nina nodded, automatically and without feeling.

"Please, Nina." I told her then of James' actions at the racecourse, explained that he had murdered a Boxer then repainted as a regular citizen by the Chinese, repurposed for diplomatic leverage, and that he had become a most valuable target to the enemy. "Any Boxer, any indignant Chinese, would have wanted him dead. Walking the streets with that distinctive laceration across his cheek, his limp still discernible even as he ran, he might have been killed tomorrow or the next day or in three months' time. Mr Millington's foolhardiness sealed his fate, and you, my dear, are utterly blameless."

"You are too kind to me," Nina said, both her hands reaching for mine. We sat a moment, our fingers entwined, her head bowed.

"Does Miss Price know what Mr Millington said to you last night?"

"No," Nina said. "She had been so ill-tempered that I did not know what I might say to her, and so I waited a while reading in the drawing room. She was asleep when I returned to bed and knows nothing but that I went to see him and then today…"

"You have done nothing wrong," I said, "but I believe it quite correct for you to keep his words a secret, for the sake of Mr Millington's dignity as much as anything else. Am I the only one who knows of this?"

Nina's eyes darted away from me, she snaked one hand out from under mine.

"Nina?" I looked at her, tense and fragile, her emotions wrought not in her expressionless face but in the hard, crooked angles of her body, in her defensive stature. How difficult the past days had been for her, how ill-suited she was to her environment, and how little I wished those women, the wives and missionaries, the citizens of a small, self-satisfied empire, to possess any weapon to use against her. Of course Nina was not to blame for James' death, but it has never ceased to astonish me how quickly, how desperately people engaged in battle search for enemies on their own side. Against a formidable, unfathomable foe, it is easier to turn against one more familiar, it is more comforting to draw divisions along habitual lines, rather than to name one's true opponent, to recognize his existence and face his vanquishing power. "Your father?" I pressed.

"Yes," she said finally.

"And where is he now?"

"He said only work might calm his mind, and so he went to his room," Nina said.

I suggested Nina go to fetch her father for dinner, promising that I would stay for the meal so she need not face Lillian Price alone. Weakly she attempted a smile and I followed her through to the drawing room, aware of the other women's eyes on her as she walked to the stairs with self-conscious gait.

"Mr Scott," La Contessa said, sudden and direct. "How are your food provisions?"

"Fine," I started, before recognizing the suggestion in her eyes, the possibilities written in the arch of her brows. "For now," I redressed myself. "I suppose I am running a little low."

"I thought as much. A man alone. I'm sure food is the last thing on your mind. Won't you take some of our supplies? My husband and I have so much and Mr Fairchild cares for us so well here. Please, come with me."

I followed, aware that Phoebe Franklin watched us, her expression quietly comprehending. How could this untouched woman perceive what the others appeared to miss entirely? La Contessa walked with purpose, her body held at sufficient distance to give me pause, to cause me to wonder momentarily if I had misunderstood her intentions. But when we crossed into the room she shared with her husband Chiara turned to me with alacrity, hurriedly pressing her lips against mine.

"Mr Scott," she said, drawing back from me. "We need a plan. We have no time now, and this is not an easy place. Your home would be better, no?"

"Yes," I said. "If it still stands after today."

"So, we are agreed."

She took a step back and I reached forward to kiss her again.

"Now we must return," she said, coyly rejecting my approach. "You shall tell them you have invited me to see your collection of… I have no idea. African hunting bows? What does a man like you keep at home? You shall collect me tomorrow." She turned from me, reaching into a box by the bed. "Here." She passed me a package of dried fruit.

In a charade of naturalness we traced our steps back down the hallway, meeting Nina and Nicholas, who appeared still stunned, stupefied, at the foot of the stairs. I told the assembled guests that I had been provided with vital nourishment and in return had offered to show La Contessa my collected African artifacts. Beatrice Moore mumbled about the safety of leaving the Legation Quarter, but her protest was forgotten as the front door opened and we heard the chiming voices of a pair of servants.

"Good evening, Mr Fairchild."

Large strides. Aggressive pace. He was approaching. And then nothing. The sound of feet pounding up the stairs. A door slammed.

"I suspect Mr Fairchild might not join us for dinner," Nicholas said. "It has been a most difficult day."

"Yes," Lillian said, and I noticed the glass in her hand was now empty. "Especially when Mr Fairchild was already so tired." She smiled bitterly then, and as her gaze settled upon Nina a small victory colored her doleful, blue eyes.

VI

I SET OUT shortly after breakfast to collect La Contessa, my
steps towards Fairchild's home accompanied by a lingering
scent of burning, that rich, woody, at times almost pleasant
fragrance, tinged with the pungent sweetness of decay. Beside
me walked Speculation; once more, my constant companion
had rouged her cheeks, painted her lips and commanded my
attention. Coquettishly she crossed my path, archly she teased
my thoughts, compelled me to return to the night of Queen
Victoria's birthday party when I had unknowingly set in motion
a chain of events that led to Lillian Price's pernicious comment
the night before. With frustration I wondered what invisible
gestures had unfolded since my first meddling with destinies,
what words had been spoken, sweet, low and unheard, between
dear, lost Nina and the steady Mr Fairchild. The assembled
group had carefully sidestepped Lillian's comment, following
its devastating delivery with discussions of the evening's
dinner menu, and Phoebe Franklin had valiantly filled the
terrible, scraping silence at the table with tales of the plight of
rural refugees, while La Contessa poured wine for each guest
in joyously exuberant measures. Nina was withdrawn, but
unyielding; and perhaps her fatigued expression betrayed no
secret feeling to the others beyond our common despair. And yet
to me, Nina's turmoil was transparent as a carp in a pond, flitting
back and forth, tail spasming in panic, fins fluttering helplessly
under threat. Jaggedly she cut the roast chicken upon her plate,

with lightly trembling grip she held Fairchild's polished silver cutlery, with tensed, curled fingers she lifted the embossed napkin from her lap to dab at downturned mouth. I watched this performance, this caricature of a normality entirely new to Nina, this unmastered impersonation of a person who existed on a diet of boiled potatoes and idle gossip, and I swelled with pride. How brave the men of the Legation Quarter considered themselves armed with guns against an enemy wielding only swords and passionate convictions, and how easily they would dismiss such quiet courage as displayed by Nina, surrounded by close, hostile foes, naked of armor, her weakness exposed.

Quickly had the assembled guests retired for the night, the efforts of feigned quotidian conversation too demanding even for such seasoned operators as La Contessa. Nicholas had walked with me to the door, leaving Nina alone in the drawing room.

"Nicholas," I began. He raised a hand to silence me. "Please, speak to her," I continued.

"Not here," he said urgently. "No, Alistair, not now."

"I do not know what Miss Price insinuated by her comment," I said in hoarse whisper by the imposing mahogany of the front door. "Yet you must speak with Nina. I do not understand what happened last night, she has told me too of Mr Millington's declaration, and I wonder if perhaps Miss Price has confused the two."

"Mr Millington?" Nicholas frowned, shook his head. "Alistair, I appreciate your intentions, but please, we must speak no more of this now."

He opened the door, and the night, cloying and thick, settled over us.

"*Yi lu ping an,*" he said. May the route be peaceful.

I recalled this exchange as I entered the Legation Quarter, my feet treading the same streets, exposed as dusty and charred now in the unforgiving light of day. I wondered, as I nodded to the young guards standing duly by, if it really were Speculation who joined me this morning, or if her plainer-faced cousin Intuition, sure and constant and true, walked by my side. For I knew now that Nina had not told Nicholas of James Millington's declaration, and yet I remained convinced that she had revealed his words to someone else. Following the incident she had remained in the drawing room, reading, she said, and which particular volume had I so recently spied in her hands? Oscar Fairchild's preferred novel, *Far From The Madding Crowd*, the tale of a woman unusual and irresistible to the men of narrow experience who populated her environs. How neatly those fragments of facts, those dimly recollected moments pulled together now, to underpin and expand Lillian Price's terrible words. Every man who has attempted seduction knows a few of its rules, and I was aware of the effective nature of flattery in literary form, of desire concealed in the intellectual cloak of poetry and prose, of the promise contained in the lending of a slim volume of Wordsworth, in the erotic charge of the shared reading experience. I had colored pink the cheeks of more than one woman with claims of love like a newly-sprung rose, women I had, in the end, not cherished until the seas had run dry. It was then, with the grudging admiration of one who recognizes his own tricks performed with impressive sleight of hand by another, and intense displeasure at such maneuvers being played upon Nina, that I knocked on Fairchild's door.

La Contessa's magnificence that morning was a welcome affront to the muted barbarism of the streets. I did not regret my return when I witnessed her posed in the drawing room with regal flair, her hair carefully coiled and arranged, her dress fitted and bustling, her frank beauty, her wild vitality a contrast to Nina, who greeted me in taciturn, weary tones, and Lillian, who in quiet hauteur awarded me only a curt nod.

"Good morning, ladies," I said to that room of melancholy smiles.

"How is it out there?" Nicholas asked, his fingers twitching over his mustache.

"The Continentals are becoming ever more nervous," I said, repeating the news I had heard when taking my nightcap with Edward Samuels at the Grand. "The French and Germans are ready to shoot their own shadows. The Austrians, in their infinite wisdom, opened fire last night and succeeded only in taking down some telegraph lines. The Boxers, of course, take the incompetence of the Austrians as further evidence of their powers of invulnerability."

"Oh, when shall this end?" Lillian said, mournful eyes turned on me. "I cannot bear another day trapped inside like this."

"Patience," I counseled. "The troops are on their way."

La Contessa came to my side, hands clasped by her waist.

"Well, I promised our Italian countess a tour of my Africa collection," I said. "So we must be on our way."

"Are you sure it is quite safe?" Nicholas began to protest. I attempted to speak with my eyes, to convey silently to him that he ought not to question me further. "Go safely," he said finally.

I was by then a great admirer of married women, and the glimpses I had had of La Contessa further convinced me of this long-held preference for women sworn by oath to other men. How they pleased me with their mature abandonment of girlish pleasures, their conversations exempt from the half-sincere judgments of others' faults. Honesty compels me to admit that other men's wives had not been strangers to me, and to recognize that despite the fleeting delight such women had provided, not one had boasted the force of personality or exquisite pulchritude of La Contessa. And yet, for all her bravado, she held my arm closely as we crossed the border of the Legation Quarter, and I perceived her apprehension in the wrap of her fingers around the cradle of my elbow. I had seen enough war by then to know how to meet the bloodied corpses; I never so much as glanced at their faces, never allowed myself to imagine their names, and I ignored the bodies on the ground, focused instead on hailing a rickshaw. Chiara struggled to aver her eyes from the bodies, those evaporated lives paused in expressions of agony, their limbs askew and bent at unnatural angles.

"Alistair," she breathed as we skirted two young girls, both with their hair pulled in tight pigtails. "There are dozens of them!"

"Look ahead," I said. "Apart from anything, you put yourself at risk when you don't look where you are going. The Boxers might approach from anywhere."

"But they are children! Women!"

"Christians," I said soberly. Her hand slipped down my arm to meet my palm, and like that we grimly, stoically walked the length of the street, looking for all the world like a married couple as we ascended a lonely rickshaw. We finally reached my home, and I was surprised that no servant came to the gate. I opened it myself, and Chiara stumbled as we entered the courtyard. I reached to catch her, my hands firm on her waist. She straightened herself.

"Is it safe for you to remain here?" she asked.

"Probably not," I conceded. "But I have no intention of being held prisoner in the Legation Quarter."

We crossed my modest courtyard and I pushed open the door to the main house, feeling the welcome darkness, the familiar coolness of my home. La Contessa stepped inside, her back to the wall, her eyes quickly taking in the surroundings: the shelves lined with books, the desk piled with papers, the still-open bottle of whisky.

"Would you like some?" I suggested, moving towards the desk. "Calm your nerves."

She followed me across the room, but as I reached for the bottle she knocked my hand away, and turned my head to face her.

"Alistair," she said softly. Her nails dug into my cheek; the pain was quick and spirited. She grabbed me hungrily and we kissed, arms and legs entangled. She pulled off her dress, my fingers fumbled on the ties of her corset. I unbuttoned my shirt, watching her, thankful to have found a complicit soul. Never is the desire for life stronger than in the shadows of death. We made love hurriedly, without elegance, pulling apart sharply when the deed was done. Then I reached for her once more, placing a last kiss upon her lips.

"Thank you," I said, turning from her to dress myself.

"I feel better now," she said. Nimbly she replaced her clothes and settled herself before the desk, scanning my papers. "What's this?" She lifted one sheet, holding it stiff between her fingers, as I poured us both two small measures of whisky. She took the drink from me, not looking up from my words.

"Oh, that." I pulled the paper quickly from her hands. "Don't worry. I have not written a story."

Naturally I did not promise that I would not, one day, write the story.

"They beheaded him?"

"You mustn't say anything to the women. We took him to a church."

She drained her glass.

"That was good of you. Those bodies on the street...just left there. In pieces. Not even human."

I kissed her forehead.

94

"You mustn't dwell on it. People think wars are won with weapons when victory really lies in the mind," I said. "Let me walk you back. I ought to visit the Germans, see if they've calmed since yesterday."

We discovered my Number One Boy in the courtyard, warily circling its perimeter. Although he appeared unsure, his display of loyalty moved me. He had been with me since my first days in China; long before I came to Peking he had accompanied my travels through Shantung in those first days of forgetting and regret.

"You're still here," I said.

"The others have left," he said, dry and severe. "They say it is too dangerous to stay."

La Contessa smiled warmly towards him, but he did not acknowledge her.

"I shall come home shortly," I said to the servant, and wondered if he would be present upon my return.

I offered La Contessa my hand as we left. She did not hesitate in taking it, pressing her cold palm hard against mine as we rode back towards to the Legation Quarter.

"That body…that person," she said at one moment. "It moves! The body moves."

"Keep walking," I said. "Remember it is in the mind."

"We must go back. If we can save one person-"

"Chiara." I pulled on her wrist and we let our hands slip out of their tense union as we neared the Legation Quarter gates. I paid the rickshaw coolie his exorbitant price, and we nodded at a pair of youthful French soldiers, guns hoisted over their shoulders, guarding our tiny patch of empire.

"Rather unpleasant, is it not?" one said as we approached. We murmured our agreement. "A few dozen Chinese already arrived this morning. Last night was terrible, they say."

Despite the destruction that surrounded its borders, the Legation Quarter boasted a semblance of routine in the absence of mutilated corpses and collapsed buildings, and yet already it felt crowded, constricted, as though too much humanity existed between its walls.

"I had meant to say," La Contessa said slowly. "You needn't worry. God decided I am not to have children. I once thought that a curse. Now I see it is a blessing."

I said nothing, and simply led her back to the Fairchild home. As I made to leave her at the doorway, I selfishly worried that the danger she had witnessed might render her somewhat reluctant to repeat our coupling. But as I turned to leave her hand snaked towards mine, the sweet ovals of her fingertips brushing against my knuckles.

"Thank you, Mr Scott," she said with a delightfully impish smile.

"*Arridiverchi*," I replied.

In my long career chasing disaster I had witnessed some impressive fires, but this, this was the most spectacular blaze I had ever seen. A day or two following my assignation with La Contessa, the sixteenth of June or thereabouts, the Boxers unleashed their full, terrifying power by unceremoniously razing the commercial heart of Peking's Chinese city. They set out to torch any "foreign" establishment, and did so according to a loose definition that included both shops that sold imported goods and those that explicitly catered to foreigners; such vague definition permitted the Boxers to destroy thousands of businesses. They burned them all: the jewelers, the furriers, the antiques and curio-sellers, the bookshops. Once again, the Chinese paid the foreign price: those who had swayed with the wind as it blew towards the West found themselves exposed and vulnerable, with neither protection nor sympathy forthcoming from their customers. The fire announced itself first in abstractedly elegant plumes of smoke, great slender flames that undulated over the merchants' quarter, but soon these converged to form a menacing, unbroken awning above all of Peking. As usual, I ran against the current, racing past the crowds that surged from the direction of fire, and sprinted towards the very heart of the blaze, imprinting on my mind the blistered corpses I saw along the way, the burned bodies of traders caught unawares amongst singed furs and blackened silks. A small collection of European soldiers had been dispatched to the scene where they milled awkwardly, coughing gently, fingers worrying the triggers of their guns.

"Don't see how we can shoot a fire," one of them commented as I slowed my pace to observe the smouldering frame of a former bookshop.

"Let's find some Boxers then," a young British soldier replied. He stood with his hips thrust forward, his eyes on the smoke-filled horizon. "You coming, Scott?"

I wiped the back of my hand across my mouth, coating my lips with ash.

"Naturally," I said, experiencing a sense of boyish pride that the young soldier knew my name.

The British soldier, whom I learned later was named Henry Cagill, led a band of variously uniformed troops behind him through streets clogged with smoke. The men ordered to protect the Legation Quarter were too few and too young to do much more than carry out patrols around the area's walls, designed more for show than for security, and they were more than content to follow someone so clearly disposed to lead. Cagill came to an abrupt stop; his arm in the air brought us to heel. We fell into muddled lines behind him, the soldiers readied their guns.

"Found them," Cagill said under his breath.

He faced a modest house, the door of which had been knocked down to leave a gaping space through which I perceived a dozen Chinese kneeling on the dusty floor. Their hands were bound behind their backs, their mouths gagged. Six Boxers with proud red turbans wrapped around their heads paced before their captives. One crouched before a man whose gag hung loosely by the side of his bruised face, exposing a swollen mouth.

"Say it!" the Boxer commanded.

The man rolled his lips over his teeth and did not utter a word.

"Say it! I am a worshipper of foreign devils. Say it!"

The man jutted his chin forward and remained silent.

"I believe in a false God. Say it!" The Boxer's hand jerked towards the sword by his side.

Silently Cagill raised his gun, and took a perfect, clean shot at the Boxer. The bullet he set forth landed in the dead center of the Boxer's forehead. The prisoners emitted screams from behind their gags; the other Boxers leapt to action. Momentarily they entranced me with their sweeping arm movements, their graceful, circular kicks, moving before us a demonic dance troupe.

Cagill punched my shoulder.

"Here." He handed me his gun. "You take one."

I held the gun, searching for a point of focus. The movements of the Boxers were fluid, rapid, their limbs blurred until I could not tell where one man's leg ended and another's arm began. All were young and slight, their sagging robes revealed slender, almost concave torsos. These were not practiced warriors, but they were young, and enjoyed all the benefits such perceived distance from death brings a man: speed, foolhardiness, an unsubstantiated belief in one's own immortality. I selected one for no reason beyond the sharp, unpleasant angles of his face. He was not an easy target; quickly he darted back and forth, twisting a two-headed blade between bony fingers.

"Go," Cagill urged.

The Boxers had ceased their menacing dance and charged towards us. I pulled the trigger. The Boxer staggered, attempted a desperate lunge towards me before falling to his knees, desperately his knife sliced at the air. Emboldened, others in our number began to fire, offering unfocused shots that hollowed the walls and pierced the furniture of that humble home. The Boxers scattered, abandoning the house. Still, my focus remained fixed upon him, my Boxer, the man who died slowly amongst it all. His body, the flesh he had been told was indestructible, clung grotesquely to life, grasping for another chance.

"Well done." Cagill's voice broke my concentration. "Here, help us untie them."

The soldiers moved quickly to unbind the prisoners' wrists and free them of their gags. One weeping woman wrapped herself around the legs of an Italian solider.

"Where do we take them?" the Italian asked.

"To the Su palace," I said. "Let me show you the way."

The sunlight was a balm as I gulped in the smoky air on the street. I ought to have felt victorious; instead dullness overwhelmed me, a vague, nameless nausea. I had followed war around the world, stood on the dividing line between right and wrong and every shade of justification in between, I had recorded every act of senseless barbarism, each final breath, yet until now I had mostly succeeded in remaining an observer, avoiding the role of actor in my own story.

"You forgot something," Cagill said, coming close behind me. He thrust a frayed red rag into my hand. "A souvenir."

We led our begrimed, bloody refugees to the Legation Quarter. They approached with awe, marveling at the young uniformed men who stood at its gates and wondering at the ordered grid of its streets. The Chinese city may have been reduced to smoldering rubble, but here our Oriental imitation of the village green lived on. The entrance to Prince Su's palace was quiet when we arrived; a cheerful hubbub came from further inside. I led the rescued Christians towards the sound, noting their murmured surprise as we passed collections of jade carvings and landscape paintings. For these escaped villagers, the simple wooden construction of the local church was likely the limit of any splendor they had witnessed. We found the residents gathered in the central courtyard, grouped around an American minister who stood above two kneeling Chinese youngsters. The pair looked to be children of tender age, their bodies were thin and hard as reeds, while their faces were round and soft. The girl wore plain dress of muddy brown and her calloused toes peeked through the broken seams of battered shoes. Yet around her shoulders was wrapped a dash of silk in brilliant bridal red. Her lips, too, had been painted crimson. The pair held hands, their eyes locked. The minister began the vows in Mandarin.

"Dearly beloved, we are gathered here in the presence of God..."

I looked up at the sky, saw that it was dense still with black smoke. I was the only one. The others, the beleaguered, the broken who had been forced from their homes, whose villages had crumbled to dust, were saved, at least momentarily, by the simple majesty of this union. The crowd clapped when the vows ended, cheering and laughing as the young groom embraced his wife with juvenile bashfulness.

Then began the unmistakable strains of the *erhu,* a stringed instrument able to produce the most wonderful or terrible of sounds depending on the talents of the one who played it. A member of Prince Su's harem knelt by the new couple, her fingers moving smoothly, expertly over the strings, her head bent in concentration, an elaborate headdress swaying in time with the music she played. Another of his women, dressed in midnight silk, stood from the depths of the crowd and sang in sweet accompaniment. I moved towards the exit as the ceremony drew to a close, and heard someone call my name. Turning, I saw Phoebe Franklin wave at me from a corner of the courtyard, where she sat surrounded by small, bare-legged children.

"Mr Scott." She stood as I approached. "I see you have brought more friends to us."

"Yes." I looked back at the group of freed captives. They were splintered now, mixing with the others, asking questions, sharing stories, enquiring as to whether anyone had seen a man by the name of Wang or a young girl called Mei.

"We found them in the Chinese city, about to be executed by Boxers. They have survived quite an ordeal."

"I don't doubt that," she said, hooking her arm around mine and steering me away from the children. "Thank you for securing the palace for our people. Such kindness shan't be forgotten, Mr Scott, I can assure you of that."

"Oh, it was nothing. I have known Prince Su a while," I said.

"Do not let kindness and truth leave you, bind them around your neck, write them on the tablet of your heart," she said, her tongue sliding easily over words often repeated.

"I must be on my way," I said.

"Wasn't the ceremony beautiful? God unites, even as man fragments," she continued.

I agitated to depart; such industrious cheerfulness at a time of tragedy irritated me. Did Phoebe and her flock not see reality? And if they did, was it faith or ignorance that meant they did they not fold under the shadows of her broad, heavy wings?

"They are very young," she said. "Perhaps they are too young. The boy told us he wished to protect the girl as best he could. A formal union, we believed, might be a source of strength for both."

"I must be on my way. Good afternoon, Mrs Franklin."

By the time night ought to have fallen, the sky still shone in a sinister imitation of day. I stopped by Fairchild's for dinner: a host of motivations, including the disappearance of my cook, the desire to speak with both Nina and Nicholas and, not least, the promise of seeing La Contessa, allowed me to reason that such regular visits to a house at which I was not a formal guest were warranted. We dined in the eerie glow of the extended day; the candles spread the length of the table were left unlit.

"I must apologize for the rather small portions," Oscar said after we were served paltry helpings of steak and mushrooms. "Supplies were already low and the fire has further disturbed trade."

I watched Fairchild closely. I hoped for some evidence of internal struggle, I wished to see some affirmation of his embarrassment, at least a modicum of discomfort, but the diplomat appeared just as before: suitably affable for a man of his position, implacably polite, decorously modest, the shadows under his eyes only confirmed his role as our weary protector, the great strategist denied sleep in the service of his countrymen.

"Quite understandable," Pietro Mancini said warmly, lifting his glass. "To our most generous host."

"Hear, hear." I too raised my wine, glancing from Pietro to his wife, who sat silently beside him. La Contessa nodded, and the symmetry of her features, from the knit of her eyebrows to the sweet bow of her lips, offered me a muted thrill, afforded an easing of tension after a trying day.

"Oh, no. I'm afraid I'm a terrible host. If my wife only knew," Fairchild said graciously.

Lillian arched her eyebrows, but voiced no rebuke. Instinctively I desired to observe Nina to my right, urged by the need to confirm the narrative that constructed itself in my mind. Would she hold her eyes unblinking, twitch her lips in dismay, or would her features remain placid, cloudless, suggesting a connection between the two of only the most shallow nature? But I could not betray her, could not expose to those smiling adversaries the suspicions my heart harbored, and so I did not glance her way.

"And what of the Chinese?" I asked Fairchild, wishing to banish visions of Oscar's wife, with her warm politeness and impeccable, trained manners, from the minds of his guests. "Surely they shall try to stop this wanton destruction?"

"I wish, Mr Scott, that I might tell you what the authorities plan to do," Fairchild said, taking care over each word. "At present I may only assure you that we are doing everything within our power to protect all foreign residents. Reading the signals such as they are from the Qing government, I hazard that we might feel fairly positive."

"Well then, why have they not extinguished the fire?" Lillian asked. "Look." She gestured to the window through which light poured as at the warmest peak of a summer's afternoon.

"They are trying, Miss Price," Fairchild said patiently. "The Chinese fire brigades were somewhat underprepared for an event of this magnitude."

"This ought to herald a change," Nicholas said, setting his glass upon the table after a long, full sip. "The Qing must respond to such aggression."

"There was a wedding today," Phoebe Franklin offered, diverting the conversation. I looked down at my lap and caught sight of the Boxer's red turban, its corners escaping from my pocket. I eased it out, turned it between my fingers, crushed it into a ball and, leaning forward slightly, I passed it under the table, draping it across La Contessa's lap. She shifted only a little as my fingers brushed her thighs. Her expression remained absolutely unaltered.

"How lovely," I watched her say to Phoebe Franklin. "A little joy amidst the terror."

I did not look away as she glanced down, as her forehead furrowed momentarily. I appreciated the curl of her lips as she recognized the origin of my offering. She raised her head to look squarely at me and offered the reward of a small smile.

Following the meal, I endeavored to speak with Nicholas.

"Really, Alistair, I have rather a lot of reading to do this evening," he said, before reluctantly leading me to his room. How strange he looked in that small space of low ceilings, its walls crowded with paintings of ships at sea and bucolic pastures of green and gray, his collection of books littered across every surface. The room seemed to diminish him, the intellectual giant so serene in his own habitual light and spare surroundings. He removed a hardbound dictionary of Classical Chinese from the bed and allowed me space to sit.

"Nicholas," I began.

"Please, Alistair, speak a little more quietly."

"But everyone is downstairs."

Nicholas shook his head uncertainly, looked towards the closed door.

"Have you spoken to Nina?" I insisted.

"I have been very busy," he said vaguely. "And she is so rarely alone."

"But you must, Nicholas."

He smiled wistfully, picked up a book and turned it over in his hands. He was a good man, a loyal friend, a devoted academic and undoubtedly a well-intentioned father. But Nicholas was not a practical man; he cared little for worldly matters, he dismissed gossip as frivolous and therefore harmless. He had been abandoned by his British wife, a woman of whom he never spoke, and had been quite unconcerned since then with foreign society in Peking. I may have looked upon most of the city's European population with lightly concealed disdain, but my contact with them was at least regular and meaningful enough to remind me of why I had abandoned the old country in the first place. I may not have admired their practices, but I was able at least to understand my people, and to recognize the roots of a scandal before its first blossom. Naturally the pruning of such infant scandals was commonly practiced by women, but in the absence of a mother or sister figure, a father would have to make do for Nina.

"Nicholas, I understand that this might be an uncomfortable subject to raise with your daughter, but you must think of Nina's future," I pressed.

"I think of nothing else," he said firmly. "I think of nothing but whether she shall live to see tomorrow. I think of the Boxers and what they might do to her, daughter of China, if she were to fall into their brutal grip. I think of the terrible things these people may say of my dear Nina, and I believe that your desperate whisperings to me in various corners of this house shall do nothing to cease such talk."

His voice was low, controlled and uncannily, uncharacteristically cold.

"Nicholas, it is precisely because of the gravity of this situation that I so desperately whisper to you, as you put it. If you might only speak with Nina then I would have no need to do so."

Wearily my friend exhaled and opened the book in his hands.

"Nina is my daughter. I know her, and I know what is right for her. Good night, Alistair."

I stood abruptly, crossed that small, cluttered room. I paused at the door, watched Nicholas place his reading glasses upon the end of his nose, sensed his proud refusal to look in my direction. I wondered what more I might say, whether I ought to remind him that a small fire is easily extinguished. But I only bowed and left, closing the door behind me with finality.

I had enjoyed many a healthy argument with Nicholas; we had sparred over the relative strengths of Taoism versus Buddhism, I had advocated the paintings of the Dutch Golden Age in the face of his robust defense of China's school of bird and flower, together we had pondered the future of China, sizing the likelihood of its fate being bound in imperial chains versus its flourishing as the world's rightful Middle Kingdom. I had stepped away from many such discussions bruised and humbled, awed by Nicholas' raw intellect and seasoned rhetoric, yet never had I felt the dismay that touched me now, the apprehension that leadened my limbs as I descended the stairs. Nicholas and I rarely entered the realm of the personal; never had I offered judgment upon his decision to raise Nina in an alien land, not once had I questioned his relationship with Pei. My attitude to the Wards' life in Peking had been one of tacit endorsement because, for the most part, I thought their unconventional arrangement rather a lovely one. Only now, in my first questioning of Nicholas' wisdom, did I see the tenacity of his stubborn determination, and realize that I must take action where he refused to do so.

Light glowed from the drawing room and I stepped towards its brilliance. The blaze still smoldered outside, and Nina read alone without the aid of a lamp.

"Nina," I said. "I am most glad to see you."

She closed the book she read - *Far From The Madding Crowd,* naturally - and looked up to me. I took a seat at the opposite end of the long chaise upon which she sat.

"How are you?" I asked. "I have been worried for you."

"You needn't worry for me," she said gently. "I am quite all right."

What then could I say? I am not a man afraid of words, I have my whole life sought to mould and model them to my desires, to make them submit to my dominance, and yet I have always maintained my respect for language, and do not consider it my place to make blunt use of a pointed tool. I took a breath and assembled my list of questions: Who else knows of James Millington's declaration of love? What has passed between Mr Fairchild and yourself? What did Lillian Price mean when she so triumphantly reported Oscar's fatigue?

"Nina, what has happened?" My final question, then, was unwieldy and unfocused, a forlorn signpost waved desperately by one entering terrain beyond his ken.

Nina bowed her head and played with the folds of her skirt. Solemnly she collected her breath, met my eye and looked to begin.

"Mr Scott, excuse me. I thought you had already departed."

Startled, Nina lifted a hand to her lips, her words faltered unspoken. Oscar Fairchild walked the length of the room towards us with easy stride.

"How strange the light is tonight," he continued. "I suspect we shall all have trouble sleeping. I came only to collect my book. Now, where did I leave it?" Oscar's gaze swept the room, before settling upon a small painted cabinet a foot from where I sat. "Here it is!"

"*Dream Of The Red Mansion*," I read the title as he lifted the volume. "Do you like Chinese literature, Mr Fairchild?"

"One must take an interest in the great novels of one's host country, do you not think, Mr Scott?" Oscar stood before me, smiling, the book gripped between his fingers.

"Absolutely," I conceded. "I only thought a man such as yourself might have greater concerns than the machinations of a fictional eighteenth century Chinese family." I cleared my throat, attempted to dissolve the burgeoning irritation I felt in the face of Fairchild's agreeable manner. His affable drawing room patter, his mask of amiable chatter, impressed and provoked me. "At a time such as this, at least."

"And yet a country's spirit lives in its authors, does it not?" Nina said. "To understand a nation, one must know its myths and fables. The people of Peking and London learn their country's values and ideals through its novels, just as the villagers of Shantung tell one another stories of the Eight Immortals in the hopes that their neighbors might emulate such giants."

"Well, yes." I regarded Nina and Oscar; they did not speak directly to one another, in fact, both appeared exceedingly careful not to look upon the other. In this conversation ostensibly involving three, I served as the only interlocutor for both Oscar and Nina and this lack of interaction gave me no recourse to assess independently the nature of their relations. "I suppose," I said, getting to my feet, "that I ought to return home."

"I shall call a servant to accompany you," Oscar said.

"Oh, no," I started, but Fairchild insisted. Placing *Dream Of The Red Mansion* upon the chaise, he went only as far as the door to summon a servant, and dashed any opportunity I might have had to speak more with Nina. Immediately she opened the book, turned its familiar pages, traced words long ago committed to memory.

"*For you are fair as a flower and youth is slipping away like flowing water...Flowers fall, the water flows red, grief is infinite,*" Nina read. "Do you ever wish you might read your favorite novel once more for the first time? I wish I might remember how I felt the first time I read those words..."

Observing her in that state so natural to her, and so infectiously joyous, I wished I might take Nina with me, return her to her rightful home, place her in the shade of the magnolia tree, allow her to hear once more the chirping of the swallows in the eaves, let her mind range and wonder with her father and Pei, permit her to spend hazy afternoons at the lake with Chang. I wished only to take her from that magnificent residence in which she had been placed, to remove her from the imperious gaze of the serious portraits upon the walls, to save her from the cruel murmurings of its inhabitants, to rescue her from gracious seduction by the cordial diplomat who stood once again before us. And yet any such rescue was impossible; even if the Boxers posed no threat and the city were secure, Nina was not a young woman to be saved. Her spirit was as majestically proud as her father's, I regretted, as I followed Fairchild's servant to the front door. Would Oscar leave her now? I wondered. Or would they remain together, bathed in false illumination, reading one another's favored tales of lands they could not fathom? Only whisky might lead me to sleep on that strange, burning night, I thought, and so I turned at a fork in the road towards the Grand.

In the morning I set out for a brief tour of the Boxers' ruination, taking in the abandoned homes and looted shops, and returned to the unnatural quiet of my neighborhood with dismayed heart. I opened the front door, starting when I saw La Contessa seated proprietorially by my desk, hands poised over my papers.

"I thought you would never come!" She rose and we embraced, but I pulled quickly away.

"Chiara, you shouldn't be here alone. It is extremely dangerous. Imagine if I were a Boxer! Here you are, entirely defenseless, not even a servant to protect you…"

"I needed to see you," she said, pressing her lips hurriedly against mine.

"And of course I'm delighted that you came to see me. But how on earth did you come to be here?"

"Mr Lovell stopped by this morning and took Miss Ward, Miss Price and I for a walk. I suppose he meant to allow the girls some fresh air, perhaps even to cheer their spirits. Naturally they were both rather disturbed by the destruction, and Nina seems very concerned about what may have happened to her home." La Contessa's fingers made quick work of the ties at the back of her dress as she spoke. "Anyway, the young soldiers guarding the Legation Quarter were most taken with our young friends and I simply slipped away. You are pleased to see me?"

"Naturally." I kissed her.

This time we retired to my bedroom and the resulting encounter was rather less frantic than the previous. Yes, we struggled against the specter of death, yes, we continued to laugh before fear, but there was a rhythm, a calm, a sense of serene inevitability to our connection.

La Contessa reclined against me, her black hair fanned over my chest.

"What news?" she asked, lifting her head. A few trails of hair remained stuck to my chest.

"The Imperial Council meets again today. There is some promise of advancement," I said, repeating what I had heard that morning on my tour of the Legation Quarter. "The diplomats say that the court officials have finally come to their senses and decided that the Boxers must be somehow… pacified. That means they ought to turn the Imperial troops against them and then…"

"It all ends?"

"Yes," I said.

La Contessa fell once again to my chest with a great sigh.

"Is it so terrible that I hope it may last a little longer?" she asked. "I wouldn't complain of spending more days like this."

"It is terrible," I said with forgiving laughter. "But I shan't tell anyone."

Chiara needn't have worried. Qing government ministers continued their debates over the following days, wavering in their support for both sides, delaying discussions until we had all but lost hope. The promised breakthrough was ultimately quashed when the Empress Dowager received a document, its contents supposedly signed and endorsed by representatives of every foreign government in Peking. I like to imagine Tz'u Hsi reading each of the demands contained in the forgery, those ludicrous wishes for foreigners to control China's military and tax matters. The document, most likely written by an anti-foreign hardliner such as Prince Tuan, spurred old Tz'u Hsi to action. War, she decided then, was the only way forward. Her hunch was proved correct when two days later she received word that the foreign powers had attempted to take the Taku forts near Tientsin; in fact allied powers had already seized them, but bad news was always sweetened when presented to the Empress Dowager. This action was perceived tantamount to a declaration of war by the foreigners in Tz'u Hsi's eyes. None was more surprised to hear of it than us, the citizens of the allied nations. We had received no word from the troops we had hoped would soon liberate us and as a result knew nothing of the events at the Taku forts. Imagine, then, the distasteful shock with which the foreign ministers opened a set of neatly-pressed, carefully addressed red envelopes, each containing a terse request for the nationals of each minister's jurisdiction to leave Peking within twenty-four hours. Leave peacefully, it instructed, and we shall permit your safe passage.

The ministers assembled in the Spanish Legation, some

still holding the red envelopes in their hands, turning them over and over, willing the words printed inside to disappear, or at least to assume a friendlier tone. They agreed to my accompanying them, and I was glad of it, not simply for the news I might be first to tell but also for the opportunity to speak on behalf of the people of the Legation Quarter. Officials, I had learned, had far softer resolve than soldiers. They possessed the scholar's natural tendency to scramble at the first sniff of war, and those first minutes of dialogue confirmed my belief that panicked men were better employed in silent consideration than in committees of joint discussion. The diplomats' voices, strained, sharp, higher than usual, sounded a discordant chorus of disagreement. We must leave, the French said. We shall be slaughtered, said Germany's von Ketteler.

"Remember Cawnpore," Oscar Fairchild said. "They killed everyone; women, children, after such a promise. The risk is far too great."

"We must go!" responded an incensed French diplomat. "Do you know when the soldiers might arrive? What do I say to my people?"

"If I may," I ventured. "As the only civilian present, it falls to me to speak for the men, women and children of no diplomatic status currently resident in Peking, and I say we must wait. I understand the reasoning of those who call for a rapid departure, of course, but we must be wise to the dangers. Even if this invitation does not constitute a plot, who knows what lies beyond Peking's walls? And what of the native Christians? Are we simply to abandon them to the Boxers? Gentlemen, I implore you. Let us wait a little longer."

I took a breath, ready to continue, when a terrific explosion sounded behind us. Fire crackled, spluttered and smoke billowed through the air. "By God!" Oscar made for the door.

"Are they here?"

The already-frayed nerves of the officials were shot through by the explosion. The Spanish Minister, Cologan, accompanied Oscar Fairchild to investigate its source. They returned to tell us that the explosion had been caused by nothing more sinister than a nearby fireworks shop catching fire. Another day, we might have laughed, but by then we had rather lost of sense of humor. And so the meeting continued, but no consensus was reached. Attempts at debate were unhelpfully punctuated by the loud peals of self-immolating fireworks launching themselves into the air.

When the meeting concluded, I walked with Oscar to the Fairchild house. He had tried to evade me, talking at great length with one especially infuriated French diplomat, occasionally looking round to see if I had departed. Eventually, he conceded defeat, allowed the Frenchman to walk away and accepted my presence by his side.

"We cannot leave," I said seriously to him. If Fairchild thought I might openly broach the topic of his relations with Nina, he was mistaken. For one, I was a seasoned enough observer of men to know that one does not expose his intentions so quickly without full knowledge of the situation at hand (one cannot accuse another of a crime not only unproven, but also unspecified), and at that particular moment my concern lay with eventualities far more terrible than a muddied reputation. Lives were at risk, and I would not stand idly by as men of great office and humble intellect led innocents towards a massacre both ghastly and wholly unnecessary.

"Of course not. Every Englishman in India is haunted by tales of the Mutiny. When one is far from home, one must take others' promises with the appropriate pinch of salt." Oscar did not turn as we passed the fireworks shop, now completely engulfed by searing flames.

"Do you think the others will agree? It is vital that we present a united front," I insisted. "If the Chinese knew of the disagreement between these supposed allies…"

"I won't leave," Oscar said firmly.

"Quite right," I said. "If the ministers let their people leave, they shall have blood on their hands."

A servant opened the door and we stepped into an atmosphere of quiet industriousness. No one read leisurely on the verandah or talked idly in the drawing room. Every guest had retreated to their quarters and was busily packing their belongings. I watched Lillian and Nina from the doorway to their room. The contrast between their approaches was marked. Nina folded clothes slowly, considering each item before resigning it to her small bag. Lillian Price, having recovered some of the color that had once pinked her cheeks, excitedly bundled dresses and blouses into imperfect squares, removing and replacing them in her valise with cheerful hurriedness.

"Mr Scott!" Lillian's smile was wide, genuine, childlike. "Have you heard? We are leaving! Oh, I cannot wait to go home!" She lifted a blouse, glancing at it quickly before rolling it, sausage-like, into her trunk. "Have you packed your belongings, Mr Scott? We must leave today or tomorrow."

"We shall not go anywhere," I said solidly. "No one is to leave the Legation Quarter. It's too dangerous."

Lillian's face fell.

"Oh no, Mr Scott. Mrs Franklin told us so. One of the ministers, French I think he was, went to Su's palace and told them all that we were to leave." Her voice was airy, hopeful.

"No. I come from a meeting of ministers and I assure you that no one is leaving. You do not need that valise."

"Where do you suppose we shall go? Should I take my

summer blouses or...?" Lillian continued.

"Miss Price. No one is leaving. Mr Fairchild will tell you the same. We may discuss this further at dinner, but for now I suggest you stop packing."

Nina nodded.

"It was too good to be true," she said, pulling a dress back out from her leather bag.

Lillian sank down onto the bed with an accusing look at her useless, bulging trunk. She neatly lifted her foot and administered a short, hard kick, causing dresses and skirts to spill over the sides and puddle pathetically on the floor.

"Damn China," she whispered fiercely.

Under the deep pink skies of dawn, German Minister von Ketteler settled himself in a sedan chair, a book in his lap and a cigar jostling at the corner of his mouth. His destination was the *Tsungli Yamen*, or Foreign Ministry. Foreign diplomats had yet to reach a consensus on whether to take the official promises at face value and so von Ketteler, who had idled away much of the past few days taking potshots at Chinese from the Legation Quarter walls, decided to take matters into his own hands. Surrounded by a veritable army of interpreters and weapon-bearing guards, he waved us goodbye with a joke about the inefficiency of Chinese bureaucratic practices, saying he might even have finished his book by the time Qing officials deigned to see him. The German's curled mustache and smug countenance as he drove off quickly disappeared from my thoughts. I had made a fresh arrangement with La Contessa; I knew Edward Samuels of the Grand to be of the utmost discretion (after all, one couldn't run a hotel on tittle-tattle) and I had decided to take a room, simply telling him that I required a quiet and somewhat secure place in which to work. I hoped a room in the Legation Quarter would permit La Contessa the freedom to slip out to see me without arousing suspicion; it was becoming nigh on impossible for a woman to leave behind the safety of the foreign district and I doubted any of the guards dotted around the walls of the Legation Quarter would allow her to step foolhardy and free into the city of unbridled conflict that lay beyond the perimeter of half-safety the foreign powers had constructed. As Edward had handed me the key, no shade of judgement crossed his face.

Chiara knocked gently. I opened the door and we faced each other for a moment.

"Thank you for coming," I said finally.

"The pleasure is mine." She pushed past me and sat on the bed, removing her shoes with one careful hand, unbuttoning the back of her dress with the other. "My husband shall be in one of those interminable meetings today." She smiled. "At least I hope it may be interminable…"

We were becoming increasingly confident and rather less wary. At first we had worried about causing suspicion when we met, but Pietro Mancini's preoccupation with the ongoing ministerial negotiations and the concerns of the other inhabitants of the Fairchild residence for their own survival meant our fears of being discovered had all but disappeared. We felt, as lovers so often do, that our secret moments together were noble and majestic, that we were protected somehow from the dangers ordinary people might face.

Nevertheless, when a swift, strong rapping sounded at the door, Chiara started.

"Who?" she whispered. I shook my head. Edward was a professional; there was no way he would allow anyone to disturb me. I motioned to Chiara, already naked, to hide behind the screen by the side of the bed. She gathered up her dress and stole behind the divider of swooping birds and drooping willows. I couldn't help but glance at her elegant buttocks as they disappeared.

"Alistair." It was Edward who waited on the other side of the door, his stocky form filling the frame. "I am very sorry to disturb you, I know you must be hard at work. I thought you should know." He looked both ways down the corridor. "May I?"

I beckoned him into the room. He stepped inside, the floorboards groaning beneath his feet.

"Von Ketteler has died. He was close to the *Tsungli Yamen* when they across some Manchu soldiers…"

"Manchus? Not Boxers?" I asked.

"No. Imperial soldiers. There was some crossfire…He died."

"Christ." I sank down onto the bed, not bothering to embarrass myself over the wrinkled sheets or the sight of my discarded socks on the floor. "So the old Empress Dowager wants war. She has turned her soldiers not against the Boxers, but against us."

"Von Ketteler killed that Chinese boy. You might say he had it coming." Edward sat beside me, placed a hand on my shoulder. We both felt the heat of La Contessa's unacknowledged presence. "Alistair, if I may… Perhaps you might think about staying here. It would be foolish now to take for granted your safety outside of the Tartar walls. I wouldn't expect you to pay for the room, I simply…"

"Thank you, Edward. I am fine at home, though I would like to keep this room for my work. It is most conducive to writing. Very quiet." I stood and guided him back towards the door. "Thank you for telling me about von Ketteler."

"Of course, Alistair." He closed the door softly behind him.

"Von Ketteler's dead?" Chiara emerged from behind the screen, partially dressed and with delightfully tousled hair. "Killed by Manchu soldiers? How can this be?"

I said nothing, put my arms around her.

"You should go back now," I said.

She left me with a brief, bittersweet kiss.

It was not long until I saw La Contessa again; deciding once more to stop by Fairchild's for dinner I encountered her instructing the servants to pour a little more wine in each glass before the guests were seated. Nina and Lillian took their places at the table, but did not speak. Lillian fanned herself listlessly. Nicholas, agitated, circled the room as we waited for the meal to be served.

"Alistair," he said suddenly, bringing his latest circle to a halt at the head of the table. "Thank God they seem to have abandoned this nonsense idea of us leaving."

"Quite," I said. Lillian regarded me from the corner of her eye as she rhythmically turned the painted fan in her hand.

Pietro Mancini announced himself with resigned exhaustion. I noted the purple hue that colored the papery skin under his eyes and found myself, I am sorry to say, quite unable to take the pride I might normally in having stolen the affections of another man's wife.

"Excuse me," he said. "I would like to speak to my wife for a moment."

Their conversation, which took place on the other side of the door, began in controlled, terse tones before giving way to more voluble accusations. Naturally, the couple expressed themselves in Italian, but the language of discontent is universal, unhappiness is more visceral than grammar.

"*Non ora,*" La Contessa pleaded, and the volume of their exchange dipped once more.

"Poor Contessa," Lillian said, setting down her fan. "He wishes for her to leave."

"To leave?" I repeated.

"Yes, that is what she told me earlier. Since that German was murdered, he believes it is too dangerous for her to remain here."

"Dangerous to remain? Yet it is suicide to leave!" My voice had risen, I cleared my throat. "A most ridiculous idea."

Lillian shrugged. "Mrs Moore told me today that she also wishes to leave, and to take her children with her too. Her husband has promised to try to secure her safe passage."

"Mr Moore did receive rather a shock," I said, remembering Benjamin, flushed and gibbering after witnessing the murder of the Japanese. "And yet he is normally so phlegmatic."

Chiara returned a moment later, her chest flushed red, one cheek a stinging shade of pink.

"Mr Fairchild has arrived," she said in hollow, controlled tones. "I suppose we might eat now."

I had seen neither Nicholas nor Nina alone for days. La Contessa had filled my thoughts, time and bed, until I had been disturbed one morning by the delivery of a neat box at the front door. My ashen-faced servant presented it to me, opened its corners with trembling fingers and revealed within its confines a severed head, eyes unblinking, flesh drained of color, its pallor a sickening, sunken gray.

"Who is that?" I demanded.

"The man I paid to take your telegraph," my Number One Boy said, his voice dull and catching. "The Boxers must have found him…"

I closed the box, thrust it back into the servant's hands.

"Take it away from here," I said severely.

My boy, unmoved, watched me with downcast eyes.

"Now. *Kuai!* Hurry up!"

He carried the box in his thin arms, walked slowly, reluctantly away from me.

Dizzied, I walked out to my small courtyard, took great gulps of the dusty air and uselessly closed my eyes against the image of that life, stilled, ended, wrenched from existence. I had seen much death by then, considered myself hardened to the inevitable conclusion of every life, and yet I could not deny the effect of this unknown man's end upon my spirit. How lightly one lives when one simply observes, and how great a weight life is to bear when one acts, when one, however unknowingly, sets in motion a chain of cause and effect. The man, whose name I did not know and did not wish to know, had died opaquely by my hand, ignorant in his last, tortured breaths, of the source of his demise.

I did not leave the house that day, but sat in the company of my guilt, and was not surprised to find Number One Boy gone by the time the sun dipped pink against the evening sky. I ate a perfunctory meal alone, and when La Contessa visited I found it impossible to muster passion, and so we simply lay together, hands entwined, her body still and calm, and I envied the peace of the innocent.

"What troubles you?" she asked me.

I could not look at her, but with my eyes fixed upon the ceiling I told her.

"It is not your fault," she said. "It is the Boxers, and I know they do not deny themselves sleep for this man's death."

I allowed La Contessa to kiss me then, to quell my spiritual agitation with the undeniable corporeality of desire, and I forgot, for the best part of an hour at least, the gruesome sight of that head cleaved from its owner, and the culpability it wrought.

The following day I committed to visit the Wards at Fairchild's home. I had gone to see Nicholas and Nina as often as my other obligations allowed. Yet never did an opportunity for conversation present itself beyond the most superficial

VII

SOME MEN cannot pass a public house without yielding to the tart whisper of its spumous barrels, others abandon restraint at the first glimpse of a generous décolletage, unbridle themselves for any painted lip or curled hair. And while I too have been partial to such common pleasures, I am equally able to resist them in pursuit of some higher objective. There is only one temptation to render me rudderless and that is the siren call of chaos, the ominous allure of disorder. We newsmen are strange creatures: masters of words and slaves to events. How it invigorated and exhilarated me to step amongst the ragged throngs that surged through the Legation Quarter in those infant hours of the siege. A thrill, foreboding but heady, gripped me as I took my place amongst the soldiers of every flag who marched the streets, barking orders at the disorientated and displaced, corralling them towards the Su palace. The Boxers had pressed closer overnight, compelling dozens more of China's forsaken peasants into the Legation Quarter and the foreign enclave now played host to thousands.

It was a short distance from the Grand to Fairchild's residence, a mere half-mile at most, and yet the journey appeared interminable as I struggled against the waves of grim-faced refugees, uselessly guided by the gilt-buttoned soldiers. I continued in determination to see Nicholas, Nina and La Contessa. In disarray I have always found great clarity; when the structures of one's life splinter, the foundations are suddenly revealed. In five years in Peking, I had made countless connections, filled leather-bound pages with names and addresses, but as the city surrendered to its crude conquerors I thought only of those three faces. Upon arrival at the house, I found Phoebe Franklin addressing the women of the household in the drawing room. All wore grave expressions.

"We must think of our Chinese brothers and sisters," Phoebe said. "I implore you to come with me, to visit them, to hold hands together in prayer!"

My natural suspicion of the religious flared. I tried to catch La Contessa's eye but her face turned blankly towards Phoebe.

"Praise be to the Lord, for he showed me the wonders of His kindness when I was in a city under siege," she continued. "We must open ourselves to kindness and serve the Lord in His plans."

"Mrs Franklin," Lillian bristled. "If it's quite all right, I think we might be better employed doing something useful. Mrs Moore told me that some of the women are making sandbags out of pillowcases, that kind of thing."

Phoebe smiled tightly.

"I see the news of our besiegement has reached you," I said as I stepped into the room.

"Naturally," Phoebe Franklin said tersely. "And we must display unity, stand shoulder to shoulder with our fellow Christians."

"And so we pray?" Lillian insisted. "We pray and hope that the Boxers shall go away?"

"Miss Price," Phoebe began, before resigning herself with a curt shake of the head and turning to Nina. "Miss Ward, I do hope that your personal history in China might allow you to see why we must support our fellow Christians. Come, girls."

"Lillian," Nina said graciously. "Let us go with Mrs Franklin."

Lillian frowned, but uncrossed her arms. Phoebe turned with

authority and the girls stood to follow her. I was surprised by Nina's compliance. Nicholas was not a Christian man, and in his decades in China had endeavored to expunge from his spirit those hallmarks the Church of England presses upon any man native to the land of its spires and greens; he had attempted, with rather notable success, to exchange public virtue for private philosophy. Nina, he had told me once, had been christened to please his wife, but Nicholas had not entered a church since that day, uncomfortable as he was to share a pew with foreign proselytizer and merchant alike. Nina had surprised me more than once with her ignorance not only of formal religion but also of its inflections in shared speech and thought. Blind to an eye for an eye, Nina knew nothing of water into wine or feeding the five thousand. She watched me meaningfully as she left, telegraphed with rounded eyes signals I failed to read. She was, I thought as I observed her leave with back straight, neck long, carriage confident and thoughts unknown, increasingly a stranger to me. I wished to reach for her, to pull her back to me, to uncover those unshared reflections that filled her mind.

La Contessa stopped in the doorway, the hem of her skirt kissed my shoes.

"I am afraid it wouldn't be right," she called to Phoebe. "I am a Catholic after all."

Her breath warm and close against my ear, Chiara extended an invitation.

"And Nicholas?" I asked.

"Upstairs," she said quietly. "Come."

We were reckless, uncaring, we went without shame to the very room she shared with her husband. Later I would justify such actions to myself, I would say that we were fearful, that we were moved by the certain death we faced, but these rational motivations came long after we pressed trembling lips together in carnal prayer. It appears ignoble to me now, naturally, but it was beautiful and pure then, our dance in the shadow of death. She dressed quickly; we were, as always after the act, both searingly conscious of our circumstances.

"Have you heard?" she asked, her voice low as I helped to lace the back of her dress. "They took an Englishman last night. Beheaded him."

I pulled the fastening tight.

"Professor Aldred. Do you know him?"

"Aldred?" I stepped away from her. "Yes, yes, I have met him several times. He lived in the Chinese city."

"And they weren't Boxers," she said, tidying her hair with quick fingers. "Imperial troops. That's what Pietro told me, at least."

"We really are at war," I said, fixing the top button of my shirt.

Chiara followed me to the drawing room where we found Nicholas, hands clasped behind his back, looking out over the sloped grooves of the city beyond the Legation Quarter limits.

"Oh, Alistair," he said gravely, turning as we entered. "I thought I was alone."

Slowly his eyes moved over La Contessa and me, taking in the high color that dappled her chest, the dampness around my temples. He said nothing, and looked once more towards the city.

"They have gone to pray, I believe," he continued, directing his words to the window. "I wonder how long God might take to resolve this particular crisis."

"God," said Chiara, "might have abandoned us to Peking."

Amidst tumult, nothing comforts more successfully than organization, and the foreigners of Peking rapidly divided themselves on that very first day of the siege into groups created for specific administrative purposes, joining committees headed by missionaries that promised stability and regulation for however long the siege might go on. A committee for water, a committee for food, a committee for health and sanitation all sprung into life as an acceptance of the inevitability of a long stay in the Legation Quarter took hold. It seethed with the discontent of the displaced; the unhappiness of the foreigners, their existences suddenly vague, incalculable, matched that of the Chinese Christians, their bodies safe but their souls wretched, their heads brimming still with memories of razed villages and charred fields. Walking back towards the Grand, I thought of the Chinese expression for a huge crowd, *people mountain people sea*: these hundreds of bodies, thousands of limbs, tens of thousands of eyes dry with tears unspilt were an unending ocean of misery. And for how long might these well-meaning committees satiate so many thousands of empty stomachs?

I observed the newly-formed food committee carry out of its first operations that very afternoon, watched as Lillian Price and Beatrice Moore gleefully accompanied a group of soldiers to raid a Chinese store within Legation Quarter lines. The discovery of huge supplies of grain led one American soldier to throw handfuls of it into the air, letting it shower down over his shoulders in a hollow and rather premature victory. I carried a sack of grain and accompanied Lillian to the Fairchild residence, where, assuming the responsibilities of her new role on the committee, the girl requested that Oscar Fairchild send his servants to gather any spare supplies from the cellar. They duly returned with a dozen bottles of wine and twenty-seven cigars.

"These will do well for the Continentals," Lillian announced with new-found vitality. She, like many of my compatriots and New World cousins, seemed to blossom within the confines and hierarchies of systematic activity. This fresh wellspring of agitation made me realize to what an extent those days of waiting, of expecting rescue, of counting deaths on tired fingers, had deflated our spirits.

Nina, however, lacked the cheerful focus of her peers. She had been assigned to make sandbags out of any and all available material: men's shirts, curtains, old bedsheets, and her enthusiasm for the task was muted. Following a dinner accompanied by one of the dusty bottles of wine from Fairchild's cellar, Nina took her unpracticed sewing to the verandah, where her fingers weaved rapidly and inexpertly over her work. An open door separated her from the party in the drawing room, and it was with familiar irritation at our permanent state of being observed that I stepped outside to join her.

"Hello, Mr Scott," she said gently.

The sky hung a low, dusty pink that cast dappled shadows across her cheeks. She looked ruefully upon the half-formed sandbag in her lap.

"Do you suppose one might learn to sew at the age of nineteen?" she asked. "Or do you think I am bound to produce such ugly stitches for eternity?"

"I believe a young woman in possession of such talents as yours ought not to waste her time on trivialities," I said, walking to the edge of the verandah and looking out to the walls that surrounded the Legation Quarter. Thin, desperate wisps of smoke rose from the Chinese city beyond our reach. "If I were First Minister I would instruct you to negotiate with the Empress Dowager herself."

"Then it is most fortunate that you are not First Minister," Nina said. "*Aiyo!*" She drew a startled, bleeding finger from her needle, lifted it to her lips.

"You went to pray?" I said, lowering my voice.

Nina rubbed at the crimson tip of her bleeding finger with her thumb.

"I wondered," she said in quiet tones to match my own, "whether Chang might have come to the Legation Quarter. Or perhaps even Pei. Of course I didn't see them, and I am glad if that suggests they are in some better place. Mrs Franklin took us to the Su palace and, oh, what misery! Poverty and hunger as you could never imagine. At least the foreign powers have accommodated the refugees, Mrs Franklin told me some had suggested they might not."

"And so you prayed?"

"It is quite straightforward," Nina said. "One simply closes one's eyes and hopes."

I took my leave once more around ten p.m., and retired to the bar at the Grand, where I enjoyed my whisky in the company of two refugee families, their sleeping bodies arranged in the corners of the rooms. Edward and I spoke in hushed tones while Hilde cleared away glasses; a group of boisterous diplomats had only recently been induced to leave the families to their slumber.

"Six men of government hopeless enough to drink seven bottles of wine," Edward said. "I believe that merits a drop more for us civilians."

Hilde handed her husband the bottle of Chivas. Just as he made to fill my glass, the door to the bar swung open. La Contessa approached with arch smile.

"Mr Scott," she said in unusually soft timbre, "I come with a request from Mr Ward."

"Well, Mr Ward ought to come here himself," Hilde retorted. "Imagine letting a woman walk alone at this time of the night. Are we not under siege? Are the streets not crawling with soldiers, are the Boxers not at the gate?"

"I like to take the air," La Contessa said simply. "Mr Scott, if you please."

We climbed the stairs to my room. I lit a lamp and closed the door; we could hear the soft roar of fire just beyond Legation Quarter limits, the resolute rumble of Boxer voices.

"What does Nicholas need?" I asked.

"And I thought you were expert in these matters," she said. She laughed, velvety and languid, as her slender fingers made quick work of the buttons of my shirt. "It appears I still have much to teach you."

Certainly her unabashed assuredness was novel for me; those other married women of my acquaintance, whilst generally accommodating and free with their affections, had endeavored still to hide their intentions from others, they had followed regular timetables, constructed excuses of afternoon teas and family visits. They had not walked, resplendent, exuberant and utterly uncaring through streets roiled of blood and despair, darkness their only cover and the ultimate betrayer of their intentions. Allow me a moment to indulge romance, and say I had never known a woman like La Contessa, and I doubt I shall ever meet another so vibrantly, carelessly individual. I submitted willingly to this sensual folly, forgetting as my lips met hers and my hands found the nape of her neck that Edward and Hilde waited downstairs. We were becoming practiced now, familiar with the desires and preferences of the other, and I felt a great swell of contented intimacy as we lay together upon my bed afterwards, the Boxer chorus, *Sha! Sha!*, accompanying our hushed conversation.

"There is something I must tell you," she said, sitting suddenly upright, her fingers reaching to entwine with mine. "Miss Ward."

She paused, looked to the ceiling, gathered her thoughts.

"Yes, Chiara? What about Miss Ward?"

"I do not judge," she said carefully. "I tell you only because I worry for her."

La Contessa explained that she had waited until Pietro fell asleep before leaving the house. It was after eleven, and she walked with silent tread through the darkened residence, her shoes cradled in her hands. Voices from the drawing room gave her pause and, wary of discovery, she stopped in the hallway. A weak, flickering light suggesting only a single candle had been lit trickled from below the door to provide a puddle of illumination. Her first objective was to avoid the light, to make no sound as she passed the doorway to exit the house. Skirting the entranceway she intended to pass right away into the night, but the conversation that filtered through the walls brought La Contessa to a halt. Two voices sounded; one, that of Oscar Fairchild, the second belonged to Nina. And yet Oscar spoke in a way La Contessa had never heard him previously. Gone was his easy, polite manner, and in its place she heard unconcealed desperation, a pleading, almost wild resonance.

"And what did he say to her?" I asked.

"I could not hear it all," La Contessa said. "He spoke of his career, said he had never intended to end up in Peking, suggested that he was unhappy, dissatisfied with his life."

"And Nina?"

"She tried to quieten him, suggested they might wake the others."

"And?"

La Contessa held my hand more tightly, pressed her palm flat against mine.

"And then, Alistair, I heard the words that concern me most. *Let them awaken,* he said, *and I shall tell them that I have never met one as beautiful, as true as Miss Nina Ward. I shall shout it until the Boxers of Shantung hear me.*"

"And then?"

"And then there was nothing. No words at least." She brought her face close to mine, brushed my lips with hers. I turned away. "I have upset you. I ought not to have said anything. It is only, if I hear them, so might anyone in the house. Her father, or..."

"Thank you for telling me." I rose from the bed, dressed myself once more. Possessed of sudden energy, I experienced a great desire to move. La Contessa watched me cautiously.

"But, where are you going, Alistair? Please, do not act without thinking."

It is remarkable how those who have known us the least time can often most effectively read our unspoken thoughts. They see us for what we are, not what we once were or aspire to become. For I might have considered myself a rational man, considered and equanimous, but I did not think, could not think, in those moments. Thoughts suggested themselves to me, but failed to gain a foothold in my fogged brain. Rage, blind, righteous and unfocused, consumed me. I angered towards Oscar Fairchild and his cruel opportunism, I cursed Nicholas' ignorance, his inaction. I maddened even towards Nina. Sweet, clever Nina; no painting or poem might save her from the frailty of the flesh, and no philosophy could protect her from the consequences of submitting to its whims. Had neither Nicholas nor Pei ever warned her that while lilies might grow amidst the mud, their petals must strain to avoid its stains?

"Please, *tesoro mio*." La Contessa rose to embrace me. "Sleep now. Tomorrow you shall speak with Miss Ward."

"Tomorrow might be too late," I said.

"Ssh." She kissed me. "I see how you care for her. To protect her, tonight you must do nothing."

Silently she dressed and left me. I poured myself another whisky and sat at my desk, one foot tapping nervously against the floor. Lillian Price had not been mistaken. Nina and Oscar. Oscar and Nina. The names merged and fell apart in my mind, conjured images I wished to expel from memory. Nina at the party in May, my summoning of Fairchild, his eyes first setting upon her unblemished form. The knife thrust towards Nina, the trail of dropped pearls across the dusty ground, my urging that the Wards seek safety under Fairchild's roof. I damned Oscar and castigated Nicholas, and yet I could not deny my hand in Nina's fate. I, with unthinking good will, I, with admirable intentions, I, with a ghastly lack of foresight, had engineered this pairing. And so I vowed that I, with concern for Nina and care for future, would dissolve the corrupt partnership.

All days in the Legation Quarter were accompanied by fire, by great, roaring flames of destruction to our north, to our east, our west and our south. Yet while smoke and heat and the splintering sounds of buildings surrendering under force had become somewhat normal for us, this fire surprised even the most jaded of residents.

The Chinese, we all agreed, valued education. We ourselves might not have appreciated their particular methods of educating themselves, indeed we scoffed at the outdated civil service examination system still in place that obliged young men to sacrifice the brightest, most tender days of their existence to memorizing large swathes of ancient scholarly works. The educated Chinese was the reverse image of that other impression of the Chinaman printed in our shared imagination: the barbarian of gnashed teeth and fearsome cry. The Chinese, we believed, could only be warriors or scholars, either savage, loathsome creatures or long-nailed, effeminate men of no practical purpose. And no place was more precious to Chinese men of books than the Hanlin Academy, a seat of learning as brilliant in their eyes as the centers of Oxford or Cambridge in ours. And still the Boxers set it on fire, launching torches onto its parched rooftops in the morning, emissaries of a fire that soon devoured the walls to reach the precious books inside, and ravaged the many thousands of printed pages contained inside them.

The blaze was abrupt and powerful. Wisdom, it soon transpired, burned even more rapidly than wood. I had planned to make immediately for the Fairchild residence in the morning to see Nina, but the fire rather interrupted my plans, and Edward and I set out for the Hanlin, located just beyond the walls of the British Legation, instead. Marines had been sent to extinguish the fire and recruited any and all willing citizens to help with the effort. I saw Nina and Lillian join a large group of people already working to assist the soldiers in their quelling of the fire. Snaking, chaotic lines had been formed, made up of missionaries, diplomats and servants, who passed buckets from one frantic hand to another, water spilling over the sides as they raced hopelessly against the fire. The marines had been dispatched to inside the compound itself, where they set about felling the walls of the Hanlin's halls in an attempt to halt the fire.

Phoebe Franklin was at the head of one of the lines of amateur firefighters.

"Hurry! Pass it here!" Her commands were invigoratingly human, untainted by her usual superiority, free from any references to the Lord or appeals to our better characters.

Edward's wife Hilde followed us from the hotel shortly afterwards, gun strapped by her side, and immediately set to work, falling into line behind the wife of the French minister. The foreigners briefly forgot their national flags in the urgency of this shared task and toiled together in harmony. Imperial soldiers kept up a steady staccato of gunfire as we worked against the blaze. These potshots from the surrounding rooftops did not constitute the finest display of firearms skills, and felled not a single foreigner. That did not matter to the enemy, however, as they were intended only to serve as a simple nuisance, a distraction from the urgent task before us.

Despite the Imperial soldiers' best efforts, eventually we succeeded in taming the fire sufficiently to ensure that the Legation Quarter itself was not at immediate risk of immolation. Then I was able to join the marines inside the Hanlin. The ruin was breathtaking: the most important works ever penned by Chinese hand had been reduced to nothing more than curled, gray dust. The Hanlin itself was a skeleton, its main library had been salvaged only by a fortunate change in the direction of the wind. I picked through the ruins, my nostrils filled with dense, black smoke. I found three marines squatting amid the ashes, bodies limp with exertion. "Look at this," one of them called to me. He gestured to a pile of books, heaped into a quivering pyramid and sprinkled with dry leaves and arid wood.

I pulled one of the books from the pile, my fingers traced the charred corners of its pages. I could not decipher the contents of the silk-bound volume, yet even a novice in the written Chinese language such as myself could easily intuit the painstaking craftsmanship of the calligraphy upon its pages.

"I simply cannot believe it." Nicholas approached, two books already placed under his arm. "If the Boxers wished to destroy Chinese civilization, well, they have succeeded."

"At least they have not succeeded in their efforts to destroy us." I placed a hand upon his shoulder, but his eyes maintained their glassy, distant expression. I had raged at Nicholas' image in my mind the previous evening, but seeing him before me restored old affections. His devastation at such savage destruction of his greatest joy, Chinese scholarship, dampened my anger.

"Alistair, will you help me?" he asked. "We must save the books, take them away from here. I fear the Boxers will return."

"Naturally."

We made our way through the ashen maze of the Hanlin, collecting volumes as we went, instructing missionaries and refugees and servants to carry the books to Oscar Fairchild's home, where Nicholas promised he would later sort the editions and find a secure place for their storage. In the main library we found Nina gazing hopelessly at her surroundings.

"Father!" She rushed to embrace Nicholas and the pair clung to one another under the high eaves that marked the entrance to the Hanlin's principal collection. "It is too awful," she said.

Softly Nicholas stroked her hair. The Hanlin was not a place she was intimately familiar with; Nina had visited the school only two or three times as a child, accompanying her father in search of texts to inform his research. Yet she had passed it frequently on her walks around the city and stopped to admire its elegant exterior, and she recalled now those happy afternoons when she had been allowed to play in the courtyards while her father spoke with the officious librarians. Then the shelves had towered above her, the ceilings had hung high and distant. Now Nina was a giant, the Hanlin trampled underfoot.

We were not alone for long. Soon other foreigners charged into the library, loud and buoyant, calling to one another in the overzealous tones that identified those witnesses to terrible events. I had seen those faces a hundred times before: shocked by the depths to which humanity can fall, delighted to be alive, rapturously enjoying the righteous outrage permitted by such events. Scholars amateur and professional scoured the shelves for remaining works despite Nicholas' protestations that no one take anything for themselves. We were not to discover all that had been removed until months later, when some of the men resident in Peking during the siege offered rare manuscripts to England's most prominent libraries.

Nicholas and I crossed from courtyard to courtyard, passing the small pools choked now with fallen rafters and discarded shrapnel, the carp that once swam tranquilly in them crushed beneath this human debris, until we reached the street. Nina followed at a distance. In her hand, dusty with ash, she held a slim volume, a mere slither of a great, historic encyclopedia.

"I shall see you at home, Father," she said, seating herself upon a low wall outside the library as the sun began its slow descent towards the night. She turned from us, shielded her eyes from the late afternoon light and surveyed the Hanlin, queen of a broken kingdom.

In Nicholas' room, every surface was already buried under volumes saved from the Hanlin, brought here by servants and sympathetic scholars. I placed a stack of books upon the desk beside a scattering of papers written in Nicholas' sharp, authoritative hand. *Popular religion has long held sway among peasants in the Chinese countryside, forming an important part of rural life despite official movements to install faith in organized religion. The Boxer movement has much in common with previous popular uprisings. The promise of religion imbues social unrest.*

"You are still studying the Boxers?" I asked.

"It is a strange feeling," he conceded. "When the subject you are studying begins to study you."

"You might say you were like a zoologist studying a tiger," I agreed. "Never thinking those fangs would be turned against you."

Nicholas laughed and we stood together in amenable quiet, looking at the most valuable library in all of China scattered around our feet. I thought of mentioning Nina, but his bewildered expression silenced me.

"If a book holds a house of gold," he said. "One might say I live in a palace."

The evening was one of subdued acceptance. Pony meat, optimistically referred to as "French beef", featured for the first time on the Fairchild dinner menu. Yet even Lillian ate her share without complaint; her work with the food committee affording her both perspective and lashings of Monopole champagne, which served to wash down the tough meat. I had also reconciled myself to circumstances; I must endeavor to speak with Nina, I knew, but until such an opportunity presented itself I ought not to take any unusual action that might imperil her further. And so, in the hopes that such an opportune moment might materialize that evening, I had returned to the house after finishing a dispatch about the Hanlin. I could imagine my editor's reaction to the telegraph when received - how could the Hanlin be a hallowed seat of learning if he had never heard of it? - and still I recorded the tale of destruction, determined as my little world grew smaller and ever more endangered to document its unshielded existence.

Talk at the table switched from the Hanlin to the latest attack upon Prince Su's palace, which had been relentlessly assaulted that day, though by some miracle it still stood. The unending violence, the nightmare of living under siege, had rapidly become so quotidian that Oscar Fairchild's guests spoke of atrocity as though discussing the weather. Types of weapon (*"Cannon or gun?"*) and death tolls (*"I suppose ten is not so many"*) filled those same spaces in conversation once occupied by shopping lists and forthcoming social occasions. The stench of decaying corpses was no longer confined to the streets, but entirely permeated the house. Death had met life, and the living bowed to its power. After dinner the remaining champagne was carried through to the drawing room where glasses were raised grimly, stoically to the day's events. Nicholas spoke of his newly-acquired library, said he would contact universities abroad, promised to find institutions that could guarantee an afterlife for these volumes, a home where they would be frequently eased from shelves, their words devoured by new generations of scholars.

My eye drawn unwaveringly to La Contessa, I determined to watch Oscar and Nina instead. Fairchild seemed circumspect, quiet, cowed somewhat by the attack on the Hanlin, but he continued to perform his official role, head nodding, lips smiling, hands dancing to the cadences of his voice. Nina spoke eloquently of her previous visits to the Hanlin, voiced disapproval of the Boxers' thoughtless ruination of China's precious canon, listened attentively when Pietro Mancini spoke of the Paris commune and the razing of the library at the Louvre. She possessed her habitual unorthodox charm; only the slight gray pallor to her skin signaled hardship. I felt her behavior a betrayal; how could she appear so unchanged? The only difference in her actions that evening was her decision to retire to bed early when usually she stayed reading alone in the drawing room. Tomorrow, I thought as she crossed the room, spine pulling straight as she passed Oscar. I would speak with her tomorrow.

The twenty-fifth of June was a strange and memorable date. The morning began with the execution of two Boxers held prisoner in the Legation Quarter. I watched unfeeling as their breathless bodies were tossed over the wall into the Chinese city. The day was pockmarked with the usual fighting and panic and disputes between diplomats concerning which positions to reinforce and which to abandon. Yet as day slipped into night, we were shocked out of our resigned pessimism by the unexpected blare of silence. The air had been so long pierced with bullets, the rat-a-tat of firing had become so commonplace, that the nature of silence had been almost entirely forgotten. I was drinking at the bar of the Grand when Edward noted the quiet.

"Something's happening," he said. Hilde, now inseparable from her gun, followed us out to the streets. There I discovered a young Chinese boy, loitering bow-legged in the street, and I asked him what the silence indicated.

"The soldiers are leaving," he said and pointed to the imperial army positions beyond the Tartar Wall, which were, just as the boy said, currently being abandoned by those who had held them. The uneasy silence was followed swiftly by a vigorous blast of Chinese trumpets. A crowd gathered around the North Bridge from where the sounds emanated, a stone's throw from the smoldering Hanlin Academy, and I spied Nina and Lillian amongst the group. I wondered if La Contessa was there; she had not returned to the hotel the previous night and I had slept fitfully, desirous of her physical presence, yes, but wishing also that I might speak to her of Nina and Nicholas, poor, crestfallen Nicholas and his collection of salvaged books.

Presently a group of imperial soldiers stepped up to the bridge, their silhouettes glimmering in the sunset. They held up a large white sign splashed with a series of bold Chinese characters. Its message was unclear; most of the foreigners could not read a word of the language. I called out to Nina, who was rapidly supplied with binoculars which she pressed against her eyes as she read the message.

"It is an imperial edict," she said, her voice resonant and unafraid in the crowd. Behind her Oscar Fairchild had appeared, his head cocked to one side as he listened to her. "In accordance with court orders the imperial forces are to stop firing immediately." Nina lowered the binoculars and looked around her. The crowd remained quiet, but bristled with restrained celebration.

"I don't quite understand," I ventured. "They are to stop

attacking us?"

"With immediate effect," Nina said, her voice level. "They shall send another message later."

"We must respond," Oscar said, taking up position at Nina's side. "Miss Ward, perhaps you could help us to formulate a response."

"Naturally."

The crowd watched with begrudging admiration as Nina's hand produced a line of dancing characters upon a piece of a paper.

"I have simply said that we have received their message and understood it well," she said, lifting her pen from the page.

"That will do for now," Oscar assented. "Until we know what to make of all of this."

The message was placed into the somewhat unwilling hand of a Chinese man who was dispatched to cross the bridge and deliver the message. Unsure, he made his way on trembling legs over to the imperial troops; their teasing calls eventually unnerved him so much it was all he could do to drop the message and steal back to safety on our side of the bridge, where he was returned with subdued applause.

The foreigners immediately broke up into smaller groups, chattering excitedly amongst themselves. Hilde placed a firm hand on my shoulder.

"Let us look across enemy lines," she said, eyes glittering at the prospect of freedom. Edward and I followed her to the very edges of the Legation Quarter, where we looked across the barricades to the fresh unfamiliarity of the old city. Imperial troops milled before us, their colors brilliant, their weapons held loosely by their sides.

"I don't quite believe this," I said to the couple.

"No, and you shouldn't," Edward said. "Look, those soldiers

appear to be strengthening their positions there. This war is far from over."

"Wouldn't it be wonderful if it was, though?" Hilde said, taking her husband's hand. "We might sleep the whole night, for once."

"Do you suppose the troops are close?" Edward said. "Perhaps Seymour and his men are within sight of the city. That would indeed be sobering for the Chinese, might give them pause."

"We can only hope," I said.

We turned back with optimism burgeoning but tempered, prisoners not wholly unwilling to return to their gaoler.

I stopped by the Fairchild residence later, where I found the guests buoyed with animated chatter as they sat down to a late dinner. The Monopole champagne secured by Lillian had once again been produced for consumption, though this time there was something more to celebrate than paltry portions of pony meat.

"I have no doubt," Lillian said. "The troops are almost here, I feel it! Finally we shall go home."

La Contessa was also in high spirits, her eyes sparkling and round, her gaze defiant as she met mine over the table. Nina, I noticed, was gripped by a more tempered restlessness, her sentiments I imagined to be as were mine: positive, certainly, but restrained somewhat by the suspicions suggested by logical thought.

"Mr Fairchild," I said. "What are we to make of this?"

Oscar cleared his throat and took a generous sip of champagne.

"We know no more than you do," he said. "My instinct tells me Seymour and his troops must be nearing. They are at least close enough to frighten the imperial government somewhat. Still, we have soldiers reinforcing our defenses tonight and they will continue to guard the Legation Quarter. One cannot be too careful."

"I agree," Nicholas said. "As the Chinese say, once you ride on the tiger's back it is impossible to alight."

"Enough!" Lillian said. "I am so tired of being careful, of being worried, of thinking I might never see another American sunrise. Let us enjoy this one night, please. A night free from gunshots, a night we can sleep peacefully."

"You are quite right," I said to Lillian, feeling suddenly indulgent, heartened by the close presence of La Contessa. I thought only of when I might next catch a quiet moment with her, if I might seal the promise of that hopeful night with a kiss. I raised my glass. "To a good night's sleep, if nothing else."

We drank a little too much champagne, eager as we were for change, we longed to try on our former selves for a time. The after-dinner talk in the drawing room was spirited, we spoke over one another, left our sentences trailing, unfinished and hopeful. Oscar Fairchild stood with his back to the fireplace and with a slender glass of frothing champagne in his hand held court over his guests.

"We shan't take any irrational action," Oscar said. "The soldiers shall remain vigilant tonight and we will see what morning brings."

"The only sensible course of action," Pietro agreed. "The imperial government, they cross us this way, that way. It is impossible to know what they shall do next."

"Miss Ward," Oscar addressed Nina directly. "What do you think might occur now?"

This surprised me, and I watched for Nina's response.

"I have been fortunate enough to experience little conflict in my life," Nina said. She raised her head, her eyes meeting Oscar's with a quiet audacity. "Nevertheless, I have learned something of the Chinese attitude to war from the books I have read. While

I may not be a diplomat or a general, I recall something Sun Tzu said in the *Art Of War*. 'Appear weak when you are strong and strong when you are weak.'"

"So you mean to say this is a pretense? That the conflict is not over?" Phoebe asked.

"Mrs Franklin, I have no idea. One action cannot reveal a person's true intention, just as the sea cannot be measured in a bucket."

"Well, this is all rather philosophical for me," Pietro said brusquely. "Though I deduce from her words that Miss Ward agrees with us that prudence is utmost in a situation such as this."

"It is just as Matthew said of sheep in the midst of wolves: be wise as serpents and innocent as doves," Phoebe said. She excused herself then and I hoped that Pietro Mancini might also retire for the night, but he remained by his wife's side. While Pietro addressed Oscar, I tried to catch La Contessa's eye, aware that while Chiara steadfastly ignored my efforts, Nina had perceived my attempts to call Chiara to attention. The frown that passed over her face was sharp, sudden, knowing. Our misdemeanors are recognized most clearly by fellow sinners.

Dispirited, I took my leave and walked back to the Grand through the uneasy quiet that enveloped the streets of the Legation Quarter. Blockades protected the foreign population from the city that encircled us, and those makeshift walls, erected to seal in our civilization, threw shadows across my path. Unnerved by the silence I turned constantly to look behind me until I reached the entrance to the hotel where I settled into a shallow sleep on that strange night of hushed tensions, of quieted threats, of stilled possibilities, until I was dragged unceremoniously from rest when the firing started once more. The entire Legation Quarter woke then with bitter hearts, with the exception of the Russian soldiers, whose liquid celebrations of peace had yet to cease. I pulled back the curtains to find to find the sky a hazy orange, the city's old hellish backdrop restored. Reality blazed undeniably over us, and no secret might escape its intractable glare.

VIII

I AM NOT a man of regret. Remorse, contrition, condemnation of the self, those are the pastimes of men who have relinquished life, who find the endeavor of existence so laced with danger that they have renounced it entirely, and instead torture themselves with the missteps of their own histories. I have travelled endlessly, I have worked constantly, I have progressed tirelessly by simply continuing to wake each morning and put one foot in front of the other. Nicholas could indubitably express this idea with more careful grace, calling upon the sages of the past, referencing Confucius' admonition to till the land one basket of earth at a time, or recalling Lao Tzu's simple observation that the journey of a thousand miles begins with a single step, but permit me, please, the indulgence to explain my philosophy in far plainer language: one must keep going. And yet the twenty-fifth of June, that strange day of silence and noise, of celebration and dread, robs me even now of sleep. Its moments unfurl themselves before me and demand justification. I am not a man of regret, but oh, if I might return to that day, if I might pull Nina to a quiet corner of the charred remains of the defeated Hanlin, if I might invite her to step out with me to the verandah of Fairchild's home, if I might slip her a secret note, or tell her with the crease of my brow or the grip of my fingers upon her wrist: stop now. If I had sent Nicholas alone to build his own library of rescued volumes, if I had set aside my glass of Monopole champagne, if I had quelled for just one evening my desire of La Contessa's charms both physical and spiritual, well, then I would not have lived the next day in its muted horrors.

I did not sleep again once the firing began, and in the first blush of dawn eventually decided to go downstairs. Hilde, bustling and efficient behind the bar, served me warm, bitter coffee. I watched the refugee families wake slowly and with dread; they had slept peacefully through the firing, so inured was their sleep to exterior disturbances, and the news of renewed fighting leadened their movements and dulled their early morning talk.

"Help me with these to the Su palace?" Hilde dragged three sacks of grain and rice across the floor. "I found them in the cellar."

"You are generous to a fault, Mrs Samuels," I said, rising from my seat.

I lifted two of the sacks, Hilde cradled one with impressive ease. The palace was not far, and even then my breath was ragged when we arrived. The prince's former residence was thick with life, raucous and rank already in those early hours, and the terrible conditions immediately dimmed any impressions of hardship we might have harbored at the Grand Hotel. The once luxuriously ample space swarmed from wall to wall with human bodies, sickly and thin, with bones that rippled under coarse skin. Hilde and I left the supplies in an austere store room, and I wandered Su's palace then from end to end, marveling at the general good spirits of its inhabitants while recoiling from the stench of the place, the cloying musk of illness and degradation. In the central courtyard I confronted the brilliant blue of the sky and thought it a day for poets: an artist's mind might see some caustic beauty in the promise of the warm, hopeful sky above us in contrast to those thick, unforgiving walls that bound and girded us; the walls of the mansion, the stern perimeter of the Legation Quarter, the Great Wall to the north of the city, and those endless confines that circled and hemmed, encroached and besieged us in Peking. But I am not a poet, and so that great open canopy seemed only a cruel joke, a celestial taunt to the wretched prisoners of the palace.

Wearily I turned towards the building's grand entranceway, desirous suddenly of the relative liberty of the Legation Quarter streets, and started at the sight of a ghostly figure walking towards me, an image so incoherent with my surroundings that I wondered for a moment if it were an apparition, if the heat and redolence of the place had finally defeated my rational mind. Silently she walked through the throngs of refugees in an immaculate summer dress of starched lilac, chin aloft and eyes unseeing. Her skin glowed translucently pale beside the earthy tones of the escapees' hardened, weather-beaten complexions. They parted as she passed, stepped aside almost imperceptibly to allow the phantom visitor to continue on her path, and she did not regard them, did not acknowledge this consideration.

"Nina," I called. "Nina."

She stopped abruptly and her eyes found mine. I stepped forward, she turned so her back faced me, a neat set of buttons from nape to waist.

"Nina." I reached for her hand, pulled her towards me. "What are you doing here?"

Slowly she craned her neck, turned her face to mine.

"Alistair," she said softly. "I am glad to see you."

The young woman who looked pitifully towards me was not Nina, but some hazy etching of her form. The features were arranged in the same manner; this person too possessed a pair of green eyes framed by bristling lashes of dark tone, lips that tapered to neat and careful bud, hair waved and dense that threatened to disobey its chignon, and yet all color was washed from this impression from Nina, as though her former self had dried out below a severe and unrepentant sun.

"Why are you here?" I asked.

"Mrs Franklin thought it best I stay away from the house today," she said, offering a wan smile. "She said my Mandarin might be of use here."

"You might fall ill," I said.

She nodded. Neither of us spoke a moment, but observed the hubbub of the courtyard; the children playing hopscotch, the elders resting with eyes closed, lips alternating between muttered curses and prayers, the mothers soothing weeping babies, pressing their offspring to dry and bitter breast.

"And so might you," she said. "Good morning, Mr Scott."

She disappeared from me then and weaved through the crowd with renewed purpose, stopping by a circle of young girls.

"Nimen shi cong nar lai de?"

She asked where they were from, knelt beside them, spoke with softly feigned animation. I watched her, thought her lost to me. Across her face was written ruin, in her thoughtless tread was printed devastation, and yet her words, mere hollow pleasantries, revealed nothing. And so with diminished spirit I made to leave. Phoebe Franklin stood by the palace's elaborate gates in earnest conversation with Hilde.

"Miss Ward is here," I observed.

"Yes," the missionary said briskly. "Miss Ward has been reading rather often of late. I do not believe it wholly salutary for a young woman to read as often as does Miss Ward."

The day promised to proceed with the same dull anguish that had colored the past weeks, but I felt a fresh, intense despair as I walked through the Legation Quarter, the mystery of Nina's strange appearance a persistent vex upon my mind. I left the Su palace wishing to rid myself of the tragedy of that forsaken place, but the streets, daubed as they were with the blood of several nations, offered no respite. The story of the siege unfolded around me, the city furnished me with unending grisly details: a child's body slumped lifeless against the Tartar wall, an abandoned, blunted sword of a Boxer, a smell so foul, so tenacious that it seemed to have permanently lodged itself inside my nostrils. Still, the wider context, the actions of ministers and nations and peoples, those prime ingredients of any history, remained indistinct, unknown. The little information we received leaked through the walls only thanks to foolhardy messengers and the occasional, bewildering missive from the Qing. We were ignorant, and today wretchedly so.

The residents of the Legation Quarter had suffered a dramatic fall from the heights of relief offered by the temporary ceasefire. Talk of war was increasingly fevered, and a sometimes glib humor edged its way into our speech. With no news of the approaching troops and every sign of true war, men were set to the dig shelters around the borders of our suffocating quarter; I heard one remark that he had never imagined digging his own grave.

"Nobody's told Queen Victoria," another said ruefully, wiping damp heat from his brow and smearing his temples with grime. "She would never allow us to suffer this."

Indeed, our abandonment had become almost shameful, particularly for those of us sheltered under the supposed auspices of Britannia. How might our nation call herself great when she abandoned her citizens to ruthless slaughter abroad? As I rounded the Legation Quarter's newly-established makeshift hospital, I tried to tell myself that anger towards the soldiers themselves would not advance their approach: their absence suggested some calamity had befallen them and I supposed they had lived worse moments than we within the relative security of the Legation Quarter's walls. Still I bitterly resented their absence as I sympathized with the newly-interned hospital patients, noting their names and injuries, coaxing from them stories of unforeseen Boxers attacks, of glinting knives in alleyways, of frantic, flying kicks and tussles over dusty streets. Those were the romantic tales, the narratives of menacing, Oriental hue, the scenes that would provoke ire and outrage in the dining rooms and railway carriages of the old country. They were, I thought, as I took scant note of those more common occurrences of imperial army bullets and legs broken in hasty retreat from enemies uniformed and regimented, the very stories that might inspire our rescue.

I witnessed young men decaying, disintegrating, giving up their lives upon blood-soaked sheets. I saw protruding bones, angry gashes, weeping cuts, these injuries incongruously wrapped in gaudy silks of joyous colors, donations from extensive, unneeded wardrobes. I heard men gabble nonsense in five languages, saw their hands clasp invisible mothers and lovers, I watched with admiration as experienced doctors and amateur nurses sewed flesh together, knowing that even as the wounds of the skin healed there would be no medicine for the ills of these men's minds. I was surprised to find Beatrice Moore there, changing sheets, cooling fevers. She tapped my shoulder, smiled coolly.

"Mr Scott, I would like to introduce you to someone." She led me to a cot tucked away in a corner of the ward. "Behold, the first child born since we have been under siege."

I looked down at the red, wrinkled face of a newborn swaddled in white. Its lips wobbled, its tiny mouth threatened screams, but it kept its silence in that room of wailing men.

"Well, hello, little chap," I said, stretching out my finger; the baby seized it with a fierce grip.

"His name is Siege," she said.

"Sorry?"

"Yes, the mother has named him Siege," she said plainly. "We only hope he will live to answer the question of how he came to be given such an unusual name."

The baby held my finger still, looked towards me with the joyous, unconcealed wonder of those newly initiated to the world.

"And you are helping here?" I asked Beatrice.

Benjamin Moore's wife was a habitually condescending and precious woman, she did not possess, to my knowledge, an ounce of character suited to either the practical or consolatory practices of the nurse. Reveling in her husband's position in trade, Beatrice usually spent her days judging and dismissing the choices of others over endless rounds of tea and luncheon, launching damning attacks upon social rivals, taking care always to deliver her rebuffs neatly wrapped and slathered with saccharine gloss. She was immensely tiresome, and I had succeeded in mostly avoiding her in my time in Peking, although my duties occasionally required I seek out her husband for some story regarding chests of tea or shipments of porcelain.

"We must all play our part, Mr Scott," she said officiously, leaning over to loosen the baby's hold of me. The fledgling looked again as if he might cry, his round eyes rolled from me to Beatrice, his tiny nostrils quivered. "Besides, I simply couldn't face another day in the house. I do so enjoy the company of Miss Price, but I rather tire of the gossip under Fairchild's roof. Ladies sitting around all day with nothing to do but chatter amongst themselves, you understand."

"I am not sure that I do."

We watched the baby as his trembling eyelids fell, curtained him from us. An apprehension built in me as I listened to Mrs Moore's brisk speech and I recalled Nina, wraithlike and shadowy in the wretched purgatory of the Su palace, feared her implication in Beatrice's words.

"Have you been to Mr Fairchild's home today, Mr Scott?"

I shook my head.

"You really ought to visit your friends the Wards." Sharply she turned from the cot and crossed the room. I followed, and over her shoulder she awarded me a spurious smile. "Miss Ward seems quite changed by the siege, and I am sure she would appreciate a token of your friendship."

Hurriedly I crossed the short distance to the Fairchild residence, momentarily blind to the tapestry of ghastly conflict spread before me. I stopped outside the house, admired the solidity of its gray structure and the uniform rows of windows that regarded me, appreciated the decorative verandah that curled the perimeter of the building, its awnings of curved wrought iron. How smooth the outward exterior of the building, how imperious and certain, and yet what obscure riddles characterized its inner workings.

Impatiently I knocked on the door, and with laudable restraint relayed my request to the slow-moving servant who greeted me, desirous as I was to push past him, to call Nicholas' name, to run to my old friend, to shake him by the shoulders, to demand he explain these uncanny events, that he reassure me circumstances were not as disquieting as they appeared. The servant offered to show me to Nicholas' room, but I declined, taking the stairs two at a time and announcing my presence with a thunder of knocks upon my friend's door.

"Alistair," he said warmly. "Do come in. I have been organizing the collection." He gestured towards the volumes rescued from the Hanlin, arranged now in neat towers across the floor. "I'm afraid I do find myself becoming rather distracted in my task. How might one resist the lure of books unread?"

"How indeed," I said drily. My acerbity was unheeded.

"Please, sit." Nicholas pointed to the only chair in the room, tucked neatly behind the desk.

"I'd rather stand."

"Very well." Nicholas settled himself in the chair, looked expectantly towards me. "You seem a trifle agitated, Alistair."

"Nina is at Su's palace," I started. Curling and uncurling my fists, I felt rage simmer, gently but irrefutably, in my gut.

Nicholas moved his spectacles to the end of his nose, looked towards me with quizzical expression. Anger reared more assuredly within me now. How might Nicholas continue his introspective, intellectual existence at this time? I wondered. How might he catalogue books and read ancient philosophy while the Legation Quarter filled with the displaced and the despairing, as disease and disorder claimed young lives, as enemies deadly and determined conspired to destroy our existence? How might he remain here in learned ignorance as those around us whispered Nina's undoing?

"So Miss Price tells me," he said calmly. "The missionary thought Nina might be of use there. I cannot imagine her sewing shall be missed."

"There is talk," I said. "About Nina. What has happened, Nicholas?"

"Talk?" He frowned. "Well, nothing." He paused, waved his hand dismissively. "Oh, I suppose they refer to last night."

"Last night?"

"Yes. You know Nina has had terrible trouble sleeping since we came here. She likes to read in the evenings, and when the firing began again, Miss Price went downstairs and found Nina reading in the drawing room. There was some terrible commotion about that; I suppose Miss Price does not like to read."

"Nina was reading?" I pressed. "Alone?"

"Yes. Well, I presume so."

"I cannot see how reading might provoke any such commotion," I argued. "We have spoken of this before, Nicholas, and I do not wish to irk you. I only ask, do you think Mr Fairchild might have been with Nina?" I hesitated. "Reading?"

Nicholas stood and with one finger returned his spectacles to rest upon the bridge of his nose.

"Alistair, do you not know Nina?" Squarely he stepped towards me. "How might you continue to make such accusations?"

"And how might you remain so resolutely ignorant of what is happening before you, Nicholas? She is your only daughter and yet you do nothing to protect her. She has no experience of men, her only suitor has been Barnaby George, his proposal was a mere month ago. How might she resist a man like Fairchild, admired, of status, knowledgeable of the world in a way she is not?"

"Alistair, please. Nina was only reading."

Reading, I thought. How zealously Nicholas read, how staunchly he encouraged the habit in his own daughter, allowing her to sample any literature, high or low, English or Chinese, how detachedly he permitted her to create her own proclivities and develop her own opinions, how innocently he had led Nina into a trap of rhymes and metaphors, towards a downfall unravelled amidst printed pages and by candlelight, a ruin unforeseen by Ts'ao Hsüeh-ch'in and Thomas Hardy when they pressed their respective pens to virgin pages.

"Nicholas," I pleaded, but he silenced me with an assertive arm around my shoulders, and guided me to the doorway.

"I would hate for us to disagree over this matter," he said. "I have asked you kindly to desist from making wild denouncements, and your frantic desire to speak with me this morning can only have created suspicion where there ought to be none."

I conceded him that; in my precipitateness and preoccupation I had not considered the impression my visit might leave on an observer such as Lillian Price, who doubtlessly waited downstairs, sewing worthless sandbags as scandal brewed and frothed around her, impatient for some further revelation.

"I care very much for my daughter, and I will not allow any harm to come to her." Nicholas reached for the doorknob. "I very much appreciate your concern, Alistair, but I believe it is misplaced."

"Nina might fall ill at the Su palace," I tried. "She did not look well."

He opened the door, regarded me with finality.

"Good day, Mr Scott."

Frustration ought to be the newspaper's man friend. Injustice, ignorance, indifference, these are the beasts we seek to slay each time we sit to compose a story. Resentment, pique and discontent, bitter as they are to the spirit, are master crafters of words, and letters turn pliant, soft under their hammer blow. And yet, returned to my censorious desk, I found no impetus to write. Motivation failed me in part because of the terrible dispiritedness inherent in knowing that even if I were to write the most brilliant, the most bloody prose, I would have no method through which to share it with the world beyond our walls. And besides, I thought, what use were my words now? Naturally I could recount those gruesome injuries I had witnessed at the hospital, of course I might retell those lurid Boxer tales the sufferers had imparted, in a moment of meagre inspiration I could even justify a paragraph dedicated to the birth of a child named Siege. Yet those were no longer the events of the day, not one of those anguished, bleeding men occupied my thoughts.

It was only Nina, Nina and her ruin, Nina and the secrets she wore as a dim halo, an aura of disgrace around her form, as she crossed the Su palace, vacant and without purpose. I wished to record her story, to understand it, to correct it somehow, set it right in neat, printed lines. Tortuously I recalled my inaction, excruciatingly I wondered what more I might do for her.

La Contessa saved me from my moroseness. I am not a man usually given to despair, but in those hours following the cessation of ceasefire I did allow myself to consider some ghoulish thoughts, to wonder if I might indeed end my days in Peking's Legation Quarter. It might only have been an hour since I had returned to the Grand, I do not remember exactly; the afternoon was already lost, wordless, dulled by the familiar salve of whisky. Her knock was knowing, possessive, and I anticipated her appearance on the other side of the door, magnificent, glorious in one of her habitual costumes of silken aplomb. La Contessa did not disappoint, crossing the threshold of my room with her lips already upon my unspeaking mouth, her exuberant figure draped in layers of royal blue, her hands, soft and wonted, close around me. Her touch was a balm, a vital potion of forgetfulness that soothed as might whisky, but equally invigorated as no manmade product could. Consoled, my insistent thoughts folded themselves away, quietened, and my mind stilled. Empty of head but full of heart, I kissed her tenderly when the deed was done, when we lay together, skin slick and spirit satiated.

"It is not so bad," she said slowly, "that the attacks have started again. At least we may have these moments a little longer."

Her voice, melodious and mellow as it was, broke the spell. My preoccupations, enlivened once more, broke to the surface of my mind. I could not stop myself from asking her about the events of the previous night. She severed our embrace, rose from the bed, began dressing herself with her back to me.

"I wondered," she said softly. "I wondered how long until you would ask for Miss Ward."

"I am concerned," I said, and she nodded slowly, wrapped her corset tightly around her waist. "Let me help you."

"I am very capable," she said, turning to face me. "I have lived many years with a husband who aids his wife in nothing."

Deftly she pulled the strings tight, and I watched her waist, already tapered and slender, shrink to impossible proportions. She smiled at this magic, and stepped into her dress, her back once more to me. I watched her reflection in the small, flat mirror as she told me of the night's events.

The Fairchild household, drowsed by celebratory champagne, had drifted into its first peaceful night of sleep not long after I had left for the hotel, only to be abruptly awoken in the most profound hours by the resumption of firing from enemy lines. Immediately footsteps and voices sounded as every guest in the house sprang, dismayed and unsettled by this sudden turn of events, from their respective beds. Lillian Price was the first to the drawing room, and her voice echoed along the hallway to La Contessa's room.

"Miss Ward!"

It was an exclamation, an admonishment, it was, La Contessa supposed, no act of intended malice on the part of Lillian Price but rather a genuine expression of surprise. Lillian was joined shortly by Phoebe Franklin; La Contessa could decipher the missionary's commanding, unflustered tone although her words were unclear. La Contessa hurried then too to the drawing room and found Phoebe arranging Nina's hair, which fell loose and untamed around her shoulders. One sleeve of Nina dress was askew, exposing the delicate ivory flesh of the upper arm. Nina's skin was flushed a tender shade of rose, her lips, La Contessa noted, looked swollen with kisses.

"Although perhaps I only imagine that," she said, her image sanguine, assured in the mirror as she spoke to me, "for the general impression her appearance bestowed."

La Contessa rushed to Nina's side, pulled her dress up over her shoulder, and assisted Phoebe in arranging Nina's thick veil of hair, dark and a little damp to the touch, once more into its customary chignon. Wordlessly Phoebe Franklin ironed out the remaining creases in Nina's dress, placed a cool palm against the young girl's hot forehead. Then she knelt to pick up a book from the floor, holding it tightly as she steered Nina towards an armchair.

"You have been reading," she said, setting the volume in Nina's lap.

The effect of this combined effort was, La Contessa felt, that Nina Ward looked more or less her usual self by the time her father appeared in the doorway, followed by Oscar Fairchild, apparently glacially unperturbed by events, but wearing, La Contessa noted, the very suit he had appeared in at dinner.

"Perhaps he changed from his pajamas," her reflection said wryly to me. "Perhaps."

"And so they had been together?" I asked.

La Contessa returned to the bed, kissed my forehead sweetly. "One assumes," she said. "You look very forlorn, *tesoro mio*."

"I only wish I might have done something," I said numbly. The horror of her words, the truth they confirmed, deadened me. So great was the emotion she stirred that I felt unable to contemplate it; instead my breath dimmed, my movements slowed, my very thoughts, terrible and undeniable, crawled, denied me immediate inspection of their contents.

"Miss Ward is not your responsibility, Alistair," she said, standing once more. "Sometimes I wonder if I ought to be envious of her."

"Envious? Whatever for?"

"How greatly you care for her reputation," La Contessa leveled. "And yet you think nothing of mine."

She left without further speech, closing the door behind her with a force I judged more pronounced than was her habit. I did not call her name.

Naturally I returned once more that evening to the Fairchild residence. How might I stay away? Nina's predicament, her discovery, her assured dissolution, occupied the intervening hours until I could bear solitude no longer. I thought of her reading, recalled the many times I had witnessed her devour a book, shaded by the magnolia tree when the sun blazed or illuminated by candlelight on those long winter evenings when Nicholas and I discussed politics and prose, her presence perpetual, undeniable, but always unobtrusive. I could not fathom that Nina's most cherished pastime, pure and admirable, learned from her father, could have so unjustly brought about her downfall. Would Nina's story have been different if her favorite narrative had not been the conventionally and respectably romantic *Dream Of The Red Chamber*, but instead the *Golden Lotus*, a Ming dynasty novel that had divided Chinese opinion for centuries as to whether it should be considered a master literary work or a collection of the most base obscenity and filth, a tale in which tender images of maidens playing men's flutes and young lovers meeting secretly in the grape arbor rapidly gave way to the terrible conclusions of jealousy, madness and death that followed the physical frenzy? I thought too of La Contessa's words, her unguarded admission of envy, as I crossed the room, a glass of my old, irresolute, malt friend gripped once more between my fingers. Her words affronted me; did she dare to suggest that I might harbor some romantic inclination towards Miss Ward, the daughter of my truest friend in that city of august charlatans? And still her accusation vexed me, for how might I explain the great panic I had lived with that day since I had glimpsed Nina, clouded and faint, walking before me in the Su palace? How might I justify my tremendous sense of responsibility for her welfare, my indubitable discountenance in response to her series of well-intentioned missteps?

The ladies of the house sewed sandbags in the drawing room, their chatter was muted, amiable in the soft glow of sunset.

"Very good, ladies," I said. I admired their creations; patchworks of old dress shirts and nightgowns attached to servants' uniforms and empty sacks from the storeroom. "You might sew together some gowns for the hospital too. Provisions there are scant."

"Have you been to the hospital, Mr Scott?" Lillian asked.

"I have indeed," I said and recounted the story of little Siege.

"How macabre," La Contessa commented. She did not sew but sat to one side, smoking a slim cigarette. She waved it in a loose circle, did not meet my eye. "The smell. The smell of death. Smoking is the only way to stop it."

"I like the spirit of the name," Nina said. "It shows some optimism, even if the poor child shall forever bear the burden of this siege."

"Siege is not a name," Lillian said, leaning forward towards Nina, who fixed at once upon the needle she held between two inexpert fingers, avoiding the other girl's stare. "I rather think they ought to call the baby James."

"James," I repeated. "In honor of Mr Millington, I suppose?"

"Naturally." Lillian nodded vigorously. "It is only right that a young man's life be honored."

"And the next shall be named von Ketteler, I suppose," I said. My comment drew ire from Lillian. Momentarily her eyes flashed, and rapidly she looked away in disgust. Nina's fingers worked rapidly, if a little clumsily, at the sewing together of two fabrics; she worked as though unhearing of our words.

"Well, Mr Scott, I am most sorry to hear you don't believe our good friend's life worth honoring. I would have thought it the right thing to do." Lillian pushed her sewing off her lap and curled one leg under the other, cat-like in her chair. "That's quite enough sewing for one day. I don't suppose a few sandbags will decide life from death when the Boxers storm the Legation Quarter."

"Miss Price, forgive me a frivolous remark. It has been a most trying day for us all," I said.

"It is quite all right, Mr Scott. I understand your opinion perfectly. You are not alone in caring little for Mr Millington's fate. Indeed, I found many of my peers most unconcerned for the welfare of Mr Millington when he so valiantly defended us from the Boxers. Each one has his own worries, one supposes. One hopes."

Nina frowned, and I allowed myself to observe her. I saw something in her then, I thought, before correcting myself. In fact, I saw neither matter nor mettle in Nina then, but rather the absence of something, the reaction I perceived in the crease of her brow was merely a further drop of nothing, a deeper layer of herself extinguished. She provided no counterargument to Lillian, and did not offer me the solace I might have expected from her, a small, private smile, the open countenance of an ally. Instead she continued her amateur sewing.

"The baby is a blessing," Phoebe said. "Hope amidst the darkness."

"Yes," La Contessa said, drawing a final breath on her cigarette. "On this we can agree."

"They ought to name him Matthias, a gift from the Lord,"

Phoebe continued.

"Well, I'm afraid he remains a Siege," I said.

A bell sounded and I accompanied the women to the dining room, where Oscar Fairchild waited at the head of the table.

"Mr Scott," he said, rising. "Delighted you could join us."

"Forgive my taking advantage of your hospitality once more," I said. "Only rations are rather low at the Grand."

"I wish I might offer you more."

With easy authority Fairchild stood to watch his guests file in. Pietro Mancini took the seat next to his wife, his hand grazed hers as she sat and he uttered a low reprimand in Italian.

"I have explained to them," she replied in English, a sweeping gesture taking in the length of the table. "I smoke only for the smell."

Mancini muttered under his breath, but our attention was diverted by Lillian, who seated herself by Nina with a theatrical sigh.

"And what might we find on the menu this evening?" she mused.

"I do apologize," Fairchild said, leveling with Lillian as he retook his position at the head of the table, "that my humble household cannot meet Miss Price's requirements under the current circumstances."

Immediately it was evident that some abnormality, some out-of-turn event, afflicted those gathered around the table. They voiced the same practiced niceties, but like a puzzle pieced together in haste, as a group they gave an impression of jagged corners, of not quite fitting together.

"Thank you all for your generosity towards a poor Scotsman," I said, raising my wine glass after the servants had placed our meals down in front of us. Gone were the days of three courses; now there was a single plate to be enjoyed, or at least tolerated, to chew over and draw out as long as possible.

"It is our pleasure," Oscar said.

"Mr Fairchild, for how much longer do you expect we shall be here?" Nicholas asked. He had not greeted me when taking his seat at the table and I recalled our earlier conversation with the chagrin of justification, wished now I might have waited to approach him with the details later furnished by La Contessa, unassailable and indisputable in the attestation they offered.

"Mr Ward, I very much wish I might give you a clearer idea, but I'm afraid that I cannot make any prediction at this stage," Oscar replied.

"Nicholas, I feel it in my bones. We shall be here least a week more," I said, looking directly towards my old friend.

"Very well. At least I shall have time to catalog the books with the care they deserve," he said gently. I nodded, he returned the gesture, and I felt our connection resumed something like an even kilter, even if the exasperation I cultivated for him had not yet subsided.

"I shall help you, Father," Nina said quickly. I noticed she had yet to touch the meat, gray and unappealing, upon her plate. "Then when we return home we shall decide what to do with them."

"A wonderful idea," Oscar said gaily, but Nina kept her eyes on her uneaten food. He directed his next question to Nicholas: "Are there some very precious books in the collection?"

"It is a little too early to gauge the extent of our collection and quite how valuable it may be," Nicholas said. "Yet one may assume that any book from the Hanlin is of great scholarly value, at least."

"You enjoy reading, do you not, Mr Fairchild?" Lillian said.

"Why, yes, yes I do," Oscar replied steadily.

"In fact, were you not reading last night when the Boxers

opened fire once more?" Without waiting for an answer Lillian continued: "When I discovered poor Nina, alone, fearful, in the middle of the night, I knew I needn't worry so much as you had likely been reading right there by her side. Is that not right?"

Phoebe Franklin's cutlery tore into a piece of meat, a high, tight sound bore into my skull. Phoebe ripped the pony meat in two rough halves, pulling it apart along its wispy, terse fringes.

Oscar cleared his throat. Nina's face betrayed nothing; her features were icily smooth.

"Mr Fairchild?" Lillian pressed him. She smiled falsely, widely and expectantly.

"Yes, Miss Price, you are quite right," Oscar said finally. "I often find myself unable to sleep these days and I prefer to read to pass the time. Miss Ward favors the same consolation, it seems, and I did indeed come across her in the drawing room. It was most *considerate* of Miss Ward to leave you to sleep peacefully upstairs, was it not?" He pushed his plate to the side and pressed a napkin to his lips.

Oscar's remarks were met with an apprehensive silence as we each unravelled his patchwork of words fashioned into a statement of innocence. Naturally the revelation struck neither La Contessa nor Phoebe Franklin as an unexpected blow, but Pietro Mancini cleared his throat uneasily and I could not bring myself to look at Nicholas, who had taken to cutting a particularly unyielding piece of meat; his knife strained against the rubbery fat of the animal. Lillian Price resumed eating, carefully, with pride, cutlery poised faintly between her fingers like a pair of sharp daggers. Nina, yet to consume a single morsel, looked ahead dully.

"Well." Phoebe Franklin rose before the servants had come to clear the plates. "Have we quite finished? How about a game of Whist?"

"A wonderful idea, Mrs Franklin," Oscar said.

Contentedly he followed the missionary. With a brief nod to La Contessa I stepped behind the pair and the Italians followed my lead. Lillian, standing languidly, stretching her arms with relish, allowed her napkin to fall to her seat, smoothed her skirts and announced that she would join us for the game of cards. How slowly, how agonizingly Nina rose from her seat, and fell meekly into line.

"My work," Nicholas said by explanation, spurning the invitation to retire to his room.

The British are masters at papering over all varieties of social unpleasantness. How else could our tiny nation come to rule half the world? Only with a sense of righteous belonging, the possession of a very short memory and by adhering to strict social dictates that forbid questioning of motives and suggestions of impropriety. No better example of this tactical British ignorance (taught to our New World cousins during our many adventures across the globe) could be found than in that evening's pointless game of Whist, marked by pockets of silence and long breaths held between each hand. Oscar Fairchild's diplomatic training dazzled, at moments one might even have described his manner as approaching gregariousness. The Italians, who constituted the most serious threat to our false peace with their more open, tolerant and frankly Continental approach to the expression of sentiment, displayed an admirably uncharacteristic submission to Phoebe Franklin's demands. Indeed, after a few rounds we were able to set the cards aside, parting ourselves from our props in order to simply talk amongst ourselves. Fairchild and I smoked cigars without troubling to leave the room. The women, despite previously-held notions that dictated them delicate creatures of sensitive olfactory senses, welcomed now the dark, woody scent of the cigars. Lillian Price chatted pleasantly, as though nothing untoward had occurred at the dining table. The implications of her words were clear to us all, and watching Nina and Oscar now, I perceived their pairing as absolutely logical. Fairchild, his eyes trained on the glowing tip of the cigar he held tightly between his lips, was dynamic, capable, intelligent, and, I would venture, handsome to many women. Nina was sharp, sure of herself, but possessed a pleasant softness of face that suggested a potential pliability to men. In another world, where Oscar was unmarried, they might have made quite an admirable couple. I suppose in those days we were living in another world.

My eyes swept the room for La Contessa as I took my leave, she shook her head gently. I bowed, left the assembled guests to their small talk. I paused at the front door, my thoughts with Nina. The night was stiff, airless, accompanied by the low rumble of violence. How might she sleep in this house, its walls close and unsparing, its inhabitants all-seeing, ever-knowing, perpetually superior? With dread I wondered if she might return later to that room in which we had constructed an edifice of the most profound pretense, if she might fall once more into Fairchild's steady arms. And why might she not, her fate already sealed, her soul condemned? I let the skies, ashen and black, and the familiar streets, coarse and stained a deadly crimson, lead me to the Grand. With a final nightcap I wooed sleep, pleaded with restfulness to relieve me, hoped as slumber eventually caressed my eyelids closed that she offered Nina the same solace, that for hours at least we might forget. *Sha! Sha!* the Boxers called, but I heard them no more.

IX

I HAVE NEVER been a keen patriot. A Scot and a man of Empire, I shrugged off the old country as easily as another man might remove his hat. Sometimes, in whisky-tinted nostalgia, I remembered the Scotland of my youth, and the damp mist that had enveloped the heather-strewn hillsides, those persistent droplets of steamed dew that settled fresh upon my skin each time I stepped outside, took on a mystical glow. I recalled those few, poor, snatched days of an approximated summer, when the midges feasted upon any inch of exposed flesh and the glens shivered, damp and unshielded, under a hazy trickle of sunlight, and I longed for it momentarily, before an instinct for progress and a desire for adventure corrected my weakness. London, where I had established myself as a young man for a little over a year, held no such wistful sway over my thoughts, in neither whisky nor whimsy. For a few months the sheer size of the place, the quantity of its people, its streets lapped by waves of faces, so numerous I eventually ignored them all, breaking a life-long habit of deciphering stories written in the bridges of noses and wishes exposed in the arches of eyebrows, calmed somewhat the intangible restlessness that had driven me from home. And yet it was not different enough; beyond the aesthetic girth and grime of the city, London's dissimilarities to home were so minor so as to be superficially inconsequential; these differences were written in a taciturn code of which I often found myself on the wrong side. At the office they teased me gently for the lilt of my vowels, over dinners they discussed the fates of names unknown to my ears, and looked pityingly upon me when I admitted my parents had considered Scotland's education system robust enough to educate my young mind. How long I had harbored dreams of my metropolitan blossoming, for years I had cradled a steady desire to mold myself a man of the world, and how London had disappointed, making me smaller, self-conscious, and creating a new, wilder thirst for the unknown. And so when my editor said Afghanistan, murmuring that there had been a bit of trouble over there again, Cavagnari killed and war unavoidable now, my mouth moved before my mind. "Yes."

The world beyond Britain's frosty seas delivered my desired metamorphosis. Under the blaze of a foreign sun, the feeble materials of which I had been made dissolved and restructured; hardened grew my limbs, darkened became my flesh, while my mind was wrenched uncomfortably open. I witnessed men of every creed, observed their unity of desires, their need to eat and sleep and find a woman forgiving of their frail prides and deficient means, and I watched them, men of every shade, surprise and betray me in equal measure. I saw an Englishman kill for pleasure and a Indian do just the same, I choked with gratitude as a son of Manchester lifted a bottle of water to my parched lips, and almost wept as a boy from Kandahar placed a scrap of naan upon my desperate palm. I suppose then I consider myself a globalist, accepting mankind as it is, recognizing that each nation holds its place in the world, believing that the men of every country deserve the same consideration and esteem as those from the place we call home, and, quite frankly, that men of all nations are often as bad as each other. Yet just because a man may not swell with pride for his country does not mean he might not cringe with shame at its wrongdoings. And so it is with heavy heart that I must report the following events, when the guardians of civilization proved themselves, in mind and in flesh, little different from the barbarous Boxers.

The following day started with familiar ennui. Living under siege, one begins to question which is more deadly: the enemy or the boredom. I looked through the window to the street below; uselessly soldiers and refugees milled, men spoke without end, and I felt the walls of the Legation Quarter press closer around me. Downstairs Hilde served coffee, remarking on my fatigued appearance.

"I took some more supplies to Su's palace at dawn," she said. "Miss Ward is there again today."

"Is she?" I let the coffee warm my throat, allowed its bitter taste to jolt my nerves awake. Immediately my concern for Nina returned, vicarious shame taking residence once more in the pit of my heart.

Edward walked through from the kitchen, nodded to me.

"Rather strange request I've had this morning," he said. "Mr Moore from the Trade Ministry asking for a room. He and his wife are with the Bloomfields, can't imagine why they might need a room here." Edward had a talent for busying himself, and immediately he set about ordering glasses and bottles behind the bar as he spoke, his feet gliding undisturbed around the small refugee children who played together on the floor. "He said something about safety, but it was all forgotten rather quickly when I explained that we were at full occupancy." He stopped, cleared his throat. "I did say you might accommodate them in your room in case of emergency. I hope you don't mind; only Hilde and I have no space anywhere else."

"Naturally. I suppose Moore did have rather a scare when he witnessed the death of that Japanese."

"I suppose." Edward looked towards me hesitantly. "Yes," he said, swallowing words unsaid. "I suppose so."

Wearily I completed my circuit of the Legation Quarter and its diplomats, soldiers and gossips in search of information, and returned to my room in the afternoon with no further clarity. The authorities were unforthcoming with their European counterparts, and no contact had been made by our savior Seymour, lost somewhere upon the great China plains with his troops. Patience, each contact counseled me, while the strain in their voices, the tremor in their hands, the red corners of their eyes, betrayed that their own measures of forbearance were close to exhausted.

Restive, I decided to stop by the Su palace as the afternoon heat started to descend from its most unbearable peak, and there I saw Nina reading to a group of scrawny schoolgirls. Her voice lifted and fell to the cadences of a book of Chinese fairytales, the worn cover and thumbed pages of which suggested the converts had likely heard all the stories several times over. Still they showed a polite interest in this retelling of the familiar, and I allowed myself to enjoy the feeling of the warmth of the sun on my back as I watched Nina read to them in the courtyard.

"She is herself again." Silently Phoebe Franklin had approached me, and I started when she spoke.

"My apologies, Mrs Franklin, I did not see you. I had become rather caught up in the stories myself."

"They adore her," Phoebe said softly. "She is younger than I, of course, but it is more than that. They are orphans, the girls, and they see that, like them, Nina hovers between two worlds. They are as Chinese as bamboo, every last one of them, but their minds and their pencils have been sharpened by American missionaries."

One of the girls inched closer to Nina as she read, and lifted a pair of slender fingers to touch a loose tendril of Nina's hair. She twisted it around her knuckle, puzzling at its wavy texture, coiling it and letting it go like a spring. Nina laughed at this innocent touch, paused her reading. The girls all laughed together, with the exception of one small, narrow-shouldered child who maintained a careful distance from the rest. Her raw-boned arms were wrapped tightly around her knees, her eyes fixed upon the ceiling rafters.

"That girl seems very quiet," I remarked to Phoebe.

"Lijun," she said. "A terrible story. Entire family murdered before her young eyes. None of us can understand how she managed to escape herself." Phoebe's face, previously open and tranquil, clouded as she spoke. "We must do all we can to protect the girls. I have insisted that they are never to leave the palace, not even to take a breath of fresh air or to see the latest news posted at the bulletin board in the British Legation. They are country girls used to wandering freely, and they do not understand the risks they face, even here in the Legation Quarter."

"That sounds eminently sensible," I said.

"For their safety and their virtue," Phoebe agreed.

Phoebe left me, and I watched Nina for two or three minutes more, willing her to look up from her flock and see me, but unwilling myself to break the spell. How sprightly she looked, how sparklingly at ease amongst the young girls, her cheeks flushed once more with vigorous color, Mandarin flowing effortlessly as she spoke. Gone was the habitual pinched expression she wore in the company of Fairchild's guests, extinguished were the uncertainty and vacillation that moderated her tone and dulled her movements in that home of strangers. And so I departed, cheered by Nina's aspect, but unable still to shake the dread of her fate that settled unbidden upon me, unyielding as a cloak around my shoulders.

I returned to the Fairchild household for supper that evening, where I noted Nina's absence with interest. In her place sat

Beatrice Moore, who had been invited by Lillian to stay for supper. Perhaps even more curious than Nina's simple non-appearance, was the fact that not a single other guest remarked upon it. Fairchild was a picture of enervation as we ate; a volley of bullets produced a ceaseless racket outside.

"They have started early tonight," La Contessa observed. Her gaze did not meet mine, and I noted her husband's close presence by her side. Occasionally Pietro Mancini, not a habitually demonstrative man, allowed his fingers to graze his wife's arm, and she awarded him small smiles, neat as gifts tied with ribbons.

"I don't hear it anymore," Lillian said, roughly dragging her knife across the tough meat on her plate. "Oh, I give up! Our cutlery and our teeth were not designed for this fare."

"Miss Price," Mr Fairchild said. "I am afraid it is the best we could do. The staff is trying with the very few resources they have at their disposal."

"Thank you for allowing me to stay for dinner," Beatrice Moore said. "I feel most guilty enjoying your provisions, but Miss Price and I had so very much to talk about this afternoon that I barely registered the time and I am certain the servants will already have cleared the plates at the Bloomfields'. When this conflict finally comes to an end, Mr Fairchild, my husband and I shall be delighted to treat you to a relative feast."

"Thank you," Oscar said. "It is nothing, the least I might do."

"Mrs Moore," I said. "I hear that your husband has requested a room at the Grand. I wish to confirm Mr Samuels' offer that in any case of urgency I will most happily accommodate both you and Mr Moore in my own humble room."

My intention was to test, naturally; Edward had in knowing silence conveyed to me some inexplicability in Benjamin Moore's desire for a room at the Grand. Yet I had not expected my question to provoke such an obvious reaction in the man's wife. A woman as seasoned in social mores as the implacable Beatrice Moore might be expected to take unexpected news in her stride, to conceal her surprise in practiced smiles and tidy diversions. But Beatrice reached immediately for her wine glass, grasping inelegantly at its stem, allowing its wide base to collide with the edge of her plate in the hurry to raise it to her lips. The overgenerous sip she took of its contents left her mouth moist and slick.

"That is most kind of you, Mr Scott," she said, fixing her eyes, dispassionate and cool once more, upon me. I realized that my words had hit upon some truth fundamental and stark, but unknown, at least in its full dimensions, to Mrs Moore. Lillian Price, loyal to the end, did not allow her friend to flounder long.

"Who is that, Mr Fairchild?" she asked, her eyes on a portrait that hung on the wall.

Oscar turned in his seat, and faced the anonymous figure in the painting.

"That is my wife's father, Miss Price," he said, without feeling.

"Oh, I am sorry, I know he has been terribly ill. Although I suppose Violet was rather lucky in the end, to have left before all the trouble."

Conversation was more or less abandoned after that. I tried and failed to meet Nicholas' eye, attempted to read the sentiment in the downturned corners of his mouth. He sat only on the other side of the table to me, yet I felt a barrier more formidable than the Tartar walls stood between us.

I desired to spend another night with La Contessa, but was unsure how I might find an opportunity to propose such an idea to her. Fairchild presented me with one such chance when he invited the men to smoke; Mancini followed him, Nicholas excused himself and I was left alone with Lillian, Beatrice and

Chiara. Lillian complained to a servant that a door did not lock properly, that the Boxers might be able to gain entry, and I took advantage of her remonstrance, which led to hysterical argumentation on Beatrice's part, to suggest in low tones to La Contessa that she join me at the Grand later that night.

"I must not," she said. "The shooting has already started tonight. I dare not."

She reached for my hand under the table, fingertips fluttering over my knuckles. Still I felt chagrined, and took my leave soon after, walking through the streets with fast yet prudent steps, occasionally ducking behind a wall when the shots grew particularly loud or persistent. Bullets flew cleanly over the walls of the Legation Quarter, but the Boxers appeared to aim so high that not a single shot threatened injury. In fact, many of us maintained a theory throughout the siege that the Boxers and their supporters amongst the imperial troops continued this steady barrage of shots not with the aim of murdering us, but instead to set us permanently on edge, to unnerve us, to make sleep impossible, to rattle our spirits but preserve our bones.

The light of a torch greeted me as I approached the Grand and I made out the figures of Phoebe Franklin and Nina. A Japanese soldier accompanied them, marching three steps ahead, holding a gun decorously, carefully, in his hands.

"Colonel Shiba and his troops have done an admirable job to protect Prince Su's mansion so far," Phoebe was saying to Nina. "However, the Japanese alone cannot fight off the Boxers. The palace is quite vulnerable in terms of location, and sickness is already spreading. Death is certain for many there."

"That does not seem right," Nina said quietly.

"It is not," Phoebe said firmly. "Miss Ward, shall you accompany me once again tomorrow?"

"Nothing would make me happier," Nina said.

"Good night, Mrs Franklin, Miss Ward," I called as they rounded the hotel.

"Oh, Mr Scott, why are you hiding in the shadows?" Phoebe said, turning towards me, the burning light of her lamp illuminating every corner of my face.

"I might be more partial to light if I thought the Boxers would not see me," I said.

"The night is nearly over; the day is almost here. So let us put aside the deeds of darkness and put on the armor of light," Phoebe said briskly. She lowered her lamp and once again she and Nina became mere silhouettes to me.

I entered the hotel just before Hilde and Edward barricaded the door for the night; each evening they blocked the entrance with a large mahogany table, a tall bookshelf and an assortment of books and other knick-knacks, calculating that any attempt to break through the threshold would cause so much disturbance that we would receive sufficient warning to mount a defense. Young male refugees slept in the hallway; by their sides was anything that might pass as a weapon: guns, knives, even a poker for the fire. They took this role most seriously, and many prayed for a Boxer attack that would allow them their vengeance against those who had driven them from their homes. So far, we had been spared.

The next few days were characterized by the absence of La Contessa in my narrow life. Devotedly I returned to Fairchild's residence every evening for dinner in the hopes that she might follow me later to the Grand. Yet she only grew more distant, avoiding me with dignified detachment and feline hauteur, weaving her form, exuberant and irresistible, in wide, careful circles around me. Pietro Mancini was forever present and seemed each day more attentive to his wife, whispering indulgently into her sweet, perfectly-formed ears, seating himself so close by her at the table that his shoulder brushed hers constantly. Tortured, I watched their supposed conjugal harmony, and left the house each night with an unpleasantly augmented feeling of isolation. Nicholas watched me stonily, Lillian Price engaged me with indifference, Oscar Fairchild approached me with cautious, fatigued amiability, and Phoebe and Nina remained steadfastly absent at Su's palace.

In fact, Nina quickly developed a routine at the old palace, where she taught lessons, served food, tended to fevers and collected clothes to deliver to the newly-established laundry, managed by none other than Russell Brazier, the Chief Secretary of the Inspectorate of the Imperial Maritime Customs. Nina usually remained at Su's former mansion until well after dinner had been served at the Fairchild residence, and sometimes stayed with the schoolgirls until all had fallen asleep. Only once was I still present when she returned to Fairchild's home. She had approached the dining table to bid her father good night. Stiff and unfamiliar, Nicholas had simply expressed his approval of Nina's efforts at Prince Su's palace and suggested, with wooden language and unnatural posture, that she may care to read a portion of his latest writing, to which she had readily assented. When I reminded her of this a few days later, Nina replied simply that he had yet to provide her with the manuscript.

Despite this separation from her peers, Nina did not seem to experience loneliness during those long days at the palace. In my infrequent glimpses of her at work, it seemed to me that she rather enjoyed her role as teacher to the young girls; indeed it appeared that she found as much, if not more, pleasure in leading her attentive pupils in their studies as the students themselves took in her well-attended lessons. She taught from Chinese and English books, and even read Bible passages to the schoolgirls, though she no doubt would have preferred to recount the more familiar tales of the God of War or Buddhism's Kuanyin. I knew, and Nina assuredly also realized, that she existed in a form of suspension, that her daily pilgrimage to the anonymous safety of the Su palace was not a true solution to the deep, wounding shame she would one day have to confront. Yet between her daily absence and the ever-present threat of the Boxers at the gates, I hoped that the foreigners might prove distracted enough to leave Nina in relative peace for now.

Only once did I see a return to that unsettled person Nina had become under Fairchild's roof. One afternoon as she gave her lessons, Hugo Lovell came to the palace. It was at that more bearable hour of the afternoon when I liked to stop by to greet Nina and ask Phoebe Franklin if any more supplies were required from the Grand.

"I heard Miss Ward was here," Hugo said to me as he removed his hat.

Standing with hands clasped and observing her with thoughtful eyes, he said no more. Hugo's face, once earnest, had now grown gaunt and weary. Nina glanced up, and seeing Hugo, stumbled over the next words she read. Hugo waited silently until she had finished reading, nodded to me and then crossed the room towards her. The girls watched his every step; Nina dismissed her pupils.

"Mr Lovell," she said. "I am most surprised to see you here."

"Well, I am rather surprised myself to find you here. Miss Price said you came here every day."

"That's right."

"It is very noble of you to help these people," Hugo said. "I suppose I mustn't keep you from your students. I am afraid I am *hors du combat,* you see, and I feel of so little use to anyone."

"Are you injured, Mr Lovell?"

"Yes. A bullet caught my leg, left a gash that is quite unsightly, but nothing to be too concerned about, the doctors say. I have been left with something of a limp, however, and even though the Boxers cannot actually fly, they are still rather fast on their feet."

"I'm sorry to hear that," Nina said.

"Yes. Well, at least I've had a luckier fate than our friend Mr Millington."

"Oh, it is too awful to think of Mr Millington," Nina said.

She stepped towards the decorated arch that led to the central courtyard, leading Hugo toward the exit. He left momentarily, and she called the girls back for their next lesson. Picking up the textbook she began reading again.

"We have just finished that lesson, Miss Nina," Lijun said accusatorially, and flustered, Nina skimmed the pages rapidly. I bowed my head, and left her with her students.

That evening, following another unsuccessful attempt to persuade La Contessa to visit me, I walked back to the Grand as a storm raged, the culmination of days of sticky rain. The Legation Quarter was restless, and the squall lent it a sensation of strangled hysteria, of repressed agitation. Dissatisfied, I circled the hotel, accompanied by an unreal feeling of invincibility; the whine of thunder muted both the Imperial Army gunshots and the Boxers' violent cries. I could not face returning to the hotel, to the small dimensions of my room, to the quiet tyranny of siege, and so I walked towards the Su palace. A Japanese soldier waved me inside, and I crossed the courtyard to the palace's main hall, where the prince's harem was gathered, dressed in their finest silks, their necks and wrists glittering still with jade, only the coarseness of their unwashed hair betrayed their hopeless confinement. Holding their instruments, the women performed a song from an old opera. I stooped to ask one spectator, a woman of sunken cheeks but warm eyes, where I might find Miss Ward.

DRAGONS IN SHALLOW WATERS

"You mean Miss Nina?" she said pointing eastwards. "In the girls' dormitory."

Quietly I entered that hushed room where already most of the girls were asleep and the old men and women whose bodies formed a protective ring around their sleeping forms gestured for me to remain silent. I saw Nina at the far end of the room, her spine a straight column against the wall and Lijun's small head pressed against her thigh. Nina ran her fingers lightly over Lijun's arm, cheek and ear, attempted to keep her locked in slumber. Cautiously she waved to me, and I crossed the room to her.

"It is very late," I whispered. "Would you like me to see you back?"

"That is most kind, Alistair," she said. "But I might stay here tonight. The storm sounds terrible. And you look rather damp."

Self-consciously I brushed my face with my sleeve, and pulled it away dripping wet.

"Then we must at least let your father know."

Nina nodded without commitment. It was then that we heard the crash of feet outside. At first I questioned whether it might be a simple burst of thunder. Then came the rise and fall of male voices; the words they formed were neither English nor Mandarin but rather a confusion of tongues, all leadened, slowed by alcohol, their consonants and vowels overlapping to create a chilling dialect. We heard the Japanese guard at the doorway remonstrate with the men; he pleaded with them to leave.

"Let us in!" a single voice cried in strangled English.

I jumped to my feet. Nina stiffened. The girls stirred in their sleep; Lijun lifted her head.

"Miss Nina, what's happening?" she asked.

"Nothing. Sleep, child, sleep."

I rushed to the door, pressed my ear against it, heard the

Japanese guard again instructing the men to leave. Nina followed close behind me, the dozen elderly men and women whose bodies had ringed the circumference of the room were also getting to their feet. Some of the girls sat upright, they whispered frantically to one another.

"They are only children," I heard the guard say.

Lijun walked unhurriedly across the room, coming to a stop by Nina's side.

"*Fangxin ba,*" she said. "Rest your heart. I shall help you."

Lijun cocked her head towards the door; a frown flickered across her face as she heard the scuffles taking place outside. Nina started at the sound of glass shattering, stepping back as amber liquid seeped under the door. Lijun did not react, letting the beer wash over her bare toes.

The door shuddered on its hinges. I pushed my weight against it, but was immediately thrown back. A dozen men charged into the room; some wore the uniforms of the foreign troops charged with protecting the Legation Quarter.

"Stop!" I cried, reaching for the man closest to me, frantically pinning him to the wall. He struggled beneath my grip, with ease I struck his jaw. Drunk, the young man's head lolled from side to side, with another punch his knees buckled. Still he tried to struggle against me, mumbling words incoherent and indignant, his impotent limbs lurching to the broken rhythm of his inebriation.

"Get out!" I heard Lijun cry in English.

I turned to look over my shoulder, and saw that the soldiers paid her no heed; they scattered chaotically across the room, some clutching bottles in their hands, others with their fingers trained around their guns. The girls ran in tottering circles as they tried to evade these pursuers, who grabbed wildly at their neat pigtails and threadbare dresses. The young man in my grasp evaded me in my distraction, cutting across the room in jagged line. An elderly Chinese man stood in front of one of the very youngest girls, shielding her on his unsteady legs; a solider in Russian uniform knocked him flat to the floor. From the old man's ear spilled a steady stream of thick, stolid blood, from his lips emitted a strangled moan.

"Do something!" Lijun called to me, to Nina, to anyone who might listen to her, but we could only watch aghast as an American soldier dragged one of the girls across the room, his knuckles wrapped so tightly around her wrist it seemed ready to splinter under his force.

"I've found a real beauty here," he boasted to another solider. "Come, little lady, come." The girl struggled under his grip, twisting and turning her small frame as she tried desperately to spin out from his hold.

"That's quite enough," I started, running towards the pair, but I was beaten by Lijun, her face set in a terrible and ferocious snarl. She bit the soldier's forearm, clawed wildly at his face.

"Hey!" he cried.

I watched as his determination to keep hold of his victim seemed only to increase and the girl's fingers turned white under his grasp. I wondered then quite what the scene was that unravelled before me; my forgiving, rational mind decided that this was mere wassailing, that the boys had drunk too much and found in the barren Legation Quarter no recipient for those amorous feelings that fester and rise in a young man far from home, that they sought only a momentary release, a singular, snatched pleasure, and I questioned the girls' terrified response, thought perhaps if they had smiled sweetly and listened to the soldiers' stories of home and tolerated their tuneless songs that such alarm might have been contained, quashed, in the immediate moments following the forced entry to the schoolgirls' quarters. And yet, when I saw Lijun, undeterred, sink her teeth into the soldier's upper arm, then rise to stand on beer-soaked toes and clasp his cheek, holding fervently to his flesh as a dog to a bone, and still he did not yield, I knew I could not so easily forgive the young men their depravity. No one might deny a soldier forgiving company and tender touch, yet these men's brutal determination, their corporeal drive, went far beyond the malady of homesickness. I stood behind Lijun, and struck the same soldier with force. Groaning, he finally dropped the girl's hand and she raced sobbing to Nina, who enveloped her in a maternal embrace.

"Do not touch this girl," Lijun said in halting English. "Never."

The man cursed Lijun, but surrendered, taking two or three steps back, and raised his palm to soothe his cheek.

"Get out," I said, striking him once more on that most sensitive spot. The soldier backed away towards the door, but surveying the rest of the room, I saw it was still in thrall to a most grotesque havoc. The soldiers chased after the girls, who sprinted from them to seek shelter behind the withered, defenseless bodies of their elders. The men, their spirits curdled with drink, laughed uproariously at this great sport, lunging after the girls and calling out salacious remarks to one another. Feeling useless, I did not know how they might be stopped. These men, the protecters of the Legation Quarter, the last defense against the Boxers, had undergone a demonic transformation. I reached once more for the man I had held first; in the dizziness of drink he once again surrendered to my grip, but I was only one man, and a dozen of those iniquitous characters ran free around us. I pulled the man closer to me, a knee to his gut forced him to the floor.

"Please," he said with sour breath. "We only wanted a little fun."

The tenor of his voice, clipped and assured, was as familiar

as it was sinister, for knelt unwillingly before me was a soldier
of Her Majesty.

Shouts from outside, barked, anguished, and in foreign
tongue, stole my attention. Through the doorway sprinted half
a dozen Japanese, called from their sentry duty elsewhere in the
palace, guns raised above their heads.

"Out, out!" they cried, and I experienced a profound relief.

The soldiers did not pause until a bullet was fired singularly
and significantly into the air. Then the men halted their chase
and filed out of the room with their heads bowed. Short of
breath, their chests heaved still and an occasional, high-spirited
guffaw escaped their lips; the Japanese greeted such frivolity by
cocking their guns in the direction of each laughing soldier. At
the doorway, the American who had suffered Lijun's rage looked
over his shoulder and called to the Japanese soldiers: "It isn't fair
of you to keep the best for yourselves."

The men were gone, but the terror they had sowed remained
in the room. Many of the girls wept, they held one another, their
cheeks were flushed feverish and pink. Lijun stood apart from
the others, her arms wrapped around herself in solitary embrace.
Nina moved towards the girl, reached out a sympathetic hand
out to comfort her. Lijun recoiled from her touch.

"Lijun, very well done," Nina offered.

"For what?" Lijun angled her shoulders away from Nina.

"You were very brave," Nina insisted.

"I am not brave," Lijun said flatly. "You might say I am the
very opposite of brave."

"Lijun, what do you mean?" Nina asked.

"You wouldn't understand," Lijun said. She shook her head,
her lips curled.

"We have had a terrible shock," Nina said. "You mustn't
forget, Lijun, that you did a very good deed. Everyone shall

remember your kindness."

"If only I had done such a good thing before," Lijun said bitterly. Nina placed a tentative arm around the girl's shoulder, but Lijun snaked her body away from Nina. "Let me be."

Nina nodded and went to console the others girls, sharing her words, assurances and embraces, aware that her offerings, however well-intentioned, were hopelessly inadequate.

Naturally, I was revolted by these events. I despised the malevolence inherent in the very act, which would have been deplorable whichever nationality had carried it out, yet I also resented the soldiers for the confusion they wrought in the morality of the Boxer conflict. I have existed as both a journalist and a simple man too long to give credence to the idea of a clear dividing line between right and wrong in any conflict. The rather trite expression has it that there are two sides to any story; my career has proved that adage to be something of an understatement. That said, the conflict had hitherto offered a fairly convincing narrative of right and wrong: we, the extended foreign community in China, were innocent, we were good, we were victims of an undeserved, unwarranted attack, while the Boxers were plainly bad. And so for our own men to molest those girls, those mere children who had lost everything, their families, their dignity, everything but the last shreds of their pitiful hope because of their faith in a religion we had imported, well, those circumstances were rather too dreadful to bear. As a foreign man standing in that devastated room, I experienced a roiling shame by association. I looked to Nina, who stood with her arms wrapped around the girl who had captured the American soldier's attention. Unseen by the girl, Nina wept silent, unending tears.

"Miss Nina," the girl asked gently between sobs, "why did the men not chase after you?"

The expression that passed across Nina's features then was grievous to observe; with great, startling immediacy her face passed from the questioning of a furrowed brow to the slack, unthinking shock of realization. Finally, undeniably, this was the moment in which she must accept that in the midst of this great conflict it mattered not that she had been born in Peking, that her feet had never trod upon the shingle at Dover. No, that night she learned the terrible truth of wars, that every conflict requires its participants to choose one side over another and as such eliminates, through physical or spiritual means, the existence of those people who prefer to inhabit the middle of any spectrum; people, in my opinion, absolutely necessary to the continued peaceful survival of any successful society. Are you one of us or one of them? the war asked, and as Nina watched the schoolgirls sob, shiver and whimper in the aftermath of the soldiers' visit, her own flesh untouched, her very skin unscratched, she knew, finally, to which side she was perceived to belong.

I helped the elders to clean the room, sopping up the puddles of beer and clearing away the streaks of rainwater left behind by the unwelcome visitors. The elderly women insisted I leave the task to them, and while they were undoubtedly more dexterous and efficient in their efforts, my contrition demanded of me some action, and I knew my natural talents did not extend to becalming the fearful girls in the room.

Nina tried to settle the girls; eventually some agreed to lie once more, letting Nina place their bedsheets lightly over them, turning reluctantly and restlessly as sleep and peace evaded them. The young girl who had been subject of the American's attack remained anxious, and refused to lie down; instead she wrapped her arms tightly around Nina's neck. Nina stroked the girl's back gently, whispering in her ear until the child eventually allowed Nina to lower her to the floor. Still she sobbed, and Nina set to plaiting the girl's hair over and over, the repetitive motion offering a salve to fear.

"Why did they do that?" the girl asked Nina.

Nina had no answer for her.

"I am happy Lijun bit that dog." The girl laughed, and the maturity, the emptiness, the lack of youth and joy in the sound she emitted, surprised and pained me. "I know why she helped me. It is not the first time she has seen men like that."

"Not the first time?" Nina's fingers worked unflagging at plaiting the girl's hair. The little girl's eyes fluttered closed and open.

"No. When she's quiet sometimes, I ask her what she's thinking. And she told me once she thinks of a man who did a very bad thing to her after she ran from the village, after the fire and after her family was killed."

Nina did not reply, but started to sing an old Chinese lullaby. I talked a short distance away with the distressed elders, advising them on how to secure the doors and windows, arranging with the Japanese for a permanent guard on duty, and yet I could not concentrate fully on the words of the young girls' guardians, so distracted was I by the words Nina sang, her voice steady, haunting, transcendent in that airless room of timidity and trepidation. Nina's mother must have sung to her before she left, but naturally Nina did not recall the words to any of those distant English songs of sheep and cradles, instead she treasured the silver-toned melodies and familiar lyrics of the lullabies the servants sang to send her to sleep as a child.

"*The moon is bright, the wind is quiet,*
"*The tree leaves hang over the window,*
"*My little baby, go to sleep quickly,*
"*Sleep, dream sweet dreams.*"

She repeated the lullaby twice, and the girl slept by the end of the second round. Quietly I approached.

"Come," I said, offering my hand. "I shall accompany you home."

I enlisted a Japanese soldier to walk with us and we followed his stocky frame through the Legation Quarter. He remained several steps ahead at all times, gun poised by his shoulder. The imperial troops maintained a steady volley of bullets as we passed, firing skywards from their posts beyond our fortifications, but the three of us progressed undetected in the shadows of the high walls and makeshift barricades that separated us from the gathered combatants. The rain fell in an unrepentant deluge and Nina struggled to fight her instinct to flinch at each roll of thunder. I was impressed, however, at how she kept her body bent in imitation of the Japanese soldier and did not so much as glance up when bullets flew overhead. The soldier bowed deeply by the doorway of the Fairchild household, took a step back and lingered, waiting for me.

"Please, go back," I said.

I accompanied Nina inside, instructing a servant to fetch her a towel and a glass of brandy. Light emitted from the drawing room as we walked towards it. I detected hesitancy in Nina's step and at the foot of the stairs she paused.

"Thank you, Alistair, but I think it is best I go to bed right away."

"Nonsense," I said. "You must dry off and have something to steady your nerves. Come, sit down a moment."

Nina's light summer dress clung to her as seaweed to a rock, and one curl, matted and wet, pressed against her forehead. Her countenance was pale and drawn, her mien faded.

"You have had a terrible shock. Come."

Nina stood firm.

"I do not wish to see anyone," she said quietly, looking with trepidation towards the drawing room. And how might I blame her? For no friend could lie on the other side of that anonymous door; who did she dread to see more, Oscar Fairchild, source of her shame, Lillian Price, instigator of her downfall, or her own father, freshly remote, newly forbidding and utterly unable to help her?

"Miss Ward."

The tone was sharp, the voice, commanding and unshakeable, belonged to Phoebe Franklin. Nina let out a breath. Wordlessly she followed me into the room, where the missionary sat alone, erect in an armchair with an open Bible across her knees. She rose stiffly as we entered.

"Thanks be to God," she said. "Tell me, child, what happened? They sent me away, I had no idea of what might have befallen you until a French missionary came by to check if you were safely returned. Oh, the horrors he told us."

"Mrs Franklin, I have come to no harm. I'm sorry to hear you were worried. I have kept you up so late."

The servant entered the room and handed Nina a towel. I held the glass of brandy as she dried her face in the folds of the towel, running it over her damp hair before returning it to the servant's outstretched hands. She shivered with the first sip of brandy, passing the rest undesired to me.

"Miss Ward, I offer you my fullest and my frankest apologies," Phoebe continued. "I never ought to have placed you in such danger. I can only hope you and your father may forgive my foolishness."

"Please, Mrs Franklin, you were not to know. It is the fault only of those men…"

"Yes, they had been drinking, I believe. At least one might hope that their governance by the flesh was a temporary failing only."

"Yes," Nina said. "The girls were frightened, but courageous. They have seen and survived much worse. I regret, however, that such a thing should happen to them in their place of sanctuary."

"Well, I heard they were Russian soldiers. It does not greatly surprise me; they are given to uncouth behavior and are particularly fond of drinking," Phoebe said.

"Actually, Mrs Franklin, they were not only Russians. I saw an American," Nina said.

Phoebe raised her hand.

"Enough, dear child. I do not wish you to relive those terrible moments; think of it no more. Tomorrow you shall stay here where you are safe and you need not return to Prince Su's palace. It was folly to take you there. You have been of wonderful service, Miss Ward, but we must do all we can to keep you away from such dangers."

"No!" Nina said with bitter vehemence. "No, no, Mrs Franklin. I must return; the girls expect me."

"It is simply impossible, Miss Ward," Phoebe said calmly and with authority. "Imagine if you had been less fortunate this evening. I wished to protect you, instead I placed you in grave danger." Phoebe turned to me with curt smile. "How very glad I am that Mr Scott was able to bring you home safely, but we cannot always rely on him to be there."

"Please, Mrs Franklin." Nina reached for missionary's hand. "I am so grateful for all you have done for me. I wish only to return to the girls at the palace."

"It is out of the question, Miss Ward. Now, to bed. You are drenched, child, and you must rest."

Nina nodded without feeling. I placed my arm around her shoulder and guided her towards the door, felt her frame weak and despairing. As we departed Phoebe said in tranquil tones: "Let the Lord be your light, child."

At that, Nina struggled free of me, surged towards the stairs and ascended them rapidly, did not look back.

Nicholas' voice called out to her from the top of the stairs and I saw my friend come into view in his long linen pajamas, a lamp flickering in his left hand. Nina ran towards him as a little girl, skipping the final steps to throw herself into his embrace.

"Nina, you are well, you are well," he said.

"I am fine, Father," she said.

"You are so very strong, my girl," he said. "So very strong, but not invincible. We must keep you safe."

He led her away then, and the landing fell black. I lifted the unconsumed brandy to my lips, swilled it until my tongue numbed, and let it tumble, welcome down my throat. I placed the empty glass upon a lacquer cabinet in the hallway and stepped once more into the night, impenetrable, tenebrous, terrible. The rain lashed my face and the gloom perplexed my steps as I hurried under that canopy of bullets to the familiar environs of the Grand, hastening gladly now towards the narrow proportions of my bed, where in sleep at least I might dream of a world in which all men were not quite as bad as one another.

X

THE STORMS had cleared and the firing of the night before had stopped, and yet when I opened the window in the first blush of morning, the smell of the city, rotting, sweet and fleshy, caused me to gag. Wearily I looked to the street below, remembered how majestically ordered the Legation Quarter had once appeared; manicured, fine and unutterably dull, an aseptic town square struggling nobly against the vibrancy of the city that surrounded it. Now the quarter hummed, whined with humanity, with the dissatisfaction of existence in all its bleakest, rawest forms, its streets stained, embarrassed by the blood of many nations. A knock at the door roused me from my dismal view. Edward, a cup of coffee in his hand, stepped into the room.

"Hilde made this for you."

A gratifying sip filled not only my mouth but also my nostrils, and the bitter, potent scent of the drink allowed me to ignore momentarily the waft of despair that passed through the window.

"I heard about the Su palace," Edward ventured. "Terrible business. The young Miss Ward was rather upset, I imagine?"

"As is to be expected. Do you know, Edward, that I cannot remember now, not really, the precise moment in which I first I recognized the true, disappointing nature of mankind. It must have been in Afghanistan, I suppose. I do recall, however, that nothing ever felt quite the same once that terrible discovery had been made. I imagine Miss Ward experiences the very same sentiment now."

Edward nodded, cleared his throat.

"I ask because I have just seen her by the chapel. She has drawn quite a crowd."

"A crowd?" I set down the empty coffee cup.

"She is...well, she is raving, one might say."

Hurriedly I navigated the narrow circuit of the Legation Quarter, that familiar maze of walls and barricades. I avoided the eyes of the young men who stood guard around its borders, recoiling at the sight of their young hands wrapped around their guns, instinctively wondering if the same fingers had wrenched at the wrists of Nina's students only half a day prior. I came to the pavilions amongst which the chapel stood, the area had become a meeting point of sorts; notices were pasted there when there was news to report, which was not often in those ignorant days. A small crowd had indeed gathered, but they did not read the messages that papered the walls, those old, false promises of safety and a swift end to fighting. No, each of that motley assortment rather had their eyes trained upon an exchange taking place in the sweeping shadow of the pavilions, a terse dialogue between Nina, her expression savage, hunted, her complexion gray and sleepless, anger mottling her cheeks, and a European man whose unsavory countenance was distantly familiar to me. His hair had grown long and unkempt, and the hunger of the past weeks accentuated his sunken, angular frame, highlighting the unpleasantly keen angles of his face.

"Forgive me, Miss. I spoke only in jest."

The man had an obscure accent that suggested much movement and few roots. This type of character, fully surrendered to the absolute dissolution possible only thousands of miles from every reminder of one's personal history, was not unusual in China, though such men were found with greater frequency in the footloose port cities than in the more restrictive confines of respectable Peking society. With practiced tranquility he lifted a pipe to his lips.

"In jest?" Nina cried. "Tell me, sir, what witticisms one might make with regards to terrified, weeping orphans, wrenched from their homes, at last in a place of safety, threatened once more by the very men mandated to protect them?"

Nina was a tiger in a trap; righteously she raged, but defeat and impotence were plain in the restrained volume of her speech, in the constrained bearing of her frame, in the small step of surrender she took backwards from the man.

"Yet it strikes a man as cruel, you see, to hide the most ravishing young ladies in one place and not to allow us so much as a glance." The man laughed, inhaled from his pipe with satisfaction.

"Sir." I pushed to the front of the crowd, displacing a Japanese diplomat from his position of privileged viewing. The nature of the disagreement I only vaguely understood; clearly Nina spoke of events at the Su mansion, but what words had birthed the conflict I did not know. I only wished to protect Nina. And yet stepping between the quarreling pair, I experienced something approaching anger towards my friend's daughter. Of course Nina was correct to challenge the man's unpleasantness, and naturally what had occurred at the palace was repugnant, but equally I wished that she might quieten her character, might tame her spirit for a short time, and allow the scandal, that sullied halo that crowned her, to fade somewhat before drawing fresh attention to herself.

"Sir," I began again. "Perhaps we ought to disperse. There are a number of people here to read the notices." I gestured to the crowd.

The man sneered, but conceded a step backwards. I hoped the argument might end there, that the gathered onlookers might turn from us and go about their day, but the man's last comment had so enraged Nina that she charged past me to face him once more, her torso held straight and tense with indignation as she addressed him.

"Ravishing? They are not ravishing! They have starved, they have crossed the great expanse of this country after losing their families. And you can think of no other word to describe but ravishing!"

"Forgive me, Miss. I have spoken out of turn."

The man shrugged then and walked away, gesturing crudely to the dozen or so people around us, suggesting with exaggerated turns of the wrist and fingers pointed in Nina's direction that she might be quite mad.

"Miss Ward." Oscar stood beside Nina now, and I realized he must have been amongst that crowd. His voice was commanding and false, a performance. "I find you on my way home for tiffin. Let me accompany you to the house."

Meekly Nina assented, following Oscar without so much as a glance in my direction, her head bowed to avoid the scrutiny of the diplomats, wives and refugees who had witnessed this public spectacle.

"You do not usually eat at home at midday," I heard her observe quietly.

The speed and serenity with which Nina had obeyed Oscar Fairchild, displaying the unthinking, untroubled devotion a loyal Labrador might show his master, alarmed me. Surely Nina, her name thoroughly blackened in the Fairchild household and already whispered with knowing disapproval in each corner of the Legation Quarter, could not bow so easily to this man, the architect of her shame. How unreservedly she had wrangled with the odious jester not long departed, how unyieldingly she had she challenged his coarse humor, and yet how lightly, how swiftly she had assented to Oscar's suggestion that he accompany her home, and now they walked the length of the Legation Quarter together, the sound of their close steps a song of scandal. I wished suddenly to follow them, and excused myself from the onlookers, noticing the source of the morning's disagreement as I extricated myself from their midst. Amongst the sun-bleached, dim notices of delayed salvation pasted on the wall was a piece of paper only recently affixed there, one of its corners loose and curling in the heat. The handwritten note announced in English that the lives of young Chinese converts resident in Prince Su's palace must be protected at all costs and that NO MEN, SAVE COLONEL SHIBA'S GUARDS, MAY ENTER THE CHAMBERS THAT HOUSE THE YOUNG WOMEN.

I walked towards the Fairchild house, but did not see Nina and Oscar on the way. I considered that they must have hurried home so rapidly that I had missed them, and counted myself fortunate, for what might I have said if I had seen them? Could I have demanded that Nina abandon the man who so generously hosted her and her father under his roof? Might I have, in my unceasing efforts to dim Nina's infamy, have instead breathed into it new life, confirmed to any casual observer the rumors that swirled around the pair and verified the disgrace, close and unflagging, that accompanied Nina now wherever she went? These were the thoughts that turned in my mind when I did then, unexpectedly, observe the pair. Nina and Oscar stood together in a slender patch of shade in one of the narrow alleyways that provided me with a shortcut to the Grand, their heads bowed so close that their foreheads almost touched. I witnessed Fairchild produce a handkerchief from his pocket, and watched as Nina raised it to dab the corners of her eyes. They spoke, or rather murmured to each other, and I stood motionless, undetected, watching them. Oscar glanced briefly around, and satisfied they remained unseen, pulled Nina into an embrace. She sobbed more forcefully then, her eyes tightly closed, a useless dam against her tears. I turned from them, and with inching shame and incipient loneliness, returned to my room at the Grand.

As we the besieged settled into the month of July, sad little events marked our days. We found a Chinese to take a message to Tientsin; he hid the missive in a bowl of rice hoping to outwit the enemy, who usually searched pockets and linings for such materials. Few expected he would return, none believed his mission would finally summon Seymour's long-delayed soldiers and yet all agreed some action, however symbolic, must be taken towards progress. One French marine offered to go himself to Tienstin, so frustrated was he with the interminable wait for death. His departure was forbidden by one of the Catholic priests, on the grounds that it would be a sin to denounce his religion if caught by Boxers and to do so would be the only way to preserve his life. By this stage I had grown rather tired of the religious fervor on both sides of the conflict, though I admired the cheery industriousness our straightened circumstances had produced in large numbers of the besieged. I witnessed this flourishing work ethic close at hand: Hilde transformed the Grand into a most productive bakery that provided hungry Legation Quarter-dwellers with dozens of loaves each day. Her management was attentive and resolute; when her head baker took a bullet to the head through a window one day, Hilde made sure his staff continued to work by holding them at gunpoint while their leader's blood congealed on the floor. It surprised some of the residents that in these most trying of moments others wished to continue as though their lives remained untouched by the Boxers, as evinced by Lillian Price's insistence on hosting a little celebration on the fourth of July. It was no great surprise to me; to abandon routine in any war is to cede that ultimate battleground to the enemy: the mind.

The American gathering afforded me the first opportunity to observe Nina at close quarters since that secret embrace. I had not been to dinner at the Fairchild house for days; a host of reasons, murky and undefined even in my own mind, kept me at bay. I experienced a sense of compunction at having witnessed Oscar and Nina together in a moment of great intimacy (for tears between lovers indicate a confidence far deeper than nudity or even poetry might) and while I missed my close friendship with Nicholas, I struggled to imagine how I might successfully restore our previous camaraderie following our recent disagreements. And then there was my pride: La Contessa had not visited me for several consecutive nights, and I hoped to prove the Chinese maxim that a short separation could draw the most established couple closer than newlyweds. Watching Nina amongst those barbed friends and smiling foes, it saddened me to see her adopt a steely indifference to us all over the course of the dinner. In fact, as geographically and culturally irrelevant as it may have been for them, only the Italians seemed able to muster any vigor to bring to the proceedings, chatting pleasantly with the handful of American officials and soldiers accommodated that evening under Fairchild's roof. I noted, with what I suppose was the justified suspicion of the transgressor, that while Pietro Mancini spoke affably with all present, and even afforded himself the occasional bout of congenial laughter, La Contessa's husband appeared to studiously avoid my eye, and reserved his mirth whenever I made some humorous observation about our trying circumstances. As the meal (horse meat, naturally, accompanied by a selection of the Grand's springiest loaves) drew to a close, a bullet pierced the window, flying over our heads and ending its course by puncturing the corner of the Queen's portrait above the mantelpiece. Whilst the Americans dived under the table and prayed to God for mercy, those of us who were subjects of Victoria raised our glasses to the incident: it recalled a similar event with the Boers at Ladysmith, when the arrival of such an ominous bullet had in fact heralded an imminent end to that siege.

The bullet shattered any remaining pretense of standard dining protocol and the guests milled freely between rooms, arms outstretched in invitation to the servants to fill their glasses.

In the drawing room I approached Nina, who stood alone by the window, observing the sun's last rays disappear over the horizon.

"Miss Ward," I said.

"Good evening."

She did not turn, but maintained her position, her face was a study of unflustered concentration.

"You have been rather quiet this evening," I started.

"That American soldier was at the palace," she said. "That night." She faced me then, her mouth drawn in a severe line. "Forgive me if I feel less than sociable."

"I'm sorry," I said.

I wished I could say I was surprised, but in every conflict countries favor blood over deed, flag over conduct, and so they turn the vilest of men into perfect saints in the name of nationhood. The solider Nina spoke of had arrived with a jade turtle, pilfered from who knows where, which he had presented with flourish to a delighted Lillian Price.

"I am frustrated," Nina said quietly. "I am idle, I do nothing each day but sew sandbags. Surely they must have sufficient numbers by now?"

"Do you not help your father in his work?"

"A little." She turned her wrists in circles, inspected the

cobwebs of veins on the undersides of her arms. "He seems to need my help less these days."

"Perhaps you might help Mr and Mrs Samuels at the Grand," I said. "The hotel has been attacked, but it remains rather safer than the Su mansion."

"Oh yes!" Nina's eyes filled with light as she finally turned to face me. "Anything rather than spend all day here."

It was with startling immediacy that I realized the suggestion might have constituted an error on my part. So far no soldiers of any stripe had swarmed the Grand in large numbers, but its position on the edge of the Legation Quarter had made it vulnerable to a series of constant, non-lethal attacks. Guests (and here I use the word loosely to include those displaced peoples who slept in the hallways and under the tables) had on several occasions heard cries from the Boxers who lay in wait on the other side of the Legation wall which brushed the corners of the hotel. Bullets pierced walls and shattered windows with alarming frequency. If Prince Su's mansion, protected by Colonel Shiba and his men, was deemed too dangerous for Nina, the Grand was little better. And so it surprised me when Nicholas gave his blessing for Nina to help at the hotel; perhaps as her father he felt her dissatisfaction and restlessness even more keenly than I did. He then suggested I might like to read the latest chapter of his book on the Boxers, and the mild rapprochement cheered me. I left Fairchild's home feeling lighter than I had for days; La Contessa had also swept by me in the drawing room and, lips grazing my ear, whispered the singular promise of "later".

She arrived close to one a.m., her limbs loose and her countenance relaxed from the wine toasted to America's independence.

"I have missed you," she said.

"And I," I replied as we reached for one another with

desperate, lonely hands.

Momentarily I paused. "Was the door not locked when you arrived?"

"Oh yes," La Contessa said, "but those nice Chinese boys in the hall were most obliging."

"You have not been to see me recently," I said.

"Oh, Alistair, do you not know that there are moments for speaking and moments for silence?"

I heeded her counsel and remained quiet, allowed her to lead me, confidently, towards the bed, where together we dissolved our fears, buried our expectations and quenched our desires. And yet even as we moved in now familiar rhythms, even as she soothed me with sweet kisses and murmured wishes, a disquiet held firm in my mind. How recklessly, how certainly, La Contessa had crossed the Legation Quarter in the most dangerous hour, how ardently she embraced me now as though no other thought intruded upon her particular plans, and yet something had prevented her from doing so in the week previous to this encounter. She kissed me feverishly, unquestioningly, paused only momentarily, untangled her form from mine.

"He shall never do anything," she muttered, her hair, loose, brushing my shoulder. "He thinks himself a lion, but I know him a lamb."

"Your husband?" I began, but she silenced me once more with febrile lips, conquering hands, and I accepted her, pressed her flesh once more to mine, and yet I could not help to think, as our breath rose and fell as one, of the refugees sleeping downstairs, and I wondered what impression this elegant foreigner of curled hair and ruffled silks had left upon them, demanding entry to the Grand in the blackest moment of the night. And, despite the insistent and calming nature of La Contessa's kisses, I could not help but to ask myself whether Hilde and Edward might too have witnessed her late arrival at the hotel.

I had told Nina to expect me in the morning; I would collect her and deliver her to the Grand where she might perform her new duties. This proved something of a logistical problem as La Contessa felt compelled to return to the Fairchild home before Nina might spy her at the hotel, and so had to hide in the side porch that morning while I called at the main door for Nina. A servant showed me through to the drawing room, where Nina waited for me, her face softer again in the glow of first dawn. She smiled warmly when she saw me. In the hallway, we happened upon Oscar Fairchild, putting on his light summer jacket, preparing himself for another day of fruitless labour.

"Good morning," he said, nodding politely towards me. "Where are you going?"

"To the Grand Hotel," Nina said proudly. "I am to help there."

"Are you sure that's quite safe?" Oscar asked, fastening the top button of his jacket.

I believed he addressed the question more to me than to Nina, but she seized upon it immediately.

"We are under siege, Mr Fairchild. Just yesterday a bullet tore through the skirts of our monarch as we ate. I am not sure anywhere is safe."

"Very true," he said. "Well, be careful."

He dipped politely as we took our leave, watching until a servant closed the door behind us.

Unfortunately, La Contessa had chosen precisely the wrong moment to emerge from her hiding place and, seeing Nina, immediately tried to steal away once more to the cover afforded by the side porch. Still her emerald skirts glistened in the orange light of morning, resplendent as they had looked at dinner the previous night.

"Is that La Contessa?" Nina asked.

"Oh no, it cannot possibly be." I held Nina by the arm and guided her away from the house. She cocked her head to one side as though she might say more, but ultimately censored herself.

I had not spoken to Hilde of my plan; it had rather slipped my mind when La Contessa had promised to follow me to the hotel the previous evening, and I hate to say that sensible, industrious Hilde appeared rather unimpressed when I presented Nina to her.

"What can she do?" Hilde stood with her arms folded at the doorway to the kitchen where a group of Chinese Christians already kneaded dough. Always fond of firearms, Hilde now had a revolver in a permanent bolster around her waist following the death of her best baker.

"You might be surprised by what I can do," Nina said promptly.

"Well, can you bake?" Hilde asked with impatience.

"I'm sure I could learn." Nina did not waver.

"She speaks better Mandarin than the Empress Dowager," I said hastily. "She was at Prince Su's palace, teaching the young girls."

"I saw her there," Hilde said mildly. "And why are you not at the Su mansion now, Miss Ward?"

"Because the Boxers are not the only depraved actors in this conflict," Nina said.

Hilde smiled and uncrossed her arms.

Nina was awarded the responsibility of overseeing the delivery of bread to foreigners around the Legation Quarter and quickly adapted to this new role. Her Mandarin allowed her to provide clear instructions to the converts who made and transported the bread, whilst her recently acquired knowledge of the foreign community within the walls, who lived where and how many mouths they had to feed, ensured the correct quantities were delivered to the right places. When not in the kitchen, Nina resumed similar duties to those she had performed at the Su mansion and entertained the children, telling them stories in Chinese and English to allow their parents some brief moments of respite. I collected her each morning and walked her to the Grand, where I left her for the day.

Whilst Nina labored in the Grand, I completed my usual rounds of the increasingly weary diplomatic corps who furnished me with neither hope nor news. In fact, so meagre were their offerings that I started to seek out the missionaries who at least shared with me tales of rural hell collected from the refugees in their care. With little political movement, I instead recorded these lurid stories of Boxer atrocities in China's hinterland: a foreign missionary forced to parade his naked form before an entire village as a prelude to decapitation, unfounded accusations that Christian converts had poisoned wells and the inevitable bloody consequences of such rumors, crude Boxer depictions of Christ as a pig on the cross. I wrote down the morbid details, wondering when I might be able to communicate them to the world outside the Legation Quarter, the walls of which now seemed to press closer upon me. In the early evening I returned to the Grand for Nina and together we would walk to the Fairchild residence; Nina always carried at least two loaves under her arm.

Working at the Grand had brought Nina somewhat back to herself. Even so, on those walks we shared, dusk-lit strolls that might have been quite pleasant had it not been for the terrible, decaying stench of the place and the unshakeable sense of foreboding with which it was permeated, she was quite honest with me. She dealt out her fears and regrets in neatly parceled words, but not once did she pronounce Oscar's name, and I avoided the topic as delicately as my powers of discretion would allow. Imagine, then, the bewilderment I experienced when upon my return to the hotel late one Tuesday afternoon Hilde told me that Oscar had arrived unannounced at the Grand that morning and asked for a tour of the premises, claiming that he would welcome the opportunity to meet the inhabitants of the hotel. Hilde escorted me to Edward's office, where she closed the door decisively and offered me a brief account of Fairchild's visit. She had been suspicious, naturally, as to why an official charged with the bodily survival of his own people would take a sudden interest in the fate of the beleaguered refugees of the Grand.

"And why would a humble establishment such as ours be of interest to an envoy of Her Majesty's government?" Hilde had asked him.

"Mr Samuels is a British subject," Oscar had replied. "Besides, at times such as these, unity extends beyond the colors of our respective flags, does it not?"

"Indeed."

Dutifully Hilde had led Oscar from room to room, presenting the refugees with yet another anonymous foreign face, another man they hoped for a moment might signal their relief, but who, like the others, was ultimately unable to tell them anything more of when salvation might arrive.

"And when might I see the famous bakery?" Oscar had asked when they returned to the lobby and Hilde had hoped to dismiss him.

I had not made a single allusion to the scandal while with my hosts at the Grand. Motivated by my loyalty to both Nina and Nicholas, I also feared any mention of it could jeopardize Nina's position at the hotel. Consequently, while Hilde was surprised by the arrival of the British secretary, she remained ignorant of his motives. Until, perhaps, she took him to the bakery.

Nina wore her customary uniform of loosely-tied apron and

scrap of fabric around her head as she walked around the kitchen where dusty clouds of dough filled the air. Her arms, exposed by rolled sleeves, were dotted with white paste and moist patches of flour created swirled patterns across her apron. She did not immediately perceive Oscar and Hilde in the doorway and continued to work free from self-consciousness, checking each finished product against her list of recipients and delivering prompt instructions in Mandarin to the boys who transported the loaves.

When Hilde announced their presence, she said the horror that seized Nina's face was instant and apparent to all. Nina stammered a greeting to Oscar, who replied in even, diplomatic tone that he was most impressed with the efficiency of the operation and thanked her with formality for her efforts to support the wellbeing of all those under siege. And yet, Hilde said, behind the decorum of his stately words glowed an affection so warm that it was detected even by the delivery boys, innocent of love and ignorant of English.

"Allow me to escort you out, Mr Fairchild," Hilde had said, but Oscar remained in the doorway, an eager, boyish smile on his face, his stance suggesting a reluctance to leave. He insisted he stay a little longer so he might take a loaf with him for lunch. Hilde acquiesced, and returned to the lobby, leaving Oscar alone with Nina and the bakers. What passed between them in those moments, Hilde did not know. She watched with her usual healthy inquisitiveness as Oscar left with a loaf tucked under his arm. No official had shown any such interest in the Grand in its new incarnation as refuge to the desperate and the faithful; most complained that they no longer liked to visit the bar, where one could scarcely rest one's feet on the floor without colliding with some poor soul from the countryside. She had proceeded to the kitchen where she observed Nina, teary-eyed and pallid, the authority gone from her voice as she instructed the delivery boys which addresses to go to next, and without the need to ask a single question, Hilde's curiosity was satisfied.

"I thought you ought to know," she said finally. "You are close to the Wards. I am not a missionary, Mr Scott, nor am I an official. But I am a woman, and I know a bad business when I see one."

Nina waited for me as usual in the lobby, her baker's guise removed, her face cleaned of any residue of the day's production. Typically I found her chatting animatedly with the refugees, but this evening she was withdrawn, her arms crossed and elbows pointed at uninviting angles. It was a brief walk through the Legation Quarter, but far from easy; the imperial troops opened fire as we were half the way home, and so we saw no alternative but to stay close by the walls, seeking the protection of sloping eaves. As we approached the Fairchild residence, Nina suddenly grabbed my arm.

"Careful," she cried. A bullet soared in a close arc over my head. We both ducked instinctively, crouching by the verandah of a small house belonging to British trade official Arthur Bloomfield. The bullet's emissary had evidently seen us and as such he followed his soft opening with a hailstorm of bullets that just passed over our heads. One bullet left a neat hole in a window; I spied the stricken face of Arthur's wife Kitty by the window, and almost as rapidly she disappeared from view.

"Lie down," I said to Nina. "There, on the verandah."

With impassive expression Nina followed my instructions and I crawled across the verandah to take position beside her. The bullets sounded continuously, but our prone position meant they soared in easy arcs above us.

"I heard Mr Fairchild paid a visit to the hotel today," I said.

I raised the topic on impulse; naturally I recognized that the environment could not have been less favorable to discussion, but there was something in the way Nina held herself that evening, in her passive acceptance of my instructions, of our situation, displaying no indication of her usual bloody determination or even simple fear, that told me the secret weighed upon her.

"Yes," she said. She rested her chin on her hands and did not look at me. "He came to inspect our little bakery."

"Nina," I said, inching closer to her. "I have no idea what may have passed between you and Mr Fairchild and I do not wish to make you uncomfortable or to insinuate anything…"

"You are quite right, Mr Scott," she said, meeting my eye with level gaze. "You have no idea."

"Yet, if you will forgive my impropriety, I only wish to help. Your father is a good man, Nina, but he knows little of these matters, and I know he would find it difficult to raise such an issue with you."

"Mr Scott, there is nothing of which to speak," Nina continued. "I did not ask Mr Fairchild to come to the Grand; in fact I expressly asked him to leave."

"Nina," I said softly. "I understand that my questions may make you feel uncomfortable, but understand, please, that I think only of you. Your relations with Mr Fairchild are already discussed in the Legation Quarter and rumors unheeded soon grow two heads. If you wish to speak to me of this matter, I assure you that you shall enjoy my full confidence. We live in suspension, but our lives will one day, God willing, be lived normally once again. And then what shall you do?"

The flurry of shooting had come to an abrupt stop as I spoke. Nina stood quickly, brushed down the front of her dress, and without looking directly towards me, said: "Come, Mr Scott."

I rose to my feet, saw Benjamin Moore through the window, occupying the same position Kitty Bloomfield had moments earlier. I waved, he turned away, and Nina and I walked in silence through those fetid, putrid streets.

I watched Nina that evening and in the days that followed, but her actions and words revealed nothing of her innermost feelings to me, or, I imagine, to any other observer who might have taken an interest in her comportment. Dinners at the Fairchild house were a studied performance in normality; Nina's pretense had become so fluent that she was able to occasionally direct questions to Mr Fairchild, just as she might have done before that terrible moment in which Lillian Price revealed the intimacy between the two. At the Grand, Nina kept up both her work and her spirits; her enthusiasm and ability never faltered. She worried still for her former students at the Su palace and asked Hilde if she might bring Lijun to help at the hotel, and soon the girl was working alongside her in the bakery. Hilde was happy for the additional support, and set Lijun tasks beyond simple baking, harnessing the girl's industriousness into cleaning and cooking, and taking advantage of her formidable temper by having her scold those refugees who failed to keep their lodgings tidy enough.

"One must never let standards slip," Hilde explained to me. "You let one piece go and the whole structure comes tumbling down."

On the ninth day of July, word reached me at the Grand that a Chinese sent out of the Legation Quarter to collect information was safely returned within our walls. I stopped by the bakery to invite Nina to come with me to the chapel where the messenger's news was to be posted. Lijun followed, tripping along excitedly behind us. We were so starved of information in those days that any glimmer of fact seemed a great promise of hope, a shaft of light to guide us out of misery and towards real, unconfined life. The notice pinned to the message board, its text set in stark relief by the midday sun, disappointed in its contents. The Emperor and Empress Dowager remained in Peking, it read, ending with the dismal sentence: "Nothing known of the approach of foreign troops." Nina's hand reached for mine and I held it tightly, feeling her palm slick. Lijun puzzled at the sign.

"The English words are too long. What does it say?" she asked Nina, who responded with only a silent shake of her head. She rested her forehead on my shoulder in the sorrowful stance that normally precedes tears, but none came. Lijun, sensing the gravity of the moment, fell away, and left Nina and I to confront the notice alone.

"Nina," I said finally. "I am so sorry."

"When shall we leave?" she whispered fiercely. "Shall we ever leave?"

"Of course we shall," I said briskly, lifting her chin with my knuckles and looking into those sorrowful green eyes. "I promise you and your father shall be back in the *hutung* before autumn."

I cannot say now if I truly believed the words I said, but they were enough, sufficient at least to propel Nina back to the Grand, arm-in-arm with Lijun, to bake more loaves of bread.

As it turned out, my words preceded some of the most terrible days of the siege. They were stifling and endless, they scratched and chafed at our collective patience. We lost lives at a steady pace as our lines of defense around the Legation Quarter continued to fall back. Friday the thirteenth of July marked the blackest day of our internment: Prince Su's palace came under sustained attack and two mines exploded in the French Legation, leaving behind a single, dismembered foot as the only evidence of the lives of two sailors. This made for a most miserable Bastille Day for the French; I spent the fourteenth at the Su mansion alongside a host of soldiers of various nationalities who had come to offer some respite to the Japanese after days of heavy fighting. When I returned to the hotel in the late afternoon, Nina peppered me with questions about the welfare of those at the palace, but I could not bring myself to tell her of the disease I had witnessed within its walls, the lingering shadow of death cast across every corner of Su's formerly august and majestic residence.

It was on Sunday morning that Oscar Fairchild once against visited the hotel. I had woken early to collect Nina: on Sundays the bakers started earlier than usual, the Chinese at the Grand were Christians after all, and they wished to worship later with their peers. La Contessa had stayed the previous night with me in the hotel, and as she fixed a diamond to her left ear she noted with soft wonderment: "Mr Fairchild. He is entering the hotel."

"Christ." I swung my legs out of bed; my feet met the wooden floor. "He has come again."

"Is he in the habit of coming here?" Chiara asked, the diamonds in her ear glinting in the gentle light of morning as she turned to me. I thought again how beautiful she was, how much life she continued to exude. She couldn't possibly have been as vibrant and vital as she had been a month earlier, hunger and desperation must have ebbed at her resources of energy and optimism, but perhaps she appeared to shine brighter as the world around us dimmed. How fortunate I was, I thought, to have found such a woman, unafraid to rise from the bed by her husband's and to steal through the darkness to offer me intimacy and hope.

"You must not say anything," I said, joining her by the window.

"I am in no position to judge," she said, stepping away from the window and wrapping her arms around me. "I suppose we had better wait for him to leave."

"He shan't leave before we do," I said. "I imagine he shall wait for me to return with Miss Ward. Very clever, installing himself in the hotel before she arrives, coming here as dawn breaks and there is no one to witness his arrival."

"Well, I have seen him now," La Contessa said simply. "And I see him sometimes, late at night, reading in the drawing room."

I descended the stairs to the lobby and intercepted Oscar on his way to the kitchen.

"Mr Fairchild," I said.

"Oh, Mr Scott." He straightened, setting his features into careful absence of expression. "I am here to make some changes to our bread order."

"I don't suppose one of your servants might have come?"

"Oh. I wanted to stretch my legs, to clear my head before the day. We have had such a terrible run this week…"

"Mr Fairchild," I said sternly. "You are here to see her, aren't you?"

He did not protest.

"I think it best for Miss Ward that you leave her be. It might also be wise for you. Politically, I mean."

We regarded one another in the hallway, quiet still in those first hours of the day.

"I suppose La Contessa agrees with you?" Mr Fairchild said archly.

I must credit his tactics; I was surprised.

"Yes, as a matter of fact she does," I replied. "I am of course somewhat freer to seek her opinions on a variety of matters, given that I am not an employee of Her Majesty's government. And there is the small fact too that La Contessa is a married woman."

"Very well," Oscar said severely. "Please pass on my regards to the bakers and request they prepare an extra loaf for us today."

"With pleasure."

"Make it two," he said.

It was approaching midnight when a knock came at my door.

I hoped it might be Chiara, but it was Hilde who waited for me; her face, usually bright with industrious cheer, appeared gray in the darkness of the corridor.

"I am sorry to disturb you so late," she said.

"Please, come in. Take a seat." I gestured to my armchair and poured her a small measure of whisky. She received it gratefully.

"Difficult day?" I asked.

"I took some of the children to the hospital," she said, her eyes focused on the bottom of her glass, seeking, as many of us did then, the light at the bottom of the well. "There is so much sickness, Mr Scott. We cannot continue in these conditions."

"I know," I said solemnly.

"I must let you sleep," she said. "I came only to speak with you of Mr Fairchild. Word reached me that he came here again this morning."

"Indeed he did."

"I do not know the particulars," Hilde said carefully. "Yet people are talking. I understand it has something to do with Miss Ward."

"Yes."

"Mr Scott, I have always cared little for the rules of society, particularly those that seek to mold the behavior of women. Yet even I see the harm such a scandal could do to a young lady like Miss Ward."

"Yes."

"We must find a way to make this problem disappear. I am no missionary myself, but we must recognize that we are in the company of the devout. I do not wish to terminate Miss Ward's activities here, but a scandal would leave me with little choice."

"Surely it hasn't come to that?" I said.

Hilde sipped her glass dry and faced with me with wearisome eyes. She had come across Phoebe Franklin earlier that day at the hospital. Phoebe had asked for Miss Ward's welfare, taking Hilde aside to tell her that some of the missionaries had expressed disapproval of Nina's intimacy with the Chinese converts living at the Grand. Nina's irreligious eccentricity might be tolerated in the name of accepting all of God's creatures, but suggestions of impropriety circled her now and such comments would only increase the closer she edged towards scandal; even her suffering at the hands of foreign soldiers at the Su palace was rewritten as a fate deserved, just the kind of thing a young woman such as Nina Ward would invite upon herself.

That there had been talk did not surprise me, though of course none of these horrified observers had taken me into their confidence. We were much together in those days, all of us, more so than any of us would have liked, but we communicated still within the confines of our social roles. Men spoke with men of military tactics and political intrigue; women spoke with women of injuries and children and sickness and, I suppose, other women. I suspected God's most loyal servants might prove even more severe in these moments in their condemnation of others.

"Mr Scott," Hilde continued. "I wondered if I might talk with Miss Ward. Of course I do not enjoy a friendship with her as you do. Yet perhaps as a woman…"

"Please speak to her," I said firmly. "I have tried, and she does not wish to discuss the matter with me."

"Very well." Hilde rose. At the door she paused and turned to me, her smile unconvinced. "I shall try my best, Mr Scott, but I fear that a fence makes love more keen."

XI

HILDE WAS a resolutely capable woman. Her skills may have resided more in the practical than the emotional realm, yet she harnessed the same expansive energy and straightforward confidence in addressing the question of Nina and Oscar with which she approached all other areas of life. Handing me my customary cup of coffee the next morning she vowed that she would speak with Nina before night fell, determining to approach her in that most quiet moment of the afternoon, the lull between lunch and the reawakening of the spirit at dusk, that hushed hour when the bakers grew drowsy and their orders tailed off, and invite young Nina to her room for a cup of tea.

I did not doubt Hilde's ability to achieve anything she might set her mind to, and yet when I collected Nina from the lobby that evening I saw that whatever Hilde might have said to Nina appeared to have wrought little impression upon her. If any shift in demeanor was notable it was that Nina appeared perhaps a little more animated than she had in recent days, greeting me with easy amiability and rising nimbly to her feet when I crossed the hall towards her.

"Good evening, Mr Scott," Hilde said drily from behind the bar, not looking up as I approached.

A more frivolous character might have felt some temptation to glance meaningfully in my direction, to raise an eyebrow or twitch a lip in veiled significance, but Hilde only continued her duties, tidying and ordering behind the bar, politely asking the refugee children who crawled and played on the floor to move aside.

And Nina offered no further clue as to what may have passed between the two women, not on our walk through the Legation Quarter, where she made idle chit-chat about the day's bread orders, nor over dinner, where she enacted her now habitual caricature of normality. I must admit that at some point I may have stopped searching for signs, distracted as I was by La Contessa, who glittered and charmed her way through the meal, and allowed the sole of her shoe to brush against my ankle just once, rewarding me with a careful smile when I met her eye. The disappointment, then, was bitter, when she passed me in the drawing room and murmured in low tones: "Not tonight".

"Why?" I returned, but she had passed me and approached Miss Price and Mrs Moore, laughing heartily as she joined their conversation.

"Talking to yourself, Alistair? I thought I was the only old man here quite mad enough for that."

Nicholas stood before me, hands clasped behind his back in his habitual, rather hesitant, social stance. When made to endure the company of others, my old friend could not hide his displeasure and discomfort at spending time away from his work; he seldom drank alcohol at dinners or parties, and certainly would never cradle a glass between his slender, academic fingers whilst engaging in witty repartee. Nicholas could not muster a false laugh no matter how great the effort at humor on the part of his interlocutor and he was given to frequently abandoning conversations, leaving acquaintances halfway through a trailing sentence as he ambled cheerily alone to some quiet corner. I was therefore not surprised by his bemused posture at the after-dinner gathering, but I was most pleased to see he had put aside his work for an hour or so to join the fray. He talked pleasantly of his book, detailing his latest thoughts on Boxer practices of spirit possession, and complained chummily of the heat while we edged warily around any subject approaching the polemical, skimming quite unusually over the topic of Nina, who was engaged only a few feet away in discussion with Phoebe Franklin about the health of those at the Su palace. My exchange with Nicholas felt congenial and fairly unrestrained, marking something, I might have said, of a return to our old footing. And so despite the disappointment I felt in knowing that La Contessa would not join me later and that I would lie restlessly alone while the Boxers burned their torches and chanted their threats, I left with a gently flourishing lightness of spirit.

Hilde waited for me at the Grand, poured me an unsparing serving of whisky immediately upon arrival and asked me to follow her. We ascended stairs at the opposite side of the building to where my room was located, and crossed a plain wooden landing, free from the brass antiques, jade ornaments and heavy, floral lampshades that filled the other corners of the hotel, and reached the doorway to what was Hilde's bedroom. I was unsurprised by the sparseness of room: the practical wooden table, the unadorned bedspread, the bare walls all matched the pragmatism of Hilde's character, but I was rather astonished that our meeting was taking place in that most intimate of settings.

"Might we not have gone to Edward's office?" I asked as she closed the door definitely behind me.

"It is better that we speak here," she said quietly, lighting a single lamp. "Edward does not know of this. He is in his office now, looking at the books." She sighed. "I have told him that while somebody might make money from this war, it certainly shall not be us."

She removed her gun from its holster and placed it upon the table, gestured for me to sit in a straight-backed chair, which wobbled unsteadily as I sat. There was nowhere else to sit but the bed, and Hilde forwent this option, standing solemnly before me.

"I spoke with Miss Ward," she said carefully, each word leaden, considered and heavy upon her tongue.

"And?"

"It is worse than I had imagined." She paced slowly across the room, turned when she reached one austere wall, retraced her steps.

"Please, Hilde, sit."

She shook her head.

"Miss Ward is in love," she said finally. "She is buoyed by promises, the most irresponsible, devilish promises, made by Mr Fairchild. He has told her he shall divorce his wife."

"Divorce his wife?" I stood now too. The words spluttered forth without thought; divorce was unthinkable, unimaginable for a man like Fairchild. The most noble of English families could not survive such scandal; an official in the narrow social confines of Peking would be utterly ruined by such a misstep. "What nonsense."

"Quite. I explained to Miss Ward that Mrs Fairchild is held in high esteem, that she had already lost a family in India to cholera, and that neither she nor her compatriots would stand for her to lose a second husband."

I sat, took a deep but unsatisfying sip of whisky. Hilde moved now to her bed, perched herself uneasily upon on its edge.

"And what did she say?" I asked.

"That she was sorry, that it had never been her intention to become mixed up in gossip and tittle-tattle, that she had never asked Mr Fairchild to come to the hotel. She has tried to finish it, she says, but he persists. She feels very alone, almost under attack from those around her. Every word she speaks is wrong, everything she thinks is at odds with them. In him she finds understanding."

"That's one way to say it," I said, the words bitter in my mouth.

Hilde bowed her head, folded her hands across her lap.

"I have proposed that she invite Mr Fairchild to the hotel tomorrow. We shall find them a quiet place to speak and then she can tell him finally to leave her be. I thought she might speak with him in your room; no one might object to her coming to see an old family friend."

"My room?" I understood Hilde's logic, but felt apprehension at any complicity in bringing the pair together, even if the ultimate aim in doing so were to cleave them apart.

"She cannot speak with him at home. Die Wände haben Ohren, as we say in Germany."

"The walls have ears."

"Precisely. Here there are only our ears. And our lips shall remain sealed."

"And Edward?"

Hilde shrugged.

"He ought to understand. After all, I was betrothed to our neighbor Stefan when a strange Englishman came to stay at the local inn and persuaded me to follow him to China. He ought to know that the heart is an untamed beast, but he can be quite proper about such matters. It is better that he doesn't know."

How I missed La Contessa that night, how I desired the mollifying effect of her kisses, the mind-clearing impression of her touch. Sleeplessly I pondered Hilde's plan, sitting by the window in the solitary midnight blue of my lonely room, watching the curled streets beyond the Tartar walls glimmer and blink red by the light of lanterns, tracing the waves of torches held aloft by the murderous Boxers, listening for the gunshots, the rat-a-tat-tat, the drumbeat of death, the anthem of our sorry summer. Whisky only confused my thoughts, swelling my anxieties, unformed, unnamed, but uncomfortably present. Of course we must help Nina. I had been trying, rather unsuccessfully, to do so since she first crossed the border from her old life to the unfamiliar Legation Quarter with its unvoiced rules and damning judgements, since I had first seen her form coherent, sympathetic arguments as to why the Boxers might have felt compelled to attack foreigners in the most barbarous ways, and watched how her empathy, her straddling of two worlds, her simple ability to hold and examine two opposing ideas in her mind at one time, provoked rejection and rebuttal and forced upon her a profound examination of identity to which there was no simple resolution.

And Fairchild, solid, respectable Fairchild, must have seemed the most implacable, the most unwavering mast to which one lost at sea might pin his colors. My anger towards him simmered in the darkness, frothing and boiling by the time the sun appeared on the horizon, coloring my room a dusty orange. Allow me to make absolutely clear that I have no issue with men seducing women (how else might the world continue to spin?) and that it is a sport in which I have much partaken myself. Yet injustice enrages me, it is endless, tireless, present in every wretched place I have visited on this Earth, a fungus that grows and spreads and clings unbidden to every corner in which it lands, and never will I accept it. All is fair in love and war, as England's fair bard observed, but my sympathies lie with Burns, that where you feel your honor grip, let that aye be your border. A man might battle a fair opponent, might lie to a cheat and deceive a tyrant, but to take advantage of one who comes to war unarmed...well, nothing disgusts me more.

In the brilliant blue light of early morning, the knock upon my door was hesitant. I opened it, saw on the threshold the melancholy beauty of Nina, felt pity at the care she had taken over her appearance. Her hair was neatly coiled and plaited in a style I had observed worn by Beatrice Moore and Lillian Price. Her dress, of stiff white silk and embroidered with blue lilies and green bamboo, was neatly pressed. She gave off a light scent of soap as she stepped into the room and looked around her, taking in the collected belongings upon my dresser, my comb, the novel I had tried and failed to read over the past three weeks, the candle burnt to a twisted stump.

"Good morning, Alistair," she said.

"Hello, Nina."

Uneasily we regarded one another. We were habitually generous with our words, our conversation ebbed and flowed, but never halted. Silence had never before stood between us; now we were both unforthcoming.

"Thank you," she said eventually, and crossed the room to the window. The Legation Quarter was quiet that morning, its residents were weary, deprived of sleep, their last hopes were withered and threatened to break.

"Well, I shall leave you now," I said. I feared speaking more, worried that any spoken admission of what was to take place would somehow make my involvement real, irreversible. As I closed the door behind me, I thought not of Nina, but of Nicholas, content in his ignorance, steeped in words, his mind and heart occupied by the drought that had ravaged the Chinese countryside, the imperial forces that had speared China's pride, and all the while unknowing, unbelieving, unconcerned by his own daughter's ruin, her future as bleak, as unknown, as unthinkable as that of the condemned villages burned to the ground by the Boxers. I have done a good deed, I told myself, descending the stairs. I have done what is best for Nina.

I could not look at Fairchild when he arrived at the hotel and passed through the lobby with easy stride, greeting me in warm tones. I left the Grand immediately and walked to the message board by the chapel in an unproductive search for news. I paced the streets as a beast caged, how small, how narrow, how constricting they felt now, under the mocking openness of the sky. I walked almost unseeing: the Legation Quarter was so familiar that I knew its every wall, pockmarked by bullets, recognized its every residence, filled with desperate, ravenous guests, circled its dismal tennis courts, empty of matches for the best part of a month. So naturally the presence of something unfamiliar startled me, shocked my eyes from their dull reverie. At the mouth of an alleyway stood a cart laden with fruit. Only a hungry man can truly appreciate the exterior of food, only a body denied the sweet, fresh pleasures of fruit could laud the ripe, promising roundness of the watermelon, describe the lush shade of forest green that colors its skin, rhapsodize of its hinted taste, imagine the blissful dissolving of its flesh in one's mouth. Only a man as hungry as I would launch himself unthinking towards the cart and reach unrestrained for one of those tender, full-bodied fruits. A foot away, I stopped myself, scanned the ground for some trap, with my rational mind instructed my physical self to wait. A Chinese man by the cart nodded his encouragement.

"A truce," he called. "They have called a truce and given us fruit!"

Euphoric refugees began to crowd around the cart, grabbing for the watermelons.

"From the Empress Dowager herself," the man said. "We shall live!"

Hastily I took a fruit for myself and hurried back to the hotel, presented the watermelon with delight to Hilde.

"Fairchild's gone," she said. "I shall ask them to cut this for us in the kitchen."

"They say the Chinese have called a truce," I said. "Are you not pleased?"

"I shall withhold judgment," Hilde said, turning from me with the watermelon cradled under one arm. "This is not the first time we have been promised liberty."

The door to my room was wide open. I had rather hoped to find Nina alone, to tell her the good news of the ceasefire and to hear from her that the affair was ended, but instead she sat upon my bed, hair loose and fanned around her shoulders, with Lijun by her side. Both ate watermelon, a plate of slender rinds sat on the bed between them.

"I see you have made yourselves comfortable," I said.

"Oh, I'm sorry Alistair. Lijun brought me some watermelon and we couldn't wait to eat it."

Hastily she rose from the bed, came towards me and offered a slice of the ripe, red fruit. I noticed that tears still dampened the corners of her eyes. I took the watermelon from her, my teeth broke the fleshy core of the fruit, its juice gathered around my chin with that first tentative bite. And then I devoured it, each swallow hungrier and less satisfying than the last until I was left only with the melon rind and a faint sense of nausea.

Oh, were we weary by then. It was not that we did not wish to believe that a truce had been offered to us, but only that we were by that late stage far beyond belief and trust and the old civilized ideal of taking a gentleman or an Empress at their word. And so we ate their fruit, but we did not swallow their words.

Oscar Fairchild decided to take advantage of the suspension in combat by going to inspect the Chinese defenses along the Tartar wall and, to my surprise, he invited me to accompany him on this look-see. I had rather planned to use the unforeseen period of peace to attempt to find a messenger who might deliver my writings to the nearest place from which telegraphs might be sent, but I am a curious man, and Oscar offered a fascinating study. And so together we admired the Tartar Wall in its solid glory, ascended it and traversed its ramparts; after just twenty minutes of inspection we were stopped by a Chinese commander in Manchu military regalia, who called to us from the other side of the wall. He held his hands out to indicate that he approached in peace. An impressive man, tall and broad, his skin was colored the deep hue of one who had battled in the back blocks of the Manchu empire.

"Gentlemen," he said. "I mean no harm. I have only a small favor to ask."

Oscar stiffened as the commander approached. His uniform confirmed my conjecture: the man before us was a leader of the fiercest tribe of imperial troops, the Kansu braves, celebrated for their swift and bloody repression of a Muslim uprising in that province in 1895, a display of ruthlessly efficient bloodshed that had earned them the status of permanent defenders of the imperial capital.

"Go on," I said in Chinese.

"I respectfully ask your permission to collect the bodies of our men. We lost them in early July." He gestured across the barricade to a pile of corpses, already mostly rotten and smothered with black flies. "We wish to bury them."

I translated the commander's request. Oscar paused. His fingers danced over his mustache and I expected he might decline.

"Of course he may," he said to me, and stepped aside to let the man cross the barricade.

The commander whistled and a number of his men climbed over the barricade and jumped to the ground, where they proceeded to gather the bodies of their peers with no discernible sentiment. Theirs was an unenviable task: as they transferred body parts over the wall limbs and bones fell away, one skull hit the ground on the Chinese side with a definite thud.

"Terrible to see," Oscar commented as we watched the Kansu Braves roll their peers in straw mats, which they balanced on their shoulders to carry over the wall. When the soldiers had finished their grisly task, the commander thanked us with a respectful bow and made to descend the wall back to the Chinese city.

"Tell him to wait, will you?" Oscar said to me, suddenly urgent.

I relayed the message. The man wavered.

"I only wish to speak with him a moment," Oscar explained. He removed a cigar from his jacket and offered it to the commander, who gingerly accepted the gift, holding it between calloused fingers and eyeing it with the healthy suspicion of a man with many enemies. "Ask him to sit with us."

The commander assented and sat beside us atop the barricade. Oscar lit the man's cigar and smoked one himself. I translated the two men's words as they smoked, the rich, woody scent of their cigars assuaged somewhat the stench of death that pervaded the lines of defense. The commander asked Oscar who the men were who wore strange hats; Oscar and I deduced that he spoke of the American marines.

"We are most afraid of them," he admitted. "We have lost a great many men to these men in hats."

"Alistair, tell him that we only seek to defend ourselves. That we did not wish to fight the Imperial army, but to protect ourselves from the Boxers." Oscar raised the cigar to his lips, his stare fixed on the commander.

"I am under the command of Jung Lu," the commander replied. "He wishes to cease fighting. Perhaps you might write to him and explain your position. You are an important man, are you not?"

"An interesting idea," Oscar said thoughtfully.

The commander shrugged and took a last inhale of his cigar. Both men rose on either side of me and marked the end of their exchange with a warm handshake. The commander disappeared back to his side of the wall, turning only once to glance at us as he retreated.

"How strange," Oscar said. "Yet somehow reassuring."

We continued along the Tartar wall; the clear, unobstructed view of Peking beyond our walls revealed the true nature of the peril we had faced over the past weeks. Of course we had known that the numbers of Chinese troops had swelled, that the Boxers had been joined by soldiers with powers of strategy and conflict far beyond their grassroots peasant abilities, but we had not known just how many soldiers flush with imperial colors peopled the low-lying rooftops that lay just beyond the Legation Quarter borders.

"Do you know," Oscar said to me, surveying the milling masses beyond the wall, "I really might write to Jung Lu. I don't suppose it can do any harm."

"Mr Fairchild," I said. "Did you ask me to accompany you for any reason this morning?"

Oscar considered this.

"Beyond your excellent Chinese skills and the hope that you might write of the exhaustive efforts of the British crown to protect its subjects under siege?"

"Beyond that," I said.

"I only hoped that we might be friends," Oscar returned. "Sometimes I fear that you have rather a mistaken impression of me, Mr Scott, and I consider it my duty to counter that."

"Mr Fairchild," I said, "we may have had our differences, but

I trust that they have now been resolved."

"Indeed." Briskly he extended his hand to shake mine and smiled warmly. "Good day, Mr Scott."

Oscar made good on his promise. He returned to his office and immediately addressed a letter to Jung Lu in which he proposed a new set of rules for any future battle, vowing, in a most generous pledge to the Imperials, that foreign soldiers would no longer shoot at the Manchu troops unless in retaliation. Oscar sent one of his servants to deliver the message to the commander we had met; given the suspension in fighting the household staff was now unafraid to wander the Legation Quarter and even take a few steps outside it. Sure enough, the next day the Kansu Braves paraded a flag along the wall announcing a truce. A letter from Jung Lu accepted Oscar's proposals.

To paint this as a diplomatic victory for Oscar would be too much, to *blow cattle*, as the Chinese might say. You or I might see his actions as just and noble and consider the waving of a flag on the Tartar wall an accomplishment that belonged rightfully to him, but it soon became evident that even in that period of supposed peace, circumstances changed hourly. Clearly some of the Imperials possessed a genuine desire to bring about an end to fighting, but there existed no unifying view across their varied ranks. Sporadic firing still took place and no other officers displayed the friendly overtures of the cigar-smoking commander. Nevertheless, spirits in the Legation Quarter remained buoyant: residents were free to wander as they pleased and many organized trips to the outermost reaches of the district, seizing this opportunity to peek out at the now unknown city beyond our walls. One afternoon I came across Lillian Price and Hugo Lovell at the Hanlin, alternately pressing their faces through a hole blown in one of the institution's old walls. Animatedly they gestured for me to observe the scene on the other side: a frieze of Boxers in battle. It took me a moment to realize that the Boxers were all slain, so anguished and alive were their faces. Their mouths were twisted in their final cries, their limbs were stretched long in combat, their garish red turbans were still affixed atop their heads.

"I have never been so close to a Boxer," Lillian said breathlessly. "How fierce they look even in death!"

"How are your injuries, Mr Lovell?" I asked the young interpreter.

"Much improving. I hope to be well enough to fight if necessary," he said.

"Oh, no," Lillian said, and took a step closer to him. "I insist, Mr Scott, that he must stop this talk of combat. I couldn't stand to lose him, not after…."

Hugo cleared his throat.

"Miss Price, we each must play our part. I already feel quite useless." He lifted his chin. "The kittens. Come."

"Kittens?" I repeated.

"Yes, Mr Lovell has found some abandoned kittens in a corner of the Hanlin. The mother must have died and left them. He says they're very sweet," Lillian explained.

"Of course," I said, shaking my head. "Kittens."

And so they left me alone with the Boxers, agonized, fearsome and terribly, terribly young, even in death.

At the hotel, I stopped by the bakery, where Nina proved more industrious than ever. The peace agreement had resulted in the availability of foods within the Legation Quarter that had been the content of wild, hungry dreams just days earlier. Eggs, fruit and even chicken, that soft, delicious meat, so easy to digest, had poured across Legation Quarter borders via enemy soldiers moonlighting as market vendors. Eggs, naturally, had proved the most useful ingredient in the bakery's activities and I discovered Nina and Lijun absorbed in the baking of a fruit cake.

"Good afternoon," I said from the doorway.

Nina greeted me with brilliant smile.

"Good afternoon, Mr Scott. What luxuries we enjoy!"

"What a delicious-looking cake. I am afraid to say I salivate just looking at it," I said. This was not hyperbole; the human body responds to starvation with an acute physicality that reminds one of how little separates us from the animals. "And how are conditions at Su's palace?" I asked Lijun.

Su's quarters [??], close to the hotel but existing in a lower chamber of hell, had become a burden of the conscience for me. I more than anyone knew that the British Empire was not built on hand-holding and respect for the natives, and that in even thinking of protecting Chinese lives I had done more than one might expect of a man in my position, but still I could not close my eyes to the suffering of the converts, knowing that I had taken them to Su's palace. Then it had seemed infinitely preferable to house them there than to see them squabble for survival on the streets, and no doubt I had prevented a handful of deaths in delivering them to the gates of the palace. Yet how many had passed to the next world within those walls?

"Poor," Lijun said simply. "More babies have died. They are so small. We go without food to provide for them, but still…they are so small…"

"Well, we must increase supplies to the palace," I said. "With the ceasefire there's no excuse for anyone to go hungry."

"Mr Samuels has been serving Qing soldiers tea," Nina said. "They popped over the wall and told us they were thirsty."

"Consorting with the enemy, eh?"

"They bring us watermelons every day," Nina said. "At a price, of course, but we appreciate it. Today they offered us a discount on rifles along with our watermelons."

I left the girls in the sweet-smelling bakery to retire to my room. I passed Hilde in the reception area, where she served bread and meat to half a dozen refugee families.

"Mr Scott," she called. "A word, please?"

With a polite nod towards the family on the floor she followed me to the foot of the stairs. "Perhaps we might go to your room?"

"Well, really, Mrs Samuels. I didn't expect a proposition before nightfall."

This roused only a feeble laugh from Hilde.

"I would like to speak with you alone," she said seriously.

We entered my room, where Hilde stood awkwardly, with an uncharacteristic air of uncertainty.

"I wish to speak with you of Miss Ward and the… arrangement we made the other day," she stated.

"Please, take a seat." I gestured to the armchair. "Too early for whisky?"

She declined the offer, but I poured myself a serve.

"As I have made clear to you in previous discussions, Mr Scott, I do not consider myself an arbiter of right and wrong. I do not pass judgement on the decisions of others, least of all their romantic choices. Here I am in Peking, thousands of miles from home. Had I married Stefan, I might never have seen a Boxer." Stiffly she sat herself upon the armchair. "I will come out with it. Miss Ward's problem continues."

"Impossible. I saw Fairchild just today and we agreed that all had been resolved. The meeting served its purpose, did it not?"

"No," Hilde said simply. "The meeting appears to have rather inflamed the situation. Miss Ward looks like one very much in love. She is so light, so happy. I fear she may do something… something reckless."

"You mean she may try to meet Mr Fairchild again?" I asked.

"Precisely. And it is not only that; I worry that she is becoming careless. One of the converts told me they had heard her teaching Lijun love poems in Chinese."

"Poetry in and of itself isn't dangerous," I countered.

"No, but it is a symptom of danger, Mr Scott."

"In that case, what do you propose?"

Hilde took a deep breath, filled her chest with the stale air of my little room.

"I believe we have two options, Mr Scott. The first is for you to speak directly with Mr Fairchild and advise that he keep his distance."

"And have him circumvent the truth once more," I said.

What an optimistic fool I had been, walking along the Tartar wall with him, shaking his hand, thinking we had come to a gentlemen's agreement, reaching an accord with gestures rather than words, when all the while I had been cheerily complicit in his continued seduction of Nina.

"And there is no reason to believe he would listen to my advice. If the man had a modicum of sense he would never have approached Nina in the first place."

"Quite. That brings me to my second idea. We allow them to conduct this... affair... here in the hotel. We contain the risk."

"Mrs Samuels," I choked. "I am not easily shocked, but you have succeeded where even cannibalism has failed."

Hilde met my gaze squarely, and returned directly to the matter.

"Mr Scott, we must think of Nina. She is naive, she is innocent, she possesses the imprudent arrogance of youth. She will not be dissuaded easily, she does not realize that her very honor rests on this affair. I more than anyone wish that she might have fallen in love with Mr Lovell, even some American soldier, but the heart is not a rational master."

She stood.

"I see I have alarmed you."

"Mrs Samuels, Nicholas Ward is one of my oldest friends in Peking. I could not do such a thing in good faith."

"In that case," Hilde said. "I implore you to speak with Mr Fairchild."

"I will," I said.

"Then it is decided." Hilde moved towards the door. "You are a man of words, Mr Scott. Convince him. For Nina."

"And for us."

What a plight Hilde set before me. What undeniable shambles we had orchestrated in our attempts to protect Nina. Blankly I looked to the wall opposite me, my mind so crowded with thoughts that I could not distinguish a single idea amongst them. I felt dread in its most physical of forms: leaden stomach, torpid limbs, numb anguish of an approaching headache. A second whisky cleared my thoughts a little, and brought one to the fore: Nicholas, dear old Nicholas, I could not betray him. I must speak to Fairchild, and end the wretched thing once and for all.

That evening I walked with Nina through the Legation Quarter towards the Fairchild household. She held the cake she had baked with Lijun in front of her chest, balancing it across two careful palms while taking even, attentive steps around the rubble strewn across the streets. Peace had descended, we were told, but it seemed bad luck to clear away any signs of the conflict so soon, a temptation too far for fickle Fate, and so the detritus of war, the crumbled bricks and blood-soaked garments, the mangy dogs and abandoned weapons, littered every pathway. I watched Nina for signs of the character-altering love Hilde had described. She seemed happy, that was certain, and a smile teased the corners of her mouth each time she spoke, but she did not strike me as entirely unheeding, indeed she appeared balanced, sanguine, controlled.

"You are content," I observed.

"Naturally. The truce has cheered me considerably," she said. "I suppose now we might even survive the summer."

"One hopes so."

I wished to speak of Oscar; the idea of going behind her back and to the man directly sat uneasily with me, but half-formed words remained dry and sour in my mouth. We arrived as the servants were preparing to serve supper: a comparative feast of broiled chicken, tinned beans and fried potatoes. Nina proudly handed over her cake to the staff: today's dessert would be more than a cigarette drawn out as long as the breath would allow. We had all grown slimmer in the last weeks, but I noticed as Nina talked with the servants that the meagre diet seemed to suit her. Her collarbones gleamed through the delicate skin at the base of her neck and the flatness of her cheeks set her green eyes in keen relief. I saw then the change Hilde had witnessed: Nina's body was deprived, yet her heart gorged itself on love.

We ate that night until sated, an unusual feeling in those days, and my full stomach left me quite uncomfortable. I had rather forgotten the sensation of a curved belly straining against buttons. I asked Oscar then if I might have a moment with him.

"I have heard some news today that may be of interest to you," I said.

"Let us retire to my study," he suggested.

Nina watched us leave, and I avoided her eye.

Oscar took a seat behind his desk and offered me a cigar. I accepted it gratefully, and let him light it for me.

"You have heard some rumors today, Mr Scott? I heard some news of the approaching troops myself, but I fear it was more wishful thinking than accurate intelligence."

"Not rumors, I'm afraid. Facts."

"Concerning...?" Oscar's smile was affable, his demeanor relaxed.

"Something rather more personal," I said, my tone light.

"Go on," Oscar said, his cigar suspended mid-air.

"Mrs Samuels and I are rather concerned about your relationship with Miss Ward."

Oscar's brow, youthful and unlined, creased.

"You must realize, Mr Fairchild, that I am privy to the facts," I continued. "After all, my room was provided as a meeting place for you and Miss Ward just a few days ago. Mrs Samuels believes that the meeting we organized with the purpose of definitively severing your relations reached a rather different conclusion." I paused, watched for his reaction.

Oscar shifted back in his chair, his cigar glowed unattended in his right hand.

"Mr Scott, I appreciate your concern. And your frankness," Oscar said. "They say the Scots are rather more direct than the English."

"Perhaps only a Scot and a German could broach this delicate subject," I said.

In truth, Oscar's statement had irritated me. It was designed to wrong-foot, to suggest that I had no right to meddle in his affairs, it was an elegant way for him to deny my judgment. And yet, did not the Boxers want us both returned as piles of ashes to the same queen?

Oscar remained silent, his cigar bled silver ash to the floor.

"Mr Fairchild, I have no desire to make you uncomfortable," I said. "You must understand that current circumstances are entirely untenable. I have chosen to speak with you not only because of my deep concern and affection for Miss Ward, but also because I recognize the danger such an affair might pose to your own career."

"Mr Scott." Oscar leaned forward, blue eyes cold now, warm congeniality disappeared. "I appreciate your concern. If I may speak in confidence, I plan to divorce my wife."

"Good God!" I said. "I thought that was only some nonsense you had said to placate Nina. A man of your position cannot divorce his wife, especially not a wife so treasured, a woman who has already lost so much. I know we live in extraordinary times, but once we are finally liberated we shall be obliged to return to normal society. And society favors Violet over Nina, you must know that. And what of Nina's prospects? This situation will likely ruin any chances of a good marriage for her."

"Nina does not wish to marry."

"Come now, that is nothing more than the silly talk of a young girl. She is a woman now, and she must marry. Let us be sensible."

Oscar sank back into his chair and took a puff on his cigar, his eyes not wavering in close observation of my movements.

A knock at the door announced a servant, who entered with head bowed. He apologized for the interruption as he crossed the room and set down a plate on Oscar's desk. A small apple tartlet sat neatly atop the dish, its surface dusted with sugar.

"What is the meaning of this?" Oscar asked.

"Miss Ward asked me to give it to you after dinner."

The servant dipped his head and departed. Oscar and I remained silent until the servant had closed the door behind him.

"Well," I said. "I suppose this proves my very point. Has Miss Ward served everyone an apple tartlet?"

"Perhaps," Oscar countered. "Perhaps they are all eating tarts downstairs."

"Then where is mine?" I tried to sound authoritative, in control, but frustration tinted the edges of my voice. I had come to tell Oscar to leave Nina be, to ask him to make a clean, graceful exit from her life before their affair damaged her future prospects. Instead I found myself tangled in my own words, my arguments lost in the plain nonsense of divorces and puddings. Oscar lifted the dessert fork from the side of the plate and cut tentatively into the tart, which crumbled from its core, spilling pastry fragments across the plate. We both stared as the small cake fell apart; tucked inside its fleshy heart was a neatly rolled piece of paper. Oscar removed the paper with careful fingers, unravelled it and read the handwritten note. I could not distinguish its contents from my position.

"Well." I stood. "I should take my leave, Mr Fairchild. I hope you shall consider my words."

"Thank you, Mr Scott." Oscar rose from behind his desk and shook my hand with a grip firm and steady. I turned to go, and he spoke again. "Suppose, Mr Scott, we are all slaughtered within the week. Wouldn't it be a shame not to have lived in the days preceding death?"

I kept walking.

I descended the stairs to delighted squeals that emanated from the drawing room. I peered around the doorway and saw Lillian Price in the center of the room, her skirts arranged around her on the Persian carpet.

"Isn't she precious?" Lillian trilled. In her lap was curled a kitten, its white fur dotted with black blotches. Nina knelt on the floor beside Lillian and the new arrival, her fingers reached nervously towards the kitten's emaciated body.

I slipped into the room and observed the assembled guests unnoticed. Nicholas turned the pages of a Chinese newspaper while Phoebe and La Contessa watched the two girls and the kitten. Pietro Mancini smoked in an armchair, his eyes fixed on the red sky setting beyond the Tartar wall. The kitten took a step towards Nina, nuzzled an inquisitive nose against her hand, then shrank away.

"Mr Scott!" Lillian said, catching sight of me. "Have you seen our new pet?"

"Is this not rather an odd time to adopt another mouth to feed?" I asked.

"She is so small, Mr Scott, she doesn't want for much. Besides, we have food for the moment. The poor little thing was living in a hole in a wall without a mother. I thought it only right I do what I could to protect it." Lillian pressed the kitten against her chest and kissed the top of a downy ear. "I have named her Liberty," she said.

"Very nice," I said, though the name moved me little. I felt that the naming of the infant Siege had been quite sentimental enough. Over Lillian's head I caught Chiara's eye, she offered me a barely perceptible shake of the head. I bowed and left, noticing that Nina did not look in my direction as I departed.

At the Grand I found Hilde finishing the last of a glass of gin in the bar. She poured me a nightcap and we retired to my room, where I told her of my meeting with Oscar.

"And?" she asked. "He will stay away from her?"

"I am afraid not." I sighed, swirling the whisky in my glass. "He tells me that he plans to divorce his wife; such nonsense as I have never heard."

Hilde shook her head, her teeth worried her bottom lip.

"Yet we must recognize that this folly is not his alone. A servant delivered a tart to him while I was present, inside was a message from Nina. A little note, rolled up and baked into a tart."

"Romance," Hilde said without feeling.

"Clearly neither party is prepared to abandon this affair," I continued. "And I quite understand their individual positions. Nina is naive and unprepared, Fairchild is intelligent and knowledgeable of our true circumstances. Any rational man in his role would have calculated by now that there is a very distinct possibility that our rescuers lie bloody and dead in a desolate field somewhere to the east of the city. He knows that while the Imperials sell us chickens and fly white flags, they also work through the night to strengthen their defenses. He believes there is a real chance of not making it out of Peking alive, and sees no harm in living his last days with joyous carelessness."

I lifted my glass; with disappointment I noticed that it was already emptied.

"What can we do?" she asked.

"Perhaps you might speak once more with Nina. I daresay she is more sensible than the First Secretary."

"May I propose again my other solution?" Hilde's finger circled her glass. "I know it sounds unorthodox, but helping them to conduct their affair in secrecy would protect Nina from the damage such a situation might inflict on her future prospects."

"Mrs Edwards! You must see that to do such a thing would be wrong."

"Only God may judge," she said simply.

"Yes, God and His Earthly followers, whom, it appears, are rather harsh arbiters. The risk to Nina is too great, Hilde."

"Precisely. The risk is huge, which is why we must seek to contain it." Hilde placed her hand on my forearm. "Left alone, there is no guarantee that either Miss Ward or Mr Fairchild will act with propriety. We could provide them with a meeting place in the hotel, take messages from one to the other, create false stories to stop the rumors."

"The risk remains," I said, shaking my head.

"There are none so reckless as lovers," Hilde said, "but lovers who expect to die."

XII

BEFORE I RECOUNT, then, the most shameful aspects of my conduct during the siege, permit me the small indulgence of an explanation. I grasp desperately to defend myself, I know, but I cannot set down on paper the following events without at least a little justification. It was wrong, I knew that as soon as Hilde said it, and yet I believed that no other option remained. Fairchild was ambitious, conscientious, dependable – a model official under normal circumstances, just as Nina was bright and shrewd and protected in her habitual environment. The alchemy of the rebellion, the surety of approaching catastrophe, altered each in turn, and bound them together in chains of the Boxers' making. And so I assented to a course of action I feared might ruin Nina, knowing reluctantly that while the potential for scandal in this plan was significant, not only for Nina but also for myself and Hilde, such disgrace would be unavoidable if Nina continued unchecked on her current path. I betrayed Nicholas, I hid my deeds from Edward, and I enabled Nina to continue the ruinous affair. But I did it for them, for us. I was duplicitous and deceitful, but only to serve a higher ideal. Such is the muck and mire of human existence.

The following morning I found Nina in the kitchen chatting animatedly with Lijun; the younger girl sneaked an occasional lick of her flour-coated fingertips.

"Miss Ward," I said. "A moment, please?"

Nina wiped her hands on her apron and followed me to the

hallway.

"Let us go to my room," I suggested.

She nodded willingly enough, but I noted the slow tread of her steps on the stairs behind me.

"Nina. You must realize your relationship with Mr Fairchild cannot continue as it is," I started, pulling the door closed behind us.

Nina, crossing the room towards the window, stopped immediately. With her back to me still she said: "Not this again, Mr Scott." She turned to face me with cool expression. "I appreciate your concern, Alistair, I do, but there is nothing for us to discuss. I can manage this myself."

"Oh, how many silly girls have thought the same thing!" I said.

"What do you know of silly girls?" Nina cried. "How unfair your words are! Is Mr Fairchild not silly?"

"Believe me, Nina, I know much of silly girls. And you protest too quickly." I took a breath, prepared myself for the words, irreparable and irrevocable, that came next. "I have a proposal for you, something rather unusual, something that does not make me happy, but may save you and Mr Fairchild from this mutual madness."

"Oh, yes?" Nina's countenance softened, she dropped her hands from her hips.

"Please, sit."

The proposition fell quickly from my lips, the words rushed into one another in my desire to expel them, to have them out rapidly enough to avoid inspection, consideration of their contents.

"It has become clear to both Mrs Samuels and myself that neither you nor Mr Fairchild is prepared to terminate this ridiculous affair. Therefore, we propose not that you end the affair but rather that you conduct it only within the confines of the hotel. We will provide you with the place, the protection, everything you need to carry on with this nonsense. I need you to understand, Nina, that I disapprove absolutely of your involvement with Mr Fairchild, but your stubbornness has left me with little choice. I am indebted to your father for his friendship and I feel obliged to do all I can to protect both you and him from the more vicious rumors about your relationship with Mr Fairchild."

"Really?" Nina asked cautiously, her lips toyed with a smile. Guilt gripped me; my stomach tightened, my hands coiled to fists, my physical self could not forgive this treachery.

"Yes," I said slowly. "But you must promise to listen to me and Mrs Samuels, to take our advice, to avoid unnecessary scandal."

"I promise," she said solemnly.

"Nina. This is not in any way an endorsement of your behavior."

"I understand," she said. "Thank you, Mr Scott."

I prepared myself to speak again, but a frantic knocking at the door stopped me. Hilde did not wait for an invitation to enter the room.

"The troops are on their way!" she declared breathlessly. "I thought you would like to know right away, Mr Scott. The Japanese have received a letter."

"Really?" Naturally I had imagined this moment in my mind dozens of times, the heralding of our rescue and the possibility of life beyond the Legation Quarter walls, but the likelihood of it coming to pass had grown more faint with each passing day. I felt almost winded by the news, as though I had taken a swift punch to the gut. "When shall they arrive?"

"In the coming days," Hilde said. "Isn't it wonderful?"

"Fantastic," Nina said, though her words lacked any such

sentiment. "Such good news."

"Nina, I must go," I said. "You understand."

"Yes, yes. But what about…?"

"Don't worry, dear." Hilde placed a maternal arm around Nina's shoulders. "You and I shall discuss that matter further."

I made straight for Su's palace, where I expected the beleaguered Japanese guards might have some idea as to what was happening. The soldiers I came across belonged to the lower ranks, but were able to confirm in a halting mix of Mandarin and English that their superiors had received word that the troops would soon reach Peking. I thanked them and stepped only briefly inside the Su mansion itself, where conditions remained bleak: there I saw children whose skin seemed to melt hopelessly from their bones, women whose hair fell in sparse, desperate clumps and cockroaches and flies that covered the walls and floors, creating a hellish, crawling tableau.

"Mister!" A girl tripped across the floor towards me, her feet heavy and graceless at the end of bowed legs. "You are Miss Nina's friend?" she tried.

"Yes, yes. I am."

"I am her student," the girl said. "When will she come to teach us again?"

"Oh, I'm afraid that I don't know. She is helping at the Grand Hotel."

"Yes, yes, Lijun tells us this. But we want her!" The girl stretched a bony hand towards me, knuckles lifting her skin in cragged peaks. "You will tell her to come, please?"

"Yes." I dipped lightly in the girl's direction, suddenly desperate only to get away from her, to obliterate the image of her helpless, starving body. As I turned to leave I saw Phoebe Franklin in a corner, cradling a baby with limpid, blemished skin. I raised a hand in greeting.

From Su's palace, I went to the chapel, where, as I had expected, large numbers of Legation Quarter residents had gathered around the pavilions to corroborate the news. I pushed my way past the uniformed soldiers and red-cheeked children to a tight group of Englishmen a few feet from the noticeboard, and waited momentarily for them to open up their circle to me. Benjamin Moore was there, unsteady enough on his feet that I wondered whether he had already taken a drink in celebration. Oscar Fairchild stood at the center of the group; he watched me closely as I took my position amongst them.

"Good afternoon, Mr Scott," he said, his voice controlled and careful.

"Good afternoon, gentlemen. Now that communication channels appear to have reopened I should very much like to submit a report about the latest developments," I said. "Would you care to expand on the news received by the Japanese?"

The group repeated what the Japanese guards had attempted to tell me, that a missive addressed to Baron Nishi confirmed the fall of Tienstin. Boxers had been slaughtered in large numbers in that city, and the troops would arrive soon to liberate us just as they had our compatriots in that city less than a hundred miles to the southeast. The letter was dated the 26th of July and recorded the imminent departure of the soldiers; the delay in it reaching us suggested our liberators may already be close. Some voices dissented from the general optimism; the Americans had received rather less hopeful letters, vague and uncommitted on when exactly the soldiers would save us. Yet none could deny that this constituted something of a breakthrough: for once the whisky I took before sundown was celebratory.

The food committee wasted no time in organizing a Legation Quarter-wide meeting to evaluate supplies the next morning. Nina and I duly attended with Hilde, who came to the meeting at the Fairchild residence with an accurate list of the hotel's stockpiles; I rather suspected that she had approached the exercise with greater integrity than others had done. The room bustled with the pleasant energy of feminine diligence: all the most helpful and practical women were in attendance. These were the ladies who had been quick to criticize the weaker members of their sex who had retired to darkened rooms over the past weeks, emerging only to eat food they had played no part in preparing and to drink wine to soothe blows they had not received.

"Good morning," Phoebe Franklin started. "We would like each household to declare their stocks. We expect to be liberated within the next week to ten days, perhaps even sooner, but we must make provisions for another month in case of any further delays. In order to design the most nourishing menus for every resident of the Legation Quarter, we must first know what each one can provide."

The women gathered in a circle and spoke one by one, their tone hushed when supplies were meagre, and round and self-assured when their residence boasted more. Beatrice Moore and Lillian Price sat outside the circle, observing the calling out of each household's inventory. Beatrice whispered in Lillian's ear after each woman had announced her stocks, raising smirks or smiles from the American girl with each comment. After Kitty Bloomfield, whose verandah had so effectively shielded me and Nina from Boxer attack, read out her paltry list of jams and grains, Beatrice's comment was sharp enough to raise a laugh from Lillian. Kitty's cheeks colored, she glanced over her shoulder at the two women; Beatrice's gaze smooth and unflinching unnerved Kitty further and she folded the list in her hands over and over until it was no more than a small square in her palm. I stood by Hilde as she proudly declared her supplies of grain, dairy and spirits. Her efforts received a brief round of applause led by Phoebe.

"Quite extraordinary, when you consider the Samuels have so selflessly given over their business to the aid of refugees," Phoebe said.

"Well, we are in the business of hospitality," Hilde said, matter-of-fact. "We started with far more."

When the comparison exercise was completed, Phoebe took a moment to read her notes silently before addressing the committee.

"Unfortunately," she began. "We appear to have rather less than I had hoped. And with only three dozen ponies left, we shall struggle to provide enough meat for everyone."

"Quite," Beatrice Moore agreed, rising from her seat by Lillian and walking to the center of the room. "Where have these supplies gone?" she asked, pushing her way into the gathered circle. "I personally find the decline in wine and tobacco quite shocking. Don't you remember, Mrs Franklin, how surprised we were by the vast quantities of such items that each household possessed at the beginning of the siege? I fear not everyone has been wholly honest about their stocks." She crossed the room to sit once more, and gathered her skirts around her with pomp.

"I do not think we can blame people for drinking or smoking at a time like this," Nina said. "The stench has been quite unbearable. Tobacco helps to mask unpleasant odors."

"I cannot stand the smell of tobacco," Beatrice retorted. "And to smoke it in such quantities, at such speed when we might be here for a... a decade! A tolerance for tobacco, well, there is another thing that you and Mrs Bloomfield have in common."

Kitty Bloomfield stared intensely at her the rounded tips of her shoes peeking beyond the hem of her dress, the color in her cheeks flushing deeper. I thought of seeing her face at the window when Nina and I had taken cover on the Bloomfields' verandah, and remembered the swift appearance of Mr Moore in her place. I saw it clearly then, understood Beatrice Moore's persistent presence at the Fairchild household, her close confidence with Lillian Price, her bitter delight in gossip, her severe judgment of character and her evident, fierce dislike for Nina, and I wondered how differently events might have unfolded for Nina had Beatrice not struggled under the burden of her own private betrayal.

"That is quite enough." Phoebe raised her hand. "We are all disappointed, Mrs Moore. I shall put together a plan for the coming days. Thank you for coming, and for your honesty. Salvation comes in helping others."

The women drifted out of the room in pairs and threes, chatting to one another as they returned to their various tasks: cooking, child-minding, nursing. Nina stood by the window, her back to the departing women, her eyes fixed on the distant horizon.

La Contessa sat alone, her expression listless and faraway. I moved towards her, she smiled gently.

"Hello, Mr Scott," she said.

"La Contessa," I said, taking the seat opposite her. "How have you been?"

"Well." She tugged on the string of pearls around her neck. "It is good news, no?"

"The food committee?"

She laughed.

"That we shall be liberated."

"Naturally," I said. "Perhaps you might like to visit us at the Grand before then? The streets have been quite safe since the truce began. We have gin and, if I do say so myself, rather pleasant company."

She nodded, but her eyes were trained in the distance, fixed on no particular point.

"I would like that," she said quietly. "Although it may be difficult now."

"La Contessa, are you sure you are quite all right?"

She raised her eyebrows in warning, of what, I did not know. I asked no further questions and left her to her meditations.

I walked back to the hotel with Nina. She was silent, but I saw that a storm brewed in her mind. She moved swiftly, arms straight by her sides.

"Why did you bother to challenge Mrs Moore?" I asked. "You know she means only to be difficult and you shall never change her mind."

She looked at me askance.

"She is an awful woman, Mr Scott."

"I don't deny that," I agreed. "But we must show tolerance towards one another. We hope the troops will liberate us soon, but you might find yourself in the company of Mrs Moore for many more weeks."

"She is cruel," Nina said simply.

"She has upset you," I suggested. "I think I may have some idea why. It is nothing personal, Nina, you mustn't give her comments more credence than they deserve."

She did not respond to me.

"You spoke to Mrs Samuels," I said. "Have you set a date?"

"This afternoon," she replied. "Thank you, again." Her face cleared, and she smiled. "Thank you."

"Nina," I said. "You must be careful. Do not rile the other women, do not encourage any more talk."

"Let them talk," she laughed. "Let them talk until the Boxers chop off their heads!"

"Miss Ward," I said, with indulgence. "You ought to learn

which thoughts should be voiced and which should remain unspoken."

"And you, Mr Scott, ought not to deny when you agree with me."

Oscar arrived at the hotel around four p.m., by which time I had already retired to the bar. Nina waited for him upstairs, and I could not meet his eye, could not allow him to read his own victory in my shame as he crossed the lobby. He left an hour later and I returned to my room, where I found Nina locking the door behind her. Her hair and dress had been carefully arranged, nothing in her appearance betrayed that she had spent the afternoon outside of the bakery.

"Miss Ward," I greeted her. "I shall join you for dinner this evening. Let me walk you home."

The meal was not jubilant exactly, yet our conversation possessed a lightness markedly absent from most of our evening gatherings. Previously any gaiety expressed had its origins in the mood-altering effects of wine, creating a hysterical jollity that belied our habitual gloom. Yet this evening even Nicholas joined the chatter about Liberty's adorable feline habits, while Oscar tolerated jokes about the poor quality of the supper without bothering to defend his staff doing their best under difficult circumstances. Nina, I was pleased to note, smiled at the appropriate moments and refrained, I was relieved to see, from any particularly barbed comments. The only one who failed to be swept along in the optimistic spirit of the evening was La Contessa, who appeared subdued, listless, her contributions to our discourse lacking their usual color.

Phoebe explained her plan for rations; small portions of white rice and slightly larger ones of yellow rice for each household, and expressed concerns that some had been rather less than honest about the supplies at their disposal.

"What concerns me," she said carefully, "is the lack of compassion for the Chinese. We are burying seven children a day at Su's palace."

"I quite agree," I said. "Have we a ration plan for them?"

"Not a formal plan as such," Phoebe admitted. "I'm afraid, Mr Scott, that I have not been able to secure the support for such a plan. For the time being, I suppose, we shall continue to send them the heads of the ponies we eat. Some of the men there have taken to shooting stray animals. Meat is meat, they say, but I fear they are stripped of their dignity."

"We shall do more for them," Oscar said gravely from his position at the top of the table. "They are foremost in our thoughts."

"Foremost in our thoughts," Lillian repeated.

Our plates were cleared and Nicholas signaled to me.

"Would you accompany me upstairs, Mr Scott?" he asked.

I felt an immediate panic of discovery, and followed him with reluctant tread, words, excuses fluttering pathetically in my throat, justifications, explanations, entreaties, all inadequate, composing themselves in my mind.

Papers and books were scattered across his room, a manuscript marked in Nicholas' distinctive, jagged cursive was spread over the desk. I lifted one of the loose sheets.

"No one party may be held entirely accountable for the rise of the Boxer movement," I read. "Rather, the Boxers, a peasant uprising with little central coordination that has grown far beyond the imaginings of even its most fervent devotees, might be considered the natural conclusion of systemic failure on behalf of those who claim to control China: the weakened Qing administration, the foreign powers which squabble over territory, the merchants who focus their efforts on the wealth of the port cities at the expense of China's hinterland and, of course, the various religious bodies that have failed both materially and spiritually to provide for their followers."

"A work in progress," Nicholas said, reaching to the take the paper from me.

"It seems a most sensible analysis," I said.

Nicholas gestured for me to take a seat. Removing a pile of books he had collected from the Hanlin, I placed them on the floor with what I considered sufficient respect, and settled myself opposite him, tried to appear natural, crossing and then uncrossing my arms. "How are you, Nicholas? I have seen little of you of late."

"Yes," he said. "I have been rather focused upon my work. And you know that I find the company of others trying at the best of times. Not your company, of course, but that of bureaucrats and women."

"Women?"

"Women like these women," he said. "Women who talk of nothing but children and dressmaking and the quality of domestic staff. Only the Italian has anything of interest to say, and her husband seems increasingly determined to keep her quiet. He speaks so very sharply to her, when I daresay he is quite the luckiest husband in this household."

"You miss Pei," I offered. Naturally I wished to ask Nicholas more about La Contessa, but a desire to protect both her and myself stopped me from enquiring further. There was another consideration too, one less noble, that I did not want details of my lover's diminishment by her husband, I did not want to imagine her, the fabric of my dreams and the source of my hope, as just another unloved wife, a woman grown older and unlovely in the eyes of the man who holds her every day.

"Very much so. I wish I had never agreed to confine myself

here."

"You would be dead if you hadn't."

Nicholas considered this, brushed his gray beard.

"Alistair, I wondered if I may talk with you of Nina."

Guilt reared then, hot and inescapable. I had convinced myself that allowing, no, arranging, permitting, one might go as far as to say sanctioning, relations between Nina and Oscar was the only solution left to a man in my position, but now, seated opposite the girl's father, doubts prickled my conscience.

"Yes?" I worked to steady my voice.

"I find my daughter rather distant at present. It is difficult to find a moment to speak with her, and even when we are alone, a terrible silence dominates." He cleared his throat. "You see her at the hotel. Does she seem quite all right to you?"

"Yes," I said simply.

"Does she speak to you of her... her thoughts?"

"Very little," I said and shifted in my chair. "I think she is a rather despondent that she cannot return to Prince Su's palace."

"Ah." Nicholas closed his eyes momentarily, shook his head. "Alistair, I fear that China shall be forever changed by the events of this summer. I doubt the future of a young Englishwoman here."

"Nina?"

"She is the case in question, naturally, but I believe that any foreigner may struggle to live a normal and prosperous life in China following this rebellion. The at first tacit, and latterly rather open, support of the authorities for the Boxer movement has created an atmosphere in which it is quite acceptable, in fact laudable, to turn against foreigners. Nina considers herself Chinese, I suppose, or some sort of Anglo-Sino hybrid, but I fear this new century is not for such hybrids."

He stopped. I nodded uneasily.

"We shall have to wait and see," I said carefully. "We cannot know what the future holds."

"Yes," he said. "I am sorry to trouble you. As usual, I am rather given to overthinking the matter. It is only that I am so removed from the old country, from that world. You have superior understanding of these things. I only ask that you might think what options could be open to Nina in England, or elsewhere. My imagination does not stretch much beyond the Tartar walls these days."

He stood and showed me to the door. "I trust you not say anything to Nina. I do not wish to alarm her."

"Never."

My heart laden now with yet more secrets, with promises I was loath to keep, I descended the stairs. Amiable conversation filled the drawing room. I paused in the doorway and watched La Contessa with a smoldering cigarette between her lips. Oscar led the conversation in the room, telling the gathered audience of letters received that day from the Qing court that promised safe passage out of the Legation Quarter for all foreigners, guarantees we were by then unable and unwilling to believe.

"We understand now the functioning of the court," Oscar said. "The pro-Boxer faction gains the upper hand and we are fired upon. Those more favorable towards us regain power and we are given watermelons. It could change tomorrow. This is no time for risk; we shall wait for the troops to liberate us."

I turned my attention to Nina. Studiously she observed Oscar, her eyes did not waver from his face, her body curved towards the warmth of his voice. I left without goodbyes.

The following day is perhaps the most difficult for me to recount. If I were a man of Christ, I might have considered it my reckoning, and if I were a Buddhist, I might have seen in those events my karma, each terrible turn more deserved than the last. As it stands, I strive to be a man of logic and reason, yet even the rational sciences cannot deny that one thing leads to another, that our actions create reactions. And how heavily, how terribly, was the force of my actions returned to me that day.

I arrived at the Fairchild household at the usual time to collect Nina for her duties at the Grand. Immediately upon stepping inside the house I sensed an imbalance in atmosphere, detected foreboding in the meek stance of the servant who opened the door for me, who showed me inside with bowed head. No pots clanged in the kitchen, no feet hurried across the floors; the entire building was in thrall to a terrible quiet. I walked the corridor to the drawing room, feeling the air heavy around my shoulders. I found Nina alone, still wearing her nightdress, eyes ringed red. She had the appearance of a phantom; long white gown gathered around her, dark hair loose and unkempt, face drawn and pale.

"Nina, why are you not dressed?" I asked sharply.

She did not reply, but regarded me with great, tender pity.

"Nina, what has happened?"

The silence of the household roared then in my ears, marched defiantly towards me, threatened the worst of fates.

"Nina. Is this to do with Mr Fairchild?"

"Oh, no. Never." A sob, ungainly and visceral, escaped her then. "Oh, Alistair, it is La Contessa." Nina buried her face in her palms, her shoulders shook as she wept. I meant to approach her, but her words stilled me. La Contessa, those two words, so joyous to the tongue, so rapturous to the ears, pronounced now at such desolate pitch. Rooted to my position, I pressed her.

"What has happened to La Contessa?"

She lifted her head, and her face, swollen with tears, moved me, and afforded no doubt that the words she spoke next were true.

"She's dead."

I laughed; gruff and coarse, the laugh of a man defeated, a man who knows that reality, dreadful and unreal as it may appear, has vanquished him.

"Impossible," I said, knowing even as I spoke that her death was eminently possible. Death was our constant companion that summer, we had mourned dozens in a few short weeks, death, in many ways, was more natural to our state than life. "How?"

Nausea overwhelmed me, I took a staggered step. Nina rose immediately, cradled my arm, guided me to a chair.

"I'm sorry," she said, kneeling before me and taking my hand. "Mr Mancini shot her. He said there were Boxers outside the house, that she asked to be saved from them."

"Mancini did it? Mancini?"

Nina raised a finger to her lips, but I could not perceive the volume of my own voice. The room around me drained away, illusory, blurred, and I heard only the terrible cry of one repeated thought: she's gone, she's gone, and my hands too are stained with blood.

"Yes, Mr Scott. I'm sorry. I don't believe La Contessa would ever have asked..."

Nina was cut short by her father, but even without hearing the end of her sentence, I knew that I agreed wholeheartedly with the sentiment. La Contessa, immortal La Contessa who stole through the Legation Quarter in the deepest hours of the night, who sprinted under a canopy of bullets to steal a kiss, who smoked and drank and laughed as though the siege were an interminable party, a sensory feast, La Contessa would never fold so easily at the sight of a mere Boxer.

"Alistair." Nicholas entered the room. "You are here."

"Yes." As I stood to greet him I felt my legs buckle weak beneath me.

"Terrible news," he said.

I made to reply, but the appropriate words eluded me. Despair had cornered me suddenly, and hopelessness threatened me. The persona I wore so well, the war-hardened cynic, the laconic observer amidst the ruins, the character I had persuaded myself I truly was, slipped momentarily from my control. Tears and self-pity tempted me, the very qualities I disdained in others. Silence offered me safety, self-preservation.

"I fear if the Boxers don't murder us we shall turn our guns on ourselves," Nicholas continued. "It is simply not healthy for us to remain in such intimate conditions."

"But remain we must." I turned to Nina. "Come, Miss Ward. Your bakers await you."

"Baking? Today?"

"Yes. Do you think that La Contessa would wish to see you so forlorn? Come with me. Fresh air and a walk will do you good."

Nicholas, constant, serene Nicholas, had returned me somewhat to myself.

"Yes, Nina. Go and dress," Nicholas said.

Nina retreated with slow, unwilling steps. Nicholas watched me carefully, stroked his beard once, twice before speaking.

"I am terribly sorry," he said softly. "I know you were fond of her."

"Weren't we all?" I matched his tone with equal caution.

"Indeed." His eyes leveled with mine. "A terrible loss for us all."

I left Nina in the bakery and retreated to my room. There I reclined on the bed and closed my eyes. Of course I understood the patterns of grief; in the many conflicts I had witnessed, I had observed the same structure repeated again and again: hysteria, denial, anger, pleas to an invisible power. I knew what recovery required, that I ought to turn over my memories of La Contessa, the images I held of her in mind, right there in that very bed, her lips bruised red from kisses, her hair a gentle tickle across my chest. But my mind wouldn't, couldn't, resurface those pictures. Instead I escaped to a mindful emptiness, and to my shame, I slept. Upon waking I fancied I could smell her bergamot scent upon my pillow, a sweet, sharp citrus that called tears unbidden to my eyes. I shook my head and went over to my desk where I poured myself my usual remedy for melancholy: a thimbleful of whisky, drawn from my diminishing supplies. Hilde, hearing my steps, knocked gently on the door and served me a plate of cool rice and pony meat.

"Miss Ward told me," she said simply. "You missed lunch."

"Thank you," I said, my voice cracking. I could not look directly at her face, round and open, shadowed with concern. Her kindness served only to stoke my guilt.

"She was a very special woman," Hilde said. "We all-"

"Enough!" I said, struck my fist on the desk before me. "Enough of this pretense! She was murdered by her husband, murdered because-"

Hilde gripped my shoulders, her stout, practical fingers pressed sharp against my flesh.

"Hush," she said. "I know, I know. But you mustn't say anything, Alistair. You must protect yourself as you have protected Nina."

"And as I failed to protect La Contessa."

"Alistair," she said sternly, hands close and firm around me. "Do not let the despair set in. Do not lose yourself, not now."

"Hilde," I said, hearing my voice faint, my spirit spent. "Please leave me to my work."

Simply, silently she nodded, and stepped back from me. She paused by the door, offered me a weak smile, and departed.

Immediately I set about writing a short article about our

imminent rescue. I could not stop myself from adding a reference to La Contessa: *Latest events in the Legation Quarter suggest Boxers are not the only threat to the survival of foreigners in Peking. An Italian countess was shot by her diplomat husband as Boxers neared the house where they had found shelter during the siege.* It was sentimental, personal, worst of all, it gave credence to Mancini's lie. I was deserving of the very criticisms I lobbed at the lowest talents in my industry, but I decided on this day to permit myself the infraction and set out with the story, hoping to find a willing Chinese to smuggle it out into the city and from there on to Tienstin, or the closest place from which telegraphs might pass unimpeded by Boxer destruction. Oh, Chiara, I thought as I stepped out into the Legation Quarter by dusk, only your kisses might lift me from these depths, and never again shall your touch bring me peace.

There is a rather trite maxim that holds that the darkest hour comes shortly before dawn breaks. In the days that followed La Contessa's death, we all had little choice but to cling to such hollow niceties and hope unfounded optimism might will them true. Phoebe Franklin further expanded our repertoire of shibboleths, furnishing us with Bible verses about perseverance: *Be joyful in hope, patient in affliction, faithful in prayer. Be faithful, even to the point of death, and I will you life as your victor's crown.* We mumbled these lines as events took a decisive turn for the worse, as though La Contessa's death had been the first of many loaded dominoes. The fighting worsened, the Qing appeared to abandon any pretense of a truce and the nights roared with thunder and gunfire. The conflict so deteriorated that Nina had no choice but to sleep one night at the Grand; returning to the Fairchild household posed too great a risk. Hilde and I sat with her in the bar until the early hours, the floor beneath us scattered with bodies sleeping and scared. Hilde had offered Lijun shelter for the night, but she had insisted on running the gauntlet to join her peers at the Su mansion. Nina explained Lijun's motives, telling us that two of the schoolgirls at the former palace had attempted to commit suicide. Despairing of ever making it out of the Legation Quarter alive and convinced they would be tortured before the Boxers would free them in death, they had jumped together from a window. They were found with their little feet bound together by a wrap of silk; likely an old adornment of one of Prince Su's harem. The poor girls did not die, but did break their legs, and now they writhed in pain, starved and delirious in the crowded palace. A visit from a Russian doctor had been promised, but they had yet to see him; the high number of military casualties amongst the foreigners kept him otherwise occupied. Lijun dreaded sleeping next to their cracked and useless bodies, hearing the moans and cries that robbed her of sleep, but she thought solidarity the only force strong enough to see the girls through the siege and so bedded uncomplainingly beside them.

"Please, Mrs Samuels. May I have some gin?" Nina asked as she ended the story.

Hilde poured her a small serving.

"To help you sleep," Hilde said.

The two shared Hilde's bed that night; the oppressive heat and unending noise meant both slept only sporadically, never reaching any true depth of slumber.

Hilde reported that Nina had posed her an intriguing question in the morning: "Mr Fairchild says that Mr Mancini shot La Contessa because she was afraid of the treatment a European woman might receive at the hands of the Boxers, that she had asked him to do so if Boxers ever approached the house. Do you suppose Mr Fairchild really believes that?"

"He is an official," Hilde said. "I am sure he says many things he doesn't believe, but I cannot begin to imagine the inner workings of his mind. You are far better placed to understand that, my dear."

Nina had only shrugged, and said no more, but this unusual query, and the insistent nature of Nina's questioning, struck Hilde as a sign of some shift in her relationship with Fairchild.

"Perhaps they have had a disagreement," she said to me.

"One can only hope," I said.

The afternoon brought about a lull in attacks from the other side of the walls and I offered to accompany Nina to the Fairchild household. We walked quickly through the Legation Quarter, yet we could not help but to notice the not insignificant quantity of bullets collected on the dusty ground and the human detritus that evinced death: rags stained with blood, clumps of hair, shoes missing their pairs. Those were for me the most doleful, miserable days of the entire bloody siege. I bid Nina farewell at the doorway, my shame was too hot still to allow myself the chance of meeting Pietro Mancini, or even to chance passing before the knowing eyes of Phoebe Franklin, whose omniscient godliness no doubt led her to at least suspect me of wrongdoing.

"Take care, Miss Ward," I said.

"Likewise, Mr Scott," she said. Then with kindness she added: "You seem tired. Make sure to rest a little this afternoon."

"After all, we may be liberated tomorrow."

She laughed. "If not," she said, and her eyes sparkled, "I may have to defect to the Boxers."

It was a terrible night for fighting; the Boxers had returned to the heights of their horror and were resolute once more in their attempts to bring about our destruction. They were unassailable in their belief that their supposed immortality would save them from death, though quite how they maintained such braggadocio at this late stage of the conflict I cannot say. That night they appeared to fear nothing, and even engaged some of our men in crude hand-to-hand combat, their high kicks and curved punches a macabre ballet before the burning sky. Colonel Shiba in Su's palace begged his men to bang pots and pans to create such a din that the Boxers might believe more fighters lay behind the building's ravaged walls. Doom had once again set in across the Legation Quarter and the Boxers denied us sleep as we kept terrified vigil.

I listened to this orchestra of chaos from my desk by the window, pen posed in my hand, whisky by my side, any attempt at sleep long abandoned. I wished to capture the shared desperation of the siege, to faithfully record the oranges, the reds, the great burning tableau of the sky, but found my words instead returning again and again to the realm of the personal, to my memories of La Contessa, to my fears for Nina, to that unanswerable question Nicholas had asked me: what might become of Nina after the siege? And then. A terrible rumble, one low, menacing crash that immediately rolled into another. The nearby scuffles paused following this deep, unusual sound, resulting in an crackling silence, a collective intake of breath that suggested neither side knew the origins of this terrible thunderclap. The sound returned; distant, powerful and menacing. I stood at once, pressed my face to the window. The ravaged scene before me did not change, but I sensed hope in those intervals of silence. It came once more, the drumroll of liberty, the commencement of freedom, and I raised my glass to the ruined city, felt my spirit soar winged and light above its blood-soaked streets. Finally, salvation.

CLARE KANE

Alistair,

Breathlessly, secretly I read your words in those moments when I am finally alone, and how I feel my heart almost stop beating when I remember those most wretched days of the siege. My poor father, he loved me so, and yet he lacked the simple words to tell me his fears.

I read this story as though it happened to someone else, I anticipate the end of the siege as though I do not know what may come to pass. Yet I know it all, I picture our future as plainly as those women in England who read fortunes in cards, or those monks in Peking who divine from the Book of Changes...I know what awaits us, and how my spirit wonders at what other destinies we might have chosen instead.

I wish I might see you, Alistair, to share with some sympathetic listener the most disturbing and stirring thoughts your words provoke in me. I think of that most apt of Chinese expressions, 触景生情, touch the past and sentiment is born.

I await your next visit and for now enjoy the company of your words.

I remain,
Your faithful and solitary reader,
Nina

XIII

I have in my career witnessed a number of historical moments; the beginnings of battles, the endings of accords, the ringing of a single bullet that heralds victory or defeat, and I have invariably found these pockets of time profoundly trivial in their lived experience. When one reads of events in the history books, one imagines each man present at the scene to be imbued with a sense of significance, one sees his flesh pimple and crawl in expectation of the great future importance of the event he observes, one pictures his eyes filling with premonitory tears. Yet I have found that time is time, and it passes just as mundanely when history is recorded upon it, in steady breaths and hunger pains and idle talk. And so while I felt great anticipation at the prospect of our release from the Legation Quarter, I was unsurprised by the damp feeling of bathos that clung to me as I stepped out onto those familiar streets, and watched, a glass of slightly flat champagne in my hand, the euphoric transformation of the Legation Quarter.

Standing shoulder to shoulder with Edward and Hilde, I watched the hotel's refugee guests fill the street in front of the Grand, their faces displaying the first genuine smiles I had seen since their arrival. These were not the usual weak half-smiles of thankfulness, of politeness, of the determined will to survive, but rather grins of unbridled happiness. They were joined in celebration by the foreign inhabitants of the Legation Quarter, who had also begun to pour onto the streets. Mr Cologan, the

Spanish minister, ran in great circles, shouting at the top of his voice: "We are saved!" The women wept, the men cheered, everyone held a drink in their hands. Edward and Hilde, a habitually undemonstrative couple, embraced and kissed, and I turned to permit them some privacy.

I do make one admission to the power of historic moments: in announcing their significance, in forcing themselves upon one's future memories, they bring about a swift evaluation of the most essential elements of one's existence. Who did I want to see in that moment? Who would I picture by my side when I rewrote my personal history of the Boxer Rebellion, when I erased from memory the lifeless sparkle of the wine and the smell of rotting flesh, and pictured only the rapture of salvation? The Wards. And amidst the happy confusion I made my way towards the Fairchild household to find Nicholas and Nina.

Lillian stood in the doorway, cradling her kitten as she watched the great carousing parade pass. Hugo Lovell, limping still but guffawing like a madman, broke away from a group of student interpreters and stopped to kiss Lillian with shameless exuberance. He left her without a word, dancing down the street with one stiff leg, and while Lillian shook her head and wagged a finger after him, she appeared radiant in the afterglow of the kiss.

"Hello, Mr Scott," she said warmly as I stepped into the house, where I found the servants wiping tears from one another's cheeks. They patted my back, called out to me as I passed down the corridor to the drawing room, where Nicholas stood alone in still, unlit environs, observing the raucous celebrations from the window.

"Not dancing yet?" I greeted him.

"You know me, Alistair," he said, his voice slow, constant as ever. "I don't like to believe anything until I see some empirical evidence."

"They have stopped firing. Is that not evidence enough?"
He chuckled.

"I jolly well hope so. What wouldn't I give to go home tomorrow?"

"Where's Nina?" I asked.

"Haven't seen her," he said. "She must be out there."

"Come, let us find her."

I took his arm as we stepped amidst the jubilant crowd that thronged the streets, and felt him suddenly frail as we attempted progress through their chants and songs, their smiles and cheers. I held him closer, increased my grip, and he did not protest, but stayed close by my side.

Champagne and wine were brought from the cellars; a number of food committee members noted that the quantities produced for the purposes of celebration appeared rather greater than those recorded in official tallies. I offered to ferry some of the supplies to the deserving Japanese soldiers at the Su mansion. The old palace, its residents long ailing, lethargic, their will almost crushed, erupted in immediate exultation in those first hours of liberation. It gave me great pleasure to see the young girls there unfurl their tired limbs to join the merrymaking, and it was in the central courtyard of the palace that we finally found Nina, her hands linked with her former students' in an elated, dancing circle under a vast dark sky of unblinking stars, their faces turned upwards with no fear of hostile fire. I recognized the familiar lilt of *Molihua*, a popular folk song: "Beautiful jasmine flower, beautiful jasmine flower, sweet, beautiful and blooming!" I raised a glass in Nina's direction, caught her eye and saw that she wept as she sang, coruscating tears of unknown nature. Did she cry with relief, like many of the embattled souls in Prince Su's palace that night, did she weep for happiness, for the hope of returning home, or were those tears bitter and sour, did she cry of regret for the affair she must now leave behind, for the future that lay unseen, unshaped before her?

At dawn the schoolgirls settled for a few hours of shallow sleep. Many of the women and children in the Legation Quarter did the same; gentle mothering hands led tiny bodies back to bed. Nina left her charges to sleep and returned home with her father and Phoebe Franklin. Most of the men, however, felt unable to sleep. Though we had wrung out our spirits in festivity and leadened our eyelids with wine, we believed it our duty to stay awake for the arrival of our liberators, whom we could only assume were drawing ever closer. I moved between the various groups of diplomats (who even in celebration divided themselves along national lines) trying to glean as much information as I could from each. I knew that our rescue had the potential to become the greatest story of my career, a defining moment that would make my name familiar not just to the best editors of Britain and the world, but also to housewives and bank tellers. This was, I felt, more my story than anyone's, and I would be damned if I let another writer in some comfortable office in London or New York profit from our hardship.

Naturally my attempts at information gathering were entirely unsuccessful. Nobody within the walls of the Legation Quarter could so much as conjecture as to what might be taking place outside, but proud men of every nation tried their best to appear better informed than their peers.

"This is quite what we were expecting."

"I should say they are around three hours away."

"Did we not say that they should arrive on the fourteenth?"

Unconvinced, I repaired to my room where I wrote a series of opening lines to the article I hoped to report later that day, preparing for what I hoped might be the most brilliant, most eminent, dispatch of my career. *On the fourteenth of August, another hot, cloudless day in the heart of China… Long-awaited soldiers today liberated the foreign population…* But with the future still concealed from my impatience, I had no choice but to leave events to fate, and fortifying myself with two fingers of whisky, made for the Tartar Wall. Hilde joined me, gun bumping against her hip, and we settled ourselves at an excellent vantage point, our eyes trained on the horizon beyond the capital.

"Do you suppose my house is still standing?" I asked Hilde.

I scanned the streets, trying to locate my modest home, only a mile or so from where we sat.

"Still standing, I'm sure," she said. "You might find, however, that it is home to a Boxer or two."

"Not after today."

We remained in amiable silence. I instructed myself to memorize the details, the few trailing wisps of white cloud across the blazing blue sky, the smell of death, still pervasive but almost sweet after weeks of acclimatization, the rubble of the Imperial capital strewn on both sides of the wall, so I might reproduce them later in my reporting. But my mind rebelled at these minor details, and I desired events grand and significant, actions swift and conclusive.

"I can't stand it," I said finally. "I'm going into the city."

"Alistair." Hilde fixed impassive eyes on me and I doubted for a moment, thought she might disapprove. "Why am I not surprised? I shall join you."

We walked together to Su's palace. Outside we found Lijun, who traced English vocabulary with her fingers in the dust. She waved to me.

"Are the soldiers here yet?"

"We're just going to see about that," I called.

It seemed another era when I had demanded Prince Su

abandon his palace to the refugees. Then they were destitute, their feet raw and bloody, their cheeks sunken and hungry. But now they were mere shadows, hovering somewhere between life and death. Seeing Lijun's gnarled fingers as she practiced her words, observing her little frame hunched and sharp as she knelt in the dust, her spine a clear, visible arc through her thin clothes, I felt shame at the fate of the Chinese Christians. Ostensibly these were the lucky ones, those who had escaped the wrath of the vicious Boxers, but I doubted they looked or felt better than those fending for their lives beyond the Legation Quarter.

Hilde and I moved cautiously around the barricades and into the Chinese city. Her knuckles grew white around her gun, though her face betrayed no fear. We found the Qing defenses unmanned.

"They've gone," Hilde said in a coarse whisper.

"Be careful," I replied, steadying myself against a wall as we turned into a main street. Here we would once have been open targets, but as we stepped carefully over the remnants of the past weeks' destruction no gun was trained in our direction, no soldier shouted our presence. The ground was uneven and treacherous, littered with scattered bullets, blunted swords, stained rags. A dog chewed ferociously on a scrap of human flesh. Its coat was matted and wiry, but its stomach swelled: a feast after weeks of famine. Beyond we happened upon a still-burning fire, bowls of uneaten rice dotted its periphery.

"They've gone," Hilde said again. "They've gone." She slackened her grip on her gun.

"I think you may be right," I said cautiously. I looked in amazement at the untouched rice, reaching out to lift a bowl that felt warm in my hand.

"The troops are really coming," Hilde said. "Finally."

She embraced me and we stood together in that ghastly street, the repulsive dog circling our ankles.

"I suppose we ought to return. Liberation awaits," I said.

Lijun waited for us outside the Su mansion. She wrote no longer, only drew swooping lines in the dust with impatient toes.

"Well?" she greeted us.

"The Imperial soldiers have gone," I said, hearing my voice distant and unreal. The Legation Quarter around me had taken on an otherworldly quality; I struggled to focus on the buildings, the people, the smell of horse meat cooking for lunch. It was true, I told myself, we were to be rescued.

"Really?" Lijun frowned, narrowed her eyes.

"Of course," Hilde said.

The girl ran suddenly towards us, jumped into my arms and wrapped her bony legs around my waist. Hilde held the girl's hands; both wept joyously, sobs giving way to laughter, tears setting upon smiles. I lowered Lijun to the ground.

"Go and tell your friends," I suggested, but already she yelled the good news from the entrance of the palace.

"Back to the wall," I suggested to Hilde. "We might watch from there and see the troops' advance."

"I would like to be with Edward," she said shyly.

"Naturally."

And so I walked alone to the Fairchild household. Nicholas and Nina were in the drawing room, their agitation palpable. They paced the perimeter of the room in interweaving circles, while a placid Phoebe Franklin read sedately in a chair, her face freshly scrubbed, hair pulled back from her weather-lined face.

"Mr Scott." Nina moved swiftly towards me, the hem of her lilac dress rustled against the floor. "They have come for Mr Fairchild. The troops shall arrive shortly."

"Wonderful," I said. "I came to tell you that the Imperial soldiers have abandoned their defenses."

"And how do you know that?" Nina asked.

"I went out with Hilde. They left their lunch uneaten. A dog enjoys their rice."

"How interesting," Nicholas said, coming to a halt opposite me. "The Empress Dowager would never allow them to abandon their posts unless defeat was considered inevitable."

"Precisely," I said. "We are free."

"Shall we go outside?" Nicholas suggested. "The officials indicated to Fairchild that the troops would arrive imminently. This is a very good story for you, my boy. You shouldn't like to miss the arrival of our liberators."

"And Miss Price?" I asked.

"She is preparing her bath," Nina replied, following her father to the door.

"A bath at a time like this?"

"Oh, let her be, Mr Scott," Nina said. "She wishes to look her best for the liberation."

The Legation Quarter shook with mirthful cries as we crossed its streets: "The British are coming! The British are coming!" The Water Gate below the Tartar Wall, so long our ultimate shield from the Boxers, lay wide open. A general stood under its arch; a line of officials waited to shake his hand. He was surrounded by a fantastical collection of Sikhs and Rajputs, Indian men majestic and regal on horseback, who spilled into the Legation Quarter, curved swords balanced over their shoulders, turbans splendid and high on their heads. They led their horses across the lawns to the tennis courts, where they were overwhelmed by the delight of the besieged. "Thank you! Thank you!" cried the newly-liberated, hands reaching for the soldiers' horses, gripping at their manes, patting their flanks. "Thank you!"

"How strange." Lillian Price appeared to have abandoned plans for bathing, and now stood close behind us, although I did note that she had tied a neat pink ribbon in her hair. "How very odd to be rescued by men of such heathen appearance."

Nina did not respond, but pressed against the bodies that surrounded her, attempted to carve a path through them. I watched as her progress was soon impeded by General Gaselee himself; the man who had led the British troops jumped down from his horse to take Nina by the hand.

"Thank God, men, here are women alive," he declared and placed an extended kiss on Nina's forehead. The crowd roared. A few feet behind the general stood Oscar Fairchild. He watched the exchange carefully, but with an expression unreadable to my eye.

One rule of my trade is that stories wither in the presence of crowds. Conglomerations appear newsworthy, and any event that draws the multitude from their usual activities does warrant some investigation, but in my experience, when all attention is focused on one place, when a story is written in numbers rather than nuance, you can be sure that the real story, the strange, course-altering development of history, is being written elsewhere. And so I slipped away from the overjoyed crowds, stepping out of the gates and once more into the city. Troops still surged towards the Legation Quarter, mostly Americans by the looks of them. They moved jauntily, guns suspended above their heads, and sounded sporadic, celebratory bullets as they progressed towards the Tartar wall. The Chinese on the streets ran in all directions, like rolling marbles they bumped into one another, repelling each another at opposing angles with the force of their contact. I attempted to root myself still amongst the movement, my eyes darted from soldier to civilian, bullets rang loud in my ears. I witnessed a Chinese man stumble as he ran, his knees sank to the grime and dust that caked the streets. An American soldier stopped, aimed his gun at the man's head.

"Hey!" I called. "What do you think you are you doing?"

"Liberating you," he said with a smile.

He pulled the trigger and the man creased helplessly at the waist, sank further into the ground.

"Why?" I grabbed the soldier by the arm. "He was never a Boxer!"

"I've seen enough Chinese these months," the soldier said, "to tell you that you never know."

He raised his gun, set free a directionless bullet, and with arrogant sweep rejoined his peers and continued towards the Legation Quarter. Bullets echoed, ricocheting from the narrow walls of old Peking, unheard within the ebullient atmosphere of the Legation Quarter. To the Chinese beyond the Tartar wall, a new terror had arrived. To appease the Boxers they had lit red lanterns, burned incense and affixed auspicious symbols to their doors and windows, but they did not know what these new invaders required of them, and so they ran, sprinted from their saviors.

I followed the American soldiers at a distance, watched as they shot careless bullets to the ground, jostled one another and joked, their skin whipped and beaten by the unforgiving sun of the north China plains, their faces etched with the grooves of much older men. As they passed through the sluice gate they broke into a run, cheering as they disappeared headlong into the open mouth of the crowd. The atmosphere of the Legation Quarter was that of absolute enjoyment, voices trilled in the manner of garden party gossip, bottles popped and glasses clinked just as they had just three months earlier when we had gathered to celebrate Queen Victoria's birthday. Away from the mêlée, I saw Nina sitting alone in a shaded section of the tennis courts. Her face was pale, and she chewed nervously at faded lips.

"Are you all right?" I asked, taking a seat on the ground next to her. "You look as though you've seen a ghost."

"Even worse," she muttered.

"Sorry?"

"I'm quite fine, Mr Scott," she said, not lifting her head to look at me. "A little overwhelmed, perhaps."

"I do not blame you," I said. "It is rather strange, however long we might have expected this day to come."

Finally she regarded me, a hand shielding her eyes from the sun.

"What happens now?" she asked.

"I cannot say, Nina," I said honestly. "Although my experience tells me that liberation shall be neither expedient nor simple. There will be a party, I suppose, and then the negotiations shall begin. The indemnity. The accusations. The diplomacy."

"You mean to say we might be here a long time?"

"Not you," I said. "Women and children, they send you away to the sounds of trumpets. The men then take care of signing papers and assigning blame."

"Well, I have no intention of going anywhere but home. Do you suppose they will allow us to return today?"

"Not today," I said, thinking of the scenes I had witnessed beyond the Tartar wall, the fleeing residents, the ravenous, flea-ravaged dogs, the blood painted fresh over old stains.

"I just want to see it," she said. "Do you think I might go accompanied by a soldier?"

"If Her Majesty's soldiers do not grant your wish, I take it upon myself to return you to your rightful *hutung*," I said, trying for lightness. "Once, and only once, all the bottles in the Legation Quarter have been emptied and you are tired of celebrating."

Nina laughed, and her pallor faded a little.

"Why don't you rest before the merriment that awaits us this evening?" I suggested. "We shall drink champagne with our horse suppers tonight."

Nina assented, rising with me.

"You will come to us tonight, won't you?" she asked, taking my arm in hers. "I would so hate for you not to be there."

"Of course," I said. "Hilde is always glad to have one less stomach to fill."

"And tomorrow...do you think we might go home?"

"Let's see."

I left her in the care of two British soldiers who appeared rather delighted to escort her back to the Fairchild residence.

"I am quite fine by myself," she insisted. "We have walked this way many times over the past weeks with bullets flying over our heads."

"We would hate to see any casualties after the liberation," one of the soldiers solemnly returned, and the pair guided her back to the house.

Hastily I wrote a report of the day's events, frustrated as I recorded each significant moment - the champagne dawn, Gaselee at the gate, the majestic pride of the Sikhs on horseback - that I knew not what these elements might portend. The whereabouts of the Empress Dowager remained a mystery, and the Boxer movement, although now undeniably frail, was, I presumed, still in existence. Did the Boxers rampage, depleted but unfatigued, across the desolate plains and leave missionaries and Christians slain, or had the foreign aggression against their cause led them to falter and fold, to accept defeat? I wrote to the emptiness, attempted to impose an order upon the few facts within my cognizance, and returned to the Chinese city where I graced a young man's palm with silver and instructions to take the dispatch to Tienstin. Whether my words would successfully travel those two hundred miles, never mind all the way to

London, I had no idea, but in the spirit of post-siege optimism I decided to pay the man's inflated price.

The air was thick with conversation when I arrived at the Fairchild household at dusk. A harried servant let me in without a word, hurrying immediately back to the kitchen where preparations were underway for this most momentous of dinners. The drawing room played host to a cocktail party of sorts, where liberating soldiers in begrimed uniforms drank wine while surrounded by the women of the house in their most splendid evening wear. Nina and Nicholas sat slightly apart, Nicholas tugging uncomfortably on a suit that now hung loosely from his shoulders, Nina twirled a loose strand of hair absentmindedly around her fingers. Her appearance was once again drawn, her cheeks empty of color, though I noticed her muted appearance did not deter the military men from stealing glances at her as frequently as propriety would allow. I made towards the pair, but was intercepted by a British lieutenant.

"Alistair Scott?" he inquired.

"I'm afraid so." I extended a hand. His right hand, unhindered by wine, shook mine vigorously.

"Quite a coup for a newspaperman, this," he said. "Imagine, you shall write the story from having lived it. Remarkable."

"Yes," I replied. I wondered if either of my reports had been successfully delivered by telegraph; I was relieved, at least, that I had not yet received a man's head in return for my efforts.

"I hope you have already reported today's liberation to England. I imagine those at home would find this news very cheering; we have had nothing but bad news from South Africa for so long now. Very dispiriting."

"I have attempted to, yes, although I admit my account of today's events was rather sparse," I said. "I am waiting for history to happen before my eyes."

"Oh, Mr Scott, would this scene alone not make a most cheering story for those at home? All these lovely ladies and refined gentlemen, preserving civility and upholding our values while surrounded by barbarism on all sides, rescued heroically by Her Majesty's loyal servants after weeks of terrible conflict in the Chinese countryside. Yes, quite a wonderful story."

"I don't deny it is a most pleasant scene," I said, "But my readers also require some of those rather less pleasant details: retribution, reparation, some indication of what comes next."

"All in good time, Mr Scott," he said. "Justice shall be done. You shall see."

I smiled, bowed lightly, and cut across the room with purpose. I felt that the arrival of these military men, swollen with the significance of their conflict, proud and arrogant despite the apparent shambles of their numerous abortive attempts to liberate Peking, had disturbed our delicate collective balance. Ignorant of our weeks of hardship, these decorated newcomers wished only to recount their own tales of bravery and courage, and I intuited that they saw the collected Britishers of the city only as guests at some quaint summer party, willowy spectators to their rugged glory. Pleased as I was to be free of the Boxer threat, their presence irked me, and I feared this arrival of Allied might would bring little good to Peking.

Nina and Nicholas stood together to greet me in their finest clothes. Their cheeks sunken, their skin wan, they appeared hollowed versions of the selves they had been that unworried night in May when Nina had first met Oscar Fairchild. Father and daughter, united once more in curious isolation, they stood hesitantly apart from the fray, unable to follow the social rhythm of the strangers around them.

"This liberation business is quite exhausting," Nicholas said, looking around at the unfamiliar faces that filled the drawing room. "They say we cannot go home yet."

"Let them have their party," I said. "They must be heroes before they can become administrators."

"Quite right." Nicholas coughed drily. "I shall enquire again tomorrow."

"Where is Mancini?" I asked.

I had not seen La Contessa's husband, and feared the direction my impulses might take if he were to appear. My grief for the loss of Chiara was hardening, and increasingly took new shape as rage.

"Returned to the Italian Legation," Nicholas said plainly. "I rather think that is for the best."

"He has certainly benefited from the distractions of liberation," I said coldly.

Nicholas nodded warily. Nina stood by us, but did not engage in conversation. Her eyes scanned the room endlessly, returning time and again to Oscar Fairchild, who remained deep in conversation with military officials. Oscar, in a crisp suit, his hair carefully waxed, was one of the few men in that sultry, clamorous room who stole no tentative looks in Nina's direction.

We were called to dinner, and under the watchful gaze of Queen Victoria we arranged ourselves around the table using a variety of chairs of all shapes and sizes collected from around the house. The food on offer was much the same, namely horse meat, but I considered the helpings of rice to be more generous than usual. An American general had been invited to this primarily British gathering due to his acquaintance with Lillian Price. Red-faced with wine, the man commanded conversation from his seat by Lillian.

"I met Miss Price in Havana last year," he said. "My wife and I were quite charmed. And to think she is now here!"

"Isn't it strange?" Lillian agreed, smiling broadly.

"Miss Price's brother is currently in Tokyo. I recently received word from him, he was most concerned for the welfare of his only sister. I kept you in my mind, Miss Price, as we made the arduous journey here. I thought of that delightful lunch we had in Havana. Not once did I consider turning back."

"Hear, hear!" The British lieutenant who had cornered me before dinner raised his glass. "We had expected to find you all in a far worse state. Imagine how happy we were to discover you in such high civility. It was as if we had stumbled across a garden party, wasn't it? All those pretty dresses and the tennis courts… It was quite magical."

Contented murmurs passed down the table. More glasses were raised, more toasts spoken. I longed to get away, feeling suddenly an urgent need to write. As the meal drew to a close Oscar Fairchild rose, pushed his chair behind him, cleared his throat and faced his assorted guests.

"On behalf of Her Majesty's government," he began, "I wish to thank the brave British troops we have amongst us this evening for their tremendous courage. Their valiant efforts have liberated us from that most ghastly of enemies, the Boxers."

More toasts, more congratulation, more elation.

"Over the past weeks we have all experienced times of terrible desperation, moments when hope appeared to entirely abandon us to a most miserable fate. We dreamed of England, we dreamed of liberty, we dreamed of unsophisticated pleasures, of walking a mile with fear of neither bullet nor Boxer. Today, you have delivered these dreams to us."

Rapturous applause. Nina rested her forearm on the table; her loose, tired fingers supported the stem of her raised wine glass.

"We have all," Oscar continued, "faced a terrible beast this summer. We did not cower, we did not doubt, we did not submit to the beast's demands. We kept a flame of hope burning in our hearts, knowing that you would come to liberate us."

Some of the military men were on their feet, they clapped and stamped, setting forth peals of good-natured laughter, exposing broad rows of white teeth.

"Yet however trying the past weeks may have proved for us here, however terrified and wretched we may have felt, however many times we complained of eating horse meat and having to ration our wine, never once did we forget that you, on our behalf, suffered far greater indignities and faced considerably graver dangers. For that, gentlemen, we thank you."

Not one amongst us remained sitting. One lieutenant started singing: "When Britain first, at Heaven's command..." By the time he reached the chorus, "Rule Britannia! Rule the waves, Britons never will be slaves", all joined him in uncurbed gaiety. Even the Americans made an effort to stumble over the unfamiliar words; only Nina's lips did not shape the lyrics.

Dinner broke up in triumphant jubilation and the guests proceeded to the drawing room for more drinking. I made my excuses and headed for the front door. Stepping outside, the evening felt cooler, the sky wider, higher somehow, now I knew that the walls that surrounded us, while still proud and impenetrable, no longer marked an impassable barrier between us and the city. I heard light footsteps behind me.

"Oh, please, may I come with you?" Nina asked.

"To the Grand?"

"Yes. It is so warm in there. I feel quite uncomfortable."

"I suppose Hilde shall be happy to see you."

Celebrations at the Grand were rather more understated. For the refugees, one state of limbo had been lifted; now another opened before them. The foreigners were liberated, but what might the pink-faced saviors do for the dead priests in the hinterland, for the burnt-out churches in nameless hamlets? The cruel histories of the Chinese Christians checked inclination towards optimism and the hotel was quiet. We found Hilde in the kitchen with Lijun. Both kneaded dough in perfect concentration.

"Still baking?" I greeted them. "Forget that and celebrate."

"And you, Mr Scott? You have returned rather early from supper, have you not? Was that not a celebration?" Hilde, knuckles dusted white, did not lift her hands from the dough.

"A fair observation, I grant you. I have returned to write."

Nina stood behind Lijun, watching the girl's wrists roll as she labored.

"Are you happy?" Nina asked her.

"It is too soon for happiness," Lijun said quietly with furrowed brow. "So many men, guns, swords, they remind me."

"Remind you of what?" Nina asked.

"Of all that came before." Lijun wiped her hands on the apron tied around her waist.

"Will you go home?" Nina asked.

"Where is home now?" Lijun shrugged. "Perhaps I shall stay in Peking."

"Let us bake these loaves, Lijun, then that shall be enough for today." Hilde turned to me and smiled. "A drink, Mr Scott? A little celebration of our own?"

The four of us moved to the bar, which was home still to a half dozen families who showed little to no interest in the bottles that lined the shelves of the room. They barely stirred as we entered, contented in their family groups. Hilde poured me a gin; Nina refused one. Hilde's glass clinked against mine, she took a hearty sip.

"So, Mr Scott, what now?" she asked.

"It is too early to say."

"That sounds familiar. I suppose men of your profession hate

279

to be proved incorrect," Hilde replied. Lijun sat at Nina's feet, her head leaning against Nina's knee, one small hand reached up to intertwine their fingers.

"I am no soothsayer," I said slowly. "Yet if I were to employ my powers of forecast, I would say that the Empress Dowager shall not withstand this pressure from the foreign powers. The troops may have taken their time, but they are here, and they have succeeded in liberating Peking, or at least the only section of it about which the allied nations care. The story shall be a sensation abroad, whether it is written by me or some imaginative chap in London with a taste for the Oriental. Fair maidens and Chinese barbarians, I can just imagine how it might be written." I paused. "The Qing shall turn from the Boxers, and leave them without state sponsorship."

"And then?"

"And then the movement shall dissipate, for now, return to the land, where it will lie fallow, hissing and crackling under the surface before it rises again."

A mother a few feet away settled two of her children on the floor to sleep, slipping bundles of clothes as pillows under their small heads.

"Come," Hilde said. "We ought to let them sleep."

To my surprise, Nina followed me when I retired to my room.

"You don't mind, do you?" she asked. "I promise I shan't make a sound."

I seated myself before the desk, an empty piece of paper accused me. I tapped my pen against the desk; I wished to write something beyond the mere facts I had filed earlier in the day, but words were timid, and they refused to reveal themselves to me.

"Oh." Soft, surprised. Nina cradled two emerald teardrops in her palm, earrings that had once hung glittering from La

Contessa's ears. She held my gaze, steady and deep, before letting her eyelids fall, defeated. When she raised her eyes to meet mine again I saw they brimmed with tears.

"Oh, Nina." I moved to the armchair where she sat, took her hand in mine. Her body shook with unvoiced tears, but she remained hard, removed, yielding nothing to the comfort I offered.

"You may have them," I said finally. "They are lovely, aren't they? Here, wear them now."

I helped her to affix the jewels, then stepped back to admire her, a glimmering, spectral apparition of watery eyes and dewy emeralds. "Beautiful," I said. She held her head proudly, defying more tears.

The sight of Nina, pale and lissom, sitting stiff and tall in that chair where La Contessa had once lounged and laughed, curled her hair loose and long around suggestive fingers, moved me suddenly, and I took a step towards her. I was gripped by a momentary madness, an unexplained impulse to not only embrace Nina but to press my lips against hers, to feel the skin of another against my own.

I denied the feeling, quelled the desire, but as I returned to the desk and retook my pen, I felt Nina watch me with curiosity.

Miss W, I wrote, *wears the emeralds of a dead woman.*

The words came then without delay and I felt myself once more able to write in vivid tones. Nina remained silent, watched me write, rose only once to light a lamp for me. The night pulled black around us, from outside we heard proud, carousing cries, we listened to songs sung in languages we couldn't understand, and we felt the release of tensions collapsing under the weight of alcohol.

Miss W wears the emeralds of a dead woman, she displays a gift she hoped never to receive, the teardrops that studded the ears of a countess passed only last week.

I pushed the paper away.

"Let me walk you home, Nina. You must sleep. I feel as though we have been awake forever."

"May I read it?" Nina said, approaching the desk.

"Oh no," I said hurriedly, placing my hand squarely on her back and pushing her towards the door. "I'm superstitious about these things. There's always a better word to use, a sentence to remove, an adjective to add. I do not like anyone to see it until it's ready."

"The Chinese call that adding feet to the snake after drawing it," she said with a shake of her head. "You ought to be careful of doing too much."

Downstairs we passed the dining room where Edward entertained a gaggle of soldiers. The table was littered with empty bottles, one teetered close to the table edge, threatening to fall and shatter. I waved quickly at Edward, noticed the weariness in his drunk eyes, the hard corners to his smile. I accompanied Nina through the streets of the Legation Quarter, where we walked now free from danger, the only obstacles in our path stumbling, singing drunks, emissaries of freedom. And I wondered, watching her cross those now-familiar streets, her steps languid where they had been hurried, how she might ever dismount the tiger upon whose back she rode that summer, and realized that I had little idea how her story might end. No words, I knew, could neatly tie together Nina's past and present, no turn of phrase could contain her experience. And yet, in my own little way that night, I had already tried to voice the unspoken.

XIV

DAWN BROKE muted and sombre over the Legation Quarter. The liberated, their senses dulled by the revelry of the night, slept through the first rising sun of freedom. Not I. I may too have partaken of wine, but it had not permitted me more than the most insubstantial of snatched slumber, and wild with impressions, frenzied with anticipation, I had risen several times in the night to continue the dispatch I had started to write. At dawn I abandoned all pretense of sleep, and reading the vivid words I had written in those darkest hours, I immediately, shamefully ripped the paper neatly in two, unsettled by how easily, how luridly my sentiments had awoken at the glistening sight of La Contessa's old earrings. I recovered my level head and began again, dispensing with all mention of glittering emeralds and unshed teardrops, and was writing the last faithful, unvarnished words for my editor (*The grateful besieged, thankfully rescued by brave troops whose sufferings have been so much worse than their own, await diplomatic negotiations to decide the indemnity for their distress at the hands of the Boxers*) when Nicholas knocked lightly upon the door and asked if I would accompany him home before Nina rose, to protect her, he explained, from whatever horror might lie in the shadows of the Tartar Wall.

We walked to the edge of the Legation Quarter in companionable silence, Nicholas muttering to himself now and again as he stumbled over rubble and detritus. Nearing the gate, a cry startled us. Nina's hair billowed loose around her shoulders as she ran towards us.

"I knew it! I simply knew you would try to go without me." She caught her breath as she reached us. "What were you thinking, Father?"

"Nina," I protested, but Nicholas raised a hand to stop me.

"Let her come," he said tenderly. "It is her home too."

The journey was short, a walk of barely ten minutes, and yet along the way we saw at least three dozen refugees, their belongings wrapped in crude knapsacks, their feet faltering over the inhospitable ground. They shielded their faces from us as we passed.

"Where are you going?" Nina called out in Mandarin to one group.

A little girl, cheeks smeared with dirt, hair pulled into hasty pigtails, turned and called: "The foreign devils shall destroy the city!" Her mother yanked on one of the girl's frayed plaits, reprimanded her for speaking with the foreign devils themselves.

"Destroy the city?" Nina repeated, turning the words, unpalatable, unsavory, over in her mouth. "Destroy the city?"

"When shall the Chinese stop running?" Nicholas asked.

I could offer no response.

From the far end of the Wards' narrow *hutung* we could see that the red door to their courtyard house lay open and ominous. As we drew closer, I noted that it hung raggedly, portentously from its hinges. I sensed Nicholas stiffen at the sight, and Nina lightly, almost imperceptibly, recoiled from the doorway, her shoulders curled round and defensive.

"I shall go first," I suggested, and Nicholas nodded.

"Very well," he said, and I left the pair in the street behind, felt their eyes on my back as I slipped into that oft-visited place with a gnawing sense of foreboding.

The front courtyard was eerily empty. The Wards' had been a

household of quiet, cheery labor, never without the gentle rustling sounds of servants passing down corridors, water splashing in pots, brooms sweeping over cobblestones. I passed through the shadeless courtyard, moving towards the main room in which Nicholas had hosted me countless times. With trepidation I stepped inside. At first glance it was as it had ever been: the same scrolls hung on the walls, the same books lined the shelves, yet everything seemed slightly awry. Pieces of furniture had moved a little, ornaments were arranged in new positions, some missed their corners, and the four walls closed around a scene at once disturbing and strangely comforting. People had been here, of that I had no doubt. The Silk Road rugs lay askew, their woven intricacy crinkled unnaturally. The floor was stained with mud, carpeted in dust, some books had fallen from their shelves, spines cracked and pages spilling. The head of a jade turtle looked up at me lost and despondent from its resting place next to the leg of an armchair. I moved towards Nicholas' bedroom. There the bed was imprinted with the silhouettes of half a dozen different bodies, the silk throw muddied and bloodied. Nina's bedroom was worse; the damage to its decorous delicacy formed a starker contrast than the destruction wrought upon Nicholas' more practical sleeping arrangements. The paintings on Nina's walls hung at odd angles, her bed was without clothes, the doors of her wardrobe were splintered and several dresses had disappeared.

"Not as terrible as one might have expected."

"Nina!" I turned. "I told you to wait."

"I would have to see it some day," she said quietly, her eyes drifting over each corner of her bedroom. "It won't take long to clean this. Everything shall be just fine, you'll see." She placed a hand on my shoulder and I held it there with my own, the two of us witnesses to an old life dismantled.

"Come!" Nicholas called. "You must see the kitchen."

This room provided the greatest evidence of alien presence: unwashed plates and bowls streaked with grease, littered with bones, suggested someone had eaten here not long ago. Most impressive was the collection of curved swords piled in one corner of the kitchen, their tips crimson.

"Good God." Nicholas lifted one from the heaped stack. The blade glittered. "Would you believe it, my girl? Our home, a Boxer hideout?" He chuckled, placing the sword down. "I don't see why we cannot return soon. The Boxers have gone, and they have at least left the old house standing."

"Oh, Nicholas," I said. "Leave it a few days. You'll need to find someone to clear all this away. Let the troops secure the city first."

"I'd like to return as soon as possible," Nina agreed. "Don't fret, Father, we shall be back where we belong sooner than you know." She smiled sweetly and embraced her father. "Mr Scott," Nina said over Nicholas' shoulder. "Might we see if Chang is at home?"

"Nina, I imagine Chang and her family will be as far away from Peking as possible. Do you really think her father would have kept the family living next to Boxers?"

"Please. Let us see."

The gate to Chang's home was locked tight. Nina and Nicholas stood back as I scaled the wall, feeling the inactivity of the past weeks in the reduced capacity of my lungs, in my ungraceful, lumbering fall to the other side. I moved towards the house, darkness through the windows warned that no trace of life would be found within its walls. Many of the family's belongings were gone; the rooms bulged with emptiness. I left quickly, the lifelessness of their household, its closed doors and stale air, somehow more discomfiting than the evidence of the Boxers in Nicholas and Nina's quarters. I climbed the wall again, shaking my head as I landed on flat feet in front of the Wards. Nina nodded, and in silence we walked back to the Legation Quarter.

It was much to my surprise and somewhat to my displeasure to discover upon my return that our saviors had brought with them a man of my profession. The young man was waiting in reception when I arrived at the Grand, feeling weary and unready for his enthusiastic pleasantries.

"Why, you must be Alistair Scott." Slim and sprightly, he sprang from his chair and proffered a smooth hand. The man's hair was a gleaming black, his skin was tanned and dry from weeks under the Chinese sun. "Imagine my envy when I discovered a fellow journalist had the luck to live through it all."

"I wouldn't necessarily describe it as luck," I said, standing opposite him, my hand hanging limp in the air where he had shaken it.

"The stories you must have, eh? Hilde invited me to stay for lunch, I do hope that's all right."

"Not my hotel." I attempted a pleasant smile, but sensed its wanness. "You're American?"

"Indeed. A New York man now, raised in Georgia. Walter Wingfield."

"Must have had a hard time getting here?"

"Absolutely. I'll tell you all about that."

And he did. We ate quietly, listening as he told of the hundreds of foreign casualties accumulated in the efforts to liberate Peking, the days without food and water, the troops who fainted while marching through wide open positions, their legs giving out under them, submitting them to the summer of death.

"I'm not a man given to exaggeration," Walter Wingfield said, chewing his words as forcefully as he did his dry mule meat, "but I don't think the American boys had seen such a fight since the Civil War."

"Is that right?" Hilde asked.

"Oh, yes. What we saw at Tientsin was much worse than any of these stories from South Africa, although I suppose the world is less interested in the fate of China than that of a jewel of empire."

"Our duty to change that, I suppose," I offered.

Walter nodded seriously.

"I hear Tz'u Hsi plans to leave Peking," he said.

"Yes, I plan to mention the departure of the Empress Dowager in my next dispatch." I placed my cutlery down. "Thank you again, Hilde."

Yet when I returned to my room I found I could muster no enthusiasm to write of Tz'u Hsi's mooted retreat from the capital, or the most terrible conflict since the American Civil War. Instead I wrote of the Wards' home, its courtyard bleached barren by the unforgiving sunlight, its rooms disturbed in elegant discomposure, its atmosphere empty of its habitual warmth, its climate devoid of its quotidian intimacy. And finally, dozens of pages filled, I allowed my head to rest upon the desk, and for sleep to welcome me.

Nicholas waited for me in the bar at Grand the next morning.

"This is becoming something of a habit," I greeted him.

Hilde had already prepared a cup of coffee, which I sipped gratefully while Nicholas explained that he planned to visit Pei, who, according to the last communication Nicholas had received from her several weeks prior, had taken shelter with an aunt.

"I am aware that it is a little further away, but perhaps you'd like to venture deeper into the city," he said.

"And Nina?"

"She sleeps," he said simply. The pause that followed his

words was meaningful, but I knew not in which way. He cleared his throat, looked intensely at his hands as he prepared to speak, the gray hair that dusted his knuckles glimmered white in the kindling light of morning. "We had more guests last night, more of the same, as you might imagine. All very jolly, celebratory. Nina was very quiet, but she stayed with the others long after I had retired. Mrs Franklin tells me she woke in the night and found Nina alone in the drawing room, that she appeared distressed."

"Oh." I took a sip of coffee. It burned bitterly against the back of my throat. I was aware that Hilde watched me, but dared not meet her eye.

"I wonder if I ought not have allowed her to come with us yesterday," he said. "I was relieved to see the house still stood, but perhaps she was alarmed by the damage we witnessed."

"It must be very hard for Miss Ward," Hilde said.

"Yes." Nicholas exhaled.

"Before I depart," I said to Hilde, "would you give this to one of the boys? And don't let Wingfield see it."

I passed an envelope to her, my latest dispatch folded inside it. I was proud of the story, it contained a great number of the elements of any good news story: intrigue (Tz'u Hsi's departure), vengeance (already the European diplomats told me of great compensation to be demanded of the Imperial authorities) and blood (I had artfully reproduced Wingfield's claim that the fighting on the North China plain had matched the horrors witnessed at Gettysburg), but I remained preoccupied by those other ignominious, unread pages, those profiles I had written of La Contessa and Nina, those descriptions of horse meat dinners and left-behind jewels. I had learned over the course of my career that both the press and the public craved stories of victory and optimism, narratives that placed their countrymen in danger long enough to lacquer events with a surface of tension, but that swiftly rescued them and painted them heroes, tales that assured that all conflict could be neatly ended and folded away, and leave behind no lingering melancholy. And yet in liberated Peking, there at the apex of Europe's vigor and fortitude, where Western fettle thundered mightily over Eastern submission, I felt nothing but a lingering melancholy, a pensive anxiety no newspaper editor would allow to sully the robust righteousness of his pages.

The streets lay quiet; Nicholas and I pushed against the silence. Every door we passed was barricaded, every window fixed shut; one could imagine trembling occupants behind those taciturn walls. Occasionally we saw figures in the street, hastening away from the Legation Quarter and its environs, meagre collections of belongings bundled in their arms.

"It gives you pause, does it not?" Nicholas said as a stooped elderly man moved past us, gnarled feet carrying him as quickly as their cracked soles would permit. "These people did not run from the Boxers, yet they flee the foreign powers."

I stopped at the squat doorway of a humble one-storey home. A Union Jack was strung across a window, a sign in unsure English pasted to the neighboring wall said, "No shoot. We are good people".

"My God, Nicholas, what's this?" I asked.

Nicholas shook his head, gestured for us to continue on our way. I followed him, but could not forget that incongruous flag.

It was when we turned the corner to the street where Pei's aunt resided that we discovered the motive for such a curious display of allegiance. A group of soldiers, British and American from the sounds of them, ran from home to home, piles of furs and silks heaped in their arms. The doors to the houses lay carelessly open, and Chinese residents occasionally followed the soldiers from those gaping mouths, darting behind the turned backs of the foreign men, handfuls of precious belongings, gold chains and books with worn covers and twills of ermine, clutched in their fists. I had seen this numberless times before, the pillage that follows victory, that flavors it sour for parties both vanquishing and defeated.

"What do you think you are doing?" I marched towards the dispersed company of young men, unable to find amidst their sprinting bodies a core that bound them, unable to identify a leader to whom I might direct my words. And so I spoke loudly, tried to capture their collective attention.

"You are aware, gentlemen, that looting is against the Hague convention?"

Some of the soldiers stopped, faced me in defensive, uneven lines, their uncaring expressions mocked me. No shame crossed their faces, no regret troubled their brows.

"Well?" I pressed. "Are you going to return these things? You are here to liberate and civilize, not to terrorize."

"Alistair," Nicholas said, his voice feeble behind me. "Let us find Pei. Please."

"One moment," I said sharply. "Well?" I demanded.

"I am sorry we interrupted the garden party you have been so enjoying this summer," one of the soldiers said with disdainful sneer. "We are simply collecting any valuable items for safekeeping. What do you suppose they make of that at the Hague?"

The other soldiers laughed then, guffawing in animal unity, half a dozen blue-green eyes trained upon me.

"Come, Alistair." Nicholas beckoned, and I followed with grudging steps.

"This is simply unacceptable," I said. "They must be stopped."

"Yes, yes," Nicholas said, but he did not break his path to Pei. The aunt's gray-walled house stood at the end of the street.

We approached cautiously, and found its wooden door swinging open to the street.

"Alistair." Nicholas stopped upon the threshold. "Do you suppose those men might have been here?"

Nicholas hesitated to enter the house, rocked uncertainly on his heels. I pushed ahead of him and into a dark hallway of low ceilings and narrow breadth. The air within the house was not stale, not faded, the windows, although they were shut tightly now, had not been long barricaded, I decided, suggesting that life had continued under the building's roof of sloping tiles as the Boxers had rushed Peking. I hoped that Pei had been here, felt this was a place unviolated. Yet as I progressed steadily down the corridor, Nicholas a few paces behind me, both of us glancing into the rooms we passed, devoid of human presence but with furniture unbroken and no evidence of looting having occurred, the ponderous quiet of the place weighed upon me.

I glimpsed the horrors of the bedroom first, saw the corner of a bed stripped of its coverings and a sheet soaked with blood abandoned on the floor. I took an intake of breath, intense enough for Nicholas to stop.

"Alistair? What is it, Alistair?" he asked urgently.

"Let me." I raised my hand and he did not move, remained in position within the confines of the corridor. I closed my eyes momentarily, gathered strength, and willed myself into the room. And there I saw her: Pei, strung from a wooden beam, feet dangling over the blood-stained bed, neck broken, dress torn. I stumbled backwards from the sight. On the other side of the bed a body lay slumped, an older woman with vacant eyes, a neat gash divided her torso from neck to navel.

"Don't," I cried. "Don't, Nicholas. Do not, do not enter."

My words came too late. Nicholas was inside the room, his face turned upwards towards Pei's corpse, his eyes round, his mouth slack.

"Alistair!" he called wildly, released an animal cry. I went to his side, supported him with my own shaking arms, but already he was collapsing in on himself, sinking to the floor.

"No, no, Nicholas," I pleaded. "Not here. We must get back to safety. Please, stay upright."

He was on his knees now, his face a terrible gray color, his lips bloodless, arms trembling under my grip.

"Nicholas," I said. "Please, try to stand."

"Who did this? Who did this? Did they do this?" His voice was thin, fissured and breaking.

"Come, Nicholas, come. We must reach safety. Pei would hate for anything to happen to you."

I tried to lift him, but his body, unwilling, resisted my efforts.

"Excuse me." A young woman's voice startled me. I relaxed my hold on Nicholas, let him fall back to the floor. She was not yet twenty, with the plain-faced appearance of a country girl. *"Ta shi Nicholas xiansheng ma?"*

"Yes, he is Mr Nicholas."

The girl knelt on the floor opposite Nicholas. In gentle tones she said: "They were foreigners. They came last night. She called your name. She said she loved you."

At this Nicholas wept, sobs tore from the back of his throat, his chest shuddered. The girl took his hands in hers.

"I am sorry," she said. "Her aunt, my mistress, she perished at their hands. Pei couldn't live with the shame, couldn't face you again after…"

"Oh no, oh no," Nicholas cried. "I would not have cared, not at all… It was not her fault, never her fault."

The girl moved closer and embraced him closely. I stood above their rocking bodies, my eyes drawn to Pei in her terrible lifelessness.

"We must get her down from there," I said.

The girl rose, standing by my side.

"I'm sorry. We have been hiding since they came," she said. "Please do not worry. We shall organize the rites. You must take him now, take him away from here."

The morning had not progressed beyond its first blushes when we returned to the Fairchild residence. The servants moved efficiently through the house, clearing away glasses slick with the residue of gin and victory, sweeping gray ash and faded embers from overflowing trays while most of the guests, including Nina, still slept. I supported Nicholas up the stairs, as he slowly, agonizingly took each uncertain step. His frame frail, he appeared a decade older than he had that morning when we had set out to find Pei. I accompanied him to his room, suggested he return to bed, but he refused, finally agreeing at least to sit, his spine straight and unforgiving, while I poured him a measure of whisky.

"Are they blind?" he said, in thick, cold tone. "Do they not distinguish between a Boxer and a civilian Chinese?"

"I do not know which is worse ," I said hopelessly, handing him the glass. "That they cannot distinguish between militant and civilian, or that they simply do not care."

"Brutes," Nicholas said. "Ignorant brutes."

Clamor rose from below us. The unmistakable voice of Lillian Price called out in high peals: "Five chickens! Eggs! Gentlemen, we have not seen such a feast for months!"

Nicholas, suddenly animated, made to stand, his legs wavered beneath him.

"They are here," he said. "Those soldiers!"

"Sit, man!" I pushed him back into the chair, poured more whisky into the glass. Reluctantly he drank it, and closed his eyes.

I left him to this dreadful meditation, and moved quietly to the room where Nina slept.

"Nina," I whispered, kneeling by her side. "You must wake now."

She stirred, an arm protruded from beneath the bedsheet. I noticed the sheer ivory of her skin, the blue maze of veins, so vulnerable and exposed, glimmering in the sunlight that streamed through the window. In sleep her hand sought mine, pulled my fingers towards her lips. She mumbled a word, or perhaps a name, that I could not understand. I jerked my hand free.

"Nina." I spoke sternly now; her eyes opened immediately, swimming in confusion.

"What? What is it?" She sat up.

"You must come to see your father," I said.

"I'm sorry, Mr Scott," she said. "I was so tired. Is it very late?"

She stood, glanced half-heartedly at her drawn expression in the looking glass, smoothed her hair.

"Nina, Pei is dead."

She stopped in the doorway.

"No," she said firmly. "It cannot be. You mean she is missing?"

"I saw her myself. I am so sorry."

She ran to her father's room. From the doorway I watched them, Nina's head in her father's lap, his hand petting her head distractedly, silent tears coursing his cheeks as Nina sobbed. Quietly I closed the door, and left them.

By then it was clear to me the fate which awaited Peking. The Legation Quarter had been liberated, but the wider city faced a terrible, vindictive crushing. Troops of every flag were issued with identical instruction to "secure the city", a command which in theory called only for the deaths of rebels but in practice proscribed indiscriminate slaughter. Whilst I have no doubts that some Boxers were exterminated in this bloody campaign, the price for one slaughtered warrior was a dozen of their helpless compatriots. Corpses piled in the street, but the fetid stink they produced proved no deterrent to the soldiers when engaged in their second most-preferred activity after killing: looting. Wealthy homes and palaces were stripped to their roofs and rafters, soldiers walked the streets with bulging trousers and awkward, arrogant gait. Not even God's messengers on Earth denied themselves the prizes of liberation, though the tactics employed by the missionaries were rather different. I discovered Phoebe Franklin removing myriad ornaments and clothes from the large home of a wealthy Chinese family. She explained that she had organized a sale of the family's belongings to Peking's foreign population and that the funds raised would be used to feed the Chinese Christians. Those were strange times, and her puzzling morality struck me as unexpectedly fair. The house would in any case be raided, the items stolen, and her actions allowed at least some good to come from the pillage of city. I handed her a coin.

"Would you like something?" she asked.

"No, no. A simple contribution." I walked away with sick heart.

The poor conduct of the foreign soldiers and opportunistic civilians continued unchecked as the various powers scrambling for the treasures of Peking bickered amongst themselves in the assigning of blame for each misdemeanor. General consensus named the Russians the most heartless and uncouth looters, though the French also provoked disdain. Many of the British asserted, despite the clear evidence in front of their own Anglo-Saxon eyes, that not one of Her Majesty's soldiers had pilfered a single item from Peking. We are gentlemen even in war, they said, and I suppressed my laughter. In a parade of rouges, what does it matter who leads?

The result was that in a few short days the count of terrible events was so high that I felt it impossible to try to record them. I did not write of Nina's visit from Lijun. The girl from Su's palace, determined to the end, arrived one unforgivingly hot afternoon at the Fairchild residence, nimble fingers drumming on the door. The servants hesitated about whether to permit entry to this ragged and sorrowful creature, but Lijun left them with little choice, tearing past them, crying Nina's name in a voice thick with tears. Between sobs she told Nina that some of her friends had jumped in a well, preferring to take their lives than risk grisly fate at the hands of Peking's liberators. While Lijun told this sorry tale the soldiers who commandeered Fairchild's drawing room from dawn til dusk, filling it with smoke and crude jest, joked amongst themselves that someone ought to shoot the female Boxer directly. Nina tried to calm her, and took Lijun to the bedroom she shared with Lillian, feeling shame as the young girl looked in wonder at the room, of unthinkable dimensions and unimaginable luxury, shared by only two people. Lillian returned from an outing to the Forbidden City, a new jade pendant swinging from her neck, and she cried in fright when she saw Lijun's tear-stained face and tattered clothes.

"Miss Ward, we are still at war with these people, are we not?" she said.

Within ten minutes Nina was at the Grand, where Hilde and I received the girl with warmth and surprise.

"Please care for her," Nina whispered, telling me in low tones of the ghastly end of the other girls. "And tomorrow, Mr Scott, you must accompany Father and I home."

In the morning they waited for me at the entrance to the Grand. I came downstairs with a jade-topped walking stick.

"Here," I said to Nicholas, who recoiled at the offer.

"That looks very much like a priceless antique," he said.

"I believe it to be exactly that. I bid on it last night. Already looted, it may as well go to a good home."

Nicholas accepted the gift, wrinkled knuckles settling around the stick's green orb. Nina was pale and quiet, but her steps grew more animated as we approached their home, and she linked her arm with mine as we turned once more down their *hutung*. The narrow street remained worryingly empty, the houses that hugged its sides were shuttered, uninhabited.

"Father," she said. "Are you happy to return?"

Nicholas nodded and used his newly-acquired walking stick to move the carcass of a dead dog from his path, its jaw open and bloody, revealing its useless teeth.

Nina and I spent several hours clearing the house of its debris, sweeping fingernails of Boxers and fragments of shattered ceramics out into the street. Nina watered the plants that shaded the corners of the central courtyard, their leaves a rusted yellow after weeks of neglect.

"This is too much work for us alone," I said to her. "Let us see if Fairchild cannot spare a servant or two."

Her head, craned over a wilted rose bush, jolted. She did not respond, but I noticed that she spilled water around the base of the pot.

It was not hard to find Oscar during those days; wherever the senior military men gathered one could be sure he was amongst them. Today they were at the British Minister's home, discussing strategy in the shade offered by the official's generous verandah.

"Mr Fairchild." I approached. "Do you have a moment?"

There was jostling, murmuring under the breath as the men observed me. Oscar did not reply, but regarded me thoughtfully, removed the pipe from between his lips. I stood firm.

"Naturally, Mr Scott," he said eventually.

Fairchild rose and weaved his way through the group of men, who turned their knees to the side to let him pass.

"Hey, Scott," one of them called to me, his uniform pulling tight over his chest as he leaned towards me. "Fairchild says there shall be a parade through the Imperial City. You might like to write a story about that, let the British read it first. We shouldn't like to lose out to that Wingfield character."

"Thank you."

Oscar led me some distance from the gathered military men, inhaled from his pipe, and closed his eyes momentarily against the glare of the sun.

"How may I be of service to you, Mr Scott?" he asked finally, meeting my eye.

"This parade," I started.

"We should be delighted if you were to write about it. It is planned for the 28th."

"And its purpose? A victory parade?"

"I suppose one might call it that, yes. It is intended simply as a message to the Chinese." Oscar pulled slowly on the pipe. "Terrible heat," he said. "Dry enough that a man might set alight."

"Mr Fairchild, I came to ask if you might make one or two of your servants available to the Wards. They have returned home and I am afraid to say that the house is still in a state of quite serious disarray. It might ease the return a little."

"They have gone?" he asked, fingers worrying the tip of his pipe.

"Yes. They felt it was time to go home."

Oscar's eyes narrowed.

"I am afraid the servants are rather busy. We have so many guests."

"Well, you have two fewer now," I replied. "Come, Mr

Fairchild. Is this not the least you might do for Miss Ward?"

"And what exactly do you mean by that, Mr Scott?" Oscar asked coolly.

"Please, Mr Fairchild," I said. "This charade is an insult to my intelligence, and to yours."

"I do not like your tone," Oscar said flatly.

"Very well," I said with exasperation. "Then we shall speak no more of your seduction of an innocent. All I ask is that you help her settle once more at home."

"Enough," Oscar said under his breath, the words controlled but live, sparking beneath their civil veneer. "I have heard quite enough." He turned his back to me, faced once more towards the men of uniform, engaged in low, murmured discussion.

"It is not fair, Mr Fairchild, that you play the victor, the emperor welcoming subjects come from afar, while Miss Ward scurries home to live amongst smashed ornaments and plates stained by Boxers."

Oscar walked. I followed him.

"The servants," I said. "Get me the servants."

I returned to the Wards with two servants in tow. We found Nina sunning herself in the courtyard; I stopped to admire her for a moment, so deeply tranquil did she appear below those old, familiar eaves. She jumped at our arrival, straightening her skirts and thanking the servants for their help. The pair moved into the quiet of the house, brooms in hand, and left me alone with Nina in the courtyard.

"Mr Fairchild sent the servants," she said softly. "That was very kind."

"Yes, very kind," I said simply.

She squinted her eyes against the sunlight.

"Perhaps Father might feel better if he were to sit out here a while," she said. "It is almost like old times."

CLARE KANE

The exodus was underway. Groups of women and children were already leaving Peking and heading east for safer pastures. Lillian Price was to be one of the first to leave for Tungchow and her departure was set for the early hours of the next day. Her trunk swelled now with new acquirements: a Siberian fur, a gold vase and a set of jade earrings among other treasures. Dinner at the Fairchild household that night was a two-hour toast to the young American, who accepted the raised glasses of the military men with happy modesty. I attended the farewell party only because I had heard that Walter Wingfield would be in attendance, and the idea that Wingfield might amongst those military men hear some significant news and better me on my own turf irked me. Word had reached the Legation Quarter that at least one of my dispatches had made the front page in London, and that the story had enthralled the general population, so fond of tales of Oriental peril and Occidental derring-do. I found the liberators keener now to seek out my company, and Oscar was careful and polite when I entered the party with dinner already drawing to a close, insisting I take a seat at the center of the table, next to Phoebe Franklin. She greeted me with fatigued eyes.

"Mr Scott," she started immediately. "I have a most wonderful collection of Ming vases for sale. Would you be interested in purchasing any?"

"Your career has moved in a rather surprising direction," I said lightly, before promising to review the collection after dinner. In the end I would agree to buy one vase from her, the purchase justified by the promise that proceeds would improve the circumstances of the orphaned converts, who existed now in unanchored liberty, caught between miserable past and hazy future.

After dinner talk in the drawing room was given over to

Lillian's recollections of the summer. Lillian, powdered and prepared for this moment, did not mention James Millington or the bullet that had torn through Queen Victoria's canvas, but spoke instead of recent jaunts to the Forbidden City and the Summer Palace. Beatrice Moore had arranged a picnic at the latter, and gathered a group to eat on the Empress Dowager's marble boat. The boat was an infamous folly of Tz'u Hsi's, its construction had stripped the navy of its budget, and being of marble the vessel of course could cross no seas. Lillian enthused about the false lake that spread across the grounds of the Summer Palace, telling us of a huge statue of the Kuanyin Buddha that she had looked upon in bemusement. "A thousand hands!"

She retired early, pleading tiredness and an early start, and watching her retreat, I regretted that these would be the stories Lillian would carry with her, these would be the memories she would tell again and again, light, giddy narratives that would obscure entirely the verity of our bloody summer. And how they would laugh. In New York, in Havana, in London. Goddesses with ten thousand arms, naps on courtiers' beds in the Forbidden City, afternoons spent watching soldiers pocket the best of the Imperial opium supply and laughing languorously with them as they slipped from reality into the cloying clouds of illusion. Wingfield filled pages of his notebook with Lillian's recollections, nodding enthusiastically as she picked over each detail. I left shortly after ten, and walked with haste to the Wards' home.

Their *hutung* was the only place I thought might bring me peace in that wretched city and so I hurried past the piles of corpses, the broken down doors, the pleading signs affixed to desperate homes: "No Boxers. Christianity", the last-ditch American and British flags fluttering outside shuttered windows, until the streets, dark, deserted, deathly, brought me finally to their quiet street. The house did not glow with the mellow warmth it had given off in a previous life; only one window was lit, and no trails of lively conversation filtered beyond its walls, yet I was glad to return. I found the main gate open (how many times had I told Nicholas that security must be better enforced now?) and allowed myself into the central courtyard, where I was surprised by the sight of a small cat, which jumped from a window ledge at the disturbance of my arrival, curving its back and stretching out its paws, instinctively moving towards me.

Nina read alone in the old drawing room, restored somewhat now to its original state, with only the most familiar of eyes able to perceive those empty spaces where treasured ornaments had once sat. I noted the book between her hands was decorated with Chinese characters:

Hung Lou Mêng, Dream Of The Red Chamber.

"No more Hardy?" I greeted her.

"I find more comfort in familiar words," she said, and called for a servant to bring me a drink. The household's stores had rather depleted in the Wards' absence, but I gratefully received the sweet rice wine I was offered.

"Your father?"

"Sleeping," she said simply. "I have become something of a night cat this summer, as the Chinese say."

"I did see a cat in the courtyard."

"Yes, it is Miss Price's kitten," Nina said carefully. "Liberty. It needs a new home now that Miss Price has left for Tungchow."

"But why is it here?"

"Mr Fairchild brought it to us this afternoon." Nina spoke softly, looked determinedly at the floor.

"Mr Fairchild was here?"

"Yes." Slowly she raised her head and glanced at me, pitiful, desperate. "He took me to the Summer Palace."

"Nina," I said sharply but quietly, aware that Nicholas slept.

"If you wish to see Mr Fairchild you must tell Mrs Samuels or myself, you cannot take such risks."

"He pleaded for me to go with him," she whispered. "It was easier simply to agree."

I am sure that Nina wished very much to see the Summer Palace, in fact I might go as far as to say that she may have desired to step within its high walls and walk its steep hills more than any foreigner in China. The Summer Palace, the seasonal Imperial hideaway, watched over Peking from a northerly distance, its treasures concealed, its happenings unknown, a delightful mystery to one as curious as Nina. I experienced a surge of anger towards Fairchild then; how clever the man was, knowing that such a temptation would prove irresistible to Nina, no matter the exhortations Hilde and I might have made for her to safeguard her reputation above all else.

"Did you enjoy it?" I asked finally.

"The air is fresh there," she said simply, and then with a sigh: "I doubt I shall see it again."

"Does your father know that you went?"

"Yes," she whispered. "But he does not know I went alone with Mr Fairchild." She studied the book in her hands, restlessly turned its pages. "Do not worry, Mr Scott, I shall not return there, or anywhere else, with Mr Fairchild." She closed her eyes, opened them once more and looked at me with chilling frankness, the green of her irises cold and expressionless. "Please, let us speak of another matter."

I took a sip of the rice wine, felt it cloying and sweet in my mouth.

"Then it is finished?" I pressed.

"What?" She turned her head sharply, irritated, and I saw that La Contessa's emeralds sparkled in her ears.

"Mr Fairchild."

She nodded.

"Good," I said.

We sat in silence. I sipped the rice wine, not enjoying the taste, but seeking some activity to occupy me while Nina's fingers restlessly traced the spine of her book. I knew when she prepared herself to speak, recognized the crease of her brow, the quiet concentration of her lips pressed against one another as she ordered and arranged words in her mind. Audibly she sighed, then leaning forward in her seat she spoke.

"You were right. I am a silly girl." Her words were quiet, controlled, devastating in their gelidity. "Mr Fairchild told me today that we could not see one another any longer. He said this was the most important moment of his career, that while he cared for me he must remain married to his wife, that a man of his position could not risk the consequences of a divorce. He said I must never speak of our...Oh, I suppose I must call it an *affair*, but what a flimsy word that seems for what we experienced together."

"Nina, I am sorry," I said, and rose from my chair.

Nina stood, placed her book on the seat behind her, and accepted my embrace.

"I promise," I whispered to her, "that you shall forget all of this, that one day it shall be a distant memory, faded and unimportant."

"I will never forget it," Nina said, and rested her head upon my shoulder.

We remained in this posture for two or three minutes, my hand brushed her back, my mouth mumbled useless words of limited comfort. I felt Nina so delicate in my hold, so wretched, a young woman on the threshold of a future hazy and uncertain, its once splendid potential overshadowed now by the tenebrous silhouette of scandal, the cragged overhang of war.

"Nina," I said. "You are not a silly girl. You are perhaps the most intelligent person I know."

"How?" she asked, and stepped back from me, revealing cheeks pink and stained with tears.

"You see it all," I said. "You see it all, the futility, the hypocrisy, the deceit with which most people live, and you reject it. You live purely, unfettered."

"You think so?"

"It will not make life easy for you, Nina, but it is a noble endeavor."

I closed the distance between us once more, took Nina in a close embrace, felt her form still, and knew her weeping had ceased. She pulled away from me, and we watched one another, eyes fixed and still, and that moment, that suspension of conversation, that departure from reality, that absolute disappearance of rationality, I have revisited it countless times in my mind, remembering, wondering, abashed at my actions. Because when I saw her face, pale and sweet, looming large before mine, and witnessed my stare reflected, green and burning, in hers, I could not help but to kiss her. Her lips yielded to mine, and together we bowed to the succor of the physical, stepping into the arms of phantom loves.

It was a kiss of shallow pleasure, rewarding the spirit and soothing the nerves as any kiss is wont to do, but it was an undoubted error. I broke the kiss, and in the pall of this corporeal surprise we stood once more in observation of one another.

"I am sorry, Nina," I said. "I only wished to comfort you."

"And I you," she responded.

"You do not want this," I said. "Not really. I ought to leave."

She smiled, warmly and sympathetically, and held me one last time.

"Good night, Nina," I said and turned to leave.

"*Wan'an,*" she called behind me. *Peaceful night.*

In the courtyard outside, Liberty wound herself around my legs, I knelt to pet the cat, crouched a moment, looking to the dark corners of the courtyard. Alone I crossed the desolate streets to the Grand, where I avoided a raucous crowd that gathered now in the bar to toast freedom, and went to that small room I called home where I wished for sleep to calm my heart.

XV

Peking, though ostensibly peaceful, was not a pleasant place as summer staggered to its end. Negotiations were underway, the officials told us, but on the streets we witnessed little change to daily life. The hunt for Boxers continued, and executions took place almost every day. I went to watch many of these dawn executions myself, but advised Nicholas and Nina to avoid them; one required the hardiest of dispositions to watch those wretched Chinese collapse lifelessly to the ground before skies of blistering red dawn. Following a particularly efficient round one morning, a British solider turned to me and said: "Not as bad as it looks, you know. Chinese don't feel pain." I did not reply as we watched a pack of dogs scrabble over the dusty ground towards the collection of freshly killed corpses.

And so it was with great surprise that I received news from Hilde one evening that a civilian visitor had requested a room at the Grand in an unanticipated return to normal business. The Chinese refugees had mostly vacated the hotel, and the Grand now functioned as lodgings for dozens of military men, who, Hilde was pleased to note, did at least have the means to pay for their rooms, even if their late-night carousing did keep her awake.

"He asked after you," she told me of the unexpected visitor. "I have sent him to your room."

I had had the pleasure and misfortune in my five years in China to meet a great host of characters, men of commerce, men of government and men of altogether more mysterious means, who might have thought to call on me when their business brought them to Peking, but I could not imagine that any of those gentlemen, however varied their desires and their debts, might have decided to visit Peking so shortly after the rebellion. Intrigued, I climbed the stairs and discovered the door to my room lying open. From the landing I perceived the outline of a young man in the candlelight, one hand clasped around a glass of whisky. I knocked lightly upon the door, and the man turned. I was startled by his appearance, at once familiar and unexpected, his features smooth and unblemished, his frame sturdy and well-fed; his evident health marked his absence from Peking that summer.

"Excuse me, Mr Scott. I hope you don't mind that I have helped myself," said Barnaby George.

The banker from Hong Kong, the young man who had asked for Nina's hand in those last days of innocence, seemed a traveler from another era, a vision from a life entirely irreconcilable with my current existence.

"Good Lord! Mr George, I did not expect to see you so soon. Have a drop more." I lifted the bottle, served him a measure. "You shall need it. Peking is not the city it was when you departed. Please, sit."

I poured myself a generous amount of whisky.

"Whatever brings you here?" I asked him. "The bank can't have sent you?"

"I am here for Miss Ward," Barnaby said shyly, looking into the depths of the glass he held.

"Miss Ward?" I repeated. "And does she know that you are here?"

Barnaby shook his head.

"I meant to see her right away, but I stopped here for a room and Mrs Samuels told me that you were also resident in the hotel. I wondered if it might not be better to consult with you before speaking with Miss Ward. I can only imagine the horrors she might have witnessed over the past weeks, the unfathomable terror..."

I placed a hand on his shoulder.

"Quite right," I said. "I must say that I am impressed. To come to Peking at a time like this speaks volumes of your character. They must have thought you mad in Hong Kong."

"Positively deranged," he said, laughing, relaxing a little. "I was due to leave for England a fortnight ago, but I decided to delay my departure. I did send a letter to Miss Ward; I suppose it was foolish to think she would receive it under siege."

"Now, Mr George," I continued. "What exactly do you plan to say to Miss Ward?"

"My plan was simply to come to Peking. Now I am here I feel rather unprepared for whatever it is that I ought to do now," he admitted.

I poured a short stream of whisky into his glass, and saw in the gentle tremor of his fingers, in the hard swallow of his throat, the opening up of an opportunity, wholly unexpected, yet magnificently timed.

"Allow me to help you, Mr George," I said.

In those moments now when the night demons visit, or in those times when I make the mistake of regarding myself too long in the mirror, wondering what quality of man I might consider myself to be, one question haunts me always. Did I believe Barnaby George to be Nina's equal in any measure? The reason this thought troubles me so is because the answer to my self-administered enquiry is so painfully, searingly clear. And yet, when I saw Barnaby George in the Grand Hotel, his appearance clean and pressed, his unobtrusive presence familiar and somehow soothing, his arrival an unanticipated solution to a persistent problem, I grew warm towards him. And so I helped him, I encouraged him, I let him try out words and phrases upon his awkward tongue until, just past a black midnight, we had a plan.

In the morning I walked with Barnaby to the Wards' home. He hesitated when we reached the gate, and so I reached for the lion head's knocker, and sounded it three times. Barnaby took a sharp inhale as we heard the approach of deliberate footsteps. One of Fairchild's servants led us to the drawing room, where Nicholas sat in an armchair, newspaper opened before him, reading glasses perched upon the end of his nose.

"Alistair," he said warmly, before starting at the sight of the man in the crisp navy suit by my side.

"Mr Ward," Barnaby said. "Good morning."

"What a surprise," Nicholas said. "Please, do come in. I shall ask Feng to fetch us some tea. I suppose that you wish to see Nina."

"Yes. If that is, if that is… quite all right," Barnaby said, his voice trailing. "And please do not trouble your boy to fetch any tea, I have had rather a generous breakfast at the Grand."

"Very well."

Barnaby and I followed Nicholas through the house, which by then had been more or less restored to its previous state: frames had been straightened, plates had been scrubbed, bedding had been washed and ironed. I wondered if Barnaby perceived a shift in the atmosphere of the place, the undeniable apprehension that I now sensed in the air.

"Here she is." Nicholas paused by the door of his study. "She has been helping me with my books. We discovered some exceptional volumes at the Hanlin."

Over Nicholas' shoulder I saw a confusion of books spread across the floor and one pale, slender leg emerging from dusky pink skirts.

"Nina, you have a visitor," Nicholas said.

He stood aside. Nina peered around her father's frame and caught sight of Barnaby. The pair regarded one another for a moment. What did Barnaby see? The girl he had left behind, yes, but there was a sharpness to her now, a wariness in the angles of her face. Her skin pulled taught across her bones, her green eyes darted restlessly. Her feet were bare, her hair fell loose and wild around her shoulders. And what did Nina see? A neatly tucked shirt, shoes of high polish, an unremarkable face comforting, I suppose, in its familiarity. Nina stood, and they approached one another as might two animals of distinct species, in cautious, hesitant circles.

"We shall leave you," Nicholas said. "I expect you have much to discuss."

"Good day, Nina," I said, and she at me in bewilderment.

Nicholas and I retreated; from the corridor we heard Nina's voice, keen and defensive.

"What are you doing here, Mr George? Peking is the last place in the world anyone would want to be right now, is it not?"

"He is a very courageous young man," Nicholas said with gentle chuckle. "One needs pluck to return to Peking, but to seek out my daughter once more…"

We walked outside, looking not at one another but rather at the expanse of the courtyard in front us, the collection of blue and white porcelain pots, the plants craning their delicate necks towards the sun, the bamboo growing in infinite spirals.

"Thank you, Alistair," Nicholas said, placed a hand upon my shoulder. "Thank you for all you have done."

His words, light and benevolently intentioned as they

were, struck me still. The siege had ended, and so too had our merciful dance of ignorance; the clement silences, the words void of meaning, the expressions not exchanged, could not sustain themselves against the stark prospects of a life post-siege. Returned to a home irrevocably, permanently altered, cleaved by terrible violence from Pei, Nicholas must have seen that his daughter's fate hung nebulously, inauspiciously before the Wards, a puzzle without resolution, and as such, salvation in the form of Barnaby George, however unimaginative, however undesirable it may have been to Nina, suggested at the very least a direction in which her unmoored existence may travel. For that, Nicholas was grateful, and in his state of more relaxed amiability he implored me to stay for a cup of jasmine tea. I wished to stay, to converse, to debate with my old friend, to return to simpler times, but I was gripped by a sudden anxiety, I felt the walls of the Wards' home press close around me, noted that familiar dread of conversations momentous but unknown taking place nearby, the foreboding of closed doors and lowered voices, and I could not stay a moment longer in that old happy house of theirs.

Barnaby George waited for me at the bar of the Grand as the day descended to dusk, one foot tapping impatiently against his chair.

"Not too early for a drink?" He rose to greet me.

"A bad day, Mr George?" I removed my hat and took a seat next to him.

"Terrible," Barnaby said darkly.

Hilde bustled through from the kitchen, gun slung across her torso.

"I heard you from the kitchen," she said to me. "Whisky?"

"Please," I said, and turned to Barnaby. His skin, habitually a ruddy shade of scrubbed pink, looked pale in the dim light of the bar, and his posture was rounded, defeated. "So, you have seen Miss Ward," I started.

"Most foolishly, yes. The answer was no. Once again."

"I'm sorry. Truly," I said.

"She told me she might never marry," Barnaby continued, and I noted the glass before him lay empty. "I told her that everyone must marry, and she said that marriage was folly, that yes, everyone marries, and then they are abandoned, as was her father, or perhaps they are betrayed. What was it she said? That married people are miserable in a prison they build with their own hands."

"Very eloquent," I said, for Nina's words did strike me as elegantly true and wise beyond her tender years, but I also spoke to fill the yawning inadequacy of my guilt, knowing no words I might say could justify to Barnaby George my hasty advice that he once more seek Nina's hand, and aware, even then, that while marriage to Mr George created an exit for Nina from her current murky circumstances, it was not one she was inclined to take.

"Miss Ward has had a terrible summer," Hilde said quietly as she filled my glass.

"I am well aware of that," Barnaby said. "It was most stupid of me to come here. I suppose I must leave as soon as possible."

"Nonsense," I said. "You wouldn't like to miss the victory parade tomorrow, would you?"

"Victory parade?" he repeated.

"Yes. I am not sure who shall be left in Peking to witness it, but the parade shall follow a most illustrious route. They shall even march through the Forbidden City."

"What is one more day after so many wasted ones?" Barnaby said.

"That is the spirit," I said.

"Excuse me, gentlemen. You may help yourselves from

behind the bar. There is someone I must see." Hilde left us, gun thumping against her hip as she moved.

I had done my best to kill the night with Barnaby, seeing him to his room just at the point when a switch from whisky to Chinese rice wine had appeared to him a sensible idea, and was preparing myself for sleep when Hilde rapped confidently upon the door. Proprietarily she strode across the room, seated herself by my desk.

"I went to see her," she said. "Miss Ward."

Hilde removed her gun from the holster affixed by her waist, placed its shining body upon the desk.

"And?" I pressed.

"We have tried, Mr Scott, we have done all that falls within our power." Hilde sighed. "She was very quiet, her father said she had not left her bedroom since Mr George's visit. It was there that I saw her, and entreated her to consider with some care the offer made to her by our young friend Barnaby. I said that he was kind, solid, secure, that she must remember that Mr George might offer her a future while Mr Fairchild could not."

"What did she say?" I asked. The anxiety of our circumstance was stifling, and I felt my breath shallow, constricted. What misery we had wreaked, I thought, Hilde and I, in the armor of good intentions. How blithely, easily I had sent Barnaby George to the fresh pain of rejection, how confidently I had believed myself the skilful puppeteer of Nina's fledgling romantic life, how foolishly, arrogantly Hilde and I had imagined ourselves Nina's guardians, her ultimate protecters, and how useless we had finally proved at the most acute moment of her wretchedness.

"Nothing," Hilde said. "Precisely nothing. Until I mentioned her father, suggested she think of him, remember his concern for her. She said then that she could not marry anyone who might take her from Peking."

"But Nicholas only desires what is best for Nina," I said.

"I told her that. But it was as though she did not hear me." Hilde exhaled, closed her eyes, and we sat silently a moment. "I took her hand," she said eventually, opening her eyes once more, "and she permitted me this. I left her shortly afterwards and told her only to remember that while you and I had protected her this summer, now she must protect herself."

"And what did she say to that?" I asked.

"She said, with some vehemence, that she was very well aware of that." Hilde stood, briskly cleaned her gun against her skirts, fixed it once more by her waist. "All we can hope, Mr Scott, is that the coming days deliver some reason to dear Miss Ward."

Had we known then how torrid, how darkly terrible the following days would turn out to be, we would not have expected them to bring reason to anyone. Dawn broke a bloody red over Peking on the twenty-eighth of August, the day selected to celebrate our great vanquishing of the Boxers. Despite official instructions that no journalists were to attend the victory parade, Oscar Fairchild had secured me the right to ride with a contingent of British diplomats, in exchange, he explained in lofty, unspecific terms, for generous and, I understood, glory-giving coverage of the event. I assented, feeling no obligation to withstand my side of the deal, given Fairchild's conduct during the siege. I walked briskly through the Legation Quarter, piecing together in my mind the dispatch I would later write. *A terrible summer draws to a close and the Chinese are taught a lesson...A magnificent display of cross-country cooperation that will surely mark the internationalist direction of the new century...*Writing the news feels at times akin to fortune-telling. Life itself unfolds as discreet, dissociated events, yet the accounts that fill the pages of newspapers require effortless linearity; as such, I often internally compose histories long before they take place, imagining paragraphs to flow in seamless succession even before the first actor has stepped onto stage. My mind drifted at times to Barnaby George, for whom I had begun to feel a real sympathy. I suspected he would still be asleep, drowsed by last night's whisky, unaware of the victory that dawned over Peking's gray roofs. And how would Nina's story end, I asked myself, matching sentences and phrases in my mind, imagining her future as it might be written in newsprint. Yet I could not read her story with clarity: too many paths opened up before me. *Miss Ward today accepted Mr George's offer of marriage...Miss Ward is to marry Mr Fairchild, who has divorced his wife...Miss Ward remains a spinster in Peking...*

The Russians had already gathered when I reached the agreed meeting point. There had been much discussion over who was to lead the victory parade, with the Russians arguing that as the most populous force they should steer the allied powers through the city. In fact, the Japanese outnumbered them, but the Russian troops, heavy, strong and determined, were granted first position. I took my place with the group of British diplomats, and patiently we waited under the beating sun for our departure. We were led by Oscar Fairchild, who took lively, spry steps through the city, a summer hat angled cheerfully atop his head. The entire event proved somewhat underwhelming: the Russian band tasked with playing each country's national anthem was hopelessly out of time, playing La Marseillaise as the Italians marched past, and the crowds lining the streets were sparse and unimpressed. Chinese faces peered in fearful bemusement, while the foreign onlookers were unable to conceal their disappointment at the rather rakish appearance of the poorly turned-out soldiers who marched behind the diplomats. The British soldiers appeared particularly shabby, wearing uniforms now too large for their scrawny frames, their faces smeared with the grime of the city. I noticed Hilde in the crowd, Lijun by her side: they surveyed the scene with blank expressions. We passed Nina and Nicholas too, eyes narrowed against the glare of the sun. Nicholas waved enthusiastically to me, Nina, with pressed lips, weakly raised her hand.

The march to victory, which under Peking's relentless sun at times felt more of a trudge to Hell, came to an end at the gilded gates of the Forbidden City, where a group of humbled eunuchs had been tasked with escorting the foreigners around the palace. Quite how this tour had been proposed to the Imperials I do not know, but in the end it was nothing more than another looting opportunity. I admit, however, that I did appreciate the chance to see that spectacular, secretive palace from the inside, to raise my eyes to its elaborate cornices and run my fingers across its collections of engraved lacquer, appalled as I was by the conduct of the soldiers who swept each shelf of ornaments, and cleared every cupboard of the finest silks.

The evening drew in humid and unforgiving and I returned to my room to produce a perfunctory report of the day's events, a series of sentences of hollow victory that I knew would please my editor. To my shame I did not include so much as a single incident of looting; perhaps by reporting it here I can absolve myself somewhat of that important omission. Finished, if not entirely satisfied with my work, I repaired to the bar, where Hilde and Lijun made sure to keep my glass of whisky always full.

"When are you going to go home, Mr Scott?" Hilde asked me. "You are very welcome here, you know that, but I may need to start charging for the whisky," she said, her smile good-natured.

"My house is ruined, Hilde. I have dared to walk past upon occasion and with each visit it seems to have fallen into a greater state of disrepair. I know it to be habitable, at least, because a number of people appear to be living there, none of whom I imagine would be enthused by my return. I have asked for reparations but in London they appear to care little for my hardship."

"I am sorry to hear that," she said.

"I have thought of appropriating one of those empty homes for myself, a nice little palace of some prince long fled, but I must say I rather enjoy the company here."

Hilde laughed.

"Stay for now," she said seriously. "I like to have you here."

We became aware then of a figure approaching us. Barnaby George walked steadily towards the bar, a bamboozled expression upon his face.

"She has asked for me," he said.

"Sorry? Speak up, boy," Hilde said.

"Miss Ward has summoned me." He paused. "To her home."

"Well, don't keep the lady waiting," I said. "Go and find what she wants."

"Do you think…" He failed to complete his question. "Yes, yes. I ought to go right away." He inhaled, steadied himself with a hand on the bar. "Yes, I shall go now. Good evening."

"Good evening, Mr George." Hilde laughed generously as he left. "Do you think," she said, "that Miss Ward might have listened to me?"

The breathless account Barnaby George delivered to us only three hours later certainly suggested something profound had happened to Nina. Barnaby had arrived at the Wards' home, trembling with nervous energy, hearing in each clipped, clear strike the lion's head knocker delivered upon the door his own wishes echo through the unseen courtyard that lay just beyond him. Nicholas had welcomed Barnaby, led him to the courtyard, which flickered warmly by the light of several clusters of candles arranged across its four corners. A table set for three stood in the middle of the space, a great lantern at its center. Barnaby dithered over which chair to occupy, and was still undecided when Nina crossed the courtyard towards him and expressed her delight at his joining them for supper. He noticed that her hair, which had fallen loose and unkempt the previous day, was carefully arranged in a tight chignon, and the light blue dress she wore appeared freshly laundered.

Barnaby watched with curiosity as the entire surface of the table was rapidly covered with enthusiastic portions of pork, beef, scallions and aubergine prepared by Fairchild's servants. Barnaby had been surprised to see Nina make deft use of her chopsticks to sweetly place a serving of each dish upon his plate. Nicholas commanded the conversation, enquiring about the bank's plans, asking whether British businesses planned to exit China. When Barnaby had replied that Shanghai, Hong Kong and the other treaty ports remained relatively stable and attractive to foreign investment, Nicholas had replied gravely: "Things shall change." He had from that point become rather morose, picking over the looting of recent days, and predicting a succession of dark years ahead for an impoverished and isolated China. The food finished, Nicholas had then excused himself and left Barnaby alone with Nina. Immediately Nina stood and moved to the seat by Barnaby's side.

"You must wonder why I invited you here tonight," she said, and when he agreed, she very rapidly explained her motives, her words quick and nimble, her eyes not lifting to meet his gaze. She told him she had been terribly affected by the siege, and had been unable to see clearly when he had asked her to marry him, and admitted that she now regretted her words.

"If your question still stands," she said, "then I wish you to know that my answer is yes."

Utterly, delightfully flabbergasted, Barnaby had required a moment of repose before his happiness could express itself in the chaste kiss he placed upon her lips.

"Let us tell my father the good news," Nina had said, and Nicholas had displayed his first smile of the evening upon hearing of the betrothal.

When Barnaby reached the conclusion of this joyful account, Hilde went immediately for a bottle of champagne, which we shared amongst the three of us. Hilde also called for Edward, who abandoned the entertaining of his military guests to join us in taking a glass; even young Lijun was woken and presented with a small serving.

"To a wonderful future," Edward said in toast.

"To Miss Ward," Hilde said, and we toasted Nina in her absence. I wished to see her, to observe her expressions, her movements, to hear the words she chose to tell of her upcoming marriage. I hoped to console myself with her happiness, to see and confirm her desire to enter into this partnership, to know she saw it as a passage to freedom and not a prison built by her own hands. But she was not there, so we drank instead to an image of her, to the illusion of the hopeful, rosy bride, and while my elation was real, buoyed by relief, its corners were firmly pinned down by anxiety, by guilt, by irrepressible shame. Hilde and I were the last ones to the retire that night, and as I made to ascend the stairs, she stopped me.

"We did right by Miss Ward," she said.

"Of course we did," I replied, but I knew not which one of us tried to convince the other, and I felt, climbing the stairs on tired feet, that we both had failed to do so.

The next day brought about the sudden onset of that activity required to organize a wedding. I had not considered the practicalities of the marriage when Barnaby had shared his news the night before, had not thought to enquire how, tangibly and feasibly, the pair expected to establish a shared life. Nina appeared at the hotel in the early morning, just as I was finishing a plate of eggs sourced by Hilde from the more functional Japanese Legation. Charily Nina asked if I might accompany her to Su's palace.

"I must speak with Mrs Franklin," she said. "And I would like to speak also with you."

Immediately I rose, embraced and congratulated her, and felt her form not cold to the touch, but certainly still, lacking the animation one might expect of a young woman in her circumstance, stepping into the thrill of a married future. Her eyes, a brilliant morning green, betrayed no emotion, and whilst she did not create the impression of the giddy betrothed, I was pleased that equally she did not appear unduly anxious or melancholy. We did not walk directly to the palace, but passed unhurried through the Legation Quarter streets, circling those familiar monuments to our suffering.

"I must try to remember it all," Nina said. "I do not wish to forget Peking when I am in England."

"You shall go to England, then?" I asked. I was not entirely surprised; Barnaby's family, his future were firmly rooted in the old country, but I was startled by Nina's easy acceptance of the inevitability of such a move.

"Naturally," Nina said as we crossed the tennis courts, empty still of matches. "One cannot marry an Englishman and not expect to go to England."

"You shall miss Peking," I said.

"Father says that even he shall miss Peking, that the city we know is finished, to be replaced by some new town, duller and sadder than before."

She led me the chapel, absent now of notices, no longer a central meeting point for the besieged, stripped of its powers as arbiter of our desperate fate.

"I wished to thank you, Alistair," she said, not looking directly at me, "for all your efforts to help me this terrible summer. I have not been an easy case, I know, I have refused your advice countless times. But I hope you see..." Here she faltered, and finally looked upon me, her eyes brimming with tears, "...that I have listened when it was most important to do so."

"I have not imparted any advice to you, young Nina, not this time. You might have listened to Mrs Edwards, Mr George, your father, and you ought to thank them. But I have done little."

"You did much before," Nina said simply. "And I know that Mr George might never have asked for my hand had you not encouraged him so. I only wish to say thank you."

I nodded dumbly, wondered if I ought to embrace her again, felt any words I might speak woefully insufficient. She thanked me, she saw the worth of my actions, she did not fight my counsel. I ought to have been delighted to see Nina survive the siege, her reputation intact, to emerge from the other side of the summer of death, alive, unblemished, prospects golden and secure unfolding before her, and yet I felt only a terrible flatness, a colorlessness of sentiment. I was pleased to see the Su mansion come into view as we approached the borders of the Legation Quarter, glad to have our conversation curtailed by the appearance of its wretched walls.

Since our liberation, many of the refugees had departed the former palace, abandoning that dismal place to rot in desperation and disease, but some found themselves in an earthly limbo following the arrival of the troops and had no idea where else they might find shelter and relative safety. And so Phoebe Franklin continued to visit the place every day and care for those still resident between its walls.

"Mrs Franklin," Nina called out as we stepped into the musty-smelling building. We found Phoebe not inside the palace, but conducting a Bible reading for a group of young girls in the courtyard. We settled ourselves a little behind the group, and listened to Phoebe read.

"Come now, let us reason together, says the Lord, though your sins are like scarlet, they shall be as white as snow; though they are red like crimson, they shall become like wool..."

My mind wandered, continued its unending stream of questions, following the cadence of Phoebe's voice until the end of the reading was announced with a heavy thud as Phoebe closed the Bible and placed it on the floor.

"Miss Ward, Mr Scott," Phoebe said, approaching us and leaving her charges to read alone. "An unexpected pleasure."

"Hello, Mrs Franklin," Nina said. "How are things here?"

"Much improved, as you can see."

"I am so glad," Nina said. She pulled nervously at a loose strand of hair that had curled itself around the base of her neck. "Mrs Franklin, I have come to ask of you a favor. Rather a large one."

"Yes?"

"I am planning a wedding," Nina said, with a bashful glance in my direction. "I thought you might recommend someone able to marry people, in the eyes of God, I mean."

"Oh yes," Phoebe said briskly. "Who is to be married? Lijun?" she asked sharply.

"Lijun? Of course not, she is a mere child. It is I who is to marry," Nina said.

"Oh!" Phoebe's eyebrows shot up momentarily, quickly she straightened her features once more. "My sincere congratulations, Miss Ward. And who are you to marry?"

"Mr George from Hong Kong," Nina said carefully, and I watched the missionary, that messenger of God who had witnessed all, to read her reaction to the news. A smile, warm and immediate, softened Phoebe's features, and she took Nina in her arms.

"Oh, wonderful, wonderful," Phoebe said. "I should be delighted to organize the ceremony immediately."

"You are sure?" Nina asked, her voice small, wondering.

"I am so pleased," Phoebe said, "that you have come to your senses. Are you not, Mr Scott?"

And she embraced me too.

A date was set only three days away. Having made the decision to marry, Nina's alacrity in organizing the ceremony came as little surprise to me; I understood that her desire to marry quickly was two-fold. To marry before anyone might say anything to give her prospective husband pause, that was one aim. To marry before she might doubt, I suppose that was the other. Nicholas suggested that Nina might wear the dress her mother had married in, and the old outfit, kept in a dusty red chest in the corner of Nicholas' wardrobe, was revealed as a yellow white, its wide skirt and the fussy, intricate detailing of its lace recalling another era, but Nina had no time for trifles now, no time for anything at all. And so the dress was taken to a laundryman, recently returned to the Japanese Quarter, whose prices had risen by a third since the siege. Nina then enlisted Lijun's help in sewing a red velvet border around the hem of the skirt; both girls believed wholeheartedly that no wedding could take place in the absence of red, whatever the ladies of England or the missionaries of China might believe.

Nicholas invited Hilde and I to the house on the eve of Nina's wedding. Hilde brought Edward and a cook with her, and together we dined in the familiar balmy environs of the Wards' courtyard. Nina's life was by then packed up in a quiet collection of trunks and boxes, but any apprehension she felt on this cusp of womanhood was concealed in her easy manner over dinner. Indulgently she encouraged her father's tales of Nina's Peking childhood, and we all laughed heartily at his stories of Nina as the cat chasing Chang the mouse from courtyard to courtyard, the two girls breaking off from their games to beg for toffee apples from street vendors, and Nina coming home to sing nursery rhymes of little fat boys and red dragonflies entirely unknown to Nicholas. It was as dinner drew to a close, and we were finishing the last of the wine, that the knock came upon the gate. I rose, and crossed the courtyard to the Wards' red door, thinking a returned servant or a neighbor robbed of sleep by our lively conversation might await me on the other side.

Yet it was Oscar Fairchild who knocked, and who, in a momentary confusion of his habitually unruffled features, betrayed surprise at my appearance.

"Mr Scott," he said, and cleared his throat. "I did not know you would be here."

"The Wards invited me to spend the evening with them," I said coolly. "I do not think they expect you, Mr Fairchild."

Oscar, unflappable and affable as always, smiled lightly.

"I have come to see Miss Ward," he said, and made to step across the threshold into the courtyard. I blocked his path. "To wish her well upon the occasion of her marriage."

"Mr Fairchild," I said sternly. "Whilst I am sure your wishes would be gratefully received, I am not convinced it is appropriate for you to address Miss Ward at this precise moment. She must rise early tomorrow, and we are still at dinner."

"I only wish to see her briefly," Oscar said. "I would like to pass on my congratulations."

"Mr Fairchild, I have asked you once to leave. I do not wish to repeat myself."

Footsteps, hesitant, cautious sounded behind me.

"Mr Scott, please." Nina tapped my shoulder, nodded encouragingly. "Allow me to speak briefly with Mr Fairchild."

"Nina," I said, rather sharply. "I have asked Mr Fairchild to leave."

"Please," Nina protested. "It is quite all right."

"Mr Scott, leave her a moment to speak with me. I promise I shall depart immediately," Oscar offered.

I looked behind me. Conversation had halted at the dining table; quizzically, anxiously Hilde and Edward looked towards the entrance where I stood in infelicitous triangle with Nina and Oscar. Nicholas did not trouble to look up, but his head hung heavy, defeated, as he toyed with the stem of his wine glass. I weighed the options, knew that a moment between the two, here, observed by us all, was unlikely to derail plans for the next day. What might Oscar dare to do before the girl's father? He had been brazen in the most terrible moments of the siege, that was true, but he had rather hastily abandoned his affection for Nina when liberation came. And so I relented, discarded my resistance, and took a few steps back, allowing the pair a moment of near privacy in the half shadows. I did not retreat to the table, did not wish to give Fairchild an impression of free rein, and so stood somewhere between the tenebrous couple and the dining party, but with my ear trained on the conversation, held in muted tones, between Nina and Oscar.

"Do not come closer," I heard Nina say calmly. "Say what you must, then leave as you have promised."

Murmured protestations followed, their specific contents undecipherable to my distant ear.

And then, Nina, forthright: "Is that all you wished to say?"

Her voice was carefully controlled, and I thought she must appear to him as decided and unrepentant, but I worried, standing between those two worlds of Nina's: the twinkling familiarity of her warm, intellectual life with her father, and the novel amusement of her illicit romance with Oscar, that upon seeing Fairchild again she may question those decisions she had taken, so very delicately balanced on unstable collections of pros and cons, and that those choices may teeter and wobble, and threaten to collapse. Fairchild spoke more; I strained to hear his words, made out a plea to wait, understood his injury at her hurry to marry, and all the time I wished him away, wondered if I ought to intervene, to step between them, but told myself to trust Nina, to believe in the power of her fragile elections.

"I am cruel?" Nina said, her voice rising. Fiercely she continued: "Since we have been liberated, I have not existed for you, is it not so?"

Anxiously I looked to the table, saw Hilde valiantly continue their dialogue, seemingly unperturbed by the distance, the distraction in Nicholas' expression.

And then I heard Nina speak the most devastating sentence of all: "I would have waited forever, Oscar, you know that."

Her voice cracked on those last syllables, and I stepped back towards the door, placed myself between the severed pair.

"You have had your time to wish Miss Ward well," I said. "Thank you, Mr Fairchild, and good night."

Nina, her eyes savage, her expression anguished, looked pleadingly to Oscar. Slowly he turned from her, and over his shoulder he called, "Good luck, Miss Ward", before disappearing into the gloom of the hushed *hutung*, the silhouette of his summer suit lost rapidly amidst the dark contours of the night. I closed the gate definitely, and numbly Nina crossed the courtyard by my side. We took our places at the table, but struggled to rediscover the uncomplicated sociability that had characterized our evening prior to Fairchild's unexpected visit, and Nina excused herself shortly, claiming tiredness. Hilde, Edward and I immediately followed and I watched as Nicholas led his daughter back inside the house, his arm mercifully, paternally arranged around her shoulders, and I saw in his slow, steady steps, in the quiet rumble of his voice, that he forgave her, forgave her everything, her moral trespassing and her imminent departure. And I hoped that Nina might sleep the sleep of the peaceful, the sleep of the assured, the sleep of the virtuous.

The morning was clear and cool, the sky an auspicious blue. We were a small group collected at Su's palace: Edward Samuels, Hugo Lovell and myself had gathered alongside some of Lijun's peers and a handful of missionaries.

"Do you know," Hugo said to me under his breath, "at one time I thought I might see Miss Ward marry James?"

I did not reply. His comment provoked a queer reaction in me; I wondered for a moment how many men in the Legation Quarter had considered that Nina might one day be betrothed to them. Prior to the siege, none could have imagined any man might remove Nina from Peking, from her father, from the half-world she inhabited between China and England, and yet here we were, waiting to see her married to a one-time visitor to Peking, a man none could dislike or discredit, but not a man we considered a match for Nina.

The Chinese schoolgirls gasped when Nina arrived: "*Lai le!* She's here!" "*Mei!* So beautiful!" We turned to see Nina on Nicholas' arm, Lijun clutching at the train of her red-trimmed skirt. Indeed, Lijun and Hilde had made Nina look her best, since the early hours they had meticulously applied cream and powder to conceal the shadows under her eyes, and had arranged her hair in elaborate coils. Nina's face was placid, her manner collected, nothing in her bearing revealed the night's turmoil. With coy grace she took her position by Barnaby, and with unhesitating words a missionary colleague of Phoebe's married the pair. Phoebe stood then before us all and read: "Love is patient, love is kind. Love does not envy, love does not boast, it is not proud. Love does not dishonor others, it is not self-seeking, it keeps no record of wrongs. Love does not delight in evil but rejoices with the truth. It always protects, always trusts, always hopes, always perseveres."

I fancied that behind Nina's veil her eyes filled with tears, but I could not be sure. Nicholas crossed next to the center of the courtyard, a piece of paper gripped between his fingers.

"I have struggled," he began, "to find a suitable passage with which to send my daughter into married life. My preferred sages, it seems, did not much favor the institution of marriage." He laughed drily. "So allow me to say some inelegant words of my own, to posit that the union of two people, like that of yin and yang, is something precious to be celebrated, a process that brings balance to two individuals."

Barnaby reached for Nina's hand.

"Unfortunately my eloquence does not extend much beyond that simple observation, so I have consulted that most wisest tomes, the Tao Te Ching, to offer Nina some advice. She is, after all, a daughter of China, setting out on untested waters, riding a wave of events that has risen unexpectedly and dramatically before her. My dear Nina, for you:

Heaven and Earth are eternal
Because they do not live for themselves.
This is the reason
they exist consistently through time.

The sage puts herself last and comes first.
She identifies with the Universal Self
And remains constant.

Isn't it this way because
she lacks personal self-interest?
This is why she will succeed
in all of her personal endeavors.

Good luck."

Nicholas stepped away, and Barnaby whispered something to Nina, who nodded, eyes fixed upon her father.

"I believe there will now be a small reception at the Ward household," Phoebe said. "Please join us for lunch and to celebrate this most delightful end to a most trying summer."

Nina and Barnaby led a merry line of guests towards the Wards' home. The city remained in mourning, its streets were unnaturally quiet, but even so a few well-wishers dotted our path, waving and whistling as the bride passed by, their number even included Beatrice Moore and her three children. Nina waved warmly to Beatrice and those gathered onlookers, and I wondered if she had noticed that there was, of course, one absent face amongst the enthusiastic passersby, that Oscar Fairchild, to my relief, had not come to see Nina one last time.

An efficient staff of refugees from the Su mansion had arranged tables around the Wards' courtyard and set out food and wine for the guests. The party was civilized and short, in the best of wedding traditions, and by mid-afternoon I was left alone with Nicholas, Nina and Barnaby. I poured Nicholas and Barnaby a finger of whisky each.

"May I borrow Nina for one last walk?" I asked Barnaby.

He granted my request, leaving a kiss on his new wife's cheek, and I stepped outside with Nina.

"Where shall we go?" I asked her.

"Let us walk to Su's palace and back," she suggested.

"Are you sure you wouldn't rather go further up to the lakes? We might take a rickshaw and sit by the water on such a beautiful day."

"No. I would rather see my streets," she said.

"Very well."

Nina had changed into a plain dress, her hair was held now in a loose plait. She walked with ease as we ambled down the *hutung* to join the jumble of streets leading towards the Legation Quarter. We stopped on a corner for toffee apples and Nina eased the sweet off her skewer with childlike enthusiasm.

"What shall you miss most?" I asked her.

"Father," she said seriously, as we continued walking. "Do you promise to visit him every day?"

"Naturally. We shall both write. He shall tell you lies, and say that he does not miss you, I shall tell the truth."

"Will you write every day?"

"Come, Nina. I do not write every day for my employers and they pay me for my words." She smiled, took a final bite from her toffee apple. "Every week, without fail."

"Thank you, Mr Scott."

"You mustn't worry about us here. You must go and make a wonderful life for yourself."

"Do you suppose I shall be happy?"

I regarded her, noticed that the restlessness that had colored her movements over the course of the summer seemed to have disappeared. She was not so much dulled as stilled, peacefulness permeated her gestures.

"It is my experience, Nina, that we are all as happy as we decide to be," I said. "And I believe you have made a very wise decision in pursuit of happiness."

"A wise decision," she repeated, as we entered the Legation Quarter and neared the tennis courts.

"Come," I said. "Let us return you to your husband."

"Do you think they shall like me in England? Or will they think me strange?"

"The best shall love you and the worst shall hate you," I said. "And long may it be that way."

XVI

NINA AND BARNABY lived in an elegant three-storey house in the fashionable London suburb of St. John's Wood, to which I had previously addressed a number of letters, but had yet to see for myself. Years of residence in unfamiliar locales had instilled in me a habit to approach places unknown on foot, allowing myself a few solitary moments to adapt to my new environs and to measure the likelihood of any hostile reception. Naturally I recognized the absurdity of descending from the hired carriage at the end of tranquil Queen's Grove, and yet a sense of continuity required that I do so. And so I traversed that tree-lined avenue on foot, passing no other person in my path, and appreciating the mild, mellow ambience of England in the last of spring's shady days, when flowers bloom unabashedly and scents continental and fresh fill the air.

I knocked upon the black door to no.11, felt apprehension as footsteps sounded unseen towards me. Nina's responses to my missives had been warm but brief; she shared light, humorous stories of her struggles to adapt to English customs and detailed the surprise with which the natives received her many faux pas. *He treats me so kindly*, she wrote of Barnaby. *His family has made me most welcome.* Still I could not imagine her, could not paint her in colors vivid and true behind that imposing, anonymous door.

"Oh, Alistair! I so hoped it might be you! I received your letter last week."

She brushed past the servant, and suddenly she was before

me, as palpable as she had been in Peking, her existence entirely undimmed. Her eyes danced green, her hands reached instinctively for mine. "Won't you come in?"

She led me to a drawing room decorated in restrained pastels. A traditional Chinese ink painting hung from one wall and through the large bay windows one could see a row of houses of identical style to her own.

"You have a beautiful home," I said as I took a seat opposite her.

"Yes. Barnaby has permitted me some reminders of China."

I allowed myself a closer observation of her then, expecting, I suppose, some physical distinction in her appearance, some shift or change in her features to indicate that she was no longer Miss Nina Ward of Peking but rather Mrs Barnaby George of London, and yet none was forthcoming. Seated before me was the same Nina I had always known, her smile irrepressible, her face open and curious, her posture trusting, intimate.

"You must meet Charlotte," she said and took my hand once more in hers. "I wished to tell you in my letters, but I simply couldn't find the words."

She called then for a servant, and a round-faced Cockney girl entered the room, a small child swaddled in her arms.

"She's sleeping, Mrs George," the girl said as Nina received the baby, pressed it to her chest.

"That's wonderful, Sarah. I do not think Mr Scott should care much for Charlotte's tempers."

Here then, cradled in Nina's young arms, was the evidence that she was not the Miss Ward I had known so long. The child was a surprise, a glorious revelation in the way that all fresh life might be; tender, vulnerable and yet utterly invincible, but also constituted to me a disappointment. The baby, gurgling now, struggling against sleep, was an event so profound in Nina's life, and yet she had not found the words to inform me of its existence.

"She's beautiful," I said, and Nina laughed generously.

"Is she really? I do worry, sometimes, that she might be terribly ugly and that I only see her as quite so adorable because I am her mother."

The servant returned then with tea, and I noted its familiar jasmine aroma. Nina handed the child back to Sarah, instructed that young Charlotte be set down once more in her cot.

"And how is my father?" Nina asked. "Tell me everything."

"Your father is well," I said simply. What more might I say? That he rarely went outside, that he spent all his time writing his book about the Boxers, writing and revising and reciting late into the night, that he sent money to Pei's family, that he muttered Nina's name under his breath?

"And his health?"

"Very good."

"I am so glad. I miss him terribly, terribly. He receives all my letters?"

"He does, and they bring him great joy."

"Good." Nina and I fell silent then, and both of us looked around the room, eyes tracing the high ceilings, the chairs upholstered in silk, the small portrait of a large-nosed man distantly related to Barnaby. "How is Peking?" she asked finally.

"Terrible. Better that you don't see it."

"I read in the paper that the Chinese refuse to pay the indemnity."

"Correct. Sixty-seven million would ruin China, impoverish the country for generations. They will pay something, though, that I do not doubt."

"But the fighting is over?"

"Yes. Not for me, of course, now that I am to go to South

Africa." I shook my head. "Let us talk no more of that ugliness. I am so very glad to see you."

"I have something for you," Nina said.

She disappeared and left me alone to contemplate the four walls that surrounded her new existence. The house was tidy, the furniture arranged neatly, the pictures hung just so, the hum of the place was muted. Nina returned with an envelope, which she proffered to me, kneeling by my side. I opened the envelope and a pile of clippings fell into my lap. I lifted one piece of paper, read closely the words printed upon it. *Latest events in the Legation Quarter suggest Boxers are not the only threat to the survival of foreigners in Peking. An Italian countess was shot by her diplomat husband as Boxers neared the house where they had found shelter during the siege.* I let the paper fall once again.

"Barnaby's mother collected any news about China while he was in Hong Kong," Nina explained. "She is rather an anxious woman, and I understand reading any news of China, however terrible, eased her nerves somewhat whilst he was overseas. I like to take them out from time to time, to read them and to remember."

"Mancini's dead," I said.

"He is?"

"A skirmish in the Italian Legation," I said. I did not look to Nina as I spoke, and I wondered if she understood the meaning in my words. "An anxious servant shot him, mistook him for a looter. Of course the servant escaped, and none of his peers have any idea as to where he might have disappeared."

"Oh." Nina collected the assorted clippings and placed them inside the envelope once more. "I would say that I was sorry, but I cannot help but feel that perhaps in this particular case justice has been done."

"That is what I thought." I reached then for her hand and held it, my thumb brushed the soft surface of her palm.

"I shall put these away," she said, making to rise, but I gripped her hand more tightly.

"Oh Miss Ward, what a terrible summer we had," I said, surprised at the strain which exposed itself in my voice.

"I know." She faced me then. Her eyelids dropped, I wondered if they were shields for tears. "Yet we must go on, Alistair. We are the fortunate."

"La Contessa was a special woman," I said finally.

"She will always be remembered by us," Nina said slowly.

"I suppose you wish to know about Mr Fairchild," I started cautiously. Nina did not reply, and I interpreted her silence as permission. "He has left China," I continued. She nodded so gently I wondered if her head had really moved at all. "He has been posted to Japan, it was posited as a reward for his work during the siege, I believe, and Mrs Fairchild has joined him there."

"I am pleased," she said, her voice falling somewhere close to a whisper. "Very pleased."

She looked at me imploringly, and her familiar features seemed to ask me a question: had another solution been possible?

"You do know, Nina," I said, "that if Mr George had not returned to Peking when he did, I would not have let you down. I only ever wished to protect you, and if I might have become your husband, well, I wish you to know that I would have done so without a moment's hesitation."

Her eyes still on mine, Nina removed her hand from our shared hold.

"Oh, Alistair," she said, and I detected a fissure, gentle but definite, in her voice. "You were never one to be pinned down."

"But...." I began to protest.

"You did so very much for me. I shall never forget it."

Hurriedly she pressed her lips to my cheek, kissed me briefly. "Thank you."

We heard the door bell ring, followed by the authoritative step of a servant. Nina stood abruptly, took a step away from me and towards the fireplace. It was with her back turned that Nina greeted her husband.

"Mr Scott!" Barnaby removed his hat in a swift, clean gesture, and stretched out his hand to meet mine. "What a wonderful surprise."

"Mr George." I said, standing to greet him. "I have had the pleasure to meet your young daughter."

"Oh yes, isn't it marvelous?" Barnaby crossed the room to his wife, kissed her quickly. "You must stay for supper, Mr Scott."

"No," Nina said hastily. "I'm sorry, Barnaby, but I believe Mr Scott has another engagement this evening."

"Correct," I said. "That is the problem with London, there is always some damned business to which one must attend."

"I'm not surprised that a man of your talents should be so popular. That is rather a shame, though. Tomorrow?"

"I'm afraid that I am leaving soon for South Africa," I said gently. "Perhaps I might stop by during my next visit. I am happy at least to know that you are both well."

"Likewise," Barnaby said cordially.

I nodded and placed my hat on my head to leave. Nina linked her arm in mine and escorted me to the door.

"Thank you," she said quietly.

"Of course," I said, though I did not know for what she thanked me. Her fingers circled my wrist still, and she held closely to me.

"I am so very happy to see you," she said, opening the door and letting go, releasing me to the balmy city.

"As am I." I paused, nodded and embraced her a final time.

"Good luck, Nina."

"*Yi lu ping an.*" May the route be peaceful.

I nodded and hurried down the stairs to meet the street, turning to see her enveloped by Barnaby. I waved, but already Barnaby had forgotten me, with his hand placed upon his wife's shoulder he looked adoringly at her. Nina watched my retreat, eyes distant, heart burdened by words unspoken.

South Africa, June 1902

Dear Nina,

I am so pleased to hear that you are all well, especially little Charlotte. The bloody mess here seems to have finished, so I hope to find myself in London again soon and very much look forward to meeting with you then.

I am most saddened by the news of your father's death. At least we have the comfort of knowing he died peacefully, certain of his daughter's future. You brought him great joy and happiness and you must never forget the very special bond you shared. I hope you may find the same peace, contentment and inspiration in your own daughter.

You asked how I am. All I can say is that I am alive. I am beginning to tire of war, I am no longer a young man, and I think it might be time for a change. I have dedicated myself of late to a manuscript of sorts that I wish to share with you. It began as a story of our experience of the Boxers, but the muses were untiring in guiding the narrative towards you, and rapidly it came to be a story about you more than any vicious Boxer or officious diplomat. It is personal, it is private, it is the true story of our Boxer Rebellion. I would not dare to publish it without your approval, and I repeat that it is highly personal, even scandalous. Yet I wonder if we might not change a few names and alter some events in order to furnish the public with a more truthful, or at the very least, a more human account of our woes that summer? I have enclosed it for you to read, and anxiously await your comments.

At first I thought it mere folly to even imagine to publish something so sensitive. Yet you, my dear Nina, are nothing short of an inspiration to me. Not for your courage or your intelligence or your beauty (though you possess much of these qualities), but for your refusal to kneel down before life, to cower in the face of death, to smooth your edges to meet the desires of others. I have lived more than a year of terrible conflict here, seen more lives wasted, more men ruined, more children orphaned, than anyone should ever care to witness. And how they fall, the men! How they fold, the women! How they submit, the children! But not you, Nina. You danced before death, you teased punishment, you laughed at eternity and scorned divinity. And for all that, you burned and raged and glittered and shone, and you lived. And for that, I love you.

Yours always,
Alistair Scott

ABOUT THE AUTHOR

Clare Kane is a London-based author who has lived and worked in Shanghai and Beijing. Her first novel, Electric Shadows Of Shanghai, was published in 2015. A former Reuters journalist, she has a First Class degree in Chinese from the University of Oxford.